A WEDDING AT THE ITALIAN'S DEMAND

KIM LAWRENCE

SEDUCING HIS CONVENIENT INNOCENT

RACHAEL THOMAS

MILLS & BOON

First Published in Great Britain 2019
by Mills & Boon, an imprint of HarperCollins*Publishers*
1 London Bridge Street, London, SE1 9GF

A Wedding at the Italian's Demand © 2019 by Kim Lawrence

Seducing His Convenient Innocent © 2019 by Rachael Thomas

ISBN: 978-0-263-27332-8

MIX
Paper from
responsible sources
FSC® C007454

This book is produced from independently certified FSC™ paper
to ensure responsible forest management.
For more information visit www.harpercollins.co.uk/green.

Printed and bound in Spain
by CPI, Barcelona

Kim Lawrence lives on a farm in Anglesey with her university lecturer husband, assorted pets who arrived as strays and never left, and sometimes one or both of her boomerang sons. When she's not writing she loves to be outdoors gardening, or walking on one of the beaches for which the island is famous—along with being the place where Prince William and Catherine made their first home!

Rachael Thomas has always loved reading romance, and is thrilled to be a Mills & Boon author. She lives and works on a farm in Wales—a far cry from the glamour of a Modern Romance story, but that makes slipping into her characters' worlds all the more appealing. When she's not writing, or working on the farm, she enjoys photography and visiting historical castles and grand houses. Visit her at rachaelthomas.co.uk.

A WEDDING AT THE ITALIAN'S DEMAND

KIM LAWRENCE

CHAPTER ONE

THE LIGHT IN the wide corridor Ivo Greco walked along was muted, but the priceless tapestries that lined the stone walls provided their own glowing illumination as he moved towards the massive double doors of etched glass at the far end. The doors had to stay closed to maintain the carefully controlled humidity and light to preserve the priceless antiques.

They provided a light-at-the-end-of-the-tunnel effect, but it was an illusion. Ivo was *not* expecting any version of a heavenly vision on the other side because the doors led to his grandfather's private apartments, to which Ivo had been summoned.

His grandfather had actually sent for him forty-eight hours ago, and people did not keep Salvatore Greco waiting!

While Salvatore was on the record as saying he respected people who stood up to him, the reality was that Salvatore, a man who possessed vast wealth and enormous power, also possessed a very fragile ego.

As an eight-year-old, when Salvatore had taken over the guardianship of him and his brother, Ivo had not understood about egos, but he had quickly realised that it was easy to make his grandfather angry.

It had actually been the day before his eighth birthday when Ivo's father had decided he could no longer live without his late wife. Ivo had found his father's body and his grandfather had found Ivo.

Amid the horror of that day Ivo remembered the strength in his grandfather's arms, the sanctuary they had afforded as he had picked Ivo up and taken him away from the scene that had lived on for years in his childish nightmares.

Even as a young boy Ivo had understood that he owed his grandfather a debt impossible to repay, and this knowledge did not disappear when he realised his grandfather was no guardian angel or superhero but a hard, ruthless man, not always fair and almost impossible to please.

But the fact remained that, no matter what he did, Salvatore was the one who had carried Ivo out of his hell. The debt remained, as did the gratitude burnt deep into his soul by the character-changing events of that day. Ivo had long ago stopped trying to please, even though he knew better than most that the old man hated to be thwarted and just how viciously he could react to any perceived insult, real or imagined. A very good reason why the people that surrounded Salvatore rarely disagreed with him, at least to his face.

Ivo was sanguine about the reception he was likely to receive, more bothered about the necessity of postponing a meeting than the tirade of abuse and invective inevitably waiting for him.

A nerve twitched along his hard jawline as, unbidden, a memory floated into his head; he had not always been so philosophical.

It had taken his brother several minutes to coax him out of his hiding place in one of the warren of attics in the *palazzo*. He couldn't remember what he had done to outrage his grandparent but he remembered not believing his brother when he had said, 'Never show him you're afraid, then one day you won't be.'

Ivo pushed the memory away, his symmetrical features hardening; the past was gone.

In his view there were few things more pathetic than people who clung onto memories until they became defined by their past. He saw them everywhere, from the people who became fixated on missed opportunities, old hurts and injustices, to the guy who constantly relived his early successes on the sports field, as if lifting a trophy at twenty defined him. All were so consumed with the past that they missed the opportunities that the future offered.

Ivo's sights were always fixed ahead, though at that moment it was something in the periphery of his vision that caught his attention.

The suited servant, a new face to Ivo, who had shadowed him since he'd entered the building, almost collided with him as Ivo came to an unscheduled halt. Ivo let the man's apologies slide off him as, head tilted back, he moved backwards to get the full effect of the glowing Byzantine image on the wall, again nearly falling over the man behind who delivered another flustered apology.

'New?'

'I'm not sure, sir.'

The response was perfectly polite but under the surface Ivo could almost feel the anxiety rolling off the man and, after one last glance at the wall, he took pity on him. Turning away, he caught sight of a look of relief on the man's face; it was that look and not his own anxiety that made him quicken his leisurely pace.

Ivo's personal spaces were minimalist and uncluttered—functional could still be pleasing to the eye or at least his eyes—but he appreciated beauty and artistic talent in many forms. He would have liked to study this testament to the skill of long-dead artisans for longer. The irony, of course, was that his grandfather would not appreciate the beauty.

Salvatore was a famed collector of many rare and precious objects—jade, art, porcelain—but for him it was all about the acquisition. For Salvatore, the pleasure came from possessing what someone else wanted. He might forget the history of an artwork or the name of an artist, but he had a flawless recall of the price he'd paid for any item and the identity of the collectors he outbid.

Once through the doors and into a brighter corridor, thanks to massive windows that revealed breath catching views of the Tyrrhenian Sea that glittered turquoise in the Tuscan morning sun, Ivo turned to his shadow.

'I think I know my way from here.'

The man hesitated; clearly Ivo's words clashed with his instructions. He began to bluster but his protests trailed away as Ivo's dark level stare held his, and after a moment he tipped his head and faded away. Ivo's grandfather's private apartments were situated in one of the older parts of the building, taking up all of one of the iconic twelfth-century square towers built by an ancestor. The massive metal banded door to the study was open and Ivo walked straight in. He was prepared; even so he experienced a moment's disorientation as he stepped over the threshold, feeling as if he'd stepped through some time portal or onto the set of a futuristic film. He almost reached for the designer shades tucked into the pocket of his suit jacket, the antiseptic white and chrome was that dazzling.

Five years earlier his grandfather had ripped out

the antique panelling along with the books that had once lined the walls, and the decor was now sleek and modern. *Efficient,* as his grandfather had said as they'd watched the monitors being mounted on the wall, the only thing left from the past the antique desk that dominated the room.

A half-smile flickered across Ivo's wide sensual mouth as he recalled the occasion he had casually admitted that he missed the old room, inviting further scorn when he had added he actually *liked* the smell of musty old books. This had apparently confirmed his grandfather's suspicion that Ivo was a sentimental fool.

Ivo had accepted the insult with a careless shrug of his wide shoulders, aware that if Salvatore had believed either of these things he would not have given him control of the IT and Communications division of Greco Industries, although *given* was perhaps the wrong word. When the grand gesture was made his grandfather had not anticipated the role would have any permanence.

His gratitude at the time had been genuine even though Ivo had known that it had been intended as a wing-clipping exercise—the unspoken but universally acknowledged expectation had been that the young upstart would fail; indeed he was *meant* to fail, publicly.

But Ivo had defied those expectations, denying his grandfather the opportunity to ride to the rescue. A source of frustration to a man who liked to be in control.

And *so far*, Ivo had been allowed a free hand.

Was that about to change?

He was not given to paranoia but neither was Ivo a believer in coincidence, and the timing of this peremptory summons, coinciding as it did with the ink drying on the new global merger he had negotiated, had raised a few warning bells. Was it significant that this merger would mean the IT division was no longer the poor relation of Greco Industries but able to challenge the leisure, property and construction arms of the company, and even make the jewel in the crown, Greco's media division, look over their shoulder?

So far Salvatore had been content to bask in the reflected glory of his grandson's success but maybe that was no longer enough. Was he about to announce he wanted to be more hands on?

Ivo approached the possibility with more curiosity than trepidation. Considering the fact Salvatore was a control freak, this scenario had always been a possibility and Ivo had already decided that, rather than surrender his control, or even share it, he would walk away.

Just looking for an excuse, Ivo?

His dark brows twitching into a frown that drew them into a straight line above his masterful nose, he ignored the sly voice in his head as he cleared his throat.

In reality he knew he would never walk away from his duty, any more than his grandfather had walked away from him. Ivo was not his father, or his brother.

'Morning, Grandfather.'

Close to eighty, Salvatore Greco remained an imposing figure. There was nothing fragile or infirm about his upright stance, but as he turned to face his grandson Ivo found himself thinking, for the first time in his life, that his grandfather was old.

Maybe it was the morning light shining directly on the older man's face as he turned, revealing the depth of the lines that grooved his forehead and etched deep the furrows carved from his nose to the downward-turning corners of his thin mouth.

The line of silent speculation vanished the moment the older man began to speak, as did pretty much every other thought. There was definitely no hint of age or softness in his voice as he delivered his announcement.

'Your brother is dead.' He took his seat in the high-backed chair behind the massive antique desk that still dominated the otherwise minimally furnished white room, pausing only to straighten the line of meticulously sharpened pencils before he continued to speak.

Ivo didn't notice a tremor in his grandfather's voice as he stared blindly ahead, and the words just rolled over him in a meaningless jumble until one sentence made itself heard above the loud static hum in his head.

'I will need you to take care of this personally, you understand?'

Ivo fought his way through the swirl of churning emotions that made their physical presence known in the fog in his head and the constricting band that felt like steel around his chest before he spoke.

'The funeral?' It still didn't seem possible—would it ever? Bruno—nine years his senior…what did that make him? Thirty-eight? How did anyone die at thirty-eight?

Outrage at the thought elicited a mind-calming burst of rage followed swiftly by denial. It had to be a mistake. Yes, that was it, some awful mistake. If his brother was dead, he'd know.

His grandfather's eyes narrowed fractionally as his lips compressed in faint irritation at the interruption.

'Their funeral was last month, I believe.'

The words ricocheted around in Ivo's head. He needed to sit down. His fingers clenched his knuckles white against the leather armrest…he *was* sitting down. He had been walking around functioning as normal for weeks while his brother was dead. How could he not have known, not have *felt* something? He tipped his head in a sharp motion of denial and cut across his grandfather, who was speaking again.

'Last month?'

His grandfather looked at him without speaking before he reached for the stopper on the crystal decanter that sat on the desk and glugged some of the amber liquid into one of the glasses that sat beside it on the silver tray.

The full glass scraped on the desk as he pushed it towards his grandson.

Ivo shook his head, not mistaking the action for empathy; he had accepted years ago that his grandparent was incapable of that. Emotional responses were, in Salvatore's eyes, weaknesses to be studied and exploited. It was not coincidental that Ivo was famed for his unreadable expression. What had begun as a self-protective device was now second nature.

'You said *their*?' Ivo's brain was starting to function, but he was not sure if that could be classed as a good thing. The sense of loss had a physical presence; he could feel it at a cellular level in a way he'd sworn never to feel anything again. As he'd coped alone after Bruno's desertion, the realisation that he could not count on anyone else had required he closed off the part of himself that made him vulnerable to such painful feelings. And now, the unfamiliar dormant feelings had exploded into painful life, blurring his normally sharp-edged wits.

'The woman was with him.'

'His *wife*.' Ivo emphasised the word as an image flashed into his head, probably not even accurate.

He'd only met the woman his brother had walked away from his own family for once, and that had been fourteen years ago. Her eyes probably hadn't been *that* blue, but the memory of that vivid colour had stayed with him even after the resentment towards Samantha Henderson had faded. Samantha was, after all, responsible for robbing Ivo of the big brother he had worshipped and the future he had dreamt of.

Not immediately, Bruno was coming to get him, he had promised, tears on his cheeks as he, Ivo, had begged his brother not to leave. How long had it taken him to realise that Bruno was never coming back?

Fool, mocked the derisive voice in his head as he thought of his younger self waiting, believing. Bruno had said what Ivo had wanted to hear. In truth, he'd never intended coming back for him; he had deserted him.

The people in Ivo's life had a habit of doing that: first his father, then Bruno. A person who invited that sort of pain and disillusion had to be a fool, and Ivo was no fool.

In a world obsessed with pairing people off, he had learnt that, far from being a deficiency, being alone was a strength. He never intended to be in a position where someone else had the power to inflict that sort of pain. He was not looking for love; love exaggerated men's weaknesses, left a man less than whole.

To this point it hadn't been difficult to avoid the infection of *love*, any more difficult than walking away from sexual encounters. The compartments in his life remained unpolluted by love, but *loyalty* was another thing.

His grandfather never demanded love but he did demand loyalty and Ivo considered he had earned it. The only person who had ever been there for him was Salvatore; a man who didn't pretend to be something he wasn't. The old man was a devil, but he didn't hide behind a saint's mask.

Bruno had been his favourite grandson.

His heir.

Ivo, who'd worshipped his brother, had been fine with that.

There had always been an expectation that Ivo would one day rebel, and, growing up, his occasional failures, while not going unpunished, were almost *expected*. It was whispered that he was like his father; that he had inherited the same weakness.

Ivo had heard the whispers, gritted his teeth and determined that he would prove them all wrong. It was not news to him that his father was weak, because only a weak man would take his own life and leave two motherless sons behind because he couldn't live without the woman he loved.

His mother must have been special, Bruno always said she was, but Ivo didn't really remember his mother at all. He didn't allow himself to remember his father; instead he despised him.

For his brother it had always been different—he was the golden boy. Not easy—the bar had been set high for the heir to his grandfather's empire and failure was not tolerated, and he'd lived up to expectations, which was perhaps why, when he'd finally challenged Salvatore, the consequences had been so extreme.

Salvatore had already had a bride picked out for his heir. It would be a profitable union, as the woman was the only child and heir of a man almost as wealthy as the Grecos and with an equally proud lineage, which for his grandfather was almost as important. He was fond of speaking of bloodlines and pointing out the proof that the Grecos, who could trace their bloodlines back centuries, were among the elite of Europe.

Ivo had been fifteen when his brother had walked away to be with the woman he loved. He'd finally re-

alised when the brother he idolised had not returned
for him that the whispers had been wrong all along.
Ivo hadn't been the one who had inherited their father's
weakness; Bruno was the one that couldn't live without
the woman he loved.

But Bruno could live without honour, and his little
brother.

His older brother had betrayed him but, even so,
Bruno had been *living* out there somewhere, some place
cold and bleak, a Scottish island, but now he wasn't.

It didn't seem possible.

'Nobody informed you?' He pressed a finger to the
groove between his dark brows, struggling to make
sense of what he was hearing.

His grandfather's bushy brows lifted. 'Obviously I
was informed, by your brother's solicitor. Oh, and the
woman's sister sent a letter, handwritten,' he added with
a contemptuous snort. 'Barely legible.'

Ivo shook his head and felt anger separate itself out
from the multi-layered raw emotions churning in his
belly. Tangled as they were with the irrational guilt he
refused to acknowledge, the physical effort of keeping
the toxic mixture in check sent fine tremors through
his lean body.

'You knew?' A muscle along his jaw clenched and
quivered as the old man simply shrugged in confirmation, feeding the flame of fury inside him. He could feel
it building. None of his feelings showed on his face but
there was ice in his voice when he pressed his point. 'And
you did not see fit to share that information with me,
until now?'

There was the slightest edge of defiance in Salvatore's voice as he met his grandson's eyes and bit out,
'What would have been the point, Bruno?'

The muscles along Ivo's jawline quivered. His grandfather seemed unaware of what he had called him, his heavy eyelids lowered over dark flame-lit eyes.

'It did not occur to you that I might want to go to the funeral?' *Would he have...?* Well, he'd never know now, he concluded with bitter irony.

'No, it didn't. You had your *closure* all those years ago when he stopped being your brother, and...' Eyes that held no expression flickered as he scanned his grandson's face. 'You're not a hypocrite.' He arched a brow, his lip curling in mild mocking contempt as he threw out the challenge. 'Are you?'

Ivo's head came up slowly, his almond-shaped dark eyes resting without expression on his grandfather's face. The surge of colour that had highlighted the slashing curves of his razor-edged cheekbones had receded. The normal vibrant olive glow had been overwhelmed by a waxy pallor that gave his features the sepia cast of an old photo; his features were utterly still. Only the nerve spasmodically clenching to the right of his clamped bloodless lips a sign of life.

He shook his head in an attitude of someone expecting to wake up. 'Bruno contacted me eighteen months ago. He wanted to meet up.' Ivo, staring blankly into middle distance, did not see the look of anger that crossed his grandfather's face. He was too consumed with the guilt clawing low in his belly.

'You met up with him?'

Ivo turned his head, the bleakness in his eyes profound. If the love he'd felt for his brother really had died when he hadn't come back, should he be feeling this sort of pain now?

Pushing the question away, he took a deep breath

and squared his shoulders. A man took responsibility for his actions. 'No, I didn't.'

A decision that he might never forgive himself for now. His brother had reached out and he had rejected him, and why? Because he had carried the anger and resentment of a youth into adulthood, because he wanted to punish Bruno?

Self-contempt quivered queasily in his belly, guilt and regret adding to the toxic sensation. The fact was he could have forgiven the desertion but he could never have forgiven the lie that had kept hope alive.

'I thought he'd given up on that,' the old man mused, dragging a hand over the grey stubble on his chin.

'Given up?'

'Bruno kept away after I took out the injunction, but the letters carried on for... Well, they stopped too...' Salvatore frowned. 'When was that...? No matter, they stopped after the lawyers made it clear that if he contacted you again I'd disinherit the pair of you and it would be *his* responsibility.'

A hand pressed against the dull throb in his head as Ivo struggled to make sense of what he was hearing. 'He came back for me?'

Salvatore snorted. 'Wanted guardianship, would you believe it?'

His expression invited Ivo to share his contempt at the idea, but Ivo was in no condition to share anything. Bruno *hadn't* lied, he hadn't deserted him.

'He came back.'

Salvatore gave an impatient click of his fingers. 'As if any court would have granted him access with his conviction.'

'Conviction?'

'I don't suppose you would know but your brother

dabbled a bit. He fell in with a bad crowd at school and was caught with a small amount…easy enough to brush under the carpet but the record remained.'

'Drugs? Bruno?' No inkling of this youthful scandal had ever reached Ivo's ears; how much else had he been protected from?

He had given up on his brother but his brother had never given up on him! The discovery left a bitter-sweet taste in his mouth.

Salvatore's comments suggested that Bruno had not just come back, he had fought, reaching out again, but this time Ivo was the one who had walked away! Ivo sat there as the guilt closed in on him, wrapping its wire tendrils around him like a cage.

He had barely begun to process this reversal of everything he had believed when his grandfather landed another shock.

'The child—'

Ivo's head whipped around. 'What child?'

'Your brother had a son, a baby, he's…' He stabbed the air in an impatient gesture. 'It doesn't matter what they've called him… This is why I need you to go to Scotland, to the Isle of Skye—presumably you know that's where your brother has been living in some shack…probably no electricity and running water. I want you to fetch back the child. He belongs here with us—the father may have been a fool and his mother…' With a curl of his lip he dismissed Samantha. 'But the child is a Greco—he has a heritage.'

'How…?' Ivo's heavy lids half lowered as he swallowed to alleviate the emotional constriction in his throat. 'How did they die?' he finally managed to push out harshly.

'A climbing accident, they were roped together apparently. A witness at the inquest said they heard him begging her to cut the line, but she didn't—' For the first time Ivo imagined he heard emotion in his grandfather's voice as he added harshly, 'Ivo always had a reckless streak.' His grandfather's eyes drifted closed.

'*Bruno* always loved the mountains,' Ivo said softly. The gentle emphasis he placed on his brother's name seemed to pass over his grandfather's head.

He opened his eyes. 'That's what I just said! And look where it led…' he intoned bitterly. 'If he hadn't climbed he'd never have met that girl… A potter, living in a hovel.'

A slight exaggeration but Samantha had seemed a million miles from the perfectly groomed models and society women his brother had previously dated.

Love at first sight, Bruno had said.

As if he'd had no choice in the matter! Ivo hadn't believed that then or now. It was the excuse of a weak man, the man he had no intention of ever being.

There was *always* a choice.

Suddenly the mantra he lived his life by had less conviction.

'I have spoken to the lawyers but there is no way to break the will.'

'So there's a will—what does it say?' Ivo struggled to express interest he did not feel. All he could think about was Bruno and the fact that he had not betrayed him out of choice. Bruno had fought for him, admittedly against stacked odds, but he had fought nonetheless.

'Not relevant.'

It struck Ivo as very relevant but he said nothing. He was thinking about the son that Bruno had left behind; the child he could not desert. He had turned his back on his brother but he wouldn't turn his back on his nephew!

'They were young, the young never expect to die, and this Henderson woman…the sister…'

Ivo hadn't known there was a sister, but then why should he? 'Does she have a name?'

'Something Scottish… Fiona or, no, Flora, I think.'

'And she is the child's legal guardian?' Ivo found himself clinging to the knowledge that Bruno had a son; that a part of him lived on. Perhaps one day it would be a comfort, one day when the pain of loss was not so raw and his sense of guilt not so corrosive. What he needed to focus on now was not the guilt, but the father-less child. *It's not about you, Ivo,* he reminded himself with a humourless half-smile.

His grandfather brought his fist down onto the desk top with a force that made the wood vibrate and drew a wince from his lips. 'It's ludicrous. She has…is…noth-ing!' he spat out contemptuously.

'You want to be a part of this child's life, maybe you should learn to say her name,' Ivo suggested mildly.

'I do not want her to be a *part* of this child's life. That family is responsible for me losing my grand-son.'

That was certainly one way of looking at it and it was the one way Ivo had been encouraged to look at it. A way he still found he was reluctant to relinquish.

'Well, how is no compromise working for you so far, Grandfather? Maybe you should be realistic and settle for what you can get.'

Salvatore's eyes narrowed. 'Is that the lesson in life you have learnt? *Settling?*' he snarled with withering contempt. 'I made her a perfectly reasonable offer—generous! She refused.'

'You offered to buy the child?' *Dio,* this got worse. His grandfather seemed to have lost the subtlety and cunning he was famed for. 'And you are surprised she refused?'

'Oh, I know what this is about. She's barren, can't have a baby of her own, so she's going to cling onto this one for dear life,' Salvatore brooded darkly. 'The letter she sent said it all…sentimental twaddle, inviting me to visit him there. I do not want *that* family in the child's life. They took him from…'

The old man's voice quivered; his eyes grew glassy and blank. The result of anger, or grief?

Or just the simple fact someone had thwarted him?

Whatever had put the quiver in his voice, it made the old man swallow and turn away. This rare visual evidence of vulnerability, the sudden appearance of frailty, struck deep, bringing the memory to the surface of the day when Salvatore had been strong. When he had rescued him from that room and the lifeless father Ivo had tried to awaken, even in his childish ignorance trying to push some of the pills that had spilled from one of the empty bottles past his father's cold lips, believing that the medicine would make him better. Not understanding until much later that the pills had been his father's weapon of choice.

Salvatore wanted to rescue this baby just as he had rescued Ivo. For Salvatore it was all about bloodlines!

Are you in any position to sneer? demanded the voice in Ivo's head. *For you, it's all about assuaging your guilt.*

His broad shoulders lifted in a shrug of acknowledgement; granted, neither motivation was particularly noble, but then the Grecos were not renowned for their nobility. His jaw stiffened—they were known for getting what they wanted, though.

Ivo stilled as the belated shocked recognition slid

through him: he *wanted* to bring up this child, this part of Bruno who remained.

He gave them both a moment to recover before responding.

'Should I ask if this information is out in the public domain, or have you accessed this woman's private medical records?'

The older man responded to the dry question with a shrug and a sour look.

Ivo did not pursue it. He wasn't that bothered about the red lines Salvatore had gleefully crossed. The fact was that, guilt aside, and with a determination to make up for rejecting his brother, there was a part of him that could identify with his motivation.

It was not something he felt the need to apologise for. Ivo possessed an Italian's pride in his culture and language, a pride he knew his brother had shared, and thinking of Bruno's son missing out on this part of his heritage drew a dizzying number of intersecting red lines in his head. Ivo's loyalty to his name was unquestioning, it went cell deep, which was why his brother's defection had hurt so much. Bruno had rejected everything they had been brought up to respect.

But he had not rejected him; Bruno had come back for him.

The regret and guilt that he would never now have a chance to thank his brother were so powerful he could taste the metallic tang like blood on his tongue. He focused instead on the *wrongness* that the child that shared his DNA was out there somewhere, knowing nothing of his history.

He had a debt to repay to his brother, and he would. Giving his nephew the sort of upbringing he and Bruno had *not* had would be his atonement.

His grandfather seemed fully recovered, delivering an irritated scowl. 'We need leverage, but she's done nothing.'

'By that I presume you mean she has no skeletons?'

'There is the suggestion of an affair with some footballer, but he wasn't married at the time.'

'So what do you expect me to do, kidnap the child?'

'Yes,' would have been less shocking than the reply he received.

'I expect you to marry the woman, and bring the child home here. The lawyers say that will give you legal rights. It should make it simple to gain custody after the divorce.'

Ivo's moment of gobsmacked incredulity found release in laughter. When was the last time he'd laughed in his grandfather's presence? he wondered as he listened to the sound...rusty, as though he was out of practice. For some reason he could hear the sound of his brother's laughter in his head, too. When Bruno had left he had taken the laughter with him.

'Have you finished?' Salvatore asked, when the room fell silent.

There had been a time when the icy disdain had tied his stomach in knots of tension but that time was long gone. 'You appear to have given this some thought.'

'You trying to tell me you couldn't make her fall in love if you wanted to?'

'Thanks for the vote of confidence,' Ivo said drily as he got to his feet to place both hands on the desk before leaning forward and saying slowly, 'I don't want to.'

He had reached the door when his grandfather's words reached him.

'I'm dying and I want you to bring my great-grandson here. Do you really want your brother's son to be brought up by a stranger, never hearing his own language? Never having the advantages that being a Greco brings? Are you that selfish?'

Ivo turned slowly, his dark eyes sweeping his grandfather's lined face. Yes, he *did* look old. 'Is that true?'

'You think I'd lie about such a thing?'

'Yes,' Ivo responded without hesitation.

The old man laughed and looked quite pleased, clearly taking the comment as a compliment. 'I would like to retain a little dignity in what is a very undignified process. I have no intention of boring you with the unpleasant details, but I am dying, and I want to see the boy. Will you do that for me?'

Ivo's chest lifted as he released the breath held in his chest. 'I make no promises,' he said, while making a promise to himself—there was no way in the world he would hand over a baby to Salvatore, but he would bring this child home and he would protect him from the full force of Salvatore's frequently toxic influence, just as Bruno had protected him.

His grandfather smiled. 'I knew you wouldn't let me down, Bruno.'

CHAPTER TWO

FLORA TIPTOED STEALTHILY down the stairs, wincing as the board beneath her feet creaked. She froze, balanced on one foot, only releasing the breath held in her chest in a sigh of shuddering relief when there was no sound of baby sobs from upstairs.

Her mum said her grandson was teething, but then she also said that Jamie was an *easy* baby.

After the past few weeks Flora was of the opinion that easy babies were fictional creatures much like elves, or unicorns, only they slept less.

Flora could *vaguely* remember what sleep was. She had begun to feel increasingly nostalgic for a time when her idea of a bad night was tossing and turning for half an hour before she drifted off.

Now she could sleep standing up; she *had* slept standing up!

Sami had made it look so easy. Flora's blue eyes filled with unshed tears and she blinked hard as she choked out her sister's name in a forlorn whisper. She was so focused on the image in her head of her smiling sister and the physical pain of loss that it took her a few moments to register the cold.

Very cold, cold she hadn't noticed upstairs, but then walking several miles up and down the cheerily furnished nursery wearing a groove in the carpet while jiggling the cranky baby and humming an irritating jingle advertising a deodorant—not a very appropriate lullaby but she couldn't get the darned thing out of her head—was one way to keep warm.

She shivered, and gathered the thick cardigan she had put on over her sweater tightly around her. Nepotism aside, she was proud of her very first project as a qualified architect. The conversion of the derelict stone steading her sister and brother-in-law had decided to convert into their home and business, a restaurant with rooms, had won her a mention, though no glittering prize, in a prestigious competition.

Heating and insulation had been a priority in the brief and normally it was warm and cosy, not to mention wildly ecologically efficient with its state-of-the-art heating system, triple glazing that muffled the sound of the storm outside, and a roof of solar panels, but tonight the cold draughts seemed to have discovered ways inside.

She didn't realise there was more involved than the storm raging outside and some uninsulated nooks and crannies until she brushed past one of the tall modernist column radiators and, instead of feeling comforting heat, her fingers made contact with metal that was stone cold.

She groaned and tried not to think of the missed boiler service she had deemed a reasonable economy, because everything seemed to be working fine and anyway it was state-of-the-art, didn't that mean something?

Easy with the clarity of hindsight to recognise a classic case of false economy.

She allowed herself a self-pitying sniff or three before squaring her slender shoulders. *Right, Flora, beat yourself up tomorrow and call the heating guy—right now stop whining and make the best of it.*

She considered her immediate options. Retreating to the small private living room, an oak-framed extension with incredible views over the water to the mainland, wasn't one because she'd not got around to lighting the wood burner in there earlier and, with the underfloor heating off and a wall of glass, it would be even colder than in here.

So maybe the best move was make a hot-water bottle, put the spare heaters in the nursery and climb into bed. It might only be eight-thirty but her body clock was so out of sync thanks to chronic sleep deprivation that it didn't really matter—yes, that was definitely a plan.

So, first things first, the heater in the nursery then make herself a hot-water bottle. Her thick wool socks made no sound on the stone floor of the reception-area-cum-lounge and informal bar space while there was a perceptible increase in the volume of the storm raging outside.

Her shiver this time was for anyone unlucky enough not to have several feet of solid stone between them and the elements. Continuing to switch off lights as she went—at least they still had electricity—she fished her mobile from the pocket of her snug-fitting jeans. With a sigh she slid it back—there hadn't been a signal since lunchtime and a couple of hours later the landline had gone too. It wasn't being cut off that was worrying Flora, it was her inability to contact her mother.

Under normal circumstances she wouldn't have been concerned about her parent; under *normal* circumstances her mother would be here helping to run the place and look after baby Jamie, while continuing to run her own pottery business. Multitasking was Grace

Henderson's middle name and Flora wished she had a fraction of her resourceful parent's energy.

But these weren't normal circumstances. Her fiercely independent mother was operating on crutches with her leg in plaster and grieving deeply for her firstborn. Flora took comfort for the fact that, although the croft was remote, her mum had several good friends who lived close enough to be called neighbours who would no doubt have checked in on her.

Flora gnawed gently on her full lower lip as she weighed the option of putting more peat on the already smoking open fire before she went to bed. It was a matter of freeze or choke. She was trying to recall where the spare portable heaters she would need to put in the baby's room were stored, when there was a loud bang on the front door she had bolted after Fergus had left, there being not much point the chef staying when all the diners had cancelled.

Feeling ashamed that her first thought was a selfish, *please don't wake the baby,* she rushed across the room, reading desperation into the loud urgent-sounding thuds. She fumbled with the door bolt, urgency making her fingers clumsy as the banging continued.

'Hold on, hold on, nearly...' As the door opened the wind blowing in off the sea loch that lapped the shore on the opposite side of the narrow road hit Flora with a full icy blast.

The physical force snatched the breath from her lips and made her stagger backwards, her arms flailing as she struggled to keep her balance. She barely heard the sound of the heavy oak door hitting the wall above the combined roar of the wind and the sound of invisible crashing waves feet away from the door.

It was to this wild soundtrack and out of the heavy swirling mist that the stranger entered.

He *was* a stranger… For one awful split second she'd thought *Callum*… It wasn't, of course. The local boy made good, thanks to an ability to kick a ball and increase the sales of everything from breakfast cereal to cars by smiling into the camera, lived in Spain—or was it Japan?—these days, and anyway there was no real resemblance beyond the impression of height, athletic muscularity, the dark hair and her imagination.

If it had been Callum she might have pushed him back out into the storm, but the man who *hadn't* broken her heart didn't look *pushable*!

He stood for a moment framed in the doorway, the top of his bare head touching the door frame, his broad shoulders filling the space as the long drover's-style overcoat he wore, caught by the wind, flared out behind him dramatically.

If this wild elemental storm had taken human form it would have looked like him.

Before her dazed brain could take in any more details he reached out, pulling the heavy door closed being him, making the effort of competing against the gale-force wind look effortless.

The deafening roar was instantly reduced to a dull distant moan and the fire, which had briefly flared to life with the influx of oxygen, died down as it blew out a cloud of acrid eye-stinging smoke, which under normal circumstances would have made Flora think about the damage it would inflict on the fresh white paintwork.

But she wasn't thinking about paintwork or actually anything else much. The adrenalin surge that held every muscle in her body taut to quivering point had thrown her nervous system directly into flight-or-fight mode, though neither would have done her much good against this man who, now the door was closed, seemed even taller.

He stood there for what felt like hours but might have been seconds, long enough at any rate for the details of his face to imprint themselves in her memory. The moisture that slicked his short dark hair against his skull trembled in droplets on the end of his dark, ludicrously long lashes and covered his face, making the olive-toned skin glow gold in the subdued lighting. Even if you had taken the incredible mouth and the dark deep-set eyes from the equation, the combination of hard planes and fascinating angles, emphasised by the shadow on his square jaw and hollow cheeks, was overtly sensual and overpoweringly male.

Refusing to acknowledge the hot sensation in her stomach as sexual awareness, she tried to kick free of the oddly hypnotic, cold, heavy-lidded eyes that held her own.

'Who are you?' she blurted when her vocal cords started working. Her voice lacked the welcoming Highland warmth that happy tourists frequently mentioned in their five-star reviews of the establishment, but, in her defence, she was in shock…or *something*?

She swallowed and brought her lashes down. Despite the protective sweep she continued to be conscious of those dark eyes with the glittering, deeply disturbing gold lights.

Oh, yes, she thought, grateful for the layers of clothing that muffled the sound of her heart hammering against her ribcage, this was *definitely* something. Not a big, significant something, just an 'opening of the door to find the most good-looking man she had ever seen or even dreamt existed standing there' something.

Was this a good time to discover that you still had a built-in weak spot for a pretty face? No, *Callum* had been *pretty*, this man was more…was *beautiful*. Too big a word…?

No, it wasn't, she decided, studying the perfect bone structure of his strongly carved face with its high carved cheekbones, square jawline and aquiline nose, her stomach dipping uncomfortably when she reached the sensual outline of his wide mouth.

Though actually what had really thrown her was the shock wave of overt sexuality his large presence in the low-ceilinged room created. The surface of her skin prickled with it and her knees were shaking.

Great! Just what she needed!

Fate decided losing her dearest sister and brother-in-law, inheriting their business and their baby son was not enough! Mr Dark and Brooding had to turn up on her doorstep and kick into life the embers of her dormant libido!

Admittedly, not dark and brooding's fault, but she struggled to view the intruder who, as supplying the *last* straw, she felt might just make her fold, with any objectivity.

Mouth closed might be a move in the right direction, Flora.

'I booked a room.'

His very low, deep voice had an almost tactile quality and held an intriguing almost accent. A wave of deep sadness tightened her throat—much deeper and harsher, but it reminded her a little of her late brother-in-law, Bruno. But Bruno's voice had been warm and filled with laughter; the stranger's voice held about the same amount of warmth as his cold dark eyes as he waited for her to respond.

She gave herself a mental shake, and dug deep into her reserves of professionalism. It wasn't normally an effort—she'd cut her hospitality teeth working shifts in a bar in Edinburgh when she was working her way through university. Several recent guests had commented online about her 'friendly efficiency and warmth'.

So why was she standing here like a tongue-tied idiot?

True, to date none of the guests she'd immediately felt at ease with had arrived wearing a suit that screamed designer beneath a long, equally expensive-looking coat that hung off shoulders a mile wide. And none had... no, she decided not to even *think* about the sexual aura he exuded, hoping that she'd wake up tomorrow after a good night's sleep and discover it was a sleep-deprivation thing. The odds of this happening were pretty good, because, though her ex-fiancé's opinion on most things counted for zero with her, on one thing he was probably right—she wasn't really a *sexual* person.

'Is there a problem?'

Beyond the inescapable fact, Ivo realised, that he had made the mistake of nursing preconceptions, having them challenged made him feel slightly off balance—not something he was accustomed to.

He didn't intend to get accustomed to it.

He hadn't even realised until the door had opened that he'd been expecting a tall willowy blonde standing there. He'd not been imagining a petite redhead, a belt holding up her snug-fitting jeans around an impossibly narrow waist.

Ivo dug his hands deep into his pockets as his long brown fingers flexed in response to the mental image of them closing around the circumference. The slight but distinctly feminine sinuous curves above and below the belt sent a fresh slug of scorching heat through his body as he studied them again before he dragged his attention back to her face.

He couldn't pretend it was a hardship to look at the woman his grandfather had casually suggested he marry.

From nowhere an image of her floating down a church aisle in white came into his head but he pushed it away. The same way he pushed away any thought of marriage. It had seemed like an inevitable prospect, something he owed to the continuation of his name… but the existence of Bruno's child, the next generation, took the pressure off.

Ivo was here, yes, but not to marry anyone!

Was his alternative plan any less insane? Actually, 'plan' might be overstating it—more a play-it-by-ear than actual plan.

So, yes, *possibly* insane, but less insane than it had seemed around the same time he had seriously contemplated abandoning his car on a section of the road that was underwater about half a mile away.

Ivo didn't believe in fate, signs or divine intervention, but when you were driving along a road that was rapidly becoming a river a man, even one who prided himself on being rational, did start to wonder: was someone somewhere trying to tell him something?

And it wasn't the first snag!

Ivo prided himself on being adaptable but today had tested him. Since he'd set out this morning everything that could go wrong had. Engine problems shortly after they had taken off from the private airstrip had forced the pilot to turn back and make an emergency landing in Rome.

When he had finally landed in the replacement jet there had been no driver willing to make the journey up to Skye with weather warnings out advising only essential journeys being made.

Considering that his journey was essential, he had been privately pretty scornful of weather warnings in the British Isles, assuming they'd probably meant heavy drizzle.

His contempt had come back to bite him. He glanced down at his ruined handmade leather shoes—the elderly couple he'd rescued after they'd run off the road had treated him like a hero—not a good fit.

And now he was here and things were still not going to plan. He focused the objectivity he was famed for—some called it coldness—on the heart-shaped face turned up to him.

To suggest that she was *not* beautiful—even taking into account that his taste in women had never run to petite and fragile—would not have been an objective assessment. He'd met women who were more beautiful, though none had possessed a heart-shaped face framed by wild Pre-Raphaelite curls, the deep titian interwoven with strands of lighter gold.

As unexpected as the vividly pretty heart-shaped face had been was the twist of hard desire he'd experienced when he'd first laid eyes on her.

Setting aside that visceral response, he continued to study the face that had drawn this reaction. It was a face that came complete with tip-tilted nose, a cute, curvy full mouth and wildly sexy and deep kitten-wide pansy-blue eyes framed by spiky, thick, straight lashes. There was the suggestion of a cleft in her pointed, determined small chin.

* * *

In response to his question, Flora lifted her eyes from the relative safety of mid-chest level. His hard stare was disconcerting.

'You're wearing a tie.'

She squeezed her eyes closed and thought, *Any moment now I'm going to say something that suggests I have more than two brain cells.*

Please make it soon!

When she opened them again he'd already unbelted his overcoat and a jacket button. The long brown fingers of his hand were smoothing the already smooth streak of his grey tie that stood out against the spotless background of white, a white made virtually transparent by its saturated condition.

She registered the shadow of dark body hair before she looked quickly away, ignoring the tingling tightness that extended even to the skin of her scalp.

'You have a dress code?'

Ignoring the sneery sarcasm in his question, though if they had had one it would have been waterproofs and walking boots, she reminded herself that it was her job to make their guests' stays happy ones, even the ones who were objectionable. Though to be fair she supposed that anyone who had negotiated the single-track-with-passing-places roads to get here, scary for the uninitiated in any weather, might have some excuse for feeling stressed.

Not that he looked stressed, quite the opposite. The aura he projected was of someone in charge, not someone who needed reassurance and sympathy. It was hard to imagine anyone offering him a cup of tea and very much easier, she mused as her eyes drifted to that mouth, to think of them offering him a more intimate form of comfort.

She tried to walk back from the image that flashed into her head—it didn't help the situation in any way imagining a man naked—and produced a half-decent professional smile. Though the effect was probably spoilt by baby sick on her shoulder...*again.*

'No, but we do have drying facilities if you venture out on the hills, though obviously not recommended in this weather,' she added hastily. It was amazing how sometimes you had to spell out the obvious and amazing how little respect some city types had for either the elements or the terrain of the island.

'Oh, and there are Ordnance Survey maps in all the bedrooms, though some of guests make use of a local mountain guide service. And if you're interested in geology there are some fascinating—'

'I'm not, and I have quite a good sense of direction.' It had enabled him to be one of only a handful of entrants to complete the arduous desert trek against the clock and the elements for charity, but perversely right now the only place it was taking him was the curve of her lush lips—every road led to the same place.

The awkward silence stretched. Flora filled it with a cheery, 'So, you're here for the fishing?' As much as they desperately needed the money, Flora found herself wishing that he wasn't here at all.

His jaw clenched. 'I'm not here for the fishing.'

Fighting the childish urge to tell him she wasn't really interested anyway, she smiled. 'Well, I hope you enjoy your stay.' She hesitated a moment before admitting, 'The truth is I wasn't aware we had any bookings. Have you come far?'

'Yes.'

I've had more interesting conversations with a brick wall, she thought, keeping her smile in place until she discovered he was staring at her hair. She fought and lost the impulse to lift a hand to smooth the tangled curls, which at some point today had come free of the tight, efficient ponytail. The time when she was working in Edinburgh and spent the twenty minutes required in the morning to religiously straighten it to a smooth, shiny, straight river seemed a million years ago.

Luxury in this life was applying some lip balm.

'Well, I think you're very brave to make the journey in this storm, or possibly very foolish…?' As the addition slipped past her guard she added a smile, which hopefully robbed the comment of insult.

You did have to wonder, though, who in their right mind made a journey in this weather, ignoring advice from every agency out there including the stretched police force, who were begging people not to make unnecessary journeys until the storm abated.

It took a special sort of arrogance, and on their brief acquaintance Flora suspected this man possessed that quality in abundance.

'Right, well, if you'd just like to check in? Card, or…' She looked towards the table where the old-fashioned leather ledger was kept beside a book inviting guests to add their hopefully complimentary comments.

The book and the flowers and twigs she'd arranged in the old zinc jug the previous day were there, but not the leather ledger.

Ivo watched as she pressed a finger to the groove above her nose, her smooth brow puckering in concentration, but it was the dark purplish smudges beneath her blue eyes that drew his attention. He pushed away a waft of feeling that fell short of being empathy but nevertheless was distracting.

And he didn't need any more distraction, he decided, the initial gut-punch reaction when the door had opened to reveal a diminutive flame-haired figure still raising some uncomfortable red-line-crossed feelings that he felt the need to rationalise. He had clearly subconsciously been expecting a replica of her sister, the tall willowy blonde who had bewitched his brother, and he was still adjusting to the reality. Add that to him not factoring in the possibility he might find the woman that stood between him and his nephew attractive.

He had acknowledged it now and moved on... It would only be a problem if he allowed it to be.

And he wouldn't.

His confidence was justified: the last time Ivo had allowed his libido to rule him he'd been a teenager and his brother had not yet abandoned everything for a woman. Ivo had been in lust a number of times but had so far avoided anything that could be termed *in love*. He'd never been in what people would call a long-term relationship, because, in his experience, before he'd ever got close to long term the woman in his bed, who had begun by telling him how much she *loved* him the way he was, had begun chipping quietly away, trying to change what she had claimed to like about him.

A massive red line of a deal breaker; the woman did not exist that he would change for. The woman did not exist that he could not live without. Even the thought drew the corners of his lips into a cynical smile.

'You *are* the person in charge?'

His words brought Flora's chin up. Obviously this guy's personality was not as perfect as the rest of him.

'I am the person in charge,' she confirmed, sounding

a lot calmer than she felt while she wondered what sort of write-up punching him on his nose would earn her.

Actually, during the past nightmare weeks, *in charge* was the last thing she had felt, but luckily she could put on a good act. She did so now as she walked confidently across to the bar, as if there were no doubt in her mind that she would find the old-fashioned bookings diary where it lay concealed on a shelf.

Luck was on her side.

'Here we are,' she said, laying it on the reclaimed wood surface.

The satellite dish meant to connect them to the Internet and the twenty-first century was arriving next week, which might make this old-fashioned ledger redundant. It was another of the outstanding bills that was keeping her awake nights.

She turned from the back where the restaurant bookings were written down, all this evening's cancellations highlighted by a red line drawn through them, to the front where room bookings were recorded. Sure enough, above one of the cancellations one of the rooms had been booked out for tonight.

She looked up, struggling to feel the professional warmth she had infused her smile with. 'I'm sorry I missed this one, Mr...?' She shook her head unable to decipher Fergus's scrawl or throw off the peculiarly strong antipathy the man had evoked in her.

'Rocco,' Ivo responded, giving his middle name as he had on the telephone when booking. He hadn't wanted to commit himself to a course of action before he'd read the situation.

'Right, Mr Rocco, sorry about the miscommunication and the welcome.'

'Or lack of it,' he inserted smoothly.

'Just so, afraid I'd assumed that everyone had cancelled due to the storm.'

His dark gold-flecked gaze slid to the window where relentless rain was lashing. 'You mean it's not always like this?'

The comment was delivered without the leavening humour which would have made it acceptable. Flora resisted the impulse to rush to the defence of her beloved home.

Her smile frayed a little at the edges as her sister's face floated into her head. Sami would have had this man eating out of her hand by now. She flinched at the physical impact as the fresh loss hit her all over again. She almost wished that Jamie would wake up so that she would have something practical to focus on to dull the pain. Maybe being too tired to think was not such a bad thing, she mused, ignoring the bleak voice in her head that told her she was only delaying the inevitable, she'd have to *feel* at some point.

'Would you like a wee dram to warm you after your journey?' She bent down to reach the forty-year-old single malt they kept behind the bar for occasions such as this.

The bottle of last resort, Bruno had called it, to be used when everything else failed with awkward or upset customers. They had very few of those, and so far it had been brought out to toast special occasions, like newly engaged couples.

Ivo watched, with what he told himself was academic interest, as the denim of the redhead's jeans stretched attractively over her taut, rounded rear as she bent over. There was nothing academic about the flash of heat down his front.

Flora straightened up, planted the bottle on the bar

so that he could see the label, but his expression did not melt… *Could granite melt?* 'On the house, of course,' she added hastily.

'No.' The guest responded to the generous gesture with a look that flattened her smile. 'If I could see the menu?'

Her expression fell. 'Menu…?'

He arched a sardonic brow and watched the angry colour wash over the fair freckled skin.

She bit her lip. 'Fergus, the chef, has gone home actually…' She stopped. Was it such a good idea to tell this bad-tempered beautiful stranger with his indefinably menacing air that they were alone but for a baby lying asleep upstairs? Feeling ashamed of the sudden flurry of fear, she lifted her chin, squared her shoulders and added a very unconvincing, 'Sorry.'

'So your kitchen is closed?' *Of course it was.* Ivo had stopped trying to imagine the urbane sophisticated brother he remembered living in this cold, misty, uninviting backwater. He sent up a silent apology to his grandfather, who he had assumed was guilty of over-exaggeration when he'd described the place his great-grandson needed rescuing from. Ivo no longer needed convincing.

From his expression she could see there was no five-star rating heading their way. 'I could make you a sandwich?' It wasn't that she *couldn't* cook, but Flora was intimidated by the restaurant's industrial-looking catering kitchen with its shiny stainless-steel surfaces and latest top-of-the-range gadgets.

She didn't ask for a translation of the sound he made in his throat, quite happy to take it as a rejection.

'Right, then,' she said briskly. 'Shall I show you to your room? We're having a little storm-related problem with the heating,' she explained putting an awful lot of effort into the lie. It was glaringly obvious by his attitude that he didn't actually believe a word she was saying. 'But I'll bring up an electric heater and you'll be toasty in no time.' She crossed her fingers while making the over-optimistic prediction. 'If you'll follow me?'

One foot on the bottom step of the staircase, she stopped as the fire chose that moment to belch a fresh flume of acrid smoke that filled the entire room. Flora stopped cursing long enough to cough. 'The wind must be in the wrong direction,' she excused hoarsely.

'There is a right direction?' he asked sardonically.

Before she could react to the sarcasm she was distracted by a sighing sound broadcast from the baby monitor, followed by a sleepy murmur.

Ivo watched as the redhead literally held her breath for a full thirty seconds before her tense shoulders sagged with visible relief.

CHAPTER THREE

'YOU HAVE A CHILD?'

He watched the shock widen her eyes. Fascinated, Ivo observed the play of emotion across her fine-boned features. His fascination was mingled with disquiet that anyone could wear their emotions so close to the surface; the idea of exposing your vulnerabilities to the world the way she appeared to was anathema to Ivo.

When her reply came a moment or so later it was tinged with surprise underlain with a hint of defiance evident in the straightening of her slender shoulders.

'Yes, that is my child.'

Flora had accepted the doctor's verdict. It hadn't been easy, and for a time she had been angry, but she had come to terms with the fact her endometriosis was so bad that her fertility was severely impaired.

She could have carried on being angry and bitter or hoped for a medical miracle. She supposed it was one of those events in life that everyone reacted to differently. Her way had been to accept what had happened, and save her energy for fights she could win, not lost causes.

That didn't mean she hadn't dreamt of saying those words...*my child*.

Ironic that when she got to say them it wasn't because of a miracle or a dream-come-true scenario but because she was living a waking version of a nightmare Flora would have given everything she possessed *not* to be saying those words now, but when she did verbalising them brought home the full reality of the situation crashing in.

It was something that happened several times a day and each time the impact felt like walking into a wall of loss and pain, and, yes, fear that she just wasn't up to the job.

Flora had never felt more desperately inadequate to any task in her life. Sure, her career had held challenges, and some were scary with an inbuilt possibility of failure, but this was different. *Parenthood* was different. Being responsible for a life was the scariest thing she had ever imagined. Could any training prepare you for it?

Or were good mothers born?

Sami had been one of those, she thought, her eyes misting as she thought of her sister, who had made it look so easy. Pushing her way through the jumble of conflicting emotions, she took a deep breath.

Doubts were distractions she couldn't afford. She needed to stay in 'one foot in front of the other' mode, and firmly focused on mundane things like paying the bills and staying awake!

Feelings and doubts were a luxury she didn't have time for.

'Oh, sorry,' she said brightly. 'Can I take your bag?' She glanced towards the overnight holdall he had dropped inside the door when he'd arrived.

Even standing on the second step, she had to tilt her head back to look him in the face. The action made her bright hair spill backwards in a tangled silky coil down her narrow back.

He knew from the file Salvatore had compiled—his grandfather was nothing if not thorough—that Flora Henderson had been forced by the recent tragic events to walk away from what was probably her dream job. He'd anticipated there might be resentment he might utilise to achieve his objective, that the role thrust on her might make her vulnerable.

Yes, she was, it was there to see in the hollows in her smooth cheeks, the shadowed unhappiness reflected in the shocking blue of her eyes and the dark circles underneath.

Yet instead of feeling satisfaction Ivo was conscious of something that came close enough to compassion to jolt him free of those blue eyes. A moment later he reassessed his reaction. Compassion required a degree of caring, and he did not care for this woman; there was nothing *personal* between them.

He only did personal with family and, aside from his grandfather, his only family now was the child sleeping upstairs. This woman stood between him and that child.

'I think I'll manage, Ms…?'

'Oh, it's Henderson.' Then, because they were listed on all the websites as providing a relaxed, informal environment, she fought her innate reluctance to provide this man with any personal details and added, 'Flora.' Facing ahead, she started up the stairs, not needing the creak behind her to tell he was following. The hairs on the back of her neck told her that.

By the time they reached the top she was breathless, in part because she had attacked them like an athlete out to break records, but mostly because of the unnerving way he had looked at her, as though he could see inside her head.

They reached the top and she paused, opening the

door of the store cupboard at the top and reaching in to pull out an electric fan heater, relieved to be able to look efficient, or at least slightly less inefficient. No need for him to know that she had only remembered where they were stored halfway up the stairs.

'Your room is the other side of the house.' Flora tucked the light heater under her arm and pushed aside a tendril of red hair that was tickling her nose. 'So, hopefully you won't be disturbed. Fingers crossed.'

'That's a very scientific attitude to customer service.'

Flora smiled through gritted teeth, rather glad she had only imagined the sympathy she had seen in his face. 'We aim more for the warm personal touch.' *Not that personal, Flora,* said the voice in her head when she realised the she was staring at the firm, sensual outline of his mouth. 'If you'd like to follow me, Mr Rocco,' she offered primly.

The selection of the room farthest from the nursery had seemed a good choice. It was the biggest and it had the best views; the size meant tonight it was also the coldest.

'I hope you'll be comfortable,' she huffed, watching her warm breath mist in the cold air as she bent forward to plug in the heater before switching it to the maximum setting. 'It'll warm up in no time,' she promised him optimistically.

'So, tea and coffee making facilities.' Her fluttering gesture indicated the tray complete with cafetière on a side table. She picked up the tin beside it. 'The shortbread is homemade.' Most guests looked impressed by this; he didn't, but Flora doggedly persevered despite the lack of reaction. *Heavens, would it kill him to smile?* 'Drinks and milk in the fridge,' she added, ticking off the items in her head. She opened the wardrobe door.

'Fresh robe and extra towels and blankets. Just let us know when you check out what you had. The prices are the same as the bar. I hope you have a comfortable night, Mr Rocco,' she said formally as she backed towards the door. 'Oh, would you like a hot-water bottle tucked in your bed?'

If there was anything he would like tucked...

He stopped the thought dead but had no control over the blood-warming image that followed in its wake, an image that involved him being warmed by her smooth limbs wrapped around him. A slow steady throb of heat slid through his body. When he was finally able to force the words out past the lustful fog that had seeped into his head, his voice had a throaty rasp.

'Do I look like I need a hot-water bottle, Flora?' What he needed was some resistance to the magnetic pull of her plump rose-coloured lips.

His grandfather's plan might have involved seduction but his wouldn't. Emotions complicated things, and expecting someone who showed every nuance of emotion on her face to have any degree of emotional continence was unrealistic.

His plan would be a business deal plain and simple... in theory at least. He was beginning to wonder if this woman could do plain and simple. Was she capable of looking through anything without distorting the image through an emotional prism?

It was his task to make sure she did. He didn't doubt his ability to make this happen and, given the fact her options were limited, it should not be difficult.

His delivery was deadpan, the tone sardonic, but it was the predatory glow in his dark eyes... She wanted to look away. She wanted to run from the room in which the *uncomfortable* factor in the atmosphere she'd coped

with up to this point by simply pretending it didn't exist
had hiked up several notches.

Ignoring was no longer an option.

But growing a backbone was.

Focusing on the sound of distant alarm bells and
not the ache in her stomach, she lifted her chin and
wrenched her eyes free of his molten stare. Or was it
molten? Was she just seeing what she wanted to?

The mortifying idea that she *wanted* him to look at
her that way cooled the sexual pulse that beat low and
hot in her belly. Her initial antipathy had not been irrational but spot on. Her chin lifted. He might remind
her of a sleek, well-fed predator, but she was damned
if she was going to act like some little cowering mouse
for his amusement.

Hope you freeze!

For one awful moment she thought she'd voiced the
vicious and uncharitably spiteful thought out loud. She
almost felt ashamed. She was neither vicious nor spiteful.

'Goodnight, Mr Rocco.'

Flora waited until she had cleared the guest wing of the
house before she leaned against the wall and released
the tension that had her body in a stranglehold grip in
a series of long hissing sighs.

Her legs felt like lead as she went back to the store
cupboard and pulled out the heaters for Jamie's room;
her energy levels seemed to have seeped away along
with the tension. She headed for the baby's room. There
were no heaters left for her own bedroom but then cooling down was probably not such a bad idea.

On tiptoe, barely breathing, Flora plugged the heaters in one of the sockets in Jamie's room. She looked

at the sleeping baby, the swell of love that tightened in her chest physically painful.

She might be a poor substitute for what he had lost but she was *determined* to give this baby all the love his parents would have if they had lived. If only, she mused wistfully, there were a handbook somewhere for people who had zero parenting skills.

Her mum was there to help and pass on her parenting skills and Flora was thankful for that, but she was also reluctant to rely on her too much. It was easy to forget sometimes, given her very youthful outlook and zest for life, that Grace Henderson had had her share of health problems. Typically, she played them down but losing Sami had taken a massive emotional toll and then she'd had her own accident... No, her mum needed to be resting and healing, not running to the aid of her pathetic daughter, which was why Flora had been glossing over any difficulties she was having and not confiding her doubts. She would tell her mum about the nightmare financial problems she had inherited after she had worked out a solution...*or they foreclosed on the mortgage*.

Pushing away the depressing thought, she took one last look at the sleeping baby, wondering if it was possible the baby just *knew* there was an amateur in charge, that at some instinctive baby level he knew that the two people who loved him most were gone.

But he'd know his parents; they would be real people to him. Flora had already begun putting items, photos and mementos in a memory book to show him when he was older. She had pasted photos of her sister growing up on the first few pages; she just wished she had more memories of his father to put in.

'Sleep tight,' she whispered, checking the red light

on the baby monitor one last time before she quietly left the room, then slipping downstairs for a last-minute check. She switched off the outside light and peered through the window just as the moon appeared through the clouds.

Her stomach gave a little lurch of dismay and her eyes grew round in horror as the silver light revealed the water level; the waves were lapping in the middle of the road just feet from the low wall.

Was this the perfect storm moment, the once every twenty years that they would flood?

She pushed away the thought. She was not the sort of person who assumed the worst, though, after the worst had happened to their family, her built-in optimism was feeling more than a little battered and bruised. It was weariness and not optimism that enabled her to dismiss the potential disaster and make her way up the stairs.

With the heater turned up full the room became, if not *toasty* as his hostess had optimistically predicted, at least tolerably warm enough to make him feel able to strip down to his shorts before he got into the surprisingly comfortable bed with the pristine white sheets.

His head had barely made an indent in the pillow before he heard the sound, the soft but unmistakable sound of a baby's cry above the sounds of the storm that continued to rage outside.

Ten minutes later the baby was still crying.

Did healthy babies cry this much?

Ivo had always possessed the ability to tune out background noise and distractions. He could sleep anywhere—at least he'd thought so. But it turned out there was a nerve-shredding noise that he couldn't tune out. Twice over the next half an hour the sound stopped only to start up again just as he had been lulled into a false sense of security and relaxed.

When it happened a third time he snapped; throwing back the quilt, he bounced out of bed and over to the door.

The temperature in the hallway was several degrees colder than his room. At some point, he supposed, this had seemed like a good idea, if for no other reason than anything was better than lying there listening to the racket that was driving him crazy. *Now you'll just look crazy!*

Quite suddenly the noise stopped. Aware it could be another false alarm, he didn't relax, neither did he turn around and crawl into his comfortable bed and get what sleep he could. He was committed to the course of action that took his feet towards the flickering light he could see spilling out into the hallways ahead.

The compulsion that drove him was stronger than logic. His brother's child, his nephew, was inside that room, the only part of Bruno that remained.

When he reached it, the door was ajar. On well-oiled hinges it swung silently inwards when he touched it. The room it revealed was small, painted a bright in-your-face yellow. The heat blasting out from the heaters that were positioned either end of it made the mobiles hanging from the ceiling spin, bringing the clowns and seals and cats to life. The effect when you added the stars and moons the night light projected on the ceiling was all a little surreal.

Ivo barely noticed.

His attention was completely focused on the spot where Flora Henderson was standing, her back turned to him, for the moment oblivious of his presence. She was holding the child, who seemed to be sleeping now;

all he could see was the dark curly top of his head and his legs encased in blue, hanging limp.

He watched as she walked barefoot across the room to where the cot was situated under a curtained window. She was wearing a thin blue cotton nightdress that ended just below her knees and was held up by thin straps that revealed the curve of her delicate shoulder blades. The fabric billowed a little as she walked, allowing him to see the narrowness of her waist and the firm curves of her bottom through it.

Later, when he examined the moment he viewed it in the light of a long, very bad, incredibly frustrating day, but at that moment he could not apply logic to the scalding heat of the hormone rush that blanked his mind totally. Just wiped it clean of everything but the sense-destroying lust that for a few moments utterly consumed him.

He had begun to claw his way back to a semblance of control when she lifted her head, the upper half of her body half turning towards him, allowing him a view, through the gaping neck of her nightdress, of the smooth slopes of her breasts and the darker shadow of her nipples through the fabric. Their glances connected, blue on black, and he felt the control he had fought for slipping through his fingers like a wet rope burning flesh as he clung on.

Then he saw the wetness on her face, absorbed the evidence of tears that she didn't seem conscious of and the gleam of intent in his eyes faded. He swallowed.

'Let me help.' Ivo had no idea where the words came from; he was immune to female tears.

So why was he reacting to them now?

The answer threw up a lot more difficult questions. He'd first set eyes on the woman a couple of hours ago so how could he be so sure, so absolutely bet-your-life-on-it positive, that the tears were not there to gain sympathy? Why did he *know* she'd crawl before she'd ask for help?

Flora's chin went up in response. She opened her mouth, the huffy rejection ready to deliver with the right degree of 'I can take care of myself' ice, when on her shoulder the baby shifted and gave a sleepy sigh.

She reacted automatically, shifting his weight so that he lay against her chest in the crook of her right arm. She flexed the fingers of her left hand, still numb and tingling from the time she had taken his weight there.

Oh, God, what was she doing, and what place did pride have in the situation? She needed a helping hand even if that hand, with the long tapering brown fingers, did seem to exert a weird and worrying fascination. Help, even if it came from a totally unexpected and frankly disturbing quarter, was still help.

And on the plus side, accepting his offer would mean hopefully he'd vanish a lot quicker.

And Flora needed him to vanish. He was too big and too...*everything* for the room. His presence seemed to alter the constituents of the air she was breathing, making it heavy, making breathing require a conscious effort.

'I have kind of lost the feeling in my left arm. If you could just pull the cot sheet back?' Her chin resting on Jamie's dark curls, she stretched out, letting out a tiny but revealing gasp as her hand felt the brush of his long brown fingers.

The electrical surge that made her eyes widen left her knees feeling weak and reawakened the shivery sensation that had originally alerted her to his presence a few heavy heartbeats before she actually saw him standing there, carrying off the tumbled-out-of-bed look like only your average sex god could.

She supposed that she should be grateful that he didn't sleep naked, though the boxer shorts he wore were not substantial enough to help her!

'Thank you.'

She had no defence mechanism to deal with the compulsion to stare at his long, lean, golden, totally magnificent body. There was not an ounce of surplus flesh to hide the perfect definition of his toned body. Her eyelids fluttered and her throat grew dry as her glance slid again over the broadness of his muscled shoulders and chest to the slabbed muscles of his belly. His legs were long, the muscular thighs slightly dusted with dark hair. The same dark hair that formed a directional arrow that vanished beneath the waistband of his boxer shorts.

Pulling in a sharp, tense breath, Flora lifted her gaze and found it connecting with his, dark shadowed and deeply disturbing. His olive skin looked warm, his carved mouth looked... She blinked hard and took a step back like someone who had just discovered they were standing on the edge of a precipice, which explained the dizziness.

He watched her lift a fluttering hand to her face, looking bemused as it came away wet. She frowned at her fingers, not seeming to make the connection between the salty moisture and her own tears.

He didn't know if the tiny negative shake of her head was aimed at herself or him, and a moment later her expression was hidden from view, the silky curtain of her flame-red hair falling in an abundant cloud as she bent forward to lay the sleeping baby into the cot, fumbling with the crumpled sheet as she tried to pull it back.

'Let me.'

Without waiting for a response, he pulled back the tangled sheet she had been struggling with, smoothing it back so that she could lay the baby down on his back.

As the baby lay there clenching and unclenching this pudgy fists, Ivo had his first proper look at his nephew, hungry to see a resemblance to his brother in the unformed features. He felt a strange tightness in his chest as he took in the details: dark hair, a snub nose and pale pink skin, eyes tightly closed, untouched by life yet and *totally* perfect.

So vulnerable.

Your father would have died for you, he thought.

Better Bruno had lived.

'I...thank you.' The light brush of his fingers lasted longer than it should this time. As for the stomach-clenching shudder that felt as though it would never go away even after his hand had moved and he had straightened up...

She took longer than she needed to smooth the sheet over the baby, giving herself some time to recover from the primal reaction that had convulsed her body when she'd seen him standing there, a confusing combination of heart-thudding excitement and fear blurred into one.

'You must be cold,' she blurted stupidly.

His mobile lips twitched into a wicked smile that made her stomach lurch.

The man looked like a fallen angel on steroids!

The impression intensified as he spread his arms wide, then slowly he glanced down, an expression of comical injured dismay on his ludicrously handsome chest. 'You have very high standards, *cara.*'

The softly drawled *cara* hit her reasoning functions dead centre, delaying her deciphering of the softly seductive insinuation.

When his meaning hit she wanted to crawl under a stone. Instead she lifted her chin and, hampered by the need to keep the noise down, whispered, 'I didn't mean...' She stopped. Of course he knew what she didn't mean. *'Funny!'* She sniffed, slinging him an unamused glance as she moved away from the cot containing the sleeping baby.

He followed her; the combination of handsome, half-naked, totally gorgeous man and small room was enough to make anyone hyperventilate. She resisted the impulse to pick a cushion from the rocker and wield it defensively. Instead she pressed a hand to her chest and willed her breathing to slow. 'I'm sorry if I disturbed you.'

It was the next best thing to pushing him through the door, an obvious signal for him to go; it was equally obvious he didn't recognise it as such. She ground her teeth in frustration and, seriously, he had to be cold by now. Despite the unbidden thought, by some miracle she kept her eyes above waist level, though the effort raised her own internal temperature by several uncomfortably shameful degrees.

She took another step towards the door and reached across to switch the lamp off, before turning the dimmer on the night light down. The room was now lit by the soft soothing silhouettes of moons and stars revolving on the ceiling.

'So, goodnight, Mr Rocco,' she said softly.

He saw the dismissal in her smile and, while part of him recognised walking away was a good idea, he just couldn't let it go and he didn't have a clue why!

She hadn't quite reached the door when his soft voice brought her to a halt.

'You've been crying.'

Her eyes flew to his face, her first instinct to deny this crazy assertion. It was a reflex. People looked at her and saw fragile; she wasn't, and if it meant acting a bit tougher than she actually was to show them how wrong they were it was a price worth paying.

Fast on the first instinct and overpowering it in a heartbeat was the realisation that letting her guard down to someone who didn't know her, and who couldn't care less, someone who wasn't going to lose sleep over anything, might be the outlet she needed.

In any event the internal debate was useless because the words came of their own volition.

'It was the blinds.' Her eyes went to the blinds with their cheery fabric of sailboats and balloons, drawn to cut out the darkness beyond. Flora had her own darkness inside and there was no hiding from that. She felt as though she'd never feel light again.

Only crazy people wept buckets about window dressings. She wouldn't have blamed him if he'd made a dash for the door—it would save her making any more of a fool of herself than she had already.

But he didn't.

'Sami, my big sister, she made them—she could make anything!' Her smile dissolved into a gulp as she rushed on. 'We shopped for the material...' It had been a girls' day out in Edinburgh. 'We had lunch, too many cocktails—it was a perfect day.'

Her big blue eyes lifted to his. It was all there for him to see: the pain, the grief, the aching sense of loss. He didn't *want* to see it but he couldn't stop looking and listening to her beautifully accented, hushed voice.

'Only I didn't know that at the time or I would have...' Her voice trailed away.

'Cherished it?'

Her eyes flew wide in acknowledgement.

'It seems to me you did.' He could have had moments to cherish but... Jaw clenched, he pushed away the thought, unwilling to allow himself the indulgence of self-pity.

He couldn't change history; he couldn't have that day with his brother; he couldn't be part, even for a short time, of the small family that had been so cruelly ripped apart, but he could be there for Bruno's son.

What do you know about families? sneered the voice in his head.

He turned a deaf ear to the voice and focused on the memory of that almost visceral rush of protectiveness he had felt when he'd seen the baby. Nothing else really mattered.

'I miss her and Jamie is missing her, too. I know he is.' Her glance swivelled to the sleeping baby, perceptibly softening as she did so. 'He's her son, not mine.' Her glance lifted from the baby to briefly touch his lean dark face.

He's a stranger—why are you telling him this?
Because he is a stranger.

'Hers and Bruno's.' Still looking in the direction of the cot, she didn't see his reaction to her mention of her brother-in-law's name, the flicker of pain that crossed his handsome face. 'I'm trying, but I don't really think I'm cut out for this. Any of it.' She had dodged the truth for so long that to say it out loud, to acknowledge it, was a massive relief. 'I make a *terrible* mother.'

The confession should, under the circumstances, have been music to his ears. Instead as Ivo looked into those tear-filled, tragic, beautiful eyes he was conscious of a totally alien and dangerous instinct to offer comfort.

He didn't like the feeling; the effort of combatting it made the muscles round his strong jaw quiver.

Flora's chest felt tight as she struggled to hold in the sob she could feel building inside her.

She was winning the battle when he touched her face. The shock of the contact melted through her, each subsequent ripple of sensation making her insides dissolve warmly. She wanted to look away but his thumb was lodged in the angle of her jaw, framing her face, his finger on her cheek.

'It must be tough…alone…' He silenced the sudden stab of guilt with the reminder that everything he had seen told him that his decision to take Bruno back to Italy was the right one. This woman was drowning under the weight of responsibility, and she'd thank him in the long run. Not that he wanted her thanks, he just wanted Bruno's son back where he belonged.

'You *are* alone…?'

Flora nodded, touched despite herself by his understanding. She had actually never felt more alone in her life.

She blinked. His chest was just there, warm and hard and solid. In her head she saw herself laying her face against his skin, feeling his arms wrap around her, resting just for a moment.

She turned her cheek into his big hand. It was a good fit; his fingers were cool against her skin. It felt like a dream and any moment now she'd wake up.

Did she want to?

Had he stepped in closer? Had she? Flora realised she had no idea but she was breathing hard and feeling light-headed as she stared up into his eyes, the swell of feeling to let go inside her surging upwards… She stepped forward, this time consciously.

The floorboard beneath her feet creaked and she froze, the sound breaking her free of the sexual thrall that had held her a willing victim…and that was the shame of it: she'd been willing. So needy she would have accepted comfort from a total stranger.

Burning with shame, she turned, and with a mumbled, *'Sorry,'* dashed for the door, picking up a throw from the chair as she went.

After a moment Ivo followed her, closed the door behind him and watched as she wrapped the blanket and her dignity around herself like a protective shield.

'I have to tell you that I don't normally—' She stopped and thought.

I don't have to tell because he almost certainly doesn't want to know, and, let's face it, the man could probably fill a book with things he really doesn't want to know about you at this point, Flora.

'Sleep deprivation. Long day. Teething…'

Could you sound more certifiably insane if you tried, Flora? she asked herself in despair.

The last word drew his attention to her teeth, the neat white upper set, which were at that moment gouging a groove in the soft-flesh plumpness of her lower lip.

'Sexual frustration…?' It was with something of a relief that Ivo diagnosed his own aberrant behaviour.

She reacted to the slow sibilant suggestion by jerking to attention. 'Pardon?' He either didn't hear the ice in her tone, or didn't care.

'Well, it's got to be tough living all the way out here? Men are pretty scarce, I am assuming? Not what you're used to. You must miss your old life, the buzz of living in a city, friends, galleries, theatre and…'

She pulled herself up to her full height of five three and glared huffily across at him, too consumed by the battle with her own embarrassment to notice the colour scoring the angle of his high cheekbones. 'Are you suggesting I was…was…*hitting* on you? And how do you know I lived in the city?'

One sable brow lifted as he looked into her cobalt-blue eyes. Nothing in his face suggested he was anything other than mildly amused by what had happened.

'My mistake,' he drawled.

She screwed up her eyes and glared. 'I'd have to be a lot more desperate than I am to—' She stopped, a look of dismay that in other circumstances Ivo might have found amusing spreading across her face. 'Not that I am desperate, that is…' She saw his lips twitch and thought, *He's laughing at me.*

And you're surprised?

She opened her mouth and closed it again, remembering the advice her mother had been giving her since she was a little girl with a red-headed temper.

Flora, when you're in a hole that's over your head, stop digging!

It was a lesson she still hadn't learnt.

'We are not exactly a cultural desert here, you know, and…goodnight, Mr Rocco.'

'Goodnight, *Ms* Henderson.' The heavy, hot desire pooled in his groin suggested this would not be a good night for him.

CHAPTER FOUR

IVO HAD EVENTUALLY fallen asleep at about four a.m., and when he woke it took him a few moments to realise what was different and then it came to him—it was the absence of noise.

It was totally silent.

The light shining through the edges of the closed blackout blind revealed a room he hadn't been in any mood to appreciate last night. The colour scheme was pale and soothing, shades of white and grey with splashes of colour in the art on the walls, which looked to be original. Besides the very comfortable and adequate-sized oak platform bed, the furniture was an eclectic mix of old and new. The exposed oak boards looked original and were softened by hand-woven rugs. A massive hand-thrown pot set on a slate washstand was filled with artistically arranged driftwood.

It was all a million miles away from the sleek modernity and uniformity of the professionally staged luxury hotel rooms he usually used as he travelled the world.

But unlike last night, this morning he was able to see the appeal. It was not hard to see why this place was popular, an opinion based not just on the ambience but the financial accounts his grandfather had *acquired*. It had a lot going for it, but Bruno had made the classic mistake of overextending himself. He'd left very little wriggle room, which meant the moment the unexpected had happened there had been a domino effect.

The unexpected had been a rise in the interest rates and—well—the fatal accident.

The place had closed for several weeks after the accident, which had punched a massive hole in the fragile cash-flow, and the situation had rapidly gone from bad to worse. Customers put off by the idea of new management had started cancelling their bookings.

The reputation could, of course, be rebuilt but not without a healthy cash flow. Without a massive injection of capital the place would go under; it was inevitable. Ivo was not sentimental about such things but he suspected, actually he was relying on the fact, that Flora Henderson was.

It seemed a safe bet.

An image of her expressive face drifted into his head.

More, it was a sure thing, he decided, a hint of disapproval turning down the corners of his mouth as he stretched to relieve the kinks in his spine and curved one hand above his head. It was a comfortable position to go over the events of last night, supported by a very comfortable mattress and safe this morning behind the wall of emotional isolation that had taken him years to build.

And one moment, one tear, one sniff, one trembling lip, to knock down.

He pushed the thought away.

It had been a perfect storm moment, and he wasn't going to make the mistake of reading too much into it. He left that to people who thought there was more to attraction than chemistry. He was not one of those people, and this morning his mind was functioning with its usual clarity and his objectivity was in place.

Lucky, because if the plan is to work you'll need to keep an emotional distance from the redhead!

It took Flora ten indulgent minutes to blur the worst of the ravages left by a sleepless night…only thirty seconds to scrub it all away; after all, she had nothing to prove to anyone, least of all a guest.

She was on her second cup of coffee when the kitchen back door opened. The farmer from the neighbouring farm stood there, a ladder casually balanced on his shoulder.

'Rough night.'

She started guiltily, the horror in her eyes giving way to embarrassment as she realised what he meant. 'Oh, the weather, you mean.'

'You've got a few slates loose, lass.'

The comment drew a laugh from Flora. 'You're not the first to suggest it.'

He grinned and half turned. 'Won't take long. See you've got a guest.' He nodded towards the small car park where a top-of-the-range car splattered with mud and complete with some spectacular scratches to the paintwork was parked beside her own battered four-wheel drive, which had so many dings that a few more weren't to be noticed.

Flora nodded.

'Ah, well, it all helps.'

Flora nodded again and wondered if *everyone* on the island knew about her financial problems. The answer, she knew, was probably. There were advantages and disadvantages to living in such a small community; secrets were a very rare commodity.

But when you needed help you didn't have to ask, she mused, deciding to delay ringing her mum until later—she might be having a lie-in.

She walked out into the bar area carrying cutlery to lay up a breakfast table, mentally practising the smooth, professional, just a little bit distant attitude she would take with her guest this morning.

She had no idea what she'd been thinking about, spilling everything like that. The memories made her cringe. The only solution to her embarrassment she had come up with was to pretend selective amnesia.

Well, what choice did she have? The option of taking the moral high ground was obviously off the table because if he had crossed any line she had virtually invited him to!

She squeezed her eyes closed in an effort to shut out the mortifying memories of her emotional outpouring and the strange intimacy of those moments.

Like the forced intimacy of two people with nothing in common, who were shipwrecked and…hell, there was no *forced* about it! Grimacing, she opened her eyes just in time to stop herself colliding with the tall figure from last night.

Standing with his back to her, he didn't immediately react to her exclamation; when he did turn around she saw what he was holding.

'That's my sister and her husband. Jamie was just hours old.' She held out her hand for the framed photo, resisting the impulse to snatch it from him.

'They look happy.' Ivo put the framed photo of the smiling couple holding a newborn in her hand and watched as she stroked the frame before replacing it on the shelf where he had seen it when he'd walked into the room.

Flora swallowed, feeling the anger rise up inside her like a wave. It was unfair—just so unfair. Why them? Her chest heaved with the silent effort of pushing those feelings back down. Newsflash: life wasn't fair—it sucked, end of story. She didn't have time to be bitter and twisted; she had a baby to care for and a business to save.

She felt those dark eyes on her and unconsciously straightened her shoulders before turning around. 'They were,' she said softly. 'I think they were the happiest people I know.' She made a throat-clearing sound before adding formally, 'So sorry we disturbed you last night, Mr Rocco.' *But not as much as you disturbed me,* she thought as an image floated into her head of him standing there in the doorway like a bronzed statue. Tthe memory was enough to create a rippling sensation low in her pelvis.

'It's Ivo.'

She acknowledged this with a slightly wary tip of her head, her brow furrowing as she wondered why that name seemed familiar. The answer was right there, then he spoke, and it vanished.

Ivo's dark brows drew into a critical dark line above his aquiline nose as he took in her pallor, and the dark shadows. 'Did you get *any* sleep?' The flash of concern in his head was filtered into accusation by the time it left his lips.

Her lips tightened under his critical scrutiny. So she looked like a wreck—did he imagine she needed telling? He, of course, looked as though he'd had a full eight hours; you could almost feel the vitality he oozed from every perfect pore. He was probably one of those irritating people who only needed an hour's sleep, she decided, nursing her resentment.

'Yes, thank you,' she lied, experiencing a flash of shame as she recalled the very little sleep she had had. Luckily for her peace of mind, only snatches of the dreams remained. *A girl can't take responsibility for her unconscious mind,* she reminded herself.

The excuse didn't really stand up to scrutiny when a moment later she found herself studying him through the sweep of her lashes. Her *conscious* mind was definitely in control as she took in the length of his legs in a pair of dark jeans and the lean, whipcord strength of his upper body showcased in a close-fitting steel-grey cashmere sweater. He looked good with clothes on too.

Head bent to hide the shamed flush that burned her smooth cheeks pink, she fiddled with the breakfast menu she had inserted into the basket of cutlery, before formally motioning him to a table beside the window that had the best view of the loch, blue, calm and beautiful on the morning that was clear enough to see the distant mainland shore.

She cleared her throat. This was always going to be awkward but she could cope. 'Or you could eat in the dining room if you prefer.' She gave a too bright smile and nodded towards an open door to her left.

It was a strange feeling to look around and think of his high-powered executive brother living here. Had he been content, happy? Had he regretted his decision to give up everything for love?

Ivo felt the flash of something that he refused to acknowledge, even to himself, was anything even vaguely related to envy as he looked around the place that had been his brother's home.

'Where would you prefer?'

At the sound of Flora's voice the ghost images of his imagination faded.

From what he could see of the room she indicated it was less dining room and more alcove, but like the rest of the place it was tastefully and eclectically furnished, the walls lined with original local artwork that had adorned all the walls he'd seen. The note beneath the ones in his bedroom had bios of the artists, and sale prices.

'Here will be fine.'

'There might be a bit of noise.'

He glanced at the road. So far this morning he'd seen more sheep wandering along it than cars—at last count two and a tractor.

'The sheep?'

Her lips tightened at the sarcasm. 'Gregory is on the roof.'

His brows lifted. 'Did he forget to take his meds or is this a quaint local custom?'

Distracted by the drift of clean male scent that tickled her nostrils, she failed to react to his attempt at humour.

'Storm damage.'

Not the only sort of damage, he thought as he studied the extent of the violet shadows of exhaustion under her beautiful eyes. The sunlight exaggerated the pallor of her skin; by contrast it made her burnished hair shine like a beacon. The combination of fragility and heat shook some nameless feeling loose in his chest.

Nameless or not, it made him uneasy...in a different way from the unease, not to mention frustration, the blind primal lust he'd experienced last night had made him feel.

'We lost a few slates last night, it seems,' she explained.

She felt a tiny spurt of relief when her brief explanation drew his glance towards the window. In her book anywhere that wasn't her face was good or at least an improvement; good would be when this disturbing guest had got into his top-of-the-range car and driven away.

It was really weird that when he looked at her with those dark eyes she felt naked... Or was that she *thought* about getting naked? asked the sardonic voice in her head.

Ivo took a step closer to the window. It overlooked the same view as the one he'd lifted the blinds to in his bedroom earlier, but from a slightly different angle.

This morning it was easier to see why this island was such a popular tourist destination. There was no doubt the scenery was stunning in an untamed way.

Hard to believe that this was even the same planet, let alone the same godforsaken spot on the map he had driven to the previous night through what had seemed like a barren moonscape of mist and rock.

The crashing waves had gone; the whirls of light mist that, with the curlew cries, had given the scene an eerie quality earlier had gone. Now the tranquil waters of the loch were totally still. The surface so mirror calm that the sentinel purple-tinged mountains to the west were reflected on the surface.

There was little to show that there ever had been a storm except for one of the branches and collective detritus along the middle of the narrow single-track road—presumably the meandering line marked the level the waters had eventually reached last night.

'Do you ever flood here?'

He was looking at her again but Flora was ready and she gave a smile that was almost cool and collected. She was in charge of very little in her life at the moment but she was damned if she'd allow her renegade hormones to get the better of her.

'Every ten years or so.'

His elevated brows suggested scepticism but Flora felt on safe ground. Bruno and Sami had needed a report on flooding risks before they'd got planning permission. They had also needed an archaeological survey, which had suggested that people had lived in this spot for centuries.

'So is there much storm damage to the building?'

'I haven't looked yet but the place is pretty solid.'

'You just took a passing tradesman's word that you're missing slates. Did you even get a quote for their work?' His frown deepened as he considered her appalling naivety. Of course, that same flaw was going to make his task easier. *Or maybe not,* he thought as he watched her chin go up at a pugnacious angle.

'He's not a passing anything, he's a neighbour and a friend. Not all people put a price on everything,' she informed him scornfully. Gregory would be offended if she offered to pay him but he would take one of the jars of honey from their bees.

'Boyfriend?' he speculated.

The suggestion drew a gurgle of laughter from her throat. 'Gregory is married,' she retorted, more amused than huffy this time, and when she grinned the little cleft in her chin deepened in a way he found he quite liked. He couldn't remember the last time that he'd seen a woman with no make-up at all. He admired her soft creamy skin. He decided that the sheer novelty value alone would account for his fascination with the sprinkling of freckles across the bridge of her nose.

How far do those freckles go? he wondered as his eyes slid as though drawn by a magnet to the neckline of her top, to the striped sweater that clung to her soft curves.

'Can I get you tea or coffee?'

His eye lifted, the thin stripes of colour banding his cheekbones hardly visible as his nostrils flared as he breathed in the aroma coming from the kitchen.

'Coffee.' He watched as she bustled away, enjoying her rear view but in a much less pure way than he had enjoyed the view from the window.

When the coffee came he was prepared for the worst but it was better than awful, which was a plus.

'I need to talk to you.'

Flora froze in 'deer in the headlights' mode, only just biting back the *Oh, God, no!* 'Last night was not… me…nothing…'

'I do not wish to discuss what happened or, rather, *didn't* happen last night.'

Flora knew this draw-a-line-in-it attitude should have been a relief, but instead she felt the mortified colour fly to her cheeks. Chances were he'd forgotten last night, not that there was anything to forget. Humiliated, she wished that the floor at her feet would open up to swallow her, or, failing that, that she could think of a flippant comeback line.

'I wish to discuss *why* I am here.'

'I thought that was a state secret, all very "need to know".' The irritable retort came out before she could stop it. 'Sorry!'

'Once more with feeling…?' he suggested drily. 'Has it occurred to you,' he drawled, 'that you're not really cut out for this sort of work?'

'It's not the work, it's—' She stopped herself, but not soon enough to prevent his smug I-told-you-so retort.

'Point proved, I'd say and, as they say, the customer is always right.'

'Or a pain in the—' She bit her lip and forced a stiff

smile while continuing to dodge his eyes. 'What can I do for you?'

Next time you feel the urge to insult paying guests, Flora, just think of the accounts, she told herself while she waited for his response. The moment stretched.

'This might be easier if I tell you my full name.'

This conversation, she decided, was getting a bit *Twilight Zone*. Was she meant to recognise him? Did he have some sort of celebrity status, a Hollywood A-lister she was meant to know? He certainly looked the part.

'You mean you signed an alias—you're not Mr Rocco?'

'My name is Ivo Rocco Greco.'

There was a twenty-second time delay before she sat down with a bump, her eyes not leaving his face as she gripped the edge of the table, not even noticing when the tablecloth slipped and sent a jug of milk onto the stone floor.

'Bruno's little brother?' she whispered hoarsely.

He blinked—no one had called him that in a long time—before tipping his dark head in a slow acknowledgement.

Denial lingered; it *still* wasn't sinking in. *'You...?'* she gasped, her voice breathy and faint as her eyes flickered over his lean muscle-toned six-foot-five frame.

He tipped his dark head for a second time in confirmation.

'This is...why on earth didn't you say so earlier?' she exploded, then a moment later, struggling to channel calm, admitted, 'This is just so weird. You're not...'

She was looking embarrassed and anywhere but at him. 'So, Bruno mentioned me?' He felt another stab of fresh guilt. From the day he had decided his brother had deserted him Ivo had never spoken his brother's name again.

She nodded, remembering the underlying protectiveness tinged by guilt in her brother-in-law's face on the occasions he had mentioned his little brother, who it turned out was not at all little. She sighed and said a silent regretful goodbye to the Ivo who had lived in her imagination—a slender, sensitive geek who was the target of bullies.

'I'm not what?'

The soft question brought her eyes up from the menu she was shredding; she dropped the pieces. 'You're... not much like Bruno.'

A good recovery that had the plus of being true.

Her sister's husband had not been above average height, his build slim and wiry, good-looking but not in a jaw-dropping sort of way. Sami said she had fallen in love the moment Bruno smiled... Flora's own smile was sad. Bruno had had a really great smile...and laugh... She fought her way through a wave of sadness.

'You're much...darker.' She shook her head, a furrow appearing across the bridge of her nose. 'I just don't understand why all the secrecy.' Wary suspicion interwoven with the first threads of anger began to emerge from the initial numbing shock that had pushed her brain into basic standby mode. 'And why now?'

It wasn't just that there hadn't been a single member of Bruno's family at the funeral, it was the fact that this brother that Bruno had spoken of with such fondness had never made any attempt to contact him over the years. Now he was here, and the question had to be, why?

Oh, hell, Flora, you're being so slow...he's here for Jamie!

CHAPTER FIVE

IGNORING THE COLD clutch of fear in her stomach, she dealt him a cool, 'over my dead body' glare.

'I thought I made it quite clear to your grandfather's lawyer that I am not about to hand over Jamie. Or,' she challenged, injecting her words with withering scorn, 'are you going to tell me you being here has nothing to do with that at all?'

'I am here on my own behalf.'

Not an exactly comforting statement when made by a man who looked a lot more ruthless than any legal letter—a man who seemed to have inherited the same lack of moral scruples that had been noticeable from her communications with his grandfather.

Her lips twisted into a bitter, contemptuous smile. 'Oh, well, I suppose you could say better late than never. Still, Bruno had plenty of people who *did* care for him and love him to say goodbye—just no one called Greco.'

He responded with a shrug. His expression gave nothing away, certainly not guilt.

'Why didn't you just tell me who you were last night?' she challenged in an accent thickened by the antagonism that shone in her sea-blue eyes. 'You lied. And save me the semantics—lying by omission is still a lie!' Arms folded across her chest, she lifted her chin and dared him with angry eyes to deny this.

He didn't try, neither did he make any attempt to defend himself, which was a shame because she'd have loved to tell him what she thought about him. She might anyway, she brooded, glaring with dislike at the too-good-looking imposter.

Actually, he seemed content to let her talk, just as he had last night. *And that turned out so well, Flora,* she reminded herself. She had told him things because he was a stranger with no connection to her; she'd revealed weakness, her fears and guilty secrets—*she was a bad mother.*

Would those words cost her—cost Jamie? she wondered. By the time the feelings of vulnerability in her mind translated into words they were angry and directed at the person responsible for her feeling this way.

Flora had never been of the 'don't get mad, get even' school of thought, she just got mad, though she liked to think it wasn't any stereotypical red-headed short fuse. She reserved her ire for people who really deserved it.

And Ivo Greco did!

This brother was as bad *as* his grandfather who had sent her the vile letter via his lawyer. The cold, subtly threatening wording had stayed with her, as had the thoughts of the blood money he had wanted to throw her way.

Hands planted on the table, ignoring the pool of milk and shattered crockery around her feet, fingers clenched into white-knuckled fists, she glared at him, hating the fact that her body hummed with awareness when she looked at him.

'Forget the bill, you're family,' she drawled. Turning away, she tossed her last words over her shoulder. 'But we just closed for the season.'

'I'd say you have another, what, two months before you close permanently.'

Shock froze her to the spot for a moment before, eyes flashing, she spun back, stamped up to the table and glared down at him.

'It may not seem much to you!' she charged, trying hard not to think of the Greco billions and the mountains that that much money could move. The wills it could find loopholes in. 'This place is Jamie's inheritance. I won't let that happen.'

He nodded. 'Good to know. Look, you're annoyed— I get that!'

Her eyes flew wide; this man was unbelievable. *Annoyed!* 'How incredibly *reasonable* of you,' she gritted with teeth-clenching insincerity. 'I'm not annoyed. I'm absolutely furious!'

And it suited her, he decided, allowing his eyes to linger a moment too long on her slightly parted pink lips.

'And don't tell me I've no right to be... *Now,*' she added with an addition of dark understanding, 'your prowling the house last night makes sense. Were you looking for ammunition to use against me in court? You may have money—' she choked '—but I have right...'

His dark brows lifted, forging a dark bar above his nose as he cut across her in an amused scornful drawl. 'You must be more naive than I thought if you think *right* always wins.'

She felt a chill run down her spine. 'Is that a threat?'

He didn't say a word, just held her eyes, the dark implacability in those still obsidian depths more threat than any words. Flora felt a shudder of visceral fear trace a cold path up her spine and fought against the panic she could feel building. She needed to stay calm and show him she wasn't intimidated...*even if she was!*

'Sorry I didn't oblige you by being drunk in charge of a baby or enjoying an orgy.'

The mental images of a private orgy with the gorgeous fiery redhead delayed his response for several moments. 'It might speed things along if you cut down on the histrionics.'

Her eyes narrowed on his face with dislike. 'You know, your family's sudden interest in Jamie seems just a little bit perverse. You've shown no interest in him before.'

'I didn't know he existed.'

She blinked and tossed out a scornful, 'You expect me to believe that?'

He shrugged, his attitude oozing the sort of arrogant hauteur guaranteed to raise her hackles as he informed her in a bored-sounding drawl, 'You can, and I'm sure will, believe whatever you wish. I have no intention of supplying you with documented proof.'

'You let me tell you about Sami and Bruno and you didn't say anything...' Her voice quivered when she thought about the other things she'd told him, thinking he was a stranger she would never see again. 'It was a cruel thing to do.'

For the first time he looked slightly, not guilty, but, at least, disconcerted, but she held tight to her anger. She had offered an olive branch to Salvatore Greco and got an insult back.

She had to assume Ivo was here because the legal intimidation and bribery hadn't worked. And on that premise, he was the physical equivalent of a legal threat.

She threw up her hands in an attitude of weary disgust and walked stiff-backed across the room before spinning back. Arms folded across her chest, where the tight knot of swirling emotions made her respirations uneven and painful, she fixed him with a tight-lipped glare, finally letting go a soft resigned sigh.

'Fine, say what you have come here to say and just go away.' She adopted an expression of determined uninterest and waited.

'My grandfather is dying.' He watched her uncompromising stance disintegrate as she tumbled from an attitude of righteous indignation to shock, before he saw her expression soften into compassion.

Had the situations been reversed, had Salvatore learnt that the woman who stood between him and what he wanted had been given a death sentence, well, *his* eyes would not be softening with sympathy, that was certain.

'I'm sorry to hear that.'

The thing was they were not just words; he believed her. She was making this too easy and making him feel *guilty*—as if he weren't carrying around enough of that! Her soft-hearted vulnerability was her problem, not his, he reminded himself, and if he took advantage she only had herself to blame.

'Is there much pain?'

He blinked, realising he hadn't asked. 'I don't know. He doesn't...confide.'

She nodded as if she understood, but of course she couldn't. Flora Henderson still believed in the basic goodness of humanity, which was where her greatest vulnerability lay. She had never really accepted that *good* was the exception, the norm was selfishness and avarice and basic 'walk all over your fellow man to claw your way to the top'.

It was inevitable that one day something would wipe the idealistic glow from her beautiful eyes. Ivo was glad that he wouldn't be around to see it...unless he was the catalyst?

'So you came.' Her slender shoulders lifted in enquiry. *'Because?'*

'He wants to see his great-grandson.'

'That was never a problem,' she pointed out. 'He didn't want to see Jamie, he wanted to *buy* him. He wanted me to give up any rights at all. I used to wonder what his family did that was so bad to make Bruno walk away, now I know.' But *this* man hadn't walked away; he was one of them. A fact that, for Jamie's sake, she couldn't allow herself to forget.

'Sami and Bruno wanted me to...' Her eyes fell, then lifted, blazing with defiance as they fixed on his face, daring him to throw last night's admission back at her as she said in a voice that shook with sincerity, 'I may not be the world's best mother, but I love Jamie, and I'm not about to hand him over for any amount of money. I'm sorry your grandfather is ill but it's not going to happen.'

Dio. Fair play seemed to be this woman's middle name, so why the hell did he feel so bad about using this to his own advantage?

'Sure, I get that.'

Her eyes widened before fluttering in confusion. 'You do?'

His gaze moved around the room before it landed on her face. 'This place means a lot to you?'

'They built it...for Jamie.'

The quiver in her voice made his jaw clench. 'Is it the life you wanted?'

She gave him a blank look and shook her head,

looking at him as though he were talking a foreign language.

'You're what? Twenty-five? Twenty-six?' He was genuinely curious; had it ever crossed her mind to refuse the burden that had been gifted her?

'You tell me, you seem to know everything,' she retorted snappily. 'I suppose you have some creepy file on my life.'

He shrugged, the smile that lifted the corners of his mouth mocking. 'It's a very thin file.' He demonstrated the point by extending his hand, holding his thumb and forefinger almost touching and watched her eyes widen with horror.

'I wasn't being serious!' she squeaked.

Welcome to my world, he thought. It was one she wouldn't fit into. 'Don't worry, there was nothing Salvatore could use for leverage, or he already would have.'

He sounded so chillingly casual that all Flora could do was stare.

'I didn't come here to blackmail you or bribe you or propose...'

'What?'

'My grandfather's favoured option is we marry, and somewhere down the line divorce, at which point I will gain full custody of Jamie.'

Her laugh was the result of nerves, not any appreciation of the joke. 'You're not *serious*?'

'*I'm* not.' But you had to hand it to Salvatore, there was a certain attractive simplicity to the plan. Not that he had for one moment considered the proposition any more than he would have considered allowing a vulnerable baby to be moulded into adulthood by Salvatore. His lips twisted into a self-derisory grimace as his glance flickered downward over himself. *Look how well you turned out!*

Her teeth clenched as she watched one corner of his mouth twitch into a lazy half-smile. 'Sorry, the *amusing* part has just passed me by. Care to share?' she tossed out sarcastically.

'Would it hurt to go along with a dying man's last wishes?' he asked, watching through the skein of his lashes as uncertainty swamped the anger in her blue eyes; followed a moment later by compassion, just as he'd known it would be.

Damping an inconvenient stab of conscience, he reminded himself that it was not his task to protect her from her own kind heart, it was hers to toughen up. The alternative was going through life being used—he wasn't the only unscrupulous bastard out there.

It had been obvious to him within five minutes of meeting her that one of Flora Henderson's flaws was that she would always do the *right* thing, even if that right thing made her miserable. She possessed the thing that made her one of life's victims—a tender heart!

He knew that she would not hesitate to sacrifice her own happiness if it was the *right* thing to do. All he had to do was convince her it was the right thing and he really didn't think it would take an awful lot of effort on his part. Not once he actually got her back to Italy—the rest was inevitable. Once she saw the sort of life the baby could have being brought up as a Greco, the sort of advantages that he could give the child, she wouldn't be able to help herself doing the right thing.

'Obviously, I'm sorry.'

He arched a brow. 'Really? You're not just a tiniest bit glad?'

Insulted by the suggestion, she stared stonily back at him.

'You're going to lose this place, you know.'

She clamped her mouth closed over a denial that she knew would be a lie.

'And then what will happen—you both move in with your mother?' He arched a brow and watched her face. 'You've thought of that, but I suppose you're also thinking she's not getting any younger, and she's already brought up her children. She needs a rest, but what option will you have? And, of course, there is no work here for an up-and-coming architect so you'll move back to Edinburgh or Glasgow?'

She fought the urge to cover her ears and shut out the horribly insidious voice putting her worst unacknowledged fears into words. 'I've not thought—'

'That far ahead?' he inserted smoothly. 'I get that, but you're going to have to when you stop thinking some sort of miracle is going to happen. Will you take Jamie with you and farm him out to a nursery?' he pressed, as he relentlessly continued to paint a picture of the future that Flora didn't want to see. 'Or leave him here with your mother? Do you think that your sister and Bruno would want any of that for their son? Do you think that was what they had in mind when they made you his guardian?'

'My mum is too old to...' Biting her lip as she felt the press of tears behind her eyes, she shook her head. 'You don't know what is best for Jamie.'

'Do you?'

Unable to respond, she turned her head away, closing her eyes to shut out his dark, relentless stare.

He saw the doubts in her face and pressed home his advantage, reminding the guilty whisper in his head that nothing he was saying was not the truth. 'How hard do you think that it will be a few months down the line, after you're late a few times to pick up the baby from nursery, or get the sack because you take too much time off when the baby is sick? How hard will it be then to convince a court that I'd be a better guardian?'

'There is such a thing as employment law and State help. Working single parents cope—'

Each word was a direct hit at his pride, but when she said cope as though that were a good thing, he couldn't hold his outrage in. He surged to his feet, swearing under his breath; the fact that she took an involuntary step back only increased his outrage. What the hell did she think he was going to do?

'I do not want my nephew to *cope*! He is a Greco, he will not *cope* on government handouts and *charity*!'

Wow...when he shrugged off urbane and reasonable he did it big time! '*Half* a Greco.'

The provocation earned her a killer glare.

'And if you think you can intimidate me—'

'I'm not trying to intimidate you!'

She let out a weak laugh; if this was him *not* trying, she wouldn't like to see him put any effort in.

'Has it occurred to you that I might be the miracle you are waiting for?' he remarked in a conversational tone.

'I do not think miracle when I look at you.'

He sketched a quick smile. 'I'm being serious.'

She viewed the change of tack with deep suspicion and rolled her eyes. 'Oh, and I suppose you want me to keep Jamie.'

He shook his head in a negative motion. 'I think you could be Aunt Flora who Jamie has holidays with on Skye and who gives him nice birthday presents.'

'Well, at least you're honest.'

In this instance honesty worked, but that didn't mean he wouldn't have lied through his teeth if it suited him in order to achieve what he wanted.

He nodded. 'I may disagree with Salvatore's methods but I do believe that Jamie should be brought up in Italy. I came here to offer a compromise of sorts that would mean your financial problems are over and my grandfather will die a happy man.' For Salvatore, happy meant getting his own way.

Flora didn't relax. She reminded herself that *this* brother hadn't rejected his heritage, his position of privilege; he was as dangerous as the grandfather.

'Unless of course you're not interested in Jamie's future.'

Her chin went up at the suggestion as she glared at him through narrowed eyes. 'Jamie's future is here.'

'Here or a bedsit in Edinburgh with no garden and noisy neighbours. And what sort of schooling would he receive? You would really deprive Jamie of everything I can give him?'

Nothing he said was wrong or even exaggerated. Flora pushed down the choking tide of panic she could feel building.

'You have a problem; I have a solution. One that isn't marry me and live unhappily ever after.'

She gave a tense nod and thought, *I'm probably going to regret this.* 'I'm listening.'

'I suggest you and Jamie come back to Italy with me—think of it as a holiday.'

'To Italy! What would that solve? Anyway,' she said, shaking her head from side to side, 'I'm not going anywhere with you.'

He dug a hand into his pocket, catching the velvet pouch that held the ring in his fingers. 'How about you hear me out?'

She responded to the sardonic request with a slow reluctant nod of her head.

'Come back to Italy with me as my fiancée.'

For at least ten seconds she managed to keep her mouth shut, until the pressure of the low heavy thud in her head got too much to resist. 'An interesting suggestion, which, in case you were wondering, is a polite way of say you're insane. Utterly mad!' she croaked with deep conviction.

'Calm down!'

'I'm perfectly calm.' The strange thing was she actually was. Her heart had slowed to a low, regular thud.

His lips twisted into a smile. She made him think of a spooked horse ready to run for the hills. One false word or move and she'd be gone.

'I have no wish to be married, though I would like to know my brother's child and have him know his heritage. He will one day inherit a great deal.'

'Jamie will...?'

'Of course, hadn't that occurred to you?'

She shook her head, recalling a couple of comments her sister had made...but seriously rich? Bruno had been so normal, his brother was not. It was not difficult to imagine this man occupying the weird world of the *uber*-rich—he was a man who made his own rules.

'My grandfather is too old to change and I see no reason he shouldn't die a happy man. Let him *think* we're getting married.'

'What on earth made him think I'd agree to marry you, that we'd...' her eyes fell as she felt a flush of embarrassment wash over her skin before tacking on an awkward '...*fall in love*?'

'He cares little about the how—it is a means to an end. And you can relax, my grandfather knows that I do not fall in love.'

The air of utter confidence he delivered this statement with, as if it were a fact as indisputable as the chemical formula of water, dragged a strangled laugh from Flora's throat, as for a brief moment her sense of humour reasserted itself.

'Sorry, you just sounded so ridiculous...' Her voice trailed off. She was guessing from his expression that he had little experience of being called ridiculous. 'Well, I suppose it is good to know I won't be expected to act loved up for his benefit.'

What did she look like *loved up*? he wondered, seeing those pink lips parted and swollen from kisses. The blue eyes glazed with passion. The effort of ignoring the flash of scalding, body-hardening heat gave his voice a throaty, abrasive quality as he explained.

'Salvatore is only interested in the parental rights marriage brings, not the merging of souls.' He tilted his head a little as he studied her face. 'Was that a yes...?'

The acrid mockery in his statement made her wince. 'Not even a maybe.' Though it was and they both knew it. The knowledge, the lack of alternatives, felt like walls closing in around her.

'Look, the deal I'm suggesting is come out with me, pretend to be my fiancée. Let Salvatore meet his great-grandson and for that I will clear the debts on this place, which will give the option of staying on or selling it as a profitable going concern. The alternative, we both know, is foreclosure.'

His fingers interwoven, he watched her, the internal

struggle being waged in her head visible in the expressive, fine-boned face.

'What will I tell people...my mother?' She reacted to the flicker in his hooded eyes and added quickly, 'Not that I'm agreeing to anything.'

'That is, *would* be, up to you.' His smile said he knew as well as she did that she was just playing for time. 'The truth or maybe a version of it that suits you.'

'You're probably better than me with versions of the truth.'

'My grandfather's dying wish is to see his great-grandson and you are taking Jamie out there—surely she would understand that? You need a holiday, some sun.'

He was right, her mum would accept that. She began to feel panicky as her legitimate reasons to resist continued to vanish.

'As for the financial problems resolving—'

'She doesn't know... Nobody—' Her long lashes lifted and he was on the receiving end of the full resentful glare of her cerulean-blue eyes. 'I *thought* nobody knew.'

'It never crossed your mind to ask for help?' Stupid question, he realised—she was too stubborn and independent to ask for a sticking plaster if she was bleeding out! 'Has anyone ever mentioned the downsides of sticking your head in the sand?'

The sarcasm brought an angry flush to her cheeks. 'If I did go along with this, this...*arrangement*...' not a bad word for insanity '... I'd need some guarantees,' she said, resisting the feeling that she was just being swept along.

He arched a sable brow. 'Such as?'

'I will need my own...space.'

His mouth quirked. '*Space* is not a problem, but you're not talking about space, are you, *cara*?' he drawled, his smile deepening as she flushed like some sort of virgin. 'You're talking about beds. You will have your own private suite, and rest assured I never enter a lady's room without an invitation.'

There would be no shortage of those coming his way, she thought with a scowl. 'Like a vampire.' There was nothing even vaguely undead about his vibrant colouring. Flora found the vitality he oozed exhausting at close quarters.

'A creature of the night, hmm?' he drawled, rubbing his chin. 'I've been called worse.'

'Of that,' she retorted tartly, 'I have no doubt.'

'So, any other demands?'

'I'd say common courtesy but I'm a realist.'

His deep, warm, appreciative chuckle tickled her nerve endings in a not entirely unpleasant way.

'So when I decide to return home there will be no attempt to prevent me...*and* Jamie.'

'*Your* decision every step of the way.'

She frowned, for some reason worried about how easy he was making this. 'I suppose...'

'So that's a yes, then, you agree.'

'But how—?'

His voice, implacably cool, cut across her protests. 'Agree or not? Leave the how to me.'

'I agree,' she said, turning a deaf ear to the voice in her head that said she had just signed away her soul for security.

CHAPTER SIX

IF HE HAD shown any hint of smug complacency she would, Flora decided, have slapped him.

But he didn't. There was zero reaction on his lean, dark face as, without missing a beat, he angled a speculative brow and said, 'How does forty-eight hours sound?'

Her hands, which had been clenched into fists, relaxed but she was mystified by his question. 'Sound for what?'

He gave a sardonic smile. 'To organise things this end.'

Her eyes flew wide, her lashes fluttering like trapped butterflies against her cheek. 'So soon? But I thought that...'

'I'd give you time to change your mind?'

Her lips tightened. 'I agreed!'

'And your word is your bond. Good to know. However, the situation is somewhat urgent. Salvatore is dying.'

The obvious response to this reminder was—when?

He couldn't see the thought but he could see the guilt that followed in its wake move across her transparent face.

This was a woman who should never play poker.

Her being too nice to press the issue worked well for him because the truth was he didn't know. The truth was

Ivo would be more shocked to learn that his grandfather was really dying than if it turned out to be another of his imaginative manipulations.

His factory setting was extreme scepticism where Salvatore was concerned, but he would deal with any surprises once he got Flora and Jamie to Italy.

'Look, I've got some things to keep me busy in London—you just organise you and the baby and I'll be back for you.'

He made it sound ludicrously simple, as if you could just walk away from your life and it would be waiting for you when you returned. 'But this place.' With a shake of her head she looked around the room. 'The bookings We have an arrangement with local artists and artisans...'

'Yes, I'd noticed. Good marketing. Symbiotic. I'll buy everything—how will that work?'

She blinked at the casual way he said it. 'That sculpture over there.' She nodded towards the window embrasure where a stone carved otter stood.

He nodded. 'Nice.'

'And expensive. Neil has five more works displayed around the place.' The local sculptor had some of his larger pieces of work displayed in government buildings.

'It looks good there.'

'So is that your plan? If there's a problem throw money at it.'

'Do you have a problem with that?'

She lowered her eyes, knowing that if she said yes she could be accused of hypocrisy—after all, she wasn't complaining about the money he was throwing at her.

'Just so long as you know.'

'Fine, then just email me the details and I'll arrange

refunds and throw in an expenses-paid break later in
the year. I can't see many people complaining.'

He was knocking down her objections like skittles
before she even had a chance to line them up. Before
she had a chance to think through the implications of
what desperation had led her to so recklessly agree to.

The desperation hadn't gone away, she reminded
herself.

Could he genuinely not see problems or was he just
ignoring them? she wondered, her frustration growing
at his leave-it-to-me attitude. She didn't like leaving it
to anyone. Flora took responsibility for her own decisions. 'But how are we going to explain closing?'

His broad shoulders lifted in a negligent elegant
shrug. 'A full refurbishment?'

'We don't need refurbishing!' she protested indig-
nantly.

'I'll think of something, don't worry.'

She bridled at the verbal-pat-on-the-head attitude;
she could almost see him moving on in his head. Well,
no one could accuse him of letting the grass grow, that
was for sure!

'Right, I'll be back Friday.' Moving towards the door,
he turned back. 'I almost forgot.'

He strode back towards her. Unprepared for the action, she didn't resist, and he caught her wrist, turned
her hand over and one by one curled her clenched fingers open to reveal her palm.

Flora was conscious of a strange, breathless sensation as she looked at his brown fingers against her own.
The breath caught in her chest escaped in a long, slow,
sibilant breath when he tipped up a velvet pouch and a
ring landed in her palm.

Her eyes lifted to the lean dark face of the man bent

over her hand. 'What's that?' she asked, her voice a throaty whisper.

It invited a sarcastic comeback but he didn't accept the invitation.

Ivo took hold of the ring and slid it onto her extended finger. 'Believe you me, *cara*, this is something I never thought I'd be doing.' Never wanted to, and yet even though his feelings were not involved, the symbolism—yes, it had to be the symbolism—made things shift inside him. 'I suppose I should be looking to you for guidance?' Why should the thought of another man putting a ring on this finger make him feel so…? Not jealous, that would have been absurd, but he just felt angry because she hadn't seen her ex for the loser he clearly was.

She stared from the finger that held a gleaming diamond to Ivo's face for a moment and back; her confusion was not feigned. For a moment she had no idea what he was talking about and then she realised… Callum!

She clenched her fingers and pulled her hand back. The ring glittered against her skin.

It wasn't as if she had forgotten, or the moment hadn't seemed special at the time, but quite crazily she remembered nothing approaching this heart-pounding shock, even though Callum had proposed prettily.

Callum's proposal had been like a well-rehearsed and smoothly stage-managed love scene in a play. And yet, perfect hadn't made her feel dizzy, just self-conscious and slightly nervous that she'd miss her cue and say the wrong thing to spoil the *prettiness*.

The irony was, Callum had been pretending. Ivo wasn't pretending he was giving her anything other than a prop; he didn't *do* love.

Then the disturbing realisation hit her, granted what she was feeling had nothing to do with love...*couldn't* have anything to do with love. No, this was about chemical attraction, and the attraction she felt for Ivo was a billion times stronger than anything she had felt for her ex-fiancé!

'So, do you always carry around a chunk of diamond in your pocket?'

'I like to be prepared.'

'Perhaps I should proofread this file? You might have got some things wrong,' she snapped waspishly.

'Oh, if you have trouble sleeping I'd recommend it.'

'I suppose your life is fascinating.'

'You're about to find out, *cara*.'

He watched her expression change as the reality came crashing in. 'You'll be ready to leave.'

It wasn't a suggestion and Flora couldn't let the order—*any* order—pass unchallenged. You gave in to an arrogant man drunk on his own power and self-importance once and he'd walk all over you—helped in no small part by her hormones, unless she took control!

She was no longer that silly romantic girl, but maybe a lustful woman was more dangerous?

'Thursday suits me better.' But it didn't, did it? It didn't suit her at all.

The moment the words left her lips, Flora wished them unsaid, but, the damage done, she fought to keep the dismay from showing. She'd established she was no pushover but that token gesture had given her one day *less* to prepare—unless he was difficult, in which case she could concede with dignity.

Please be difficult!

He studied her, a flicker of a smile moving across

his face, though when he responded it was with perfect solemnity. 'Absolutely, whatever you say, *cara*.'

Flora took Jamie to say goodbye to her mum, leaving herself plenty of time to be back in the time that Ivo had said he'd arrive.

Flora, feeling guilty as hell for lying to her mother, had gone for the partial-truth option.

When Flora had explained the situation her mum, being family orientated herself, had agreed that of course Flora must take Jamie to meet his Italian family, even though she would obviously miss her grandson but, as her sister was coming to visit from Australia, she wouldn't be lonely.

It wasn't until Flora was making her last farewells that she realised she might have spoken more than she realised about Ivo Greco.

'I know you were hurt, Flora,' her mum said quietly, 'by that wee idiot, Callum, but not all men are alike.'

Startled, Flora finished strapping Jamie in his car seat and turned back, one hand on the door.

'I'm not, Mum. What made you say that?'

'The way you were talking about Bruno's little brother.'

Flora hurriedly did a mental review of their conversation. Had she been talking about him...*that* much? 'Oh, Mum, he's not little. He's—'

'Fair enough, and it's true I've never met the man, but in my experience there is a big difference between an *arrogant* man who loves the sound of his own voice and can't stop boring you with how marvellous he is, and a man who is quietly confident and listens to your opinion.' Balanced on the one crutch she had been promoted to, she hugged her daughter.

* * *

Some people listened to music when they drove, some people liked company. Ivo liked neither. He enjoyed the solitude of driving, the fact that he could legitimately ignore an email or phone, and call it being a considerate law-abiding driver.

If he'd actually been travelling with the woman he was to marry he supposed that he might have felt obliged to make conversation, but he wasn't.

Basic civility required that he respond if she spoke but he had no intention of encouraging conversation, and definitely not initiating it!

The baby had fallen asleep almost the instant he'd been strapped into his baby seat in the back, and Flora had been totally silent.

There was more than one sort of silence.

This one was not relaxing. He recognised the perversity of his reaction when he even started feeling irritated by the fact she seemed to feel no need to break it.

'Are you all right?'

Flora started, her head whipped around his way, the fat, shiny plait she had her hair confined in today landing with a *thunk* on her shoulder. 'Yes.' She glanced at the baby in the back, before training her eyes once more on the side window, wrapped up in her own thoughts.

He let the monosyllable lie another ten minutes before the compulsion to prod her into a response overcame him. It was not about hearing her voice, although the light accent was pleasing on the ear.

'Babies don't travel light.' The boot of the car was capacious but it was full to the brim of clutter that was apparently essential for babies. Loading it in had been like a military operation. There had barely been room for the small bag that Flora had brought—either she did travel light, which would make her a very unusual woman in his experience, or she wasn't expecting to be staying long.

'No.' This time she didn't even turn her head.

His jaw clenched as the conviction the silent treatment was deliberate grew.

He didn't speak again until they had passed a sign that said the airport was another ten miles. They'd made good time. 'I'm beginning to think you're ignoring me, *cara*?'

Flora almost laughed...*ignore*!

As if there were any way in the world she could have ignored six feet five of vital masculinity in this enclosed space. Air-conditioning or not, she could feel the warmth of his skin and smell the warm clean male scent of his body. The combination did not make for a relaxing journey.

'You usually have a lot to say for yourself.'

Callum had once said something similar, accusing her after a meeting with friends that she had hogged the conversation. The irony hadn't struck her until later that Callum liked talking about himself so much that she rarely got to contribute to any conversation. She didn't have to. He enjoyed worshipful silence.

And she'd been stupid enough to supply it!

Her eyes slid to her travelling companion. While Ivo Greco's arrogance entered a room before he did, he could not be accused of bragging, but her mum was wrong. The fact that any personal information had to be dragged out of him didn't mean he couldn't have taught lessons in arrogance.

'I was thinking, wondering, if I'm not doing the most stupid thing I've ever done in my life.' She'd also been trying to figure out a way of asking how long her stay was likely to be without making it sound as if she were wishing for his grandfather's death.

So far she hadn't come up with one.

His brows lifted. 'I suppose, *cara*, it depends how stupid the most stupid thing you've done previously was.'

Her lips moved in a whisper of a smile, which vanished like smoke as she admitted ruefully, 'It was pretty stupid.' Falling for Callum was stupid. Believing he'd loved her was even more stupid.

A bit of hero worship, at fifteen, was one thing. She wasn't the only local girl who'd had the local boy who'd become an international football legend on her bedroom wall. She wasn't the only one to compete for a glimpse of him on his rare visits home to see his parents who still lived in the house he'd grown up in.

But she *was* the only one who had bumped into the sporting hero a few years later in Edinburgh. She'd been flattered when he'd recognised her and in a state of disbelief when he had invited her to dinner.

One short month later he'd proposed. Walking on air, she'd accepted, but even before she'd had a chance to share the news, it had been over. At least the humiliation had been private.

Her gaze flickered to the man beside her. How many hearts had he broken? she wondered. Did he keep count? she mused cynically. Did he even remember their names?

A pothole in the road that jolted her made her realise how long she'd been staring at him, in a way that could, to the casual observer, be confused with drooling. Ashamed and a little alarmed at the conscious effort it required to drag her gaze from his patrician profile, she rubbed the ring finger on her left hand hard.

It was only at the last minute that she had remembered to take off the ring Ivo had produced and slipped onto her finger before he'd left. She'd just managed to stuff it in her handbag before her mum had appeared from the pottery.

Handbag! She experienced a flurry of panic…hadn't she?

The noise of Flora scrabbling in her handbag drew his attention sideways for long enough to register the panic on her face.

'What's wrong?'

Heart thudding with trepidation, Flora shook her head and dumped the entire contents of her handbag onto her knee.

'The ring…was…is it real?' She aimed for casual and produced shrill panic.

'You mean is it fictitious?'

Irritated, she cut across him. 'I mean, is it a real diamond?'

He arched a brow. 'You're worried I'd fob you off with a fake?' He shook his head in an attitude of mock hurt. 'You think I'm cheap.'

'I think you're…' She inhaled a deep relieved breath and sank back weakly in her seat as her fingers closed around an object that had slipped into a hole in the bag lining. A moment later it was in her shaking hand. 'Thank God!' she breathed in fervent relief as she slipped the rock onto her finger.

'It fits well.'

'Yes, but I'd feel a lot happier if it was in a bank vault,' she said darkly.

'It looks better on your finger.'

Flora, who was repacking the collection of female

essentials that had spilled onto her lap, turned her head. 'I thought I'd lost it. I nearly had heart failure.'

'It's just a ring.'

'Oh!' An explanation for his relaxed attitude occurred to her. 'Is it insured?'

'I hadn't got around to that.'

The pucker between her feathery brows that had been sitting there all morning deepened as she remembered her mother's comments. She was not ready to admit that there wasn't any commonality between the two of them, but on the subject of expensive rings the two reacted *very* differently.

Callum had had no hesitation accepting the ring that she had slid off her trembling finger after he'd dumped her. She could still hear the moral indignation in his voice as he'd accused her of tricking him, of hiding the truth from him.

'I mean, kids, a family, what other reason does a guy get *married* for?'

'Oh, I don't know—love?'

He'd laughed, actually *laughed* at her then, explaining the way you did to a small child or someone not very bright, 'There are plenty of girls out there for love. A wife is different—a man puts her on a pedestal.'

She didn't know about the pedestal but he had put the woman he had married two months after he'd dumped Flora in a mansion, several, actually, and, just as he'd said, there were still plenty of girls out there giving Callum love…or at least *sex*. Callum had never had any intention of changing his lifestyle for something like marriage…he believed he could have it all, and he did.

The wife *had* to know about the girlfriends. It wasn't

as if Callum was discreet, and there were always cameras and phones around to record any social-media-worthy action of an ex-premier-league footballer, but did the beautiful blonde know that the ring she wore had once been on someone else's finger? Flora wondered, staring down at the diamond glittering on her own finger.

She had been devastated at the time but Flora appreciated now that she'd had a lucky escape. She only wished it was good judgement and not a biological failing on her part that was responsible.

'Stop worrying.'

Her eyes lifted and made fleeting contact with Ivo's dark stare. *He can't read your mind,* she soothed herself, managing a huff of scornful laughter.

'Easy for you to say!'

At the wheel Ivo stiffened in response to being snapped at. The women in his life purred and smiled, and the novelty value of having this redhead snarl up at him had limited novelty value. Before he could react in kind there was a grumpy snuffling sound from the back seat, followed by a wail.

'See what you've done now,' she reproached, ignoring his indignant growl of, *'Me!'* as she twisted around in her seat and murmured soothingly, 'Hush, Jamie, we're nearly there.'

Actually, they were there.

It took seconds for him to park up in the small terminal.

There was no struggling with bags this end; what appeared to be an army of people arrived and began to unpack the luggage. Their progress through customs was equally swift and effortless and it felt like moments later that they were on the plane with no airline logo, though inside Greco was discreetly evident from the headed notepaper to the coasters on the table.

Ivo told her to make herself at home and vanished, leaving her to cope with the baby. She'd have liked to call him selfish but there were several hovering staff offering her assistance.

Having read up on travelling by air with a baby, Flora spent take-off and the next part of the journey feeding Jamie, who didn't appear to suffer any problems with the change in pressure. She had just got him changed and back to sleep when Ivo appeared.

He wasn't alone.

'This is Cristina.' The young woman smiled. 'She's one of the nannies.'

It would have made less sense to Flora if he had said the woman was part of a boy band. 'What do you mean, *the nannies*?' The plural part hadn't passed her by.

'Well, Nanny Emily is getting on, though don't let her hear me say it.' The young woman beside him smiled. 'And—'

Flora cut him off mid-sentence. 'If you think I'm handing Jamie over to anyone, you are off your head!'

After scanning her angry face, Ivo turned to the young woman and said something in Italian that made her vanish. 'I'm trying to make your life easier here,' he said, struggling to hang onto his temper.

Flora flung back the plait, and shook her head, causing stray red curls to drift across her face. Ivo, distracted by those golden-tinted wisps, fought a strong compulsion to push them back.

'No, you are trying to take over my life. Jamie's life.' Give him an inch and she'd be asking his permission before she decided what dress to wear. This man was so typical of the breed, she decided, forgetting she had ever imagined for one second that she had misjudged him.

'Where is the harm in having a nanny?' Not accustomed to considering anyone's convenience but his own, Ivo had rationalised the efforts he had made to make the journey and stay as comfortable and stress-free for Flora as possible by telling himself it had nothing whatever to do with sentiment, it was simple practicality.

The last thing he wanted was her gratitude. He just wanted Jamie. Admittedly they came as a package but *that*, he hoped, was a temporary situation.

Not gratitude, but the last thing he had *expected* was her spitting fury!

Flora compressed her lips. 'No harm at all if you live in the nineteenth century,' she agreed with a smile that aimed for provocation, and if the tightening of the muscles around his mouth was any indication she succeeded.

'Ever heard of delegation?'

'Ever heard of consultation?' she retorted, planting her hands on her hips as her chin lifted another defiant notch. 'Ground rules, Ivo, where Jamie is concerned I make the decisions. Is that clear?'

The look of astonishment that flickered across his incredibly handsome face might have been funny in other, less fraught, circumstances.

'Was that an *ultimatum*?' he grated, clinging to his temper.

'Excellent,' she approved. 'You're catching on. It's possible you're not as stupid as you look.' About halfway through she sort of knew she'd gone too far, but she was on a roll and couldn't stop. She knew she was shaking; it was always that way when she let her anger get the better of her.

He didn't say a word, he just looked down at her. The colour that had flamed in her face had faded, leaving it washed pale; her eyes were blue pools, the defiance in them now tinged with wariness. With no warning his anger snuffed out.

She looked so tired but she was so stubborn. In his head an image materialised of him holding her until the stiff rigidity in her shoulders dissolved, she dissolved against him, warm and... He gave his head a sharp jarring shake to dislodge the image and the emotions that went with it.

'I was trying to help, but if you enjoy being in a state of permanent exhaustion—fine!' he said, wrapping up his misplaced concern in irritation. 'Your choice. But for God's sake sit down before you fall down!'

Flora did, not because she was grateful for his reminder that she looked awful, but because her knees were shaking in reaction to the emotional confrontation. *Probably the first of many, Flora girl, so you need to toughen up.*

'I should have discussed it with you.'

The concession made her eyes widen.

'But I just assumed...'

'What, that babies have an army of nannies and live in nurseries?'

'I did,' he said.

'And look how well that turned out!'

He responded to her soft taunt with a grin that literally took her breath away. Wow, if Ivo Greco decided to seduce a girl she'd be seduced, Flora realised, no if, but or even maybe.

In her anxiety to push away the thoughts and the insidious warmth unfurling low in her belly and confusing rush of feeling that came with it, she said the first thing that came into her head, a question that was already there but she'd never intended actually to ask.

'How old were you when your parents died?'

His smile vanished to be replaced by a more familiar hauteur. She bent her head, waiting; she could almost *smell* the chilly put-down coming her way.

It didn't come.

'I was a few months old when my mother died.' Her head came up with a snap. 'She was diagnosed with breast cancer when she was pregnant, but she delayed treatment until after I was born... So you could say I killed her.'

His father had.

He'd apologised the next day, tears streaming down his face as he'd said over and over, *'I didn't mean it.'*

It was not a memory he accessed voluntarily, though the smell of stale alcohol on someone's breath always brought the moment back.

'Only if you were a total idiot!' she retorted, hotly indignant—furious! Surely *no one* would allow a child to think that? To potentially carry that sort of guilt through life and into adulthood?

Eyes misted, she turned her head sharply, embarrassed by the emotions that threatened to find release in tears, emotions that only intensified as her eyes drifted towards the figure of the sleeping baby.

She might never know what it felt like to hold her own baby but she could imagine—imagine being willing to give anything for the life you had created.

'I remember my dad,' she said to fill the silence that was growing. 'Though it's hard to know when the memories are mine and when they are stories mum and Sami told me, if you know what I mean.'

'Our father didn't tell us stories. He drank and he

wept, spent weeks in bed and then he killed himself because he couldn't live without her.' *And you are telling her this* why, *Ivo?*

The fact that this tragic information was delivered in a tone that was totally devoid of any emotion made it all the more shocking.

Flora's tender heart ached in her chest; she hurt for the boy he'd been, the pain real.

'Poor man,' she whispered, thinking of poor boys left to be brought up by an army of nannies and a grandfather who, if the Internet opinion of him was even half true, was not exactly warm and cuddly. Flora was *really* trying hard to reserve judgement, but it wasn't easy.

'Poor man…' Ivo ground out the words as he surged to his feet.

Flora sat still and silent. His intimidating height advantage was emphasised even more than normal by the confined environment. 'I just meant—'

'*Weak* man,' he bit back in a clear, cold, contemptuous voice before dark lashes veiled the anger and pain she had glimpsed in his eyes and he delivered the abrupt addition. 'To allow a child to find him—' He stopped, an arrested expression stealing across his face as if he had just realised what he had said.

'You…*you* found him?'

His face was wiped clean of all emotion as he met her tear-filled gaze; everything inside him rejected the one thing he hated above all else: pity. 'I have work. Anything you want…'

And he was gone, striding into the next compartment of the private jet, leaving Flora wondering about the revealing moment and the little boy scared by seeing something no child should.

CHAPTER SEVEN

'WOULD AN OFFER of help get my head bitten off?' Ivo was all for self-sufficiency, but she took it into the realm of the ridiculous.

Flora, who hadn't heard him come up behind her as she tucked the baby into his buggy and adjusted his sun hat, gave a startled jump at the sound of his voice at her shoulder.

She didn't realise how disturbingly close he was until she straightened up and half turned, finding they were standing almost touching. The sensation that made her head spin sizzled along her nerve endings and sent her stomach into a violent dip.

Her eyes made the slow journey from mid-chest level up to his lean, dark face. There was no trace of the emotions that had blazed earlier in his enigmatic stare; his expression was inscrutable.

But now she had glimpsed past the mask she couldn't help but wonder what else his impregnable shell of control hid besides a toxic relationship with his late father.

None of your business, Flora girl. He's not your business. The romance is fake. It's not your job to understand him or heal him. He'd laugh in your face at the idea he needs healing.

And maybe, she mused, he was right.

His voice cut across her internal dialogue.

'Well, are you?'

She looked at him blankly. 'Nervous?'

It wasn't what he'd asked and if he was honest not something he had even considered. The acknowledgement came with a stab of guilt tinged with irritation. He didn't need to change. He didn't want to change. Any changing and compromise would be hers to do. *Dio*, why the hell did she have to be so in touch with her feelings about everything anyway? he wondered, ignoring the fact that it was this aspect of her personality—the soft heart, the desire to put the needs of others above her own—that he was relying on to deliver his nephew into his care.

Flora shrugged and dodged his dark brooding stare. If she hadn't been nervous she was now, and not only of what waited outside.

The earlier conversation had made her think of him in a new light, not as a man who was invulnerable but someone who might actually have some weak spots. Just when she had got comfortable with thinking of him as a man who was one of life's takers, a Callum, a man she could comfortably dismiss, a man she wouldn't allow herself to be attracted to.

'A bit.'

He took a half-step back and she almost wept, so intense was her relief to put a few more inches of air between them. She had to ask herself whether the problem lay with him or her… No, actually, she didn't have to ask herself anything—and she wouldn't.

Resurrecting a little defiance, albeit a slightly less focused version, she lifted a hand to her face and absently brushed a curl from her cheek. The braid in her hair was unravelling as fast as she was!

'Do I have time to freshen up?'

His heavy-lidded gaze slid over the soft curves of her face, lingering a second or two too long on the plump fullness of her lips before he ventured a response. 'You look fine to me, but if you need—'

Flustered by the way he was looking at her, she shook her head. 'No. I'm fine.'

He watched through his half-lowered lids as she tweaked the baby's cap, even though it didn't need tweaking. She looked, he decided, better than fine.

A lot better!

He recognised the compulsive element as his glance slid over her slim figure, but he didn't have an appetite to fight it.

He *liked* looking at her. It was a weakness he was ready to admit to and looking at her was infinitely preferable to having her loose in his head, even if he had invited the invasion by revealing far too much. He still didn't know what madness had possessed him to make him open up that way.

During the flight, while he'd renewed his acquaintance with the pilot, he'd tried and failed to analyse why she acted as some sort of catalyst to feelings he had buried—best thing for them—and failed.

He'd settled for a slightly unsatisfactory verdict: that it wouldn't be happening again, but he could carry on looking.

And where was the harm?

Except to his blood pressure.

Today her hair was tied again, though in a looser plait affair that left curls trailing down her neck and around her face. She had opted to wear a shift dress with a swirly pattern of soft blues and greens that showed off her slim arms and incredible legs. Looking at the slim calves reminded him of the only other time he'd seen her legs. The memory of the sizzling tension of that night still retained enough residual heat to make his skin prickle and his gut tighten.

'Are you going to accept some help?'

She straightened up gracefully and did the flip thing with her hair. Every time she did it he thought about unwinding that plait and spreading the hair... 'Help,' he exclaimed abruptly.

In response to her bemused expression, Ivo nodded at the stroller where Jamie was doing his impression of a perfect baby, kicking his legs and looking cute and smiley. 'Do you want to negotiate the steps or...?' He arched a satiric brow and added drily, 'In case you were wondering, this is me discussing it with you.'

Flora decided to ignore the sarcasm. Instead she nodded to the two uniformed figures waiting to carry the buggy down the steps.

'Thanks so much.'

Ivo watched the men melt as she smiled at them.

Behind her Flora heard Ivo swear; it was an impressive bilingual effort. She half turned to look at him as the men hoisted the buggy between them, a questioning frown painting furrows in her wide smooth brow.

'What happened?'

'It hasn't yet—this is the first test.'

She lifted her face and quivered nervously. *Test?* It had an ominous sound and brought back the terrible weeks of revision before her finals, then the elation of passing before she'd realised that exams were only the first step. Next came experience.

She'd been lucky and got a job offer after her first interview, a firm based in Edinburgh but with their heart and much of their work in the Highlands, domestic and commercial.

She'd joined a team of young and enthusiastic architects with innovative ideas for affordable but aesthetically pleasing homes in the Highlands.

She had seen her future as mapped out and then… Well, it just went to show that you should live in the moment. She had walked away from her dream job and did she regret it? She looked at the crumpled sleep suit in her hand and lifted her chin. Not for one second did she regret her choice.

'We are in love, remember.'

The soft words jolted her back to the moment with a thud. She dropped the sleep suit, gulped and tried to match his insouciant tone. 'I didn't think you'd care what the help thinks, and you've already told me that your grandfather doesn't believe in love…or is that you? You know, a person could be forgiven for thinking the brooding Latin lover doth protest too much.'

'I'm not your lover.' The blush she had held at bay couldn't withstand this provocation or the dark chocolate, velvety voice. 'As for the help, just don't smile at them the way you did those two.'

'Smile?' She shook her head, bemused by his comment. 'I don't…' Her voice faded as he took her arm and propelled her towards the open doors and onto the metal platform in the open air. 'My jacket!' she protested.

She didn't need it. The heat after the air-conditioned atmosphere of the flight hit her. She lifted her hand to shade her eyes against the sun. The men carrying the buggy were on the tarmac waiting; so were several other people. Oh, hell, she realised, a reception committee! All it lacked was a brass band and some sexy baton-twirlers.

This was more awful than any of the scenarios she had dreamt of.

'I'd assumed low profile,' he hissed through clenched teeth.

She felt his low chuckle, low *heartless* chuckle, and then his fingers tightened around her shoulder in warning, as though he had expected her to turn and run back into the plane. *Serve him right if I did,* she thought viciously.

'You might have warned me there would be...'

She had half turned and was tilting her head back when his hand moved from her shoulder to the back of her head, his long fingers curling into her hair and his thumb coming to rest on the angle of her jaw, making her forget what she was about to say.

He bent forward, the gleam of intent in his dark eyes telling her what was about to happen a split second before it did.

He was going to kiss her.

Then he did, and she stopped thinking.

His mouth was warm, his kiss managed to be slow and sensitive and yet possessive, a statement saying, 'She's mine,' to anyone watching.

Flora wasn't watching, she was *feeling*. It was as if her nerve endings had been exposed as she fell bonelessly into the kiss and him; resisting never even crossed her mind.

The hot stream of desire coursing like wine though her body was both terrifying and the most exciting thing that had ever happened to her.

His arms were like steel, holding her close, moulding her to his hard body, *very* hard. Knowing he was aroused—that he *wanted* her—only escalated her excitement, her *madness*.

And then it was over. The anticlimax had the physical impact of an icy plunge pool after a sauna. She couldn't breathe, normality still felt a long way off and her brain was blank.

'You all right?' he asked as she swayed.

Bit too late to be concerned now, she thought as she glared her dislike up at him. Even in the open she was conscious of the electrical charge that still surrounded them. 'I don't like heights,' she retorted, swaying coltishly away from his steadying hand. The one that planted itself firmly in the small of her back was impossible to evade.

'All about first impressions, *cara*,' he whispered, running his lips up the curve of her neck. 'There are people here who will be reporting back to my grandfather.'

She was dimly aware in the distance of Jamie making his own first impressions as he kicked off—*loudly*!

'Jamie...'

He nodded and speared his free hand through his hair, wondering as he did at what point he had actually thought he was in control.

He was acting like some sort of hormonal teenager... or his father.

Short of hugging an iceberg, nothing could have exerted a more blood-cooling effect than the second possibility.

Flora listened as he responded to a question from someone standing inside the plane with what sounded like orders issued in his native tongue. She used the moments to gather her wits.

'Sorry about that,' he murmured as the person vanished.

'For kissing me?' she said, managing to sound cool, even slightly amused.

Was he sorry?

He ought to be. She was, it turned out, *exactly* the sort of woman he'd spent his life avoiding, the sort of woman of whom he could imagine men becoming reliant on the sound of her voice to start the day.

He wasn't one of those men. He had no emotional connection, it was just sex…or it had the potential to be.

'You'd be insulted if I said yes.'

Flora met his dark, hypnotic gaze and was lost. Great big holes appeared in the composure she had managed to gather around herself. Lowering her gaze was the only protective option left and that wasn't as easy as it should have been. By the time her eyes were safely fixed on her toes her skin was covered by a fine sheen of perspiration.

'I'm sure you enjoy performing to your adoring audience but, like I said, I'm not good with heights.'

'Come on. Watch your step.'

His hand stayed an inch clear of her elbow as she walked straight-backed down the steps, close enough to steady her should it be required and far enough away to avoid having another of her displays of pig-headed independence.

The meet-and-greet, the VIP fast route—actually everything that happened between walking down the metal stairs and getting into the middle one of the half-dozen cars that seemed to be reserved for their party—was a bit of a blur.

Was this what it felt like to be a celebrity? If so, Flora couldn't for the life of her work out why so many people wanted this dubious status.

She knew she'd been introduced to people she'd never seen before, and wouldn't know again, even though their names were drifting like flotsam through her head. She knew she'd smiled in what she hoped were appropriate moments.

Ivo spoke to the driver for a few moments before the screen separating them slid silently into place. He leaned back in his seat.

'That went well.'

Flora held out a toy, zooming it in to tickle the baby's tummy and nuzzle his cheek to distract him.

Ivo's proximity was bothering her too much. She really hoped this was a short journey. 'I think your idea of *well* and mine might be pretty far apart.'

'The kiss?' Head against the deeply padded leather rest, he turned his head.

'Yes, the kiss.' She had decided to treat it just like any other line that had been crossed. Making a big thing of it would *make* it big thing or, and that was what she was afraid of, make him realise that it *had* been a big thing for her—nothing short of a revelation.

He had tapped into a *passion* inside her. A *hunger* that she hadn't known existed. Even when she had imagined herself in love with Callum she had never considered herself a particularly sexual person. If she had been she might have been less appreciative of what she had idealistically assumed was his *consideration*. She'd realised later, of course, that he simply hadn't been into her that much.

'You want me to ask next time?'

'A little warning would have been appreciated, and maybe a breath mint.'

She was just feeling pleased with herself for keeping things light when he laughed; the deep vibrant sound sent illicit shivers down her spine. Then he touched her cheek and the contact seemed both natural and intimate. His eyes dropped to her lips. 'You tasted like strawberries.'

She fought the magnetic pull with a shocked little gasp to break the contact, before flopping back in her seat, breathing hard.

'So, what happens now?' she said, putting all the cool and practical at her command in her voice.

'Try catching up on some sleep.'

Her eyes went to the baby. 'I couldn't.'

'It might help some of those frown lines smooth out.'

'I suppose I might come across as a bit overprotective.' The concession came reluctantly and drew a short, hard laugh from her travelling companion.

'You think?'

She gave a little shrug. 'He's my responsibility and I was worried about him flying.' Not worried enough, she thought with a fresh rush of guilt.

The possibility that the tiny defect in his heart detected at Sami's twenty-week scan and confirmed at birth might make air travel an issue had not occurred to her until *after* Ivo had left that first morning.

Obviously she had contacted the family GP immediately, who, declaring himself unable to see a problem, had in turn checked with the paediatric cardiac consultant who had overall responsibility for Jamie's care.

His advice had been the same: there was no reason Jamie could not fly.

'Babies fly all the time.'

It was annoyance at his dismissal that made her toss back, 'Not all babies have a heart defect.'

The indolent pose he'd adopted vanished as his posture stiffened. 'A heart…' His chest lifted as he inhaled deeply before training his accusing stare on Flora. 'Why am I just learning of this?'

'Possibly because you never asked, or maybe because it's none of your business?' she charged back, angry at his display of *how very dare you?* hauteur.

The muscles in Ivo's brown throat rippled as he swallowed. He was still in the grip of shock, not just because of the information she had casually dropped into the conversation, but because of the overwhelming surge of protectiveness that had hit him without warning.

'Is he…is it bad?'

She shook her head. 'At Sami's twenty-week scan they discovered a small defect in the baby's heart. Something they call a VSD, and the rest of us call a hole in the heart. Sometimes it's vanished by birth, but Jamie's hadn't. He was referred to a top cardiac paediatrician.'

It took a supreme effort but Ivo managed to stop himself asking any of the myriad questions that were hovering on the tip of his tongue. He knew that letting her speak would tell him what he wanted to know quicker, and she was being concise as she gave the information in a carefully neutral voice.

'It isn't that rare. In more severe cases they surgically intervene on infants. Jamie's isn't severe and there is every chance it will close spontaneously over the next few years. It's a wait-and-see policy at this stage and he has no symptoms.'

'So he is in no immediate danger.'

'No, the doctors are quite relaxed about it.'

'But you're not,' he said, leaning back into the leather and half closing his eyes. 'You have to relax. Babies pick up on that stuff.' He opened one eye and saw she was looking at him in astonishment. 'I've been doing a bit of research.'

The slightly embarrassed look on his face as he made

the admission made her smile. It was weird—she had never known her emotions to be on such a roller coaster and it was all the unpredictable man's fault. One moment he was yelling at her and being totally unreasonable, the next he was being disarmingly sweet.

Her smile deepened as she realised she'd just thought of Ivo Greco and *sweet* in the same sentence.

'I did a lot of research when I first…' Her eyes skittered away from the understanding in his. 'When I became guardian. I knew nothing about babies. I never thought I'd be a parent. I never had a five-year plan or anything. I just sort of fell into things—right place, right time.'

She made it sound as though she had sleepwalked into a great job at an incredible firm of architects and graduated in the top three in her class quite accidentally. *God save me from British self-deprecation!*

Scottish self-deprecation, he could almost hear the pride and reproach in her voice as she put him right—as she undoubtedly would do, were he reckless enough to voice his complaint.

He opted for a middle ground.

'Modesty… I don't come across that very often.'

She scowled. He made her sound like some sort of old-fashioned freak. 'And definitely not when you look in the mirror.' Her eyes flew wide, her hand going to her lips in an attitude of comical dismay. 'Sorry. I didn't mean that as an insult.'

Amusement danced deep in his eyes as he studied her face and then faded like a snuffed-out candle as he found he was able to see all too clearly her checking and double checking on the sleeping baby, her glorious hair swinging loose around her narrow shoulders, tense from the burden that had fallen on them. He could almost see the individual lines of worry etched on her youthful, beautiful face as she searched fearfully for signs and symptoms the doctors had told her to look out for.

Fighting his way free of the uncomfortably empathic moment, he managed a forced smile.

'God help me when you *do* mean it, Flora Henderson.' His glance slid to the baby lying between them just as his head lolled; this time he didn't jerk himself awake as he had on the last half-dozen times.

'Why don't you take a nap while he's asleep?'

'I couldn't,' she said, meaning it.

Two minutes later he heard her breathing deepen.

CHAPTER EIGHT

'I SLEPT!' FLORA YELPED, coming to with a jerk after several moments of pleasant drifting.

One hand meshed in her tangled curls, she clenched the fingers of her right hand as her glance went straight to the sleeping baby. Seemingly satisfied, she relaxed, or at least went down from red to amber alert status...

When had she last relaxed?

Not his business, Ivo reminded himself. She was a consenting adult and if she chose to... Feeling his anger build, Ivo closed the laptop on his knee with a decisive snap. The illusion that he'd actually been working was false. The face of his sleeping travelling companion had been infinitely more appealing than emails or financial breakdowns.

He supposed there was an element of guilty pleasure, though mostly pleasure, in being able to stare at her unobserved. To study the curve of her cheek, the elegant arch of her brow and the pink bow of her mouth. He remembered how she tasted and wanted to taste her again. He imagined himself waking her up with a kiss.

Despite the Sleeping Beauty analogy, in his head there was nothing chaste or fairy-tale-like about the kiss, or her response! It involved warm pale limbs wrapping around him, sinking into...

'Are we nearly there?'

Wrenched free of the sensual, erotic images, he clamped his lips tight over a strangled laugh, and watched her *almost* press her nose to the window.

They'd been *there* for at least ten minutes. The fertile land dotted with fig groves and larger stretches of vineyards belonged to his family.

But he knew what she meant.

'We've just left the village.' At the foot of the craggy outcrop that the Castello was built on, much of the village still belonged to the Greco estate. 'Just wait a minute and you'll see it.'

She followed the direction of his pointing finger and turned her head.

Beside her Ivo said, 'About—now!'

He heard her breath catch; it was a common response to the first sight of his family home, but the awe on Flora's face made him think of a child seeing a Christmas tree.

Flora realised a moment too late that the openmouthed look was not the height of sophistication, or for that matter a good look on anyone except, perhaps, her travelling companion, who would look incredible no matter what.

At least this was an example of life's unfairness that she could smile at, and she did smile as she shifted in her seat to face him.

'It looks like something out of a fairy tale. The towers…' Head shaking, she glanced back at the square stone towers at each of the four corner of the monumental building.

'They were there a couple of hundred years before the actual Castello. There's a view over the sea from up there, but it's not bad from here either.' He nodded past her and she turned again.

She'd been aware of the steep incline of the winding road but not the village, built on the edge of the water, it revealed or the glittering aquamarine sea scape it was set against.

Wow hardly seemed adequate—when he had spoken of Jamie's heritage she had never imagined anything like this. On this scale the historic grandeur was intimidating. 'So this is the Greco ancestral home.'

'There have been Grecos here for centuries. This place's fortunes followed ours, land sold, land bought back, disrepair and grandeur, but our family originally didn't build the place, an ancestor won it in a card game, or so the story goes. A tale probably invented for the tourists.'

'Have you always lived here?'

'We lived here as children, but these days I have an apartment in Florence. It's more convenient for when I'm in Italy, but I travel a great deal. I could give you a history but as an architect you'll probably know more about it than me.'

'I am an architect,' she agreed, wondering absently if this was the wrong tense, or maybe, considering the sick feeling in the pit of her stomach, to describe her as a *scared* architect would have been more appropriate. 'Not an art historian.' That said, she did recognise the massive double entrance that had come into view on top of an impressive flight of stone steps as a pretty incredible example of pure Renaissance.

The melding of styles over the years had given this place a unique look, in the same way the melding of genes over the years had given Ivo a unique look.

The thought drew her gaze towards the man whose genetic make-up had produced...well...perfection, and she found he was looking at her. He wasn't smiling and there was something in his eyes that made her heart beat faster.

She lifted her chin in response to the silent challenge glittering in his eyes. 'So what now?'

'Now we get you and Jamie settled. I'm assuming that Salvatore will want to see you both.'

An invitation where non-attendance was not an option.

Her spiky, thick lashes half lowered, her plump lower lip caught between her teeth, her soft mutter of, 'I can hardly wait,' was obviously not as under her breath as she intended because he responded drily.

'In order to avoid any misunderstandings, I should mention that my grandfather is not likely to get *irony*, or, for that matter, humour.'

'Any more tips?'

'Don't overthink this, and don't look so guilty.'

She silently tacked on *and don't throw up* as she nodded to the uniformed figure holding the door open and slid out of the car.

A moment later Ivo joined her. He was carrying the car seat. She was actually grateful for the light pressure of the guiding hand in the small of her back as they approached the shallow flight of stone steps with the elaborate wrought-iron railings.

This was what Bruno had walked away from. Seeing it up close made her appreciate for the first time just how much he had turned his back on for the woman he loved, just what he had sacrificed.

She had thought that the home and business his parents had built was Jamie's inheritance, preserving it had been her focus, but now she was here she realised that *this* was Jamie's birthright too.

She glanced down at the baby sitting contentedly,

his sun hat slightly askew on his dark curls, and experienced a moment of mind-clearing clarity.

Her chin lifted. Yes, she would fight to keep the business going, so that, unlike his father, Jamie would never have to choose. 'None of this actually matters. Jamie's true birthright is his parents' love.'

She hadn't been aware that she had voiced the realisation out loud until the pressure against her spine increased and Ivo's deep-voiced cynicism, etched in every syllable, floated down to her, making her wince.

'You put a high price on love.'

She was still blinking as she waited for her eyes to adjust to the more subdued light after the brilliant sunshine outside, when a man approached. *Neat* was the word that popped into her head when she saw him. Everything about him was precise, from his neatly trimmed beard to the parting in his slicked-back hair; she could have seen her reflection in his highly polished shoes.

'Ramon.'

'Sir.' He greeted Ivo with a deferential tip of his head.

'Flora, this is Ramon, my grandfather's major domo, who makes this place run like clockwork. Ramon, this is my fiancée, Ms Flora Henderson, and Jamie.'

'Hello.' The way he looked at the hand she had extended made Flora wonder if she had broken some sort of etiquette, but his smile was genial as he took it in a dry-handed grip.

'If you're here as an escort, Ramon, explain to my grandfather—'

'Jamie needs feeding.' Flora had been watching the baby push his chubby fist into his mouth. Experience told her they had about five minutes before the hungry wailing started.

'There, you see, my grandfather will have to wait.'

The older man cleared his throat. 'Of course.' He nodded his head as three people appeared. They responded to instructions he delivered in his precise voice with lots of nods. 'Actually, sir, I was hoping… The doctor is here and your grandfather has given him permission to speak with you.'

Flora felt Ivo's splayed fingers tighten in the small of her back; her eyes went to his face. His features were still. Despite the lack of any discernible expression at all on his face, or maybe *because* of it, Flora sensed the emotions under the surface.

If everyone had a secret fear, she decided then that Ivo's was anyone who suspected he was human.

'You go,' she said, drawing the attention of the older man to herself. 'We'll be fine.' She stepped away from his supportive touch and curled her fingers around his on the handle of the baby carrier. 'I can manage,' she said and turned, while around them the rest of the luggage and baby paraphernalia was being carried up the stairs and along one of the wide galleries that ran around the upper floor perimeter, before vanishing.

'I can manage,' she repeated with another tug.

Ivo didn't release his grip but he did put the carrier down on the floor. 'Give us a moment, will you, Ramon?'

The other man moved away to a discreet distance.

Flora glanced over her shoulder towards him and, pitching her voice low, said softly, 'I'm sorry.'

He arched a brow. 'What for?'

'That your grandfather is…'

'What? Dying? Well, that's why you're here, isn't it? Smile, *cara*, this might be good news for you. I know you were too *polite* to ask how long but this does looks promising for you, so fingers crossed.'

It wasn't just the sneering intonation in his voice or the coldness in his eyes as they swept over her face, it was the fact that she hadn't seen it coming. She focused on stopping the tears she felt pressing at the backs of her eyes and told herself it was ridiculous to feel this level of hurt.

'Why are you being so hateful?'

He flinched inwardly at the unconscious dignity in her stance, but he ignored the guilt nudging his conscience and refused to even acknowledge the odd wrenching sensation in his chest as he looked down into the reproachful blue eyes that shimmered up at him, bright as jewels.

He gave a negligent shrug. 'What can I say? They tell me it's one of my talents.'

'Odd. I get the impression you're working hard at it.' The bewilderment in her face was genuine. 'Why are you pushing me away?'

Wishing the words unsaid, not even knowing where they had come from, Flora veiled her eyes as she pushed her way through a wave of cringing embarrassment by sheer force of will.

Pushing you away...! It was the sort of thing that people in a relationship said. She twisted the ring on her finger and reminded herself it was very much for show.

He flinched inwardly, then dealt with the direct hit the only way he could—he ignored it. 'Ramon.'

The other man hurried over.

Flora was aware of Ivo saying something to him but it wasn't until the dapper bearded figure reached for the baby carrier that Flora reacted. Possibly he was slow because he thought the request was beneath his pay grade, but Flora got there before him, tugging up the carrier in two hands and holding it against her front.

'I can manage.' Anger shimmered through her as she walked, stiff-backed, towards the staircase. A lot of things were uncertain but one thing she knew for sure: she was not going to waste her sympathy on Ivo Greco again, or imagine he was something he was not.

The doctor, actually two of them, stood outside his grandfather's bedroom. One he recognised as Salvatore's personal physician, the other was a stranger. If he'd had any doubts remaining, their professional expression, that blending of gravity and sympathy that all medics perfected, said it all.

Ivo took a deep breath and dragged a hand through his hair, banishing the lingering memory of the hurt in Flora's eyes that had plagued him as he'd walked down the corridors feeling like a total heel.

What was the British saying? *If the hat fits...*

Well, it did, he decided, removing his hand from his hair, not bothering to smooth down the spikes. Flora's only sin in this instance was being in the firing line when he had realised this wasn't one of the old man's games, he really *was* dying, and rather than admit even to himself that he cared, his reflex had been to hit out.

Obviously at one level he had known that it was a possibility that for once in his life his grandfather was being forthright, and he should have been prepared, but deep down he had never actually believed that Salvatore, who had always seemed so indestructible to him, was dying.

The irony was he hadn't even known he was in denial until the moment he had heard the truth in Ramon's voice.

This wasn't just another of the old fox's schemes. It was for real.

Not quite the classic case of the boy crying wolf but a toxic, twisted version of it.

'He is waiting for you.'

Ivo never had responded well to authority, and this went double for the white-coated variety. He was not impressed by medical degrees. Men with more degrees than wall space had not stopped his damaged father killing himself or his mother dying. 'And yet you are out here.'

'We wanted to speak to you before you go inside. Actually, we wanted to speak to you much earlier, but we were constrained by your grandfather's wishes.'

That would be right, Salvatore would always have the last word, even if that word was a dying word...'Is it cancer?'

The men glanced at each other, then the one he didn't recognise cleared his throat.

'I'm afraid not.'

Afraid? What the hell could be worse than cancer? Ivo wondered.

'Your grandfather has dementia.'

Ivo looked at him and laughed, not an amused sound. 'That's the most ridiculous thing I've ever heard. My grandfather is as sharp as a tack. He can run rings around someone half his age, physically and *mentally*.'

'Your grandfather can have long periods of lucidity.'

Meaning he doesn't know where he is the rest of the time. The grinding pain pressing into his temples was no longer the beginning of a tension headache, it was full blown. Ivo looked coldly at the man who spoke before transferring his attention to the familiar face of the family doctor, who up to this point had seemed reasonably reliable.

'I don't know where you dug this joker up from, but I want a second opinion.'

The older man flushed and looked embarrassed as he sent an apologetic grimace to his colleague. 'This is Professor Ranieri—'

Ivo arched a brow; the degree of reverence had only increased his antagonism. 'Is that meant to mean something to me?'

The younger man stepped forward. 'I'm a professor in neurodegenerative conditions and dementia, Mr Greco, and I *am* the second opinion.' He flashed his colleague a look. 'Or would I be correct in saying third is more accurate?' The older man nodded unhappily. 'I diagnosed your grandfather three months ago,' he finished quietly.

'He's suspected it for some time,' the older man added to back up his colleague. 'When he finally consulted me, well, the tests were all conclusive.'

Ivo's chest lifted, and he swallowed; his brain still refused to accept what he was being told. First Bruno and now Salvatore, a double whammy.

His family was vanishing.

He had not seen his brother for years, and he saw his grandfather as little as he could. Alone was the way he liked it, he reminded himself.

'I would have known.' He clung stubbornly to the belief because the option was believing what these men were saying.

'Not necessarily, Mr Greco. People with dementia will hide their symptoms—even those closest to them don't always notice. Some changes can be subtle.'

'No.' Ivo remained firm. 'We spoke last week, he was... He called me Bruno...' The recovered memory took on a new significance as he replayed highlights of

the conversation in his head. Suddenly the clues were
there, the minor errors evidence of his memory loss.

Ivo stood there breathing hard as his defences against
the ugly truth disintegrated. He could no longer stop
himself thinking of the tough old man with a razor-
sharp brain losing part of himself and knowing it. It
was the ultimate horror; fear clawed at his own belly
just thinking about it.

Dio, Salvatore must have been desperate!

'Look, we appreciate this is a lot to take in.' The
older man stepped forward to place a reassuring hand
on Ivo's arm but was stopped by a look from those dark,
hooded eyes. 'You'll need time to digest and there will
be questions. We are accepting your hospitality for the
night, so whenever you're ready?'

Ivo's jaw tightened. 'How about now?'

The older medic cleared his throat and adjusted the
wire-framed spectacles perched on his nose. 'Actually,
I believe you are expected inside.' He nodded towards
the bedroom door. 'We are here at the behest of your
father's lawyer.'

'Rafe is here?' Was he the last to know? Just how
many people had known before he had?

'You grandfather wishes, I believe, to sign over
power of attorney to you. That is why we are here,
to confirm that his mind is… That he is able to make
such a decision with sound mind and without any ex-
ternal pressure.'

Ivo struggled to hide the devastating impact of the
wave of shock that rose up inside him like swirling
filthy flood water. 'That is hardly urgent.' Right now,
his priority was learning all there was to know about
what his grandfather was facing.

Knowledge was power. There was always an alternative; this wasn't something that you meekly accepted.

It was the younger doctor who responded. 'Can I be frank with you?'

Ivo said nothing, he just looked.

'Right, well, tomorrow, Mr Greco,' he said gently, 'we might not be able to confirm that your grandfather has the mental capacity to make that decision. Time is running out, I'm afraid.'

CHAPTER NINE

IT WAS TWO hours before the lawyers, and Ramon who had acted as a witness, had the documents signed.

'Well, that's done.'

Ivo didn't say anything.

'So how does it feel, boy, to finally have the old man where you want him?' Salvatore mocked.

Suddenly Ivo was angry, too angry for a moment to respond. 'Is that what you think I am?'

'No, it isn't. I would be happier if you were. You're soft, Bruno, you always were. You allow emotions to get in the way of good sense.'

Ivo's anger dissolved as quickly as it had flashed. 'I'm Ivo, Grandfather.'

The old man looked away. 'What's in a name…? I didn't tell you because I didn't want anyone to know, for anyone to know that Salvatore Greco is a feeble-minded dribbling idiot who needs feeding.' His voice cracked.

Ivo turned away while his grandfather fought the tears that filled his eyes. He had never seen his grand-father cry. He was filled with a sense of helplessness he had never felt before.

'You will not tell anyone. Swear to me, Ivo.'

Ivo turned back to face him. 'I swear.'

'Give me a little while longer before my enemies start celebrating. So, what is the child like?'

'Jamie is a…nice baby.'

'And you're marrying the girl.'

Ivo shook his head. 'No.'

'I thought as much. You're a devious devil. You get that from me. Is the baby like…his father?'

It wasn't seeing his grandfather struggle to remember his grandson's name, it was watching him try and disguise the fact that it felt like a body blow as a fresh stab of toxic guilt consumed him.

How could I not have seen this?

Ivo moved impulsively across the room to his grandfather's side. 'Grandfather—'

The old man held up his hands as though warding off danger, his lip curled in a snarl of distaste. 'No soft stuff and sentiment. I'm not totally ga-ga yet.'

His expression blank, Ivo drew back.

'That's better. I think I'll sleep. When does the boy arrive?'

'They are already here.'

'We will have dinner tomorrow, then.' He gave a little chuckle and threw his grandson a knowing look. 'Are you bedding her yet? Oh, my God, when you look down your nose at me you look just like my father. I was a major disappointment to him, you know, never good enough for him.' His voice trailed away. 'Too crude and vulgar.'

It was several minutes before Ivo realised he'd fallen asleep.

Ramon was waiting outside the door when he emerged. 'He's asleep,' he said.

'He tires easily.'

They exchanged a nod of understanding. Ivo took

steps before the reality began to kick in; the entire empire was now his responsibility. The buck stopped with him.

The suite of rooms she had been allocated covered three floors, and had, as well as the master suite, two guest suites, a dining room, living room, kitchen, a kitchenette, a day nursery, a night nursery, lift access to the nannies' rooms and one to the ground floor.

When asked was it suitable she gave a cheery smile and said, 'Just like home.'

Nobody smiled at her joke but they did leave her in peace.

She focused on the immediate priorities. Bathing and feeding Jamie were top of the list, after which he'd immediately fallen asleep.

A hot shower was calling her. It was a relief to strip off her creased clothes and step into the shower after resisting the temptation of the massive antique copper bathtub. A long luxurious soak was for an occasion when Ivo was not likely to appear to bear her off to the awful interview with his grandfather.

When she walked back into the sitting room, wearing a soft robe from the bathroom, there were hot coffee and tea, tiny sandwiches and a selection of pastries on one of the tables.

She poured a black coffee, took a sip and, picking up one of the sandwiches, she went to the bedroom and walked over to one of the massive wardrobes. The scent coming from the lavender sachets that were hooked around the rail tickled her nostrils as she opened it. Someone had unpacked her clothes before she'd even reached the room and they looked pretty lost sitting there in the cavernous scented space.

Eating the rest of her sandwich, which was very good, she selected a dress similar in design to the creased one she had just taken off, though the neckline on this one was squarer and the fabric plain white with a discreet diamond pattern picked out in silver.

She fished out some fresh underwear and wriggled her way into it. It required a few contortions to reach the zip but once on she smoothed down the fabric and looked at herself in the mirror. She was playing a part. Did she look like the sort of woman a man like Ivo Greco proposed to?

The answer was quite obviously no, not when you considered the long-legged model types she'd seen hanging on him, quite literally in some instances, in the collection of photos available online for anyone interested enough to type in his name.

Now, if you were talking taking to bed...?

Fastening onto the unbidden thought came a flashback to that kiss, as her gaze drifted to the big bed that dominated the room. She walked across and laid her hand on the smooth, pristine silk quilt.

Through half-closed eyes she visualised two figures lying there, limbs entwined. She shook her head to clear the erotic, illicit hallucination. A shiver ran through her body as she lifted a hand to her lips, running her finger along the outline, her eyes half closed.

What was happening to her?

Her breath came shallow and uneven as she fought against the pressure exerted by the knot of tangled emotions, among them a yearning she didn't want to acknowledge, all lodged behind her breastbone. It was as if that one kiss had released something inside her. Something she didn't seem to have any control over.

She wandered across to the dressing table and picked

up a silver-backed brush. Removing the pins that had held up her hair in the shower, she began to brush it, focusing on the long soothing strokes and not the depressing realisation that that kiss had been the most mind-blazingly erotic experience of her life. Which had to make her one of the saddest twenty-five-year-olds in the world.

How many twenty-five-year-old *virgins* were left in the world, outside convents?

'You're an anachronism, Flora...and yet,' she told her mirror image, 'you look quite normal.' She waved the brush at the mirror. 'Freckled, and very ginger, but normal.'

She brushed until her hair prickled with static, a fiery nimbus around her face.

And she could still taste that kiss.

With a small, angry cry of self-disgust she threw the brush across the room. It landed bang in the middle of the big bed.

'This has to stop, Flora!' she told herself as she stalked across to retrieve it.

For some reason Flora found herself reluctant to put a crease in the pristine bed linen so, leaving one foot on the floor, she pushed her other knee through the folds of the dress and put it on the bed before she stretched out to reach the brush.

She was in this position when Ivo walked into the room.

What he had intended when he walked in, he'd never know because the moment he saw her there, the provocative image of her rear, the smooth curve of her bare thigh, the cloud of copper curls, he didn't fight it. It was a done deal.

It was with relief that he embraced it, actually ran full tilt at it. He wanted the mindless oblivion of sex, and that was all it was.

Wanting her.

She didn't see him. She saw his reflection in the mirror on the opposite wall and immediately lost her balance and pitched forward to land in a sprawled heap on the bed.

With a grunt of dismay she fought to pull the dress over her legs as she twisted over onto her back. Levering herself semi upright on her elbows, she looked across the room to where he stood. A combination of shock and excitement slithered through her, the way he was standing, the way he was breathing... She could feel the tension that was written in his face and in the tense muscles on his powerful body; the sense of danger that she'd always been conscious of in him was there but there was nothing potential about it, it was raw and real.

There was a moment of total silence as their eyes clashed, and connected, and then he was striding across the room, making her think of some sort of ancient Roman warrior.

He stood for a moment beside the bed, not saying a word. She looked at him, his image filtered through the skeins of hair that had drifted across her face, until he bent forward.

'I want to see you.'

The contact of his cool brown fingers on her hot skin as he brushed back the hair from her face was like a lightning strike. Every muscle in her body tensed, electrical shocks zigzagging through her.

'That's better,' he breathed, drinking in the delicate features turned up to him.

His voice seemed to be coming from a long way off, but it wasn't because she could feel his breath warm on her cheek as he pressed the heel of his hand against the centre of her chest and pushed her backwards onto the bed.

It felt to Flora as though she were in slow motion. Everything had slowed, even her heart; each fresh beat of blood around her body felt like a drumbeat in her temples. She was more conscious of her own body than she ever had been, conscious of everything from the heat pooled between her legs to the fine downy hairs that stood on her arms.

Arm over arm, he dragged himself up the bed until his face was level with hers. With his body suspended over her she felt cut off from everything but this man, this man who released all these wild, raw, primal feelings inside her.

She squeezed her eyes shut but the feeling didn't go away.

'I don't feel like me,' she whispered.

He kissed her paper-thin, blue-veined eyelids.

'I didn't mean for this to happen,' he rasped.

If you didn't want anything to happen, why walk into the room, Ivo? No, this is exactly *what you wanted to happen, what you have wanted to happen from the first moment you set eyes on her.*

'I want you.'

The throaty purr of his words sent a primitive thrill through her body.

Her blue eyes blinked open; the primal glow in his dark eyes sent her insides melting. Her breath came harder and she could feel his breath hot on her face. Though they were not touching she could feel the quiver of tension in his lean body.

The leashed power, his sheer maleness, filled her with a longing she had no name for. Every cell of her body ached for him. She had never felt anything like this in her life.

When Callum had wanted to wait, he said because

he *respected* her, she hadn't pushed it. She hadn't questioned it, because there had been a small part of her that had been relieved. She certainly hadn't felt as though she'd die if she didn't give herself to Callum. There had been no yearning, no desire to surrender totally to the hunger roaring inside her, to ease a deep, aching inner loneliness she hadn't even known was there until now.

She felt frightened and excited, the only reason she held back the burden of her embarrassing inexperience. Should she tell him? It was the possibility that he might reject her that tipped the balance. She couldn't risk that. She needed this to happen too much.

'I want you too,' she whispered, as, framing his face with her hands, she kept her eyes open as she kissed him.

For a moment he did nothing as her lips moved across his, then she felt a groan vibrate deep in his chest and he kissed her back with a frantic hunger, a driving desperation, that forced the air from her lungs and drew frantic little moans from her own throat.

He slid down beside her and, one hand hooked behind her head, he slid his free hand down over the curve of her body and pulled her hard against him to face him. He stopped kissing her long enough to tangle his fingers in her hair, to pull her face away so that he could look at her. She just stared at him raptly as he swept away the strands of hair from her face.

She touched his face, smoothing her fingers over the stubble on his cheek and jaw, fascinated by the strength, the beauty, of the angles and hollows.

Her throat ached as she looked at him. 'You're beautiful.'

His jaw quivered in reaction to her awed whisper. This might be just sex but he needed it—*her*—as much as he needed the oxygen he was dragging into his lungs.

He had never experienced a passion as powerful and as all-consuming as the one that drove him now.

The whispered touch of his breath on the skin of her face before he kissed her was a delicious torture and she was so ready when he did cover her parted lips with his own that she whimpered with relief, the sound lost in his mouth.

Still kissing her, his mouth moving in a series of open-mouthed, warm kisses down the graceful column of her neck, he slid his hands under the dress she wore, easing the straps off her shoulders and exposing the angles of her collarbones and the upper slope of her breasts. Her skin had an alabaster glow, the clarity enhanced somehow by the sprinkling of freckles.

Desire roared inside him like an inferno as he held her passion-glazed eyes and then suddenly, expertly, he pulled them both to their feet so that he could reach around her to ease the zip of her dress undone. He watched hungrily as the garment slid to the floor, leaving her standing in just her underwear. She shivered as the cool air hit her hot skin…and then shivered again when his hooded glance dropped to her chest. Her nerve endings reacted to the sensuous sweep of his hooded eyes as it would a touch.

'You're beautiful.' He reached round behind her, unclasping her strapless bra, and watched appreciatively as her breasts were fully exposed to him.

He tilted her back towards the bed and laid her down. His hands resting either side of her shoulders, his body was suspended above her, not touching… She wanted to touch him.

Did she say so? She had no idea, but he suddenly kissed her hard and levered himself off her and stood by the bed.

Her dismay switched to relief as he began to tear off his clothes.

Lying there, her only covering a tiny pair of pants, her breasts lifting and falling in time with her short, shallow inhalations, she watched him kick himself free of trousers and fight his way out of his shirt. The intoxicating wildness pumping through her bloodstream made her feel light-headed, reckless, unlike herself. She was literally paralysed with lust and longing. It infiltrated every cell of her body, every inch of her skin.

She ached for him in a way she hadn't known existed.

He paused for a moment by the bed, giving her greedy eyes the opportunity to gloat over his streamlined perfect body, every muscle beautifully defined under skin that glowed gold.

One knee on the bed, he leaned over and ran his fingers under the waistband of her knickers, sliding them slowly down over her smooth thighs.

The first skin-to-skin contact made her gasp then sigh as he kissed her, his tongue slipping deep between her parted lips.

She grabbed his head to deepen the pressure of her tongue meeting his.

The soft keening moan of protests when his head lifted dissolved into a deep moan as he cupped one breast in his big hand, and, drawing a thumb up to the aroused rosy peak, he covered it with his mouth. By the time he moved to apply similar treatment to the other breast, she was writhing. The only thing stopping her floating away was his hand on her hip.

'Look at me, *cara*,' he slurred thickly.

His searing stare held her blue eyes tight as his hand slid between her legs.

'You feel ready for me,' he said, stroking her.

'I feel on fire,' she rasped. 'This is too…too…much!' Her eyelashes fluttered against her cheek as he eased a finger into her.

'So tight,' he murmured against her ear. 'Incredible.'

She moved restlessly, pressing against his hand, not realising what else he was doing until he curled her fingers around him.

A choking sound of shock vibrated in her throat.

'That's how much I want… I need you. I want to be inside you, *cara*.' He could not remember wanting a woman this much in his life. It felt like a fever roaring in his blood, driving him to the act of possession. Teeth clenched, he fought the need, wanting her to need this as much as he did. His skin was slicked with sweat by the effort of staying in control.

No woman had ever tested his control this much.

The dark, driven need in his face increased her excitement. Her skin was on fire…she was burning up with need from the inside out. 'I need you too,' she gasped faintly.

As he rolled her beneath him she arched up into him. The touch of his body against the curls at the apex of her legs brought her eyes wide open and on a collision course with his hot, hungry stare.

'Please,' she said simply.

She felt the deep, animal groan building in the vault of his chest and it emerged at the same moment he slid into her.

She jerked, gasped and wrapped her legs around him. Eyes tight, focused on each advance and retreat, each thrust taking her deeper into herself. She focused on the places he was touching that had never been touched, the muscles that clenched by instinct, building the pressure, the pleasure, the nerves that were singing, the tension that was building and building.

She forgot where she ended and he began and it felt as if she couldn't bear any more, and then she saw explosions behind her closed eyelids, bursts of light as the heat and pleasure rocked through her body, as the pleasure centre in her brain went into overload.

The floating back to earth was gentle, as was his kiss before he rolled off her. They lay there, side by side on their backs, fingertips touching as their sweat-slick bodies cooled.

'So.' He propped himself on one elbow and looked down at her deliciously flushed face, remembering the look of concentration on her face as the heat had built inside her. His body stirred lazily, and then not so lazily as his glance slid a little lower. The sheet ended just below her coral-tipped, perfect breasts; they quivered as she covered her face with both hands.

The *lazy* element vanished at the quivering. His hunger for her had flared into full, hot life.

'Look at me, Flora.'

She dropped her hands and did. It would always be a pleasure to look at him, but right now it was a struggle to meet his gaze.

'I suppose you're talking about the virgin stuff.'

'You suppose right…' He adjusted a pillow and put it behind his head. 'I was under the impression that you'd had a love affair, were engaged.' He'd certainly not imagined there had been only one man in her life, so the discovery that he was her first lover had been one of the biggest shocks of his life.

He looked down and found she was looking up at him quizzically. 'Do you mind?'

Mind?

On one level it was possibly the most erotic thing in the world to know you were a woman's first lover... maybe modern man was a myth?

He swallowed. It fascinated him that this seemed a bigger thing for him than her. 'A heads-up might have been an idea. It's not usual to be a virgin at your age unless you have just come out of a nunnery.'

'Or you had a Callum in your life.' She sighed, with an eye roll and a supple feline stretch that sent a fresh slug of lust through his sated body.

She made him greedy.

'Callum?'

He'd never liked that name.

'All the girls at my school had a crush on Callum. He was seven years ahead of me, so he left as I arrived at high school. But his dad was our postman and his mum worked in a chemist in Portree. You'll ken that Skye isn't such a big place.'

'I ken.'

'Are you mocking me?'

He held up his hands in mock horror and promised solemnly, 'I wouldn't dare.' It flickered through his head that sleeping with a virgin wasn't the only *first* for him today; he'd never enjoyed, and, yes, he *was* enjoying, a post-coital conversation quite like this before.

Actually, his experience of post-coital conversations was pretty limited. His lifestyle was not about lingering, more perpetual motion. Lingering for him generally involved checking his emails.

'Anyway, I had a massive crush on him.'

At this artless confidence Ivo felt some of the pleasure of the moment slip away.

'We all did. I was in my second year at uni when I bumped into him, and, well, a month later we were engaged.' She closed her eyes. 'I know it sounds crazy. And it was. It turns out we expected very different things from marriage.' Callum wanted kids and she couldn't give him them.

Ivo caught her hand and nudged the diamond on her finger with his own. 'We were engaged in one day.'

She pulled her hand away and bent so that he couldn't see her face as she twisted the diamond around on her finger. 'That's not the same. *This*—' her clear blue gaze lifted to him '—is a...not a real...not real at all,' she finished awkwardly.

What had just happened felt *very* real. It felt very *right*.

'So, we just had imaginary sex.'

She flashed him a look. 'You know what I mean.'

He knew more than she realised. Reading between the lines it was pretty obvious that she'd told this Callum guy she couldn't have kids and he'd said, thanks but, no, thanks!

The bastard, he thought viciously.

'Well anyhow he...' She hesitated, after the Callum fiasco she had told herself that in the future she would tell any potential partner upfront that she couldn't have children. She hadn't quite worked out the timing yet, should it be on the first date, third, before you'd got to like him?

But she reminded herself before self-pity kicked in that timing was not an issue here. Ivo wasn't a potential partner, he was her lover. Her marvellous, incredible lover, but this was just sex, at least for him.

She felt a sudden spurt of panic and she didn't want to go where that acknowledgement was leading.

'Dumped me.'

Ivo's jaw began to ache as he watched her produce

a smile that invited him to share the joke. Ivo did not feel in a joking mood, he recognised there was no reason for her to confide in him, he was the last person in the world to advocate trust, which begged the question, why? Though for a while there he had been holding his breath willing her to.

'I suppose it turned me off the whole dating thing, and since then I've been too busy to do anything about it.'

'So why didn't your mad, passionate love affair involve sex?'

'Other than the obvious truth I know now, that he just wasn't that into me? I think Callum is one of those men who think there are two sorts of women: the ones you sleep with and the ones you marry and then cheat on.'

'Charming guy.'

'I have terrible taste in men,' she agreed, snuggling into his side. No longer sweat-slicked, his cooled skin had a satiny texture that fascinated her, as did the movement of fine muscles just below the silky surface. Everything about him fascinated her to a point that she would previously have called obsession.

'Thank you.'

'Oh, it's fine. I'm not looking for a keeper and that was… Actually, you were totally marvellous.' It wasn't as if she was telling him something he didn't already know.

'You just insulted me and buffed my ego in one sentence. That takes skill.'

'So do you.'

At the last moment she lost her nerve and lowered her gaze.

'I am quite happy to pass my skills on.'

Her head lifted. 'Yes, please.'

CHAPTER TEN

Ivo FOLLOWED RAMON out of the room. Flora had already vanished into the bedroom to change, ignoring his assurance that the jeans and silk shirt she was wearing were fine for breakfast with his grandfather.

'So, breakfast? I was under the impression that we were coming to dinner.'

Ramon tipped his head in acknowledgement. 'Yes, your grandfather informed me of this last night and asked me to arrange matters, but—'

'But...?' Ivo prompted.

'This morning he... He had forgotten.'

'Does this happen often?'

'More than it did,' said the other man, unhappily.

'What else have you noticed?' Ivo gave a brooding frown. He would respect his grandfather's wishes but it was inevitable that people would start noticing.

'Well, some mood swings—he can be quite...irritable.'

'Not exactly unusual.'

'Indeed, but, well, he can get ideas. Take against people.'

'Such as?'

'This is different. It is...'

'Go on, say it.'

'I am not a medical man, but it's more like *para-*

noia. There was a new staff member, young, really very promising, and your grandfather decided that he had stolen his watch. He became quite abusive and accused the lad of being part of a conspiracy. The watch was in his dressing room where he always keeps it.'

'You smoothed things over?'

Ramon nodded.

Ivo, his expression sombre, heaved a sigh. 'I'm grateful and I'm sorry. This is not your job. I'll speak to the doctors, ask about extra staff. More qualified staff.'

A look of visible relief passed across the other man's face. 'That seems like an excellent idea, sir—and, sir, I suggested breakfast because that's a good time for him usually."

Madre di Dio, things really were that bad, and they would only get worse.

His grandfather would suffer, but for how long the doctors had been frustratingly vague.

And he could do nothing.

Except keep his grandfather's secret.

Ramon cleared his throat delicately and nodded past Ivo, looking at the half-closed door. 'May I ask, does Ms Henderson...?'

'No, not yet.'

Would it be the right thing to do in this situation?

The question in his head wasn't what was the right thing to do. Or even was there a right thing...he left moral philosophy for the better qualified.

If she knew the truth, what would her reaction be?

One thing was for certain: it wouldn't be a selfish one. If he'd learnt anything about the woman who had shown more passion in his bed than any other lover he'd had, it was that she was a born giver. She had to have arrived in the world with a note saying 'use me' in her chubby little hand.

And he had and furthermore he had enjoyed it. She was right, she did have terrible taste in men but *he* wasn't about to kick her out of his bed.

What a saint, admired the ironic voice in his head.

All right, he was no saint, but he was not this Callum guy who, he suspected, she might still have feelings for. The idea might have bothered a jealous man; luckily Ivo was a stranger to that emotion.

'I see.'

Ivo tipped his head in acknowledgement and began to step back inside the room, but it appeared that the relief of being relieved of some of the burden he'd been shouldering had made the normally taciturn Ramon uncharacteristically talkative and emotional.

'That must be hard for you.'

It didn't seem to require an answer so Ivo said nothing.

'Keeping secrets from the person you love, not being able to share the burden, your grief. I had someone once, but no longer… I envy you.' Ramon gave another precise little nod, slightly embarrassed-looking this time, and walked away.

Ivo watched him go. If he'd felt the need to reach out to Flora…a woman, *any* woman, he would have crushed it instantly. He had no desire to be part of a relationship where two people blurred into one. The mere idea was anathema to him. He realised this romantic ideal of a joining of souls was what many dreamt of, but to him it represented a loss of control, of sanity, of the essence of his individuality.

The only merging he wanted was of bodies.

When he walked back inside his face was carefully blank, denying there was any struggle going on inside him.

Ivo was tense about the breakfast; the conversation with Ramon had made him realise that his grandfather was a lot more unpredictable than he'd realised.

It sounded as though his behaviour was such that, had he not been who he was, rich, powerful and pretty much a law unto himself, had he not surrounded himself, with a few exceptions, with people who would have agreed if he'd called day night, people might already be asking questions.

Or if you, his only family, had been around a bit more.

Ivo took the hit of guilt, pretty sure he deserved it.

He need not have worried; the breakfast couldn't have gone better. Nobody meeting Salvatore for the first time would have known there was anything wrong. If he misspoke a few times…well, people did.

He was charming, funny and full of praise for Flora and the job she was doing. And he was emotional when he got to hold his great-grandson, who he decided looked exactly like his father, at which point he became tearful.

His tears evoked a sympathetic response in Flora, who didn't know that Salvatore never usually cried.

Ivo, worried about the mood shift, found himself moving protectively to Flora's side as she lifted the baby off his grandfather's lap, whereupon Jamie began to cry.

Ivo could have kissed the baby for his excellent timing. Salvatore did and then began to weep again.

'He's lovely,' Flora said, sending up a reproachful look to the man walking beside her. 'I can't believe how nervous I was, and he looks quite well…?' She hesitated a little before adding huskily, 'He's not in pain, is he?'

Ivo shook his head. Then, seeing the look of concern on her face as she pressed her fingers to the back of the baby's neck, he asked sharply, 'What's wrong?'

'Does he look flushed to you?'

Ivo didn't say anything. Jamie clearly did to her.

She touched his neck again. 'He feels hot to me,' she fretted.

Ivo could hear the panic in her voice. 'He looks fine to me.'

She shrugged off the hand he'd placed on her shoulder and shook her head, missing his reaction to the rejection.

'You're worried?'

She shrugged her slender shoulders and lifted her troubled eyes to the figure standing with his back to one of the windows against the distant background of the blue sea.

He looked so big, so solid and so calm that she felt a little of her panic subside.

'Sorry, you must think I'm crazy.' She loosed a self-mocking laugh. 'I used to wonder how I'd cope if Jamie was ill and I was alone, now I know I'd panic.'

'For starters, we don't know he's ill and you're not alone…or panicking…' He shook his head. 'Borderline at best.'

Not alone. She didn't make the mistake of reading anything into that, although the wistful feeling his words had shaken loose remained.

'It's just his heart. I'm sure it's nothing to do with that.'

'You'll feel a lot surer after the doctors have seen him. Leave it to me.'

Despite the fact she had told herself that morning that one thing she was not going to do was become too reliant on Ivo, she found herself sighing with relief.

'Thank you.'

This time she turned her cheek into the hand that an instinct he couldn't control had made him place on her shoulder, despite the earlier rejection. The reaction to feeling her soft cheek against his skin was just as strong and unexpected a reaction as her earlier rejection had been.

He let his hand fall away and stepped back.

'I'll organise it, then. You have the name of your GP and Jamie's consultant?'

She nodded and gave them. 'I don't have any paper.'

'Don't worry, I'll remember them.'

When the doctor arrived, a mere thirty minutes later to Flora's relief, she was dreading having to explain, especially if there was a language problem.

There wasn't and he seemed to have a full grasp of Jamie's medical history.

A very short time later, and after a thorough examination of the by now cranky baby, he confirmed that the baby did have a mild fever and diagnosed a virus... basically a cold.

'And his heart?'

'No problem there that I can detect. When is his next appointment?'

'Six months' time.'

'Well, you are in good hands and this young man has a fine set of lungs. I knew Bruno, a good man, tragic, so tragic.'

Flora, her throat thick with emotion and unshed tears, nodded.

'So the analgesic syrup four-to-six hourly, keep him cool and lots of fluids, any problems, you know where I am.' He glanced towards the sitting room where Ivo, who had not accompanied him into the nursery, was waiting. 'Or at least Ivo does. Those of us who know him were pleased to hear about his engagement and I am even more pleased now I have met you.' His charring smirk faded as he added, 'Ivo has few friends but those who are would die for him. He pretends he doesn't care but he—well, I don't have to tell you this, do I? Have you known him long?'

Blinking at this extraordinary endorsement and realising that nothing he'd said had surprised her, Flora shook her head. She already knew that Ivo's mask of toughness, and coldness, hid deep feelings, but she also knew that he'd never share those feelings, or at least not with her. 'No.'

'Well, it doesn't take long, does it, when you meet the right one?'

'No, it doesn't.' Flora said the words quickly because she didn't want to think about them too hard.

Quickly, but not quick enough to stop the flood, the relentless stream of images that began to flicker across her retina.

She blinked, her jaw tight as she struggled to halt the slide show. It felt as if a tug of war were going on in her head. She was pulling one way and...*truth* was pulling the other.

She couldn't have fallen in love; she hadn't put Ivo on a pedestal; she wasn't blind to his faults. She didn't even like him a lot of the time. She was just getting carried away by the great sex.

'So, everything good?'

She started guiltily and swung around, the rope of

plait that hung down her back whipping around a moment after she did, landing with a thump over one shoulder.

She saluted him with the bottle of baby medicine in her hand. 'Yes.' Jamie, lying in the crib, chose that moment to give a cranky cry. 'He has a cold.'

'Let me.'

She watched as he bent over the crib, lifting the sobbing baby with the sort of care normally reserved for an unexploded bomb, his expression fierce concentration as he arranged the baby against one broad shoulder and began to pat his back gently. The sight of Ivo cradling his tiny nephew made her smile despite the hand squeezing her heart.

One day he would have babies of his own; crazily the thought made her want to cry.

He glanced across, a look of self-conscious enquiry drifting over his face when he saw Flora standing there staring. 'Am I doing it wrong or something?'

Flora swallowed the lump in her throat. How crazy to get choked up, but the sight of this big tough man being so gentle with the baby scored a direct hit on her tender heart.

'No, you're doing it perfectly,' she said, grabbing the first thing to hand, which was a baby blanket. She began to fold it as though her life depended on perfectly aligned creases. 'You know, you're welcome in Skye any time. You should be part of Jamie's life.'

Even before she heard his steely, 'I intend to be,' Flora sensed the change in the atmosphere. Maybe Jamie did too because he gave another whimper as Ivo laid him carefully down in the crib.

He watched Flora drag a chair over to the crib. They'd found mind-numbing passion together, and it was the thought of losing that and nothing else that had made him react to the idea of her vanishing back to Skye. That, after all, was the plan. Flora was to vanish out of his life, out of Jamie's life.

Was he being fair to Jamie?

A child needed a female influence and not just one supplied by nannies. There was no doubt that Flora was utterly devoted to the baby. He shook his head; in some ways his grandfather's plan was simpler.

Simple because Salvatore is losing his mind. The real question is: are you, Ivo?

He took a deep breath. He really needed to show her what an excellent life Jamie could have without her. It shouldn't be that hard. He'd show her the glossy brochure of the really excellent school he'd picked out for Jamie, Ivo decided.

What's the betting she disapproves of boarding schools?

'He might take a while to settle.'

'You planning on spending the night there?' Ivo pointed to the lift doors at the end of the room, the ones that led to nannies on tap. 'Or are you going to take some help?'

She pushed away a frivolous mental image of nannies lining up to slide down a pole like firemen, white frilly aprons fluttering, and started to shake her head.

'Look, I know you have strong feelings on the subject.' As she did on everything. 'But there is help there ready and waiting if you change your mind. I know I'm probably wasting my breath, but you have nothing to prove. Everyone can see you put the baby above everything else.' How many men would see that as a problem? An image of some future lover being jealous of Jamie drew his dark brows together in a frown.

'But you can accept help. You don't have to be a

wonder woman or too tired and worn down to do fun things with the baby.'

Was he telling her that she looked worn down or she wasn't fun, or both?

'Or I could help?' he heard himself say.

The offer made her smile. 'Do you know one end of a nappy from the other?' she asked, ignoring the fact that a few weeks back she hadn't either. It was quite nice to feel superior for once. 'Stick to what you're good at.'

'I'm good in bed, or so someone told me not so long ago.'

The blush on the outside was visible but it was the heat deep down inside that was more of a problem for Flora, who brought her lashes down in a protective shield, but not before Ivo had seen the aching longing reflected in the blue depths.

Inhaling through his flared nostrils, he fought to leash his libido. In another woman he might have imagined the look of silent yearning was a calculated seduction technique, but Flora didn't have a clue what she was doing, or what power she was wielding.

It made her a very dangerous woman.

'Do you really think this is an appropriate moment for that sort of…?'

The striking contrast between the silent sensual message of her eyes and the prim, prissy delivery drew a laugh from his throat. 'Thing?' he suggested. His shoulders lifted in an expressive shrug. 'You could be right.'

She decided one concession deserved another. 'Maybe another pair of hands would be useful. Ones who know what they're doing, that is.'

The girl who delivered her meal gave a shy smile as she placed the tray down on the table on the balcony.

'Nanny Emily says you need the calories, that you're too stick thin. Me, I think you have a lovely figure,' she added daringly, straying from the party line.

'Thank you.'

Flora lifted the silver dome. Whatever was in the herby tomato sauce smelt good. She looked at the label on the wine bottle beside the single glass; presumably Nanny Emily saw nothing wrong in being drunk in charge of a baby.

And it would have taken a brave person to argue with the woman who radiated a reassuring sense of calm and spoke fluent Italian with a Yorkshire accent, which was fascinating to listen to.

She had made the day a lot easier but Flora had insisted that she take the night shift, rejecting the offer of a night nanny.

Finding it weird and a little worrying how quickly she had accepted the existence of night nannies and night nurseries, she had not objected when Nanny Emily had had a bed made up for her on the day-bed in the nursery.

She ate her lonely supper, picking at the food and allowing herself one glass of the really excellent red, which might have been a mistake because she found her thoughts veering towards self-pity. It wasn't as though she hadn't got plenty of practice eating alone, and Nanny Emily had offered to stay and keep her company.

Only it wasn't Nanny Emily she was imagining sitting opposite her in the empty chair.

She shook her head, tossed back the dregs of the wine and wandered back to the bedroom. The whole place was wired for sound; she'd have heard Jamie if he'd cried, but she went to check on him anyway. He was fast asleep, his poor little nose bright red, but when she touched the back of his neck he seemed cooler.

She adjusted the speed on the cooling fan and went over to the neatly made up bed. She didn't bother undressing, even though someone had brought night clothes from her room. Instead she lay on top of the covers intending to just rest her eyes.

Apparently, his grandfather hadn't been sleeping. His valet, a sombre-faced little man who'd been with his grandfather for ever, had to know something was wrong and yet when he asked him what he was doing standing in the corridor at one o'clock in the morning, the man had replied with no expression at all that his master had locked him out, as though it was the most normal thing in the world—it probably was for him.

'I'm just waiting to see if—'

Ivo shook his head. 'You go to bed and I'll check if he wants anything.'

'I need to put his clothes out for tomorrow.'

'Go to bed.'

The door was locked, but Ivo found his way in via a side door that led directly to the study. The study was empty but what seemed significant to Ivo was the debris of paper spread across the desk. He'd never seen that desk without neat piles and sharpened pencils in neat rows.

The TV was blaring in the drawing room but it too was empty. He eventually found his grandfather sitting on a stool in the bedroom, staring out into middle distance.

'Not sleeping.'

Salvatore didn't seem to find it strange to see his grandson standing there. 'Can't seem to these days.

I think,' he added in a conspiratorial tone, 'they put something in the water. I'm seeing the baby tomorrow. Have they arrived?'

'Yes, Grandfather, they have. The baby has a cold.'

'Don't call the doctors, they're damned quacks.'

Ivo's knuckles turned white as he clasped them in front of himself. This was the man who had always seemed like a giant to him growing up, feared, but respected. To see him reduced to this was more than heartbreaking; it was tragic, it was cruel.

There were still people who clearly respected him, perhaps even loved him—what else but love would make someone carry on serving him with unquestioning loyalty?

The man they were loyal to was vanishing.

'How about you go to bed?'

It was an hour and a half later before Ivo finally left; his grandfather was asleep and Ivo knew he couldn't offload the responsibility that was his. He needed advice from people who knew about this evil disease.

He needed... He walked past the corridor that led directly to his own suite.

The lights in the nursery were turned down low when he entered. He walked over to the cot where the baby lay and then past it to the day-bed where Flora, fully clothed, lay sleeping.

He stood there for a while looking down at her, conscious of the ache located in his chest as he studied her sleeping face, the delicate contours and fine bones. Her beauty was compelling, the misleading fragility rousing protective instincts even though he knew she was a lot tougher than she looked.

Something inside him responded to her beauty the way it had from the first moment he'd seen her. He'd been as powerless to control it then as he was now, as he felt the swell of a nameless emotion build in his chest.

A shudder passed through him.

What the hell are you doing here, Ivo?

He was in no mood to analyse; emotionally drained dry by the encounter with his grandfather, he was operating on autopilot. Instinct had brought him here and the same instincts kicked in now.

The day-bed was narrow but he slipped into the narrow space beside the wall, slid a hand under her waist and pulled her back into him. Her soft body adjusted into his angles as she turned her head, her eyes opened and she saw him.

'Ivo!' Her voice, thick with sleep, was barely more than a husky whisper.

He put a finger to her lips and whispered, *'Hush.'*

The tension drained from her body as she closed her eyes, pushed her head against his shoulder, gave a sleepy murmur and went back to sleep.

Lying there with the scent of her hair in his nostrils, her body curved into his, he felt a strange sense of something close to peace drift over him.

He had no idea what had driven him here, or maybe pulled him here. The idea of losing himself in a woman's body made sense, but this physical but non-sexual embrace was outside his experience. Before he could sort it out in his head he fell asleep to the sound of Flora's soft, even breathing.

He slept deeply, before fighting his way through layers of sleep and into painful wakefulness; the arm she lay on was numb and heavy and there was a sour taste in his mouth.

He slid his arm from under Flora and slipped off the narrow bed. He looked down and felt the emotions inside him swell and begin to seep out, his jaw clenched as he tried to tap into his ability to turn his feelings on and off.

Nothing happened.

Instead he was forced to reel them in through sheer-minded willpower. The effort brought a sheen of sweat to his face but at least he had control again.

He'd been on the point of falling into the inevitability trap; 'the heart wants what the heart wants' nonsense was pretty much a version of crossing your fingers when you lied through your teeth.

A lie was still a lie, and a bad decision was still a bad decision. It all stemmed from the mawkish need for people to romanticise what was a basic primal drive.

He wanted, he *needed* sex. They had chemistry—strong chemistry. There was nothing wrong in wanting sex; the *wrong* came when you imagined it was going to last a lifetime.

A man had a choice, he reminded himself. He didn't *have* to fall in love. There was strength in being alone, not relying on anyone else to make you happy. He was already complete. Love was a trap that he was not about to fall into.

He'd always been able to separate his emotions from basic needs, like sex, before. Then it came to him, so obvious that he didn't understand why he'd not seen it earlier!

The only reason this felt different was the fact there was another factor between them. His eyes went to the cot. He felt a connection because there *was* a connection, not a deep, meaningful, heavenly choir-singing one, but a physical one. Jamie!

He let out a long hissing sigh of relief.

He didn't look back because he didn't want to. He wasn't trying to prove anything to himself.

* * *

The cold morning light was seeping into the room through a window where the blind had not been drawn. She could hear the sound of the dawn chorus outside. She yawned and stretched, easing the kinks out of her spine.

Her eyes suddenly snapped open.

Had she dreamt it?

The memories drifted through her head like smoke, the impression of being held, of feeling warm and safe.

'Good morning, my dear, did you sleep? How was he?'

'Nanny…' Flora pulled herself up into a sitting position and swung her legs over the side of the narrow metal bed. 'He slept through, and so,' she admitted, removing a sharp object that had been sticking into her arm from her top, 'did I.' She rubbed her arm, was about to toss the object into the waste-paper basket when a glitter caught her eye.

She opened her palm.

It hadn't been a dream.

It hadn't been a dream—the beaten copper cufflink she had first noticed gleam against the pristine cuff of Ivo's shirt lay in her hand.

She slid it into the pocket of her jeans, got to her feet and went over to the cot. Her thoughts were racing. When had Ivo come and how long had he stayed?

'You go and have a shower, dear, and take your breakfast. I'll feed him for you and wait for the doctor.'

CHAPTER ELEVEN

Ivo HAD STOPPED by his grandfather's office on his way to the nursery. He'd made some tentative enquiries today. If yesterday had taught him anything it was that he was going to have to bring some people in on the secret.

And therein lay the problem: it *was* a secret.

Her evening meal arrived at the same time as the previous evening. She had just lifted the dome when the door opened. Ivo took the cover from her hand and put it back down over the food.

'That looks terrible.'

She pulled in a taut breath before she lifted her gaze to the man who stood there looking out-of-this-world attractive.

The sight of him in a beautifully cut pale grey business suit, the formality softened by the open collar of his white shirt, was a signal for her hormones to go wild.

She swallowed, but found there was no moisture in her mouth. Instead she ran her tongue nervously over her dry lips. 'It looks delicious.'

He picked up the wine bottle and looked at the label. 'I think we can do better than this.'

'I'm not drinking.' She really didn't need her inhibitions loosening; she needed them shoring up. 'Help yourself.'

'I'm driving.'

'Don't let me keep you,' she said, feeling pretty stupid for assuming he was here to keep her company.

He pulled out a chair and straddled it. 'We're eating out.'

She shook her head. 'I can't.'

'Why?'

'Isn't that obvious?' she flared back.

'Humour me.'

'Jamie…'

'They tell me his temperature is down and he's looking much better.' He arched an interrogative sable brow. 'Is that not right?'

'He needs a familiar face…he…' The impact of his male aura was so strong that she was only just seeing the tension in his face evident in the fine muscles around his jaw and the lines etched around his sensual, sculpted mouth.

'He what?' he prompted.

'I wouldn't feel comfortable leaving him at the moment.'

'Has it occurred to you that poor Jamie might need a break from you?'

She fought the urge to respond to his smile.

'Look, you've been here a few days now and you've seen nothing but the inside of the nursery. If there's a problem we'll only be five minutes away. Come on, you're going stir crazy, admit it.'

'Jamie still looks very pale.'

'So do you.'

The hungry intensity of his scrutiny made her stomach flip. She lifted a self-conscious hand to her face.

If he thought this was pale he should have seen her before she'd put the blusher on, but then he had—he'd seen her in the night.

'But—'

He surged to his feet, all restless energy and testosterone making her feel dizzy. He looked, she decided, like a man with a lot on his mind.

'No buts, it's all arranged. Nanny Emily will take first shift and Olivia will sleep in the nursery. You need a night off.'

'But I'm not dressed.' And she had the start of a tension headache—lack of sleep, probably.

Lack of *something*!

Sadly, she was dressed.

He watched as she smoothed down the fabric of the slip dress over her thighs with a telling nervy, jerky motion, while calculating which would be the quickest way to remove it. Slide the straps over her shoulders and tug, or over her head in one smooth motion?

Both images were pleasurable enough to send a roar of heat through his bloodstream. So strong that it took all his willpower not to reach out for her there and then.

'If we don't spend any time at all together Salvatore is going to start smelling a rat,' he lied. 'I already told him we had a date night.' He pushed away the memory of his grandfather's bewildered question, *Flora who?*

She gave a defeated sigh. 'Oh, all right, then.' She got to her feet at the same time as him. 'But I need my bag.'

He stood waiting, the display of foot-tapping a bit over the top considering it had taken her barely five minutes to pick up her bag and a light wrap and swop her flat ballet pumps for a pair of sandals with heels.

'I looked in on Jamie,' she said, hating that she felt

the need to justify herself as she panted to keep up with the long-legged pace he set as he led her out into the courtyard and over to a long, low-slung, power-statement convertible.

'This is yours, I think.' She held out her hand.

He looked at the cufflink but there was nothing to read in his expression. 'Thanks. I stopped by last night to look in on the baby. You were asleep.'

She wanted to ask him if she'd only dreamt being in his arms, dreamt his heartbeat, but she couldn't risk the answer being yes, and looking like a total idiot who dreamt of him—even if it was a fairly accurate assessment.

The top of the car was down as they drove down the winding road from the Castello to the small town beside the sea.

It seemed to Flora that the farther they got from the Castello, the more relaxed Ivo became. The tension left his shoulders, even the lines bracketing his mouth relaxed.

His next comment confirmed her observation.

'That place...' He glanced at the reflection in the rear-view mirror. 'It's oppressive.'

It seemed a strange way for anyone to speak about their home. 'It's very beautiful, but if somewhere has bad associations, I suppose—'

'My father killed himself in his flat in Rome, if that is what you mean by bad associations, and I do not live in the past.' He was living in the present. The problem was the present was not a very uplifting place to be; witnessing the disintegration of his grandfather was agonising. 'I simply have no taste for living in a museum.'

The drive had taken only minutes. They were already passing under a massive stone arch and into the town, at which point the feeling of freedom and wind in her hair vanished. They slowed to a snail's pace.

'They've pedestrianised the old town, which is good, but it's kind of moved the problem out here,' Ivo explained above the cacophony of car horns.

This part looked pretty old to Flora. He slammed on the brakes and threw out a curse as a scooter cut across them. The driver looked back and grinned. 'I'll park here and we'll walk in. It's only a few minutes, even in those heels.'

'I didn't think you'd noticed.'

'I was meant to, then?'

She slung him a look and he chuckled softly as he turned off the road and pulled the car onto a cobbled area and went round to open the passenger door for her. She managed a graceful exit, even though he was looking at her legs.

'Yes, very good shoes.'

Flora made a snorting sound.

'It's this way. I think you'll like it. It's right on the water and the seafood is excellent.'

They walked down the cobbled streets that became narrower as they got nearer the waterfront. The place was buzzing with a mixture of holidaymakers and locals, the atmosphere relaxed, almost festive.

'This is really lovely but are you sure us…this…? It wasn't part of our arrangement. Things are getting a bit, well, blurred.' She gnawed nervously on her lower lip, gave an awkward little grimace and lifted her eyes with appeal to his. 'Don't you think?'

'Are you regretting sleeping with me?'

Her eyes flew wide. 'No, of course not.'

'Then I don't see a problem.'

He stood aside and let her enter the restaurant ahead

of him, then as he joined her he placed his hand lightly in the small of her back.

The restaurant owner appeared almost immediately, greeting Ivo by name.

Ivo in turn introduced Flora, then the man personally led them past the diners inside to a table beside the water.

A romantic spot, or it would have been but for the tables joined together to accommodate a large family group who were having a celebratory dinner.

The manager said something to Ivo, who translated for her benefit.

'It's the grandmother's eightieth birthday. He asked if you'd prefer a quieter spot?'

'I'm fine...if you are?'

'You all right with the noise?' Ivo asked as the table began to clap the arrival of a large birthday cake laden with candles.

Before she could assure him she was fine, that she loved the atmosphere of the place, a toy car landed in the dish of olives in the centre of the table, splashing Ivo with oil.

She didn't know what she expected his reaction to be but laughter wasn't it. One of the adults at the table had got to his feet but Ivo was quicker. He picked the car up and, wiping it on a napkin, he walked across to the table.

She watched, her expression growing wistful as he handed it to a toddler in a high chair and said something to the adults that sent up a roar of laughter. He was so good with children.

It was no struggle to see him with his own one day, a brood to carry on his family name and a wife he could be proud of.

For some reason she felt her eyes fill.

Some reason? Really, Flora, who are you kidding?

Her heart ached because she would never be that woman, but Ivo was born to be a father.

'You want to move?' he asked softly when he returned to the table and retook his place.

Flora blinked hard. 'No, I'm fine, unless you—'

She was interrupted by a loud shout from a man across the restaurant. 'Little brat! This is a disgrace! Hey, don't you people know how to control your kids? People are here to escape their kids... Never heard of a babysitter, mate? You... Hey, you... I want to see the manager! Don't you know who I am?'

She could see the look of contempt on Ivo's face and was sure that it was an expression mirrored around the place.

'I'm sorry about this,' Ivo murmured.

'What have you to be sorry about?' she asked. 'Anyway, he's a Brit—maybe *I* should be the one apologising. I think he's trying to impress his lady friend. You know, he reminds me of someone I used to know,' she confided, lowering her voice to a confidential murmur.

'Who?'

She gave a shame-faced grimace. 'Callum. He always liked to be the centre of attention, too.'

Ivo didn't seek attention but he commanded it. She felt a stab of disbelief when she remembered comparing the two men in her head.

She must have been blind!

Her eyes went to the strong, beautiful man sitting across from her and the idea of falling in love with someone you had only known for a matter of days no longer seemed something to laugh at.

It was no joke.

It was real.

It was a fact.

She felt weirdly light-headed as she embraced the sense of relief, along with the pain she'd been avoiding.

She suddenly felt more alive than she had done in an age. She had so much to give, she knew that—the sadness was he didn't want to take, not her heart anyway. But she'd give him what he did want, which, for the moment at least, was her body.

Afterwards, she'd deal with the hurt.

Her glance lifted from the glass of wine she was clutching to where Ivo sat across the table. She wanted to say, Let's leave. Take me to bed, love me.

She was framing the bold words in her head but when she saw his face, her resolve faltered and faded.

The contempt she'd seen stamped into the aristocratic angles and planes was still there but the overwhelming impression now, as he looked past her and into the main dining area, was chilling hauteur that, as she watched, tipped over into anger as the tipsy tourist launched into the second act of his tirade, his voice drowning out the clearly pacifying responses of the manager, who was attempting to calm the situation.

One of the children at the table started crying and Ivo, mouth compressed, eyes like ice, put his glass down and glanced over at Flora.

'If you'll excuse me, this won't take a moment.'

'No!' Without thinking she reached across the table and grabbed his sleeve. 'Don't go, please, leave it. Let someone else.' Of course, she knew that Ivo wasn't the person who *let someone else*.

He *was* the someone else.

He smiled into her worried face. 'It's fine. I'm not

going to ask him to step outside.' Unless absolutely necessary.

She watched as Ivo approached the table, somehow managing to look urbane and darkly menacing at the same time.

She couldn't hear what he said to make the tourist go quiet but whatever it was didn't stop the wife taking a selfie of herself with Ivo.

Ivo received several nods of approving gratitude as he walked back to the table.

Leaning down, he caught Flora's hand, brought it up to his lips. She was caught unawares; the tingle from the contact went all the way down to her curling toes. The hypnotic tug of his dark eyes was utterly irresistible, and she sat transfixed by a wave of lustful sheer longing.

'What did you say to him?'

'I told him we were newly engaged and were enjoying a private dinner. A private, *quiet* dinner.'

Their glances connected. The pupils of his dark eyes had expanded dramatically, and she could hear his laboured breaths—or were they her own?

Flora felt the well of love inside her expand until she could barely breathe; the noise of the rest of the room faded out.

It was Ivo who broke the spell.

'Let's get out of here,' he growled.

She didn't say anything, she couldn't; she just nodded.

They both stood up. Ivo peeled notes from a money clip in his pocket and laid them on the table, grabbed her hand and together they walked out.

'You paid and we didn't eat.' She realised as they reached the car.

His dark eyes flickered her way. 'You want to go back?'

'No, I want you to make love to me.'

Without a word he walked around the car to her side, put one hand behind her head; the other he curved over her bottom and pulled her tight into his body, sealing them at hip level before he covered her mouth with his.

When he lifted his head, he pinned her with a stare like hot smoke. 'That's what I want too. I hope you noticed.'

She gulped. 'I noticed.'

'I should go.' Head pressed into the pillow, one hand curved above her head, she studied the dark intense features of the man lying beside her. She reached out and touched the rough shadow on his jaw; there were places on her body that were red from the abrasive contact with the stubbly growth.

The first time they had literally fallen into one another, ripping off clothes in a frenzy of desire, the coupling had been equally raw and her climax, when it had come, so intense that she'd thought she'd faint.

Then later it had been much slower, slow and sensual. He had explored every inch of her body and encouraged reciprocation. Encouraged experimentation. Learning what pleased him had only increased her own pleasure.

'Go?'

The fingers moving in sweeping arabesques up the warm, still slightly damp skin of her back stopped for a moment, and then continued their nerve-tingling progress.

'Why?' he asked, lifting a skein of bright hair from her cheek so that he could see her face.

'Because you've already said you have an early flight and the doctor is dropping by first thing to see Jamie.' And hopefully pronounce him fighting fit.

'Stay a little longer…?'

She sighed—who could resist?—and curled into him, pressing a kiss to his stubble-roughened cheek. 'I really thought that the other diners were going to cheer you tonight.'

He gave a grunt and stroked her hair.

'What did you *really* say to him?'

'I don't remember.' His hand stilled. 'Did he hurt you, your ex?'

She lifted her head and raised herself up on one elbow to look down at him. 'That was a bit out of the blue.'

'You said the loser in the restaurant reminded you of him…'

She settled back down, pressing her face into his chest. 'He dumped me because I can't have children. It seems he wanted a *real* woman.'

He responded to her little sigh with a low growl and flipped her over onto her back before settling over her. 'You are a very *real* woman…' Pinning her arms above her head with one hand, he curled a hand around the side of her face and kissed her hard and long, as if he could drain the pain from her.

She closed her eyes as he slid down, pressing his face into her neck as his body came to rest heavy and hot on her. She loved the musky smell of his warm, damp skin, the weight of him pushing into her. She wanted to hold onto the memory of this moment.

They lay there for a while, she wasn't sure how long, when she sensed the tension building in him.

'I would have come to the funeral, you know, but I didn't know. Not that Bruno was dead, not about Jamie. I would have known, if…'

Lying very still, hardly daring to breathe, Flora silently willed him to go on.

'Bruno reached out to me. He wanted to meet up. I think he wanted to tell me about the pregnancy, Jamie, but I refused.'

She felt a deep sigh shudder through his body.

'I was punishing him, you see, because when he left he said he'd come back for me and he didn't, but it turns out he did.' His bitter laugh was muffled in her hair.

'You didn't know,' she soothed, aching for the pain she heard in his voice, the fact that he was beating himself up for something that wasn't his fault. 'I miss Bruno too, and Sami.' She felt the tears she couldn't stop seep out from her closed eyelids; after a moment, so did Ivo.

His arms slid around her as he pulled her onto her side so that they were lying facing one another. The sound of her sobs made him feel as though his heart were being dragged out of his chest. It was unbearable. He lay there holding her, feeling more helpless than he'd ever felt in his life and conscious that none of this felt like safe, meaningless sex.

The next time she said she should go to her own bed, he didn't object.

CHAPTER TWELVE

'SO, HE IS FINE?'

The doctor smiled. 'The picture of health.'

'And his heart—has the virus caused any damage?'

'None whatsoever.'

'Sorry, I'm a bit paranoid.'

'Not at all, it's perfectly understandable.' He extended his hand. 'Well, I hope the next time we meet it will not be in a professional capacity. Good morning, Ms Henderson.'

The bang on the door came so soon after his departure that she assumed the doctor had forgotten something and returned.

In the middle of changing Jamie's nappy, she was about to call out when the door crashed in, loudly and violently enough to make her protective instincts kick in.

She grabbed the baby and rose to her feet with him clutched in her arms.

The downgrading of her alarm when she saw that it was Salvatore standing in the doorway was brief because this was a very different Salvatore from the benign, smiling, jolly figure from their breakfast earlier in the week. He actually looked generally dishevelled, unshaven; his silver hair didn't look as though it had seen a comb for some time.

'Good morning. Is there anything wrong?' she asked, noticing the splodges of something down his shirt front.

'Is it true?'

She shook her head, bemused not just by the question but by the aggressive way it was delivered.

'I'm sorry, I don't—'

'I've no time for this. I have meetings…*important* meeting to go to. Do you deny that you are barren?'

The brutality took her breath away. 'It's true that I can't have children.'

'And that this child has a defective heart?'

'Jamie has a minor heart defect, yes.'

'Grecos do not have defects. Grecos' hearts are strong. Grecos are strong!' he bellowed. 'I know what your game is… You can tell them I know…'

Close to tears by this point, she hugged Jamie close to her. 'I haven't got a game. There is no *them*.' She shrank back as the old man stamped towards them, stopping a few feet away, but close enough for her to see the spittle on his lips as he waved his fist at her.

'Ivo will give me strong heirs. If you marry him I will disinherit him.' Having delivered his parting threat, he turned and stomped away.

Flora's knees just folded under her and she sat down cross-legged on the floor with the baby clenched against her chest.

She had woken this morning feeling so much hope, so much optimism. Last night, in her head at least, had been a breakthrough. Ivo had actually shared something with her and she had confided her secret to him; he hadn't recoiled in horror… She scrunched her eyes tight shut and let out a low wail of anguish as she rocked with Jamie clutched to her chest.

No, he'd not recoiled, instead he'd gone straight to

his grandfather and shared the intimate, private information! That hurt far more than the old man's ranting and cruelty. Maybe Ivo had gone seeking advice? How he could extricate himself from this barren creature? Oh, she was good enough for the odd tumble but she was getting ideas there might be more.

'And I was,' she told her waxen reflection in the mirror. 'I thought he might be growing to care for me... love me.' Back against the wall, she pushed herself to her feet, feeling old as she walked across to the mirror, pushing her face towards it as she sneered, 'You idiot... Flora, you stupid fool.'

Ivo was halfway to the airport when Ramon's voice-mail reached him.

'Sir, there has been an incident with your grandfather. I think you should get back now.'

'Sir!'

Ramon was waiting as he burst into the hallway.

'Your grandfather, he has confronted Ms Henderson, and I think—'

Ivo swore. 'Talk and walk.'

The older man did talk, though in a series of gasps as he struggled to keep pace with Ivo's long-legged stride.

By the time Ivo reached the door to the nursery wing there were some gaps but he knew enough not to be surprised when he walked in and found Flora, wearing a coat and stuffing baby clothes in a bag.

'What are you doing?'

She turned. The tear stains on her cheeks gave lie to her calm expression and the oddly emotionless delivery of her response.

'I'm going back home. Jamie's all better and I don't think we are very welcome any more.'

'I don't know what he's said—'

She held up a hand to stop him. 'No, I'm grateful really, your grandfather just explained things to me, things like how you need a *proper* woman with all the equipment in full working order. Oh, and he's not overly struck, it seems, on *defective* babies...'

'Flora—'

Ignoring his agonised cry, she held him off with an outstretched hand and a narrow-eyed stare of loathing before he'd taken more than a step towards her.

'Do *not* come near me!' she snapped. 'You know, I actually think I hate you, you know that? I thought, I actually thought, that you c-cared!' She swallowed and bit down hard on her wobbling lower lip. 'How long was it before you rushed to tell him about my defectiveness? Oh, the ring, I almost forgot and I don't know why you were so worried—it's not as though we were really engaged so there's no chance he'll disinherit you.' She twisted it off her finger and flung it onto the top of a bureau.

'Disinherit?'

'Oh, did I miss out that bit? Well, you can tell him that there is no chance we are getting married, that there never was, so problem solved.' Just the little matter of living with regret and sticking together the pieces of her broken, disillusioned heart.

She stood there looking brittle and fragile and *hurting*, stood there looking at him as though he were a stranger, and Ivo wanted to rush over her and hold her.

If only he'd spoken last night when she would have listened, but he'd bottled it, he told himself in disgust, remembering the thing close to panic that had gripped him when he had realised the actual extent of his feelings for Flora. The *real* reason why he had felt her pain more keenly than his own.

If only he had not let her go last night.

If only he'd never hidden Salvatore's condition.

Well, you can speak now, so what are you waiting for?

'I won't tell him that.'

Her eyes flew wide. 'Why on earth not? You want me to put it in writing?'

'No, because it wouldn't be true.'

The tears quivering on her eyelashes, shining in her swimming cerulean eyes, snapped something inside him.

'Cara mia...!'

'Don't come near me, Ivo, just let me go,' she wailed.

'I'm not going to tell my grandfather anything because it is likely he has forgotten what he said to you.'

She pulled the baby vest she had absently blotted her tears on and stared at him. 'What do you mean, forgotten?'

'My grandfather has Alzheimer's disease, Flora. You know what that is?'

Her eyes flew wide in horrified comprehension.

'He has never been a nice or kind man, he is ruthless and a stranger to empathy, but he is my grandfather and once, when I was small and in a very bad place, he rescued me.'

'Your father...?'

He nodded. 'And now he is the one who is scared. He knows that he is slipping away and he can't do anything about it. He forgets, he remembers, he tries to hide it, but the paranoia, the conspiracy theories are a new development. He does not want people to know. He hates the idea of being an object of pity and I agreed. I see now, of course, that I should have warned you. As for the threats of disinheriting me, he gave me power of attorney, with just such an event as this in mind.' He glanced towards the baby. 'Jamie's inheritance is safe.'

'I am very sorry about your grandfather. I was really confused but it makes sense now. Is there anything I can say or do to make it easier for him? For you?'

'You are a really good person, Flora, you know that? The thing is he will have forgotten he said it by the next time you see him.'

She walked across to one of the cases and shut it.

He frowned at the symbolic gesture.

'I really don't think we should risk that, Ivo, do you?'

He growled out, 'You're not going!'

She went across and touched his arm. She could feel the quivering tension in the taut muscles through the fabric of his jacket. 'I would stay, I really would. I'm having the best time with you, but the thing is I need more than this half-love thing. I love you and you... Well, you don't love me. I'm not blaming you,' she added hastily when she saw his expression. 'I understand, and to be honest it's probably for the best given my...' Without her realising it, her free hand had gone to her stomach. 'You have so much to pass on, not just all this, but love—you should have children, Ivo, and I'm not going to deprive you of that.'

'Have you finished?'

She nodded.

'Good, because I have some things to say, too. And for the record I always knew you couldn't have children. It was one of the things that Salvatore told me and then forgot and then presumably remembered in some twisted way. As for an heir, I already have one.' He took both of her small, cold hands in his and looked down at the baby kicking on the rug.

'I need a son, Jamie needs a father. It is my intention to adopt him after we are married.'

'I love Jamie,' she choked out, 'but I'm not marrying you for him.'

'I am not asking you to. I'm asking you for me.' He pulled her captured hands up to his chest and pressed them over his heart so that she could feel the echo of his life force thudding beneath her fingertips.

She looked into his eyes and for a moment she forgot how to breathe because the love shining down at her was so all-consuming.

Could this really be happening?

'I have spent my life seeing love as a weakness to be guarded against. I told myself that I was the strong one and others were fools.' His mouth twisted in a grimace of self-contempt. 'I was the fool, not strong, but weak and scared. You have taught me that, and there is more you can teach me, I'm sure. Meeting you has changed my life. It's set me free. I'm not offering you a half-life or half-love, *cara*, I'm offering you complete love. My whole heart.'

By the time he had finished the tears were streaming unchecked down Flora's cheeks.

'I love you, Ivo, with all my heart I love you.'

He smiled a slow smile that made her heart flip. 'You'll marry me.'

'When?'

'Tomorrow.' They'd done everything so far in a short period of time and he didn't see any reason to stop now.

'That would not be a good first impression to make on your mother-in-law.'

'A compromise...a week?'

'A month.'

Eyes dancing, he nodded. 'Deal.'

She held out her hand. 'Should we shake on it?'

Grinning, he grabbed her arm and jerked her towards him. 'Kiss on it.'

With a deep sigh Flora fell into his embrace.

EPILOGUE

FLORA HAD BEEN dozing when the door opened.

'Hello, there.' She smiled and pulled herself upright as Jamie entered the room, his dark hair slicked back, his shoes freshly shined, a posy of flowers clutched in one chubby hand, the other enfolded in the hand of the man who walked in beside him.

'You've come to see your new baby sister?'

Jamie shook his head, though his eyes kept swivelling to the cot at the side of the bed.

'No, I've come to see you, Mama, because you're my favourite person and I have to make a fuss of you or you might get jealous.'

Flora's laughing eyes turned to her husband. 'Thank you, darling, you are my favourite person too.'

'I know,' the little boy said smugly. He crept in closer and, lifting his hand to his face, lowered his voice. 'But we won't tell her,' he whispered. He glanced back towards the tall figure behind him. 'It wouldn't be kind, and I will always be kind to my little sister. Is she nice?'

'I think she might be. Now, tell me about your day and then if you like you can hold your sister.'

'My day was good, I helped Nanny Emily pick up toys 'cos she's incredibly old—maybe even thirty?' He glanced to Ivo for conformation and received a solemn nod in return. 'I thought so, and Nana Grace told me the story about how my mummy Sami once fell in the sea with all her clothes on...*cold* sea...and when she was born she had golden curls. Does Samantha have curls?' He edged his way towards the cot.

'She does.' Flora, a lump of emotion in her throat, glanced towards Ivo, who smiled back at her with his eyes. It was amazing but she knew he was remembering, as she was, the moment their miracle baby had put in her appearance.

She lifted a hand to her own head. 'But I'm afraid they are like mine. See for yourself.'

Ivo lifted Jamie up so the boy could get a better look at the sleeping baby. 'So, what do you think?'

'She's cool...but a bit small.'

Ivo looked over their son's head at his sleeping daughter who, for the first four months after her conception, Flora had been convinced was a *grumbling appendix*, or else something too bad to put a name to.

He had gone with her when she had booked herself a doctor's appointment, prepared for the worst and determined to be strong for his wife of two years.

The first clue they'd had was when the doctor had asked if they'd been trying for a baby.

Flora had told him that she wasn't able to have children and then he'd dropped his bombshell. It had taken the scan to convince her, the image of the tiny life inside her on the screen.

They'd left the office shell-shocked.

Ivo liked to think that his grandfather had understood when they'd told him they were having a baby, but it was hard to tell as by that point Salvatore had needed twenty-four-hour, round-the-clock care.

He had passed away in his sleep a week later.

But there was a permanent monument to his memory: they had just completed the transfer of the Castello and its contents to charity, which was going to open it to the public as a museum.

They had moved to a sprawling farmhouse in the hills more suited to a family home. His clever wife had overseen the entire renovation and designed the massive modern extension with the glass walls that looked out over olive groves and the Tuscan hills.

'Can I wake her up?'

'Ivo!' Flora exclaimed. 'I'm going to remind you of that in two weeks' time when you're walking around like a sleep-deprived zombie. You'll be longing for the days of peace and quiet.'

'I've had enough quiet in my life, enough of being alone. I like my life noisy and messy and filled with my family.'

It sounded like a winning formula to Flora, who was too happy to protest when he scooped his baby daughter out of the crib.

* * * * *

SEDUCING HIS
CONVENIENT
INNOCENT

RACHAEL THOMAS

PROLOGUE

Spring in London

LYSANDROS DRAKAKIS WATCHED Rio Armstrong, the woman he wanted above all others, as she took her seat at the piano. An expectant hush fell over the room as everyone waited for the recital he'd arranged for his business clients at one of London's top hotels to begin.

Rio was beautiful. Her tall, slender body was full of poise and elegance and as she sat at the piano all eyes were on her. Everyone else in the room was waiting for her to play but all Lysandros could do was imagine her in his arms, kissing him with an unrestrained passion she'd so far resisted. Every time they'd kissed the hints of desire had lingered on her lips, tormenting him.

His younger sister, Xena, had introduced them, claiming them to be perfect for one another, and for the last two months he'd been the personification of a gentleman with this alluring beauty. He'd also been patient, allowing their relationship to unfold at Rio's pace. Not at all his usual style, but this was the first time since his disastrous engagement to Kyra ten years ago that he wanted to consider more than just physical gratification.

That uncharacteristic restraint since he and Rio had

started dating was having serious side effects. Not having done anything more than kiss her, his mind was constantly filled with the image of their naked bodies entwined with desire, and as Rio's fingers began to caress the first notes of her performance from the piano, he closed his eyes, forcing himself to calm his ardour, try to halt the thoughts of her touching him, caressing him.

Rio had warned him, from the first moment he'd made his interest in her known, of her concert commitments, the need to put in hours of daily practice, and more recently had used those commitments as the reason she wasn't ready to take their romance further. But with summer approaching and the concert season ending, Lysandros was determined to whisk her away to his home in Greece. Once there he wanted to allow the attraction between them to bloom like the flowers on his island retreat.

A ripple of applause swayed around the room, dragging his thoughts back to the present. How long had he been wrapped in heated thoughts of making Rio his? Rio stood and took a bow, smiling at the audience's appreciation of her playing. She was a rising star in the world of classical music and small performances like this were her way of bringing the joy of the genre to new listeners.

As the audience slowly dwindled away, heading to the hotel restaurant or bar, he walked towards the large black grand piano where Rio was gathering up her music. She glanced up, smiling at him, and he could almost believe that she could be, as Xena had more than hinted at, the woman to overthrow all the disbelief in love with which his ex-fiancée Kyra had filled him.

'Excellent entertainment, Lysandros.' The gruff voice of Samuel Andrews, a man with whom he'd just signed a lucrative deal to supply his company with ten luxury yachts, invaded the moment.

'Indeed.' He glanced at the older man before looking over at Rio, who was almost ready to leave. He couldn't let her go without telling her how wonderfully she'd played—and arranging dinner tonight. 'If you will excuse me.'

He didn't wait for a response. The only thing that mattered now was being with Rio. In just a few days he would return to Greece, where he had a full schedule of meetings for the next few weeks, and it shocked him to realise how much he would miss Rio during that time. This was all such new territory for a man who'd done nothing but play the field for the last ten years.

Rio looked up at him, that sensual but shy smile on her lips convincing him further, if he needed it, that time together in Greece with this woman was exactly what he wanted.

'You were wonderful,' he said as he stood in the curve of the piano, its lid lifted. 'You play so beautifully.' He watched her, admiring her grace and elegance in the long black dress she wore, one shoulder bare, as the silky fabric swept across her breasts, a frill of black silk over her other shoulder. Her hair was pulled back at the nape of her neck in a tousled chignon he found so very sexy as he imagined setting it free during the passion of sex.

She gathered the last of her music up and clutched it to her, the softness of her brown eyes filled with happiness. 'Thank you.' Her voice was light and teasing, the sparkle in her eyes flirtatious. Finally, he was breaking through her reserve. Soon this innocent beauty would be his in the most intimate way. That thought intensified the heated lust already raging inside him after his imaginings while she'd played. 'Does that mean you will take me to dinner tonight?'

He stepped closer to her, not able to resist touching her, and brushed back a stray piece of hair, lifting her chin gently with his thumb and finger. His eyes held hers briefly, and then he brushed his lips over hers before answering. 'It most certainly does, especially as I have to return to Greece at the end of the week.'

'Next week?' Her voice was husky, proving she wanted him as much as he wanted her. 'So soon?'

'Yes, *agape mou*, so soon.' He wanted to take her in his arms and kiss her until that infernal barrier she hid behind came crashing down.

'I have to meet with Hans now, the conductor. He wants to go over some of the pieces with me, but afterwards I'll be free.' She paused. 'Free to make the most of the last few nights together.'

'Last few *nights*?' He couldn't miss the blush that had crept over her face or the sudden shyness that made her look at him from lowered lashes. He swallowed hard against the need to crush his mouth to hers, to kiss her until passion consumed them both, until desire doused them in flames.

'Yes, Lysandros.' Her whisper was husky and so very sexy. She moved closer to him, her gaze locked with his, the fire of their attraction almost crackling in the air around them. Did she have any idea what she was doing to him? How she was tormenting him? 'I want to be with you tonight. All night.'

He looked into her eyes, desire filling them, darkening the soft brown until they were almost black. 'Are you sure?' he asked softly, wanting her to know that he was willing to wait, that he understood this wasn't something she did lightly. He wanted her to know he was prepared to take things as slowly as she wanted to.

'Absolutely.' The certainty in her voice was all the reassurance he needed. Tonight, this beautiful woman, with an aura of innocence, would be his.

He kissed her gently, allowing her to taste his passion, his desire for her, and when she responded with as much need for him, he had to force himself to step back from her as the crazy need for her threatened to overcome him. 'I will make tonight very special for you, *agape mou*.'

'Just being with you will do that.' She blushed and hugged her music sheets tighter. 'But first I must sort this out.' She allowed the sheets of music to fall forward, as if providing the evidence for what she had to do. 'You know how hard Hans works us. And, besides, you need to mingle with your guests.'

He watched as she walked away, turning to look back at him, smiling, her step light with happiness. The same happiness that had made him feel a different man since he'd been dating Rio, sparking off conversations about engagement with his sister. Xena had been convinced that, ever since that first date with her friend, an engagement would be a question of when, not if.

Rio felt crazy and reckless with the anticipation of all that tonight would hold. Tonight she would give herself, give her virginity to a man who was everything she wanted. He might be her best friend's brother, might have already been engaged once, but he was the man who made her feel alive. Even though she knew he wasn't looking for any kind of long-term, emotional commitment, he was the man she wanted to be with above all others.

She pushed open the door of the grand room where practices were held and crossed the wooden floor to the piano, her heels echoing in the vastness of the room. Hans had insisted they go over some of her pieces for the final concerts of the season. She was early, so there was time to enjoy just playing, for no other reason than she wanted to.

She hadn't wasted time changing from her black gown. She'd wanted to get the meeting over and done with and back to Lysandros. For the first time in her life, she was irritated by the need to do such things, annoyed by the fact that it meant she couldn't be somewhere else, doing something else. Something else she was finally ready for. Even knowing Lysandros was only interested in her physically, she wanted to be with him, wanted to know the pleasure of a night in his bed.

As she sat at the piano she thought of Lysandros, of the way he'd kissed her before she'd left. Even if he hadn't promised her tonight would be special, it had been there in his kiss. Her heart fluttered with anticipation as she began playing, losing herself in the romance of the piece, letting all her emotion pour out through her fingers as she played.

As she ended the piece her whole body was humming with need for Lysandros. She closed her eyes and sat, hands lying on her lap as she savoured the moment.

'Now, *that* was beautiful.' Hans's voice came from behind her. Very close behind her.

She gasped and turned around, annoyed that he'd

invaded her private moment. She felt vulnerable. Exposed. He'd watched her as she'd given free rein to her emotions, as she'd allowed all the desire she felt for Lysandros to pour into the music.

'You should have said you were there.' She couldn't keep the irritation from her voice.

'And ruin such a moment?' He looked at her, his gaze sweeping down her body. 'You looked so beautiful. So passionate.'

He stepped closer to her as he spoke and for the first time ever Rio felt threatened by a man's presence. The smell of alcohol hung around him and she didn't like the way he looked at her, the way he'd wiped away the purity of her feelings for Lysandros. Mentally she shook herself. She was overreacting. Embarrassed at being caught off guard.

'Shall we go through what you wanted to discuss?' Desperately she tried to get the practice session back on track.

'Play something for *me*.' He seemed to be goading her. As if he'd known she'd been playing for someone else. For Lysandros.

She swallowed down her nerves, sure her embarrassment must be making her see things that weren't there. As she turned on the piano stool and sorted her music, she was aware of him moving even closer. She glanced over the grand piano towards the big bay window and the parkland beyond, which was coming to life now with spring. In the summer it would be full of people enjoying the sunshine. Now it was empty.

'That one,' he said as he leant over her shoulder, moving one piece of music to the front.

Play, she told herself. *Just play and he will step back.*

She took a breath and placed her fingers lightly on the keys. After a few seconds' pause, she began to play. At first it was stilted, emotionless as the uncertainty of the moment took over. He hadn't moved at all. Was she just being panicky? Gradually, even though he remained behind her, she began to relax, and the music flowed more naturally round the vastness of the domed room.

She finished the piece and sat looking at the keys, not daring to look up at him. When his hand rested on her bare shoulder she stiffened, her eyes wide. What was he doing?

She turned and looked at his hand, unable to move any other part of her body. She should get up, should step away, but she couldn't. Paralysed by fear, she dragged in a ragged breath.

As if her stillness had given consent, his hand moved lower, down over her chest, and she gasped, moving backwards on the stool, only to come against the firmness of his body.

'Don't,' she said, snatching at his hand as it slipped alarmingly lower. Inside the fabric of her gown. Instinctively she curled herself inwards, hoping the movement would prevent what he was trying to do, but the fabric slackened, enabling him to fully grasp her breast.

'What are you doing?' she shouted.

The room echoed with the sound as she tried to avoid him, but his grasp tightened painfully on her breast and she was trapped between his body and his arm. How could this be happening?

'I'm giving you what you want.' His voice had changed, become hard and menacing. His face was so close to hers now she could smell stale alcohol on his breath.

'No. No. This isn't what I want.' She struggled again and his grip on her tightened, his free hand now pressing down on her other shoulder.

'Don't be shy, Rio. I know you want it.' He groped at her breast. Pain shot through it. Sickness filled her. She had to stop this. Had to get away.

She pushed against the piano with a discordant jangle of keys. Her heels making it difficult, she scrambled to her feet. Finally, she was free of him, but so shocked by what had just happened she stood there, panting wildly as she looked at him.

Too late she realised her mistake. She should have run when she'd had the chance. He moved quickly, his body pressing hers against the keys, his mouth claiming hers in a cruel kiss. He roughly pulled her dress up, his hand grasping at her thigh as his body pushed her even harder against the piano.

The sound of her dress ripping galvanised her into action and she pushed against him. 'Get off.'

He was too strong for her. 'I like it rough,' he said as he tried to kiss her neck, his stubble scratching her skin, his foul breath making her retch.

'No,' she screamed as panic tore through her. He couldn't do this to her. He couldn't. She fought harder, screamed louder. 'No. Stop it.'

'What the hell?' Another voice mingled with her scream and Hans let her go. She sagged in relief as his weight suddenly moved away from her. Anger took over and she watched Hans being manhandled off her by two other members of the orchestra. Then shock set in. The whole thing had lasted only minutes, but it had felt like hours. Rio slithered to the floor, her arms clutching the piano stool as if she'd been cast into the sea and it was all she had to hold on to.

She rested her head on her arms, not wanting to watch now as the scuffle continued amidst Hans's angry accusations. How could he accuse her of leading him on? How could he say she had been up for it?

Tears slipped from her eyes. What had just happened?

'Are you hurt?' A woman's voice, gentle but filled with anger, made her lift her face. Rio glanced around the room like a scared rabbit. 'He's gone.'

'Thank goodness.' She shivered, the shock of her ordeal really taking effect now. 'God knows what he would have done if you hadn't shown up.'

'Evil bastard,' the woman snapped. 'Thank heavens the room was double-booked and that I had Philip and Josh with me.'

'Double-booked?' She looked up in confusion, not really knowing where she was any more. Nothing seemed to make sense.

The older woman placed her jacket round Rio's shoulders, which, instead of comforting her, only made her shiver even more. 'Don't worry about that now. Just be safe in the knowledge that as soon as the police get here he will be locked up and will never be able to do this to you or anyone else again.'

'What do you mean?' Her eyes were wide with fear and shock, tears threatening once again.

'The police will need your statement, as soon as you are able to, that is.'

'The police?'

'Yes. I called them whilst Philip and Josh wrestled him off you.' There was a hint of humour in the older woman's voice now and Rio gave a weak smile, finally realising who the woman was. Judith Jones, one of the company's newest members, a fabulous conductor and now her saviour.

Rio tried to stand, the ripped front of her dress falling away. She gasped in shock. Had he done that to her? Hans? 'My dress.'

Judith hugged her. 'The dress isn't important, Rio. All that matters is that we found you in time.'

Rio sniffed as the reality of Judith's words sank in. 'If you hadn't come along…' The implication hung in the air.

'But we did,' she soothed. 'And you can give your statement to the police.'

'Yes,' Rio said shakily.

'After you have done that, you will come to my home. I will personally take care of you tonight—unless there is someone else you'd rather be with, because you shouldn't be alone.'

'No,' Rio whispered sadly. How could she go to Lysandros now? After all she'd just promised him? She couldn't spend the night with him now. How could she even see Lysandros, let alone begin to tell him what had happened? Xena was busy this evening, and there was no way she could tell her yet either. 'No, no one is home tonight.'

'That's settled, then. You will stay with me,' Judith said firmly.

Rio smiled weakly. She should be with Lysandros tonight, should finally be discovering the joy of giving herself to a man. But how could she do that now? How could she allow any man to touch her again? Even the man she was beginning to fall in love with?

CHAPTER ONE

It HAD BEEN six weeks since Rio had seen Lysandros. Six weeks since she'd said to him with her new-found flirty confidence that she wanted to spend all night with him. And six weeks since her world had been torn apart, destroying that confidence, ending her fragile hope that she and Lysandros could be beginning something special.

That life-changing moment after the recital had left her no option but to stand up the man she'd lost her heart to, the man she'd been ready to give everything to. She'd ended things between them, refusing to see or speak to Lysandros. That afternoon had been the last time she'd played the piano, the events that had unfolded as Hans had arrived in the practice room now making it impossible for her to go near a piano, let alone play.

Now another life-changing event meant that at any moment Lysandros would come striding into the hospital room where his younger sister—her best friend, Xena—lay sleeping, looking battered and bruised from the car accident late last night.

'Xena.' Lysandros's voice snapped Rio from her thoughts as he surged through the door of the dimly lit private hospital room, his focus completely on the sleeping form of his sister.

Rio's heart pounded hard as she watched, almost in slow motion, Lysandros walk back into her life. She couldn't move, couldn't speak, couldn't make her presence in the large comfortable chair in the corner known. Instead she watched as he stood on the other side of Xena's bed, looking down at his sister. His stubble-covered jaw clenched, giving away the hurry in which he must have left Athens. He spread a hand over his chin as if he was trying to gain control, trying to work out what to say, what to do. He still hadn't even realised she was there.

With a sense of desolation more profound than she could have ever dreamed possible, Rio sat silently, watching the man to whom she'd lost her heart. As if that very thought made her presence felt, he turned to look at her, the emptiness in his eyes breaking her heart.

'Rio?' For a moment he seemed speechless, unable to say anything. 'When did you get here?'

'Early this morning.' She didn't know what to say to him. The way he searched her face, looking into her eyes for the answers she couldn't give him—answers about more than what had happened to Xena—almost tore her heart in two.

'How much longer is she likely to sleep?' His voice was firmer now, his shock at seeing her gone, as he walked to the bottom of his sister's bed. His height dominated the room, crowding her thoughts. The dark grey suit he wore only emphasised his muscular physique, reminding her how it had felt against her body when he'd kissed her. It had felt good. Right. But that had been before. That had been when she'd been a different person.

Aware that he was waiting for an answer, she dragged her thoughts back in line and resisted the urge to stand up and try to match his height. Instead she remained seated, hoping it would give off the message that she was as totally unaffected by him as she'd claimed when she had broken things off.

'When she first came round, she was very distressed. She couldn't remember anything, so the doctors gave her a sedative.' Rio focused her attention on Xena. She couldn't look at Lysandros. Not into those coal-black eyes. She didn't want to see the questions. The accusations. 'They said she will be sleepy for some time and are worried the knock on her head has affected her memory.'

'Her memory?' She had his full attention now. And the full force of his scrutiny.

'She doesn't recall the accident, or any other recent events, but as she knows who she is, the doctors are saying it's her way of coping. She is blocking it out.' Rio gulped back a wave of emotion. She had to be strong, had to focus on what Xena needed. Right now, nothing else mattered, not even her and Lysandros.

'What happened?' The question was firm, but by the look on his face she knew he was struggling to comprehend his sister's injuries, intensifying her own guilt at what she'd done to him. She didn't know how she was going to answer that and keep Xena's recent relationship from him. A relationship that was now over. It might be the reason why Xena was here in hospital, but it was no longer of any importance or relevance. Just as all she and Lysandros had shared was no longer of importance.

Last night, when Rio had arrived at Casualty, Xena

hadn't recalled the promise she'd extracted from Rio. The promise not to tell Lysandros about her romance with Ricardo, a married man. A promise she'd never envisaged being brought into play, but last night Xena had been confused and distressed, unable to piece together recent events—or even Ricardo. The doctors had assured her it was almost certainly temporary, but it still upset Rio to see her friend like that and she knew she would do anything to make it better for her. Even keep the truth from her powerful and commanding brother. Just as she'd keep her true reason for ending their relationship from him.

Rio fought frustration and guilt as it welled up inside her. If only she'd been able to convince Xena that her married lover had ended the affair in order to make his marriage work. That he wouldn't leave his wife. Then maybe the accident would never have happened. Xena wouldn't be here now. But she hadn't been able to convince her. She and Xena had fallen out over it and Xena had slipped out after Rio had gone to bed and now Rio blamed herself for being too hard on her friend.

'What happened?' Lysandros demanded again, his tone more insistent this time, dragging her back to the present.

'A car ran the lights. It hit her car hard. Spun it round.' As she thought of it, of the distress Xena must have felt, she closed her eyes, pressing her fingers to her temples. She was tired. Upset. Seeing Lysandros again was too much on top of Xena's accident.

'Are you okay?' Lysandros's voice was so close it made her jump.

She opened her eyes to see him crouched before her, his hands holding the arms of the chair either side of her.

Trapping her. Instantly all she could think about was the moment Hans had trapped her against the piano. No, she couldn't allow that moment to rule her. Not ever. She just needed time to get over it.

'Rio?' Lysandros laid his palm on her lap, genuine concern in his voice. The heat of his hand grounded her, making her feel peculiarly safe.

She looked at him, almost bereft when he withdrew his hand, but this wasn't a time to focus on her or what she wanted or even needed. The only thing she had to do now was be there for Xena, doing and saying whatever she needed her to say.

'It's Xena who needs your concern, not me.' Even to her own ears, her voice sounded cold and emotionless.

He stood up, his long legs making him intimidatingly tall as he towered over her. She looked up at him, straight into the black depths of his eyes. She couldn't look away. Couldn't help herself wondering. Did the desire that had once filled them lie beneath their lacklustre darkness?

She forced her attention back to Xena's sleeping form, desperate to focus her emotions. She looked up at Lysandros again, the man she could have been so happy with if other things hadn't got in the way. 'I have spoken to the doctor. She should start to come round soon. Her broken arm and fractured wrist are expected to heal, although her injuries will mean she won't be able to play the violin for some considerable time.'

If only he knew the full truth of it all. Playing the violin would not be what Xena worried about as she recovered. It would be the loss of the man she loved that would fill her mind, her heart. If she remembered him. Tears sprang to Rio's eyes and she blinked rapidly to hold them back. Jumping up, she went to the window, looking out over the city bathed in glorious spring sunshine as the day began. Anything to get away from his scrutiny.

'Why?' He glanced at Xena, sleeping peacefully, blissfully unaware of the storm brewing around her. She'd promised Xena her secret would be exactly that until she was ready to tell anyone. With a clarity and determination she'd never felt before, Rio knew she would do whatever she had to for Xena. That was what friends did and she knew without a doubt that Xena would do the same for her.

She looked at Lysandros and refused to quake at the power that radiated from him, refused to bow to his superior command. This wasn't a business transaction—this was his sister's life. Xena's future. All Rio wanted was to be there for her.

'Even without the amnesia, the injuries Xena has sustained will require time to heal. She may not even be able to play when the new season starts in the autumn.'

Rio calmly laid the foundations, which, although true, was not the reason why Xena wouldn't want to rejoin the orchestra. Ricardo was part of the stage crew and amidst a torrent of tears Xena had clung to Rio before they'd fallen out, saying there was no way she could be part of the orchestra now. Rio's heart still broke to remember the pain in her friend's voice, knowing it came from losing the man she loved. A pain she also knew—because if she was truthful with herself, she had loved Lysandros.

'Then the best option is for Xena to return to Greece.' Lysandros looked at his sister, then back at her. The firm tone of his voice left her in no doubt that he did not expect his decision to be challenged— by anyone.

Rio had no intention of challenging him or his superiority. Relief flooded through her. If Xena left London and went to her island villa to recover, then any chances of gossip about her and Ricardo would be lessened. Ricardo certainly wouldn't be the one to say anything. He was a married man and stood to lose everything. Xena would be able to recover in peace, and although the thought of saying goodbye to her friend at such a time hurt, it was the best solution.

'Yes, I think that would be exactly what she needs in the circumstances.' Rio's voice had lost that determined edge, but she was acutely aware of Lysandros's scrutiny.

He moved back to the window, looking out over London for a moment before turning to face her. Like an animal trapped in the beams of car headlights at night, she froze to the spot. Was he going to demand an explanation? From her? Was he now about to demand to know why she'd stood him up that night?

'And what about you?' He spoke gently and she swallowed down her guilt. She didn't deserve his concern. She might not have been directly involved in the accident, but she blamed herself. 'I can see this is affecting you too.'

He moved closer to her, his handsome face softened by the kind of concern she guessed those he did business with rarely saw. She wanted to back away, wanted to keep as much distance between herself and this man as possible. But she couldn't. He mesmerised her, made her want things she couldn't have now.

'I will stay in London.' Her voice was barely more

than a whisper. He reached out and pushed the stray strands of her hair back from her face, just as he'd done the last time he'd seen her. Before he'd kissed her.

She caught her breath. Her pulse raced so fast she couldn't say anything. All she could do was look into his hypnotically sexy black eyes.

'You have had a shock too. You shouldn't be alone.' His words were heavy with his Greek accent, making her body's reaction to him, to his nearness, even more intense.

She stepped back from him, away from the strange power he had over her. 'I will be fine here.'

'I am sure Xena wouldn't want that,' he insisted, his eyes dark and watchful, as if he was trying to tell her *he* wanted her there.

'No, I should stay here.'

Lysandros took in Rio's face, unusually bare of make-up, and along with the casual jeans she wore with a sweater, she had an air of complete innocence. What was it about this woman? Why did she affect him like this? Why did he want to take on the challenge she'd unwittingly issued when she'd stood him up and then told him it was over? Her response to his kiss after the piano recital had promised him so much. So what had changed that?

Xena stirred and he forced his mind from those questions. Instantly Rio was at his sister's side, her attention focused completely on her friend. He should be giving Xena the same attention, but he couldn't keep his eyes off Rio. Her hair, loosely pulled back, looked tousled, giving away the haste in which she'd obviously left her bed early this morning. She might well have been here for hours, but she looked beautiful. Breathtakingly beautiful. His heart wrenched.

'Lysandros is here,' Rio said softly as Xena opened her eyes, a look of bewilderment on her pale face.

Xena winced as she tried to slide up the partially elevated bed. Rio fussed with her pillows, going to great lengths to make them right. Anything, it seemed, to avoid looking at him. Anything to avoid that sizzle of attraction that still sparked between them, despite the current situation.

'Lysandros?' Xena asked shakily as she turned to look up at him.

'I came as soon as I heard,' he said, taking her hand in his. He knew Rio was watching him. Every nerve in his body was tuned in to her.

'But you only just returned to Greece,' Xena said weakly as she looked at him, then at Rio. Lysandros's heart sank. He'd been in Athens for the past six weeks. Xena obviously didn't remember much at all.

'Do you think I would stay there when I had just been told by Mother that you had been involved in an accident?' He glanced up at Rio.

'I was in an accident?' The panic-laced question confirmed all Rio had just told him about Xena's memory loss.

'Yes,' Rio added gently, and Xena looked at her. 'A car accident.'

'I don't remember.' Xena shook her head. Then her eyes widened. 'I don't remember anything.'

'Don't panic,' Rio soothed, and Lysandros marvelled at her command in the face of Xena's fear. 'You've had a bump on the head. I'm sure it's perfectly normal not to remember things straight away. I'll go and find the doctor now, get him to come and reassure you.'

'Don't go yet,' Xena pleaded, and Rio hesitated. 'There is something else wrong, isn't there? Something is wrong between you two. I can feel it.'

'Don't worry about us,' Rio said soothingly, again fussing with the bedsheets.

Xena laughed softly. It was such an unexpected sound that Lysandros looked at his sister, not sure what was coming next. Tears maybe, as the shock of the accident set in.

'Well, I hope you two haven't fallen out.' Xena rested her head back against the pillow, her face as pale as the white sheets. 'Because you do realise you were meant for each other?'

Lysandros didn't dare look at Rio. It wasn't just the accident Xena didn't remember; she didn't remember he and Rio were no longer dating. 'Of course we haven't fallen out. Far from it.'

He looked at Rio across the bed, shocked to find how near they now were. Their concern for Xena had drawn them physically so close he only needed to lean forward a little to kiss Rio. And he wanted to. She still had that effect on him, still raised the desire in his blood until it almost boiled.

'Fallen out?' Rio frowned, her gaze locked with his, and he saw the moment she realised what he was doing, that he didn't want to panic Xena or worry her by explaining they had done exactly that six weeks ago. He let out a breath of relief when she laughed softly, looking at Xena, apparently happy to conspire with him. 'Of course we haven't.'

Lysandros straightened away from the temptation of

kissing Rio once more and looked at her. 'You will, of course, come to Greece with Xena. I'm sure it's what she will need to aid her recovery.'

Rio's eyes snapped to his. 'I don't think that is necessary,' she said firmly, a clear challenge in her voice.

Lysandros should be worried about Xena, should be anxious about her amnesia, but all he could think about was getting Rio to his Greek island. Getting her alone. Then he could convince her that what they'd had before she'd stood him up had been good, worth continuing. He wanted Rio. Couldn't get her out of his mind. It was not just because she was the only woman to have stood him up. It was more than that. He couldn't make sense of his reaction to her. All he knew was that this might be the only opportunity to discover the pleasure of making her his.

Rio took a step away from the bed, away from him. As if she sensed his ulterior motives. As if she knew the reason he wanted her in Greece was because he couldn't accept that she didn't want him.

He damn well couldn't.

Not when desire had sparked within every smile she'd bestowed on him. Not when she had seductively let him know she was ready to take their relationship to a different level.

Even now, in the hospital, with his sister's suspected amnesia looking ever more likely, the air was filled with sexual tension, pulling him and Rio together, invalidating her claim they were over. How could he turn his back on something so powerful, something that had promised to be amazing? The disaster of his engagement had loomed over him for ten years, but whatever it was between him and Rio, this was the first time that shadow had been eclipsed.

'Xena, do you want Rio with you in Greece?'

'Most definitely,' Xena said, her voice still wobbly as she looked from one to the other, as if she couldn't make out what was happening.

'Then I will make arrangements immediately for you both to travel to Greece.' He turned to leave. He couldn't stand this close to Rio and not touch her, not try to convince her with a kiss that they needed to explore the attraction between them. They needed to extinguish the fire of desire and he knew exactly how. 'I will speak to a doctor right now.'

He strode out of the room, not expecting Rio to follow him, but he knew she had. He sensed it with every taut muscle in his body. He continued to walk briskly down the hospital corridor, wanting to be completely out of Xena's hearing before he turned to face the onslaught of Rio's anger. Anger that radiated up the corridor after him.

'Lysandros, will you wait?' She was angry all right. He turned slowly to face her, keeping his expression devoid of emotion. 'Why are you allowing Xena to think we are still together?'

'Because I don't wish to upset her.'

'I can't just go to Greece and pretend everything is right between us.' The defiant tilt of her chin should have annoyed him, but instead it set light to the fuse of lust once more. Why did this woman drive him so wild with desire? Her lack of experience with men had been evident from the first day Xena had introduced them. So why did he want her so much when he'd always preferred experienced women? The kind of woman who wouldn't demand anything more than a night of exquisite pleasure? No questions, no longing for happy endings, just hot, passionate nights until the desire cooled.

'Rio.' He'd always liked the feel of her name on his lips and moved closer to her. 'Xena needs you. You are her closest friend.'

She folded her arms across her slender body, adding to the aura of defiance—and the spark of lust in him.

'I should be playing the piano each day, even though the season is over.' He didn't believe the hostile glint in her eyes for one minute. Just as he didn't believe that excuse. There was an emptiness in it that warned him she was hiding something.

He smiled at her weak excuse. Was she afraid of what was between them? Afraid of its power? 'Xena has a grand piano in her villa, which I am sure she would love you to play.'

He didn't go on to say that he also had a piano in his Athens apartment. That would deter her further, but the thought of her playing it—just for him—fired his lust higher.

She shook her head. 'No. I need to stay in London.'

He moved closer still, putting temptation in his path once more. He couldn't allow that to distract him, not when he knew Xena would want her friend with her if she had to return to Greece. If she had to face the reality of not only her loss of memory but being unable to play her violin while her wrist and arm healed, she would need Rio.

He would need Rio there too. As hard as it was to admit, he found it difficult to emotionally connect with anyone, even Xena. Angered that his flaw had surfaced, that maybe it had chased Rio away, he drew on the few facts he knew about the accident.

'Why was Xena out alone when she wasn't familiar with driving in a big city at night?'

Rio's eyes sparked with anger, her soft lips pressing into a firm line. For a moment he thought she wasn't going to answer. 'I had no idea she'd gone. We'd…had words.'

'Was she meeting someone?' He might still want Rio in a way that unnerved him, but right now she was the only person who could help him understand what had happened last night.

'I think so.' He heard the pain in her voice and a twinge of guilt spiralled through him until he reminded himself he was doing this for Xena. She would have been furious with him for upsetting her friend, but he needed to know and right now Xena was unable to talk for herself.

He gentled his tone. 'Who?'

'Just a friend.'

'And what were you doing at this time?' He hated himself for needing to know just where Rio had been that night. Xena had assured him Rio hadn't dated anyone else since their split and he'd accepted that, had given Rio the space she'd asked for. Maybe now he'd get the answers he wanted, maybe even continue where they'd left off.

'I went to bed, assuming Xena had too.' Rio looked boldly at him, daring him to challenge her explanation. And he would. He hadn't got where he was now in business by not taking risks. His world-renowned luxury yacht company had pushed him to the limits and beyond as he'd fought to bring his father's declining shipping company into the twenty-first century and expand it. There was no way he was going to allow Rio to undermine him. He wouldn't allow her to keep him from the truth about last night—or any other night, for that matter.

'You said you'd had words. What about?' His usually all-too-effective charm slipped into his voice and he watched as a flurry of emotions crossed her face.

'It doesn't matter now.'

He hadn't expected that. 'And why would that be?'

She inhaled deeply then moved a pace towards him. A valiant attempt at bravado.

'It was nothing; you don't need to concern yourself.' He hadn't anticipated the innocent and somewhat shy Rio Armstrong to have such a sting in her tail.

'My sister is lying in a hospital bed, unable to recall the accident and obviously other things too. I have every right to concern myself.' He looked back up the corridor to where Xena's private room was, giving weight to his argument.

'We were talking about a man.' She paused as if contemplating her next words carefully. 'That's all you need to know.'

So Rio *had* spurned him, only to move on to a new lover. 'And this man is the reason you stood me up?' He waited for her answer, the unexpected turn in the conversation working in his favour.

'That's not important now.' Rio skilfully avoided the issue, but he wasn't going to let her get away with not answering him that easily.

'Why did you stand me up, Rio?' The need to know surged forward, pushing all other thoughts to one side.

'Because you kissed me? Told me you wanted to spend the entire night with me?' He taunted her mercilessly.

She gasped, her gaze meeting his, indignation in her eyes. 'No.'

'Why did you change your mind?' If only she could admit there was something between them. 'What are you afraid of, Rio?'

'I'm not afraid of anything. I simply don't want a man in my life—any man.' Sparks of anger filled her words, but he refused to allow them to penetrate his armour. He'd do precisely what he'd done for the last six weeks and wait for the right moment. This was a conversation to have later, in Greece, on the island, when she would have no option but to talk to him.

'Xena would want you to come to Greece and help her through this difficult time.' He pushed home his point, satisfied when he saw her conflicted expression. 'The last thing Xena needs right now is to think you and I have fallen out. Whatever has happened between us, we owe it to her to be there for her in Greece—as a couple.'

Rio wanted to crumple to the floor. She was ensnared in a trap of her own making. Damn Lysandros. He'd led her right to it and she'd obliged, stepping in. Yet despite all this she knew he was right. Xena would need her, and if that meant going to Greece and pretending she and Lysandros were still together, then that was exactly what she would do. Not because Lysandros had asked her but because of the bond of friendship between her and Xena.

Lysandros had a business to run and she knew he preferred to spend his time in Athens, where he notoriously played as hard as he worked. Surely he would return to that life once Xena was settled into her island villa? Surely he wouldn't pursue her or the promise she'd once made. Not when he could have any woman he wanted.

'That's unfair,' she defended herself as he regarded her from dark and unyielding eyes. If only he wasn't so striking, so handsome. If only he didn't make her heart flutter so wildly. If only she didn't find him so attractive and hadn't almost given herself so completely to him. 'I'd do anything for Xena.'

His brows rose in disbelief. 'Except come to Greece and spend the summer with her—because of me.'

'You really are very arrogant.' She grappled with the way he made her body tingle as he moved closer. He searched her face, his eyes darkening, reminding her of the moment she'd told him she'd wanted to spend the entire night with him.

Her pulse leapt wildly as that moment clashed with this, confusing her after his annoyance. She wanted to turn away, wanted to conceal the attraction she had for him, but she couldn't. As hard as she tried, she couldn't fight the way he made her feel.

'Right now, all that matters is that Xena gets well and regains her memory.' Rio forced herself to look away from the handsome Greek who was wrong for her on so many levels. She couldn't allow herself to fall for him all over again. She didn't want that kind of power held over her.

'As soon as the doctor tells me she is well enough to travel, we will go.' His deep and sexy accent sent ripples of awareness over Rio, but she refused to feel them, refused to react.

'What if I agree—just for a while?' She was torn between what Xena needed and protecting her fragile heart.

'Not for a while, Rio. For the entire summer,' Lysandros added with icy calmness. 'That is what Xena will want—and need.' He knew she wouldn't refuse to give Xena what she needed. Damn him.

'No, I can't.'

'But you will come, won't you, Rio? Because you will do anything to help your friend.' Rio couldn't believe how he was manipulating the situation—or the way her body reacted just from having him near her. Had she been too hasty in ending it all after what Hans had done? Would Lysandros have understood if she'd told him?

The questions chased each other through her mind. There was no way she could have told him, not when their relationship had been nothing more than just another affair to him. She'd never been foolish enough to believe otherwise.

'Very well. I will, but not because you have asked, or should I say bullied, me to do so, but because I want to be there for Xena.'

The look he gave her made Rio realise that everything she'd ever been afraid of happening if she saw him again was happening. She was still attracted to him. Still wanted to be with him, but things had changed. Things he didn't know about—couldn't know about.

'And because we have things to sort out?' The question sounded casual, but the look in his eyes was far from that.

'We don't have anything to sort out. We won't even

need to see one another.' Rio folded her arms, desperate to stand her ground, prevent her body from betraying her.

'Xena believes we are together. I don't think making her worry about us will help her recovery, Rio, and we will be seeing each other, of that you can be sure.'

CHAPTER TWO

FOR TWO DAYS, Xena's Greek island retreat had been a haven of tranquillity for both Rio and Xena. Now Lysandros was due to arrive from Athens and Rio's nerves were threatening to get the better of her. He'd be disappointed his sister's memory of the accident and previous weeks hadn't yet returned.

Rio glanced at Xena, compassion for her friend's predicament filling her. Xena didn't recall anything that had happened in the weeks leading up to the accident. She had blocked out everything bad. Ricardo's rejection of her. The assault Hans had attempted on Rio. The break-up between Rio and Lysandros. Even blocked the accident itself. Xena lived under the illusion that none of those things had happened.

'It's so frustrating,' Xena said as she looked up at Rio. 'Why can't I remember anything?'

Rio sat down beside Xena. 'It will come. The doctor said you just need time—and rest.'

'I can remember that Lysandros will be back from Athens today and we are all going to visit my mother,' Xena said brightly, recalling the arrangement that had been made as they'd arrived on the island.

Rio, too, could remember that Lysandros was due

to return to the island today, but for very different reasons.

'Maybe you could play a little,' Xena said, pulling Rio from her thoughts. 'It might help me remember something.'

Rio looked at the grand piano, forlorn and abandoned since they'd arrived. 'Later, perhaps,' she soothed, trying hard not to let her fear of even going near it show.

'I am rather tired.' Xena stifled a yawn. 'I think I will go and have a lie-down before we visit my mother. Gather my strength again.'

Rio watched her friend go with a heavy heart. If only there was something more she could do to help. She missed the confident and bubbly girl Xena really was.

For the past two days, while Lysandros had been in Athens, it had been easy to allow Xena to think that she and her brother were still a couple. But once he was here, it wouldn't be so easy. She was still far too attracted to him, still longed for the dream of happiness she'd glimpsed before it had been cruelly snatched away by Hans.

With a sigh of frustration she turned and walked to the large glass doors that opened up onto the terrace with a view of the sea. As she looked out over the sparkling waters she saw the sleek white speedboat slowing and moving towards the island. She pushed her thoughts aside, watching as Lysandros stepped onto the jetty. Her heart leapt as he looked towards the villa and she quickly moved out of view. She didn't know if she could do this, even though deep down she wanted nothing more than to go back to that moment after the recital.

Footsteps sounded on the marble floor as Lysandros entered his sister's villa. Rio forced brightness into her voice that didn't echo in her body despite the idyllic Greek island setting and the early summer sunshine.

'Hello, Lysandros.' She kept her voice firm, refusing to allow her nerves to show in any way. Whatever Xena believed about them, she needed to keep him at a distance and he had to know that.

'Hello, Rio.' The cool edge to his voice contrasted sharply with the darkening of his eyes as his gaze swept over her, creating a trail of tingles almost impossible to ignore.

Power radiated from him and despite his relaxed attire she knew he was anything but. The hard line of his clean-shaven jaw gave so much away. The courage she'd managed to summon up during the first days on the island began to slip away like the retreating tide. How could she be around him and be indifferent to him?

'How is Xena?' He moved a little closer, convincing Rio he knew she was still attracted to him.

'She has gone for a lie-down.' Rio let out a slow breath of relief as he walked away from her, giving her some much-needed physical distance between them.

'Has she remembered anything yet?'

Rio shook her head. 'Nothing.'

'Nothing?' She heard the despair in his voice. Despair that matched her own.

'She sounded so frustrated when we talked on the phone,' he said as he walked towards the baby grand piano. Did he have to bring it so starkly to her attention?

'It is frustrating for her.' Rio watched Lysandros, the man who still held her heart if only she was brave enough to give it to him, as he turned and frowned at her.

'I understand that.' He spoke again, snagging her attention back to him. 'But it's just as frustrating for me to know how much this is worrying her.'

'This is a big ordeal for Xena,' Rio said, watching Lysandros as he stood by the piano looking out towards the sparkling sea beyond the garden of the villa. He resembled a predatory wild cat, intent on luring its prey ever closer. Or was she imagining him drawing her in? 'She's lost some of her memory, maybe even her career, and she can't even pick up her violin and seek solace in playing.'

'Xena tells me you don't play either, even though you claimed daily practice was essential.' The sound of waves rushing onto the soft sand beyond the villa punctured the silence as she met the suspicion in his eyes. He was throwing her reason for not wanting to leave London back at her.

As he looked at her the hot sultry air suddenly crackled with undeniable tension between them. That strong attraction she had to ignore but was finding it ever more difficult to. He knew it too. He was far too astute, far too in control to be easily fooled.

'It's true. I should be practising every day.' She paused as she thought of Hans, of what he'd believed she'd wanted. Hans had been so adamant she had been leading him on, giving him the come-on. She hadn't been able to touch the keys, let alone play, since then. The piano and that moment were far too painfully linked. Even though she knew she'd done nothing to encourage him, she couldn't bring herself to sit at the piano, let alone play it.

Neither was she ready to tell Lysandros why she'd stood him up, why she'd coldly ended their relationship when it had been so good, so right. Xena didn't recall how she'd consoled Rio, how she'd tried to persuade her to tell Lysandros, and right now that suited Rio. She needed to avoid that painful conversation for as long as possible.

'So why are you not practising, Rio? Xena loves to hear you play. As do I.' He began to walk towards her, stopping when she backed away.

'I… I…' she faltered, not knowing what to say without telling him exactly why she didn't want to go near the piano.

'At least you can still physically play the piano—if you choose to.'

His accusation hit home and she dragged in a breath. Did he have to make her feel worse? Play on the guilt she felt about the night of the accident? About him? Them?

'This isn't about me. This is about Xena.' Desperately she pushed back her pain, her raw emotions, trying to bring the conversation back to Xena.

He took another step towards her, bringing him so close she could smell the citrus tang of his aftershave, and it made the memory of their last kiss collide with the guilt for all Xena was going through, as well as her own fear. She tried not to recall how lightheaded Lysandros had made her feel when he'd smiled at her, reminding herself he was well versed in the art of charming women.

Yet he'd been prepared to take things slowly with her. At first, she'd thought it was simply because of her friendship with Xena, but soon she'd wondered if it was more than that. He'd respected her. He'd showed patience and kindness totally in contrast to the playboy past Xena had told her about. He'd treated her as if she was special.

'Is it, Rio?' His voice had deepened, become so sensually soft he could be seducing her.

'Of course it is. I'm here for Xena, not myself—or us. Not that there is an us any more.'

'What happened after the recital, Rio? What are you keeping from me?' His question hung in the air and she hated the way he made her feel, the way she wanted to confide in him, tell him what had happened. But she couldn't. It was over between them and there was no point in going over that night now. She was here only for Xena.

'There is nothing to tell,' she said quickly, hoping he wouldn't keep asking, be able to tell she had been doing exactly that.

'Let's take a walk on the beach while Xena is resting.' He changed the subject so fast Rio felt dazed.

'Xena and I are due to visit your mother today.' She grasped at that. 'Maybe we should wake Xena now.'

'As I am the one charged with the task of getting you both there, we can spend a while walking on the beach first.' He paused and looked at her, the intensity in his eyes changing, making her pulse leap with awareness she wasn't sure she was ready to acknowledge yet.

'I ought to leave Xena a note. In case she wakes.' Rio began to write a quick note and Lysandros stood over her, so close her body began to tremble, not with fear, as she'd expected, but with anticipation. Need. For him.

'Make sure you mention you and I are together.' His voice had dropped to almost a whisper and was so sexy she had to close her eyes against the tingle that rushed up her spine.

She put the pen down and turned, her gaze locking with his, holding it.

Lysandros knew Rio was keeping something from him. He'd known it since he'd first arrived at the hospital after the accident. He'd seen it in her eyes. Sensed nervousness in every move she'd made. Now that Rio was here with Xena, he was going to get to the bottom of what had happened the night she'd left him waiting alone at a romantic and secluded table for two.

The sunshine was gaining in strength as he stepped out of the villa, across the terrace and onto the sand. Beside him Rio adjusted her hat, and while he accepted it was necessary to protect her pale complexion from the sun, he sensed it was much more about erecting a physical barrier between them. He put on his shades. If the way his body was reacting to her nearness was anything to go by, the more barriers between them the better. For now at least.

'What really happened the night of the accident?' He plunged right in as swiftly as if he'd just dived into the cool waters from his yacht.

'I told you. A car ran a red light and hit Xena's.' The defensive tone of those short, sharp sentences gave so much away, but that wasn't what he wanted to know.

'I know the details of the accident itself.' He couldn't keep the impatience from his voice. He had to know just why his sister had been driving around London alone so late at night.

'So why ask?' He sensed her looking at him, but he kept his focus ahead, sure that if he didn't put her under the spotlight she would tell him the finer details of that treacherous night.

'Because I'm Xena's brother and I want to know what happened before the accident.'

Her pace faltered and she stopped, forcing him to do the same, but she didn't look at him. Instead she stared out to sea. Yet another avoidance tactic. 'There is nothing more to tell.'

'Are you sure, Rio?' The question caught her attention and she turned to face him. He wished she didn't have her sunglasses on, wished he could see the expression and emotion in her soft caramel-brown eyes.

She sighed and he watched the smooth, pale skin of her throat move as she swallowed. At least he could now be certain he was finally near the truth. 'You might be able to manipulate others into doing what you command, but it won't work with me.'

The passion in her voice was intense and she moved away, holding her hat in place against the playful, warm wind. Her long limbs were outlined as the wind flattened the blue sundress against her, testing his resolve far too much. He couldn't allow himself to be distracted by the attraction she still had for him. Not yet. Xena had to come first.

'Manipulate?'

'Yes, you try and control everything. Everyone. Even Xena.'

'I resent that accusation. What I do for Xena I do out of love.'

'Love?' She abandoned her attempts to hold her hat in place and took it off, exposing her subtly highlighted hair, which had been pulled back into a rough ponytail. The wind whipped stray strands of hair across her face and he scrunched his hands against the urge to push them back from her lovely and beguilingly innocent face.

Whatever it was that had changed things for Rio after the recital, he sensed she was fighting hard against her attraction to him. An attraction he still felt, still wanted to explore. Patience was all he needed.

'I don't think a man such as the mighty Lysandros Drakakis, CEO of Drakakis Shipping and Luxury Yachts, does anything for love, does he?'

Her taunt had the desired effect but he resisted the urge to respond with anger. He was well aware of his inability to emotionally connect with his sister or mother, let alone with another woman. Rio might have challenged that on so many levels, but he wasn't going to allow her to know it right now. 'Love for my family is an entirely different thing from passionate love. That kind of love is built on sexual attraction and heated desire.'

She blushed and looked away. He smiled at the sense of satisfaction that ruffling her feathers had brought him. That sexual chemistry was still there. Buried but alive. 'For you maybe.'

'So you are holding out for true love, are you? Is that why you stood me up so spectacularly? So publicly?'

He could still taste her rejection, something he wasn't at all used to. If he wanted a woman it was usually only a question of when, not if. Rio had refused point-blank to see him after that night, cementing her status as the first woman to turn him down. The only woman to wound his male pride since his early twenties, when his first taste of love had been soured by deceit.

'Yes, I am holding out for true love and you would

hardly be the perfect candidate. Not with a string of broken hearts behind you.' She smiled in that *so there* kind of way the English were so good at. 'But I'm not here for us. In case you have forgotten, I'm here for Xena.'

'And what we had isn't of consequence?'

Rio looked uncomfortable and a heavy sense of seriousness filled the warm air around them. 'My friendship with Xena is more important than anything else. I don't want *us* to get in the way of that.'

She looked as though she was holding her breath, as though she was waiting for him to piece together whatever it was in her mind, but the mention of his sister served only to direct his thoughts back to his original purpose of bringing her out here to talk alone.

'I don't think going over the accident will help anyone right now. She has blocked out everything from the last two months. It's as if she is stuck at a happy point in her life.'

'I agree on that. That is why I believe it will reassure Xena if she thinks that we are in love.'

'In love? You and me?' She stumbled over the words, her fingers fidgeting with the hat she clasped as if it were a lifeline. 'Is that really necessary?'

His mind raced. All his sister had ever wanted was for him to meet someone and fall in love, and the attraction between him and Rio had been so obvious, so intense he'd allowed Xena to revel in her role as matchmaker. Allowed her to believe there was a future for him and Rio. She'd even suggested that this time he should use their grandmother's engagement ring, saying that Rio wouldn't want the flashy diamonds Kyra had demanded.

He should have told Xena there and then that he

didn't want any kind of commitment, but he hadn't wanted to destroy her happiness then, just as he didn't want to now. 'It would be what Xena has always wanted for us and maybe it could actually help Xena to feel more emotionally secure, which might enable her to remember things again.'

Rio's heart raced. How could she pretend to be in love with Lysandros when just being around him sent her pulse racing?

She sighed heavily, determined not to dwell on her problems but to focus on Xena and the heartache she had endured when Ricardo had ended their romance, and the worry of how she'd react when she remembered all about it. 'I'd do anything to help Xena, but pretending we are lovers?'

'What are you scared of, Rio?'

'I'm not scared of anything.' She swung round to face him square on, every muscle in her body tense as if ready for a fight, forcing her to remember a time and a man when a physical fight had been necessary. The clamour of her memories, the guilt of the accident and the secret she had to keep for Xena became one big storm cloud, fully laden and ready to spill everything out around her.

'Really?' His voice softened, and he moved closer to her. She thought he was going to touch her face, brush her hair back and then kiss her. Heaven help her, she wanted him to as much as she didn't.

She couldn't become enslaved by the attraction. She needed to divert his attention. 'You blame *me* for all that's happened to Xena, don't you?'

'I think you are doing an admirable job of that already.' His eyes were granite hard as his gaze fixed her to the spot.

She thought back to Xena's distress before the accident as she stepped back from Lysandros, needing the sparks of attraction to stop so she could think clearly. She could still hear the desperation in her friend's voice.

'Ricardo wants us to finish. He wants to sort everything out between him and his wife.'

'Rio.' Lysandros took her arms, turning her gently to face him, the heat of his touch sending skitters of awareness, mixed with trepidation, hurtling through her. She couldn't bear that she still had that kind of reaction to him. It was in total contrast to what she'd vowed after the attack. She just couldn't be at a man's mercy again and most certainly not one as powerful and attractive as Lysandros Drakakis. 'What are you keeping from me?'

Rio looked down and away from his scrutiny but he didn't let her go. When she looked up he was far closer than she had thought. Too close. She backed away as much as she could while his hands still held her upper arms, determined to show control and restraint.

'I'm not going to tell you anything if you don't let me go.'

He did as she requested, but his expression warned her not to push him further, not to test his patience. 'I apologise.' The words were sharp and accented, proving this whole situation with Xena was as upsetting for him as for her. Xena had often told her he was the ultimate big brother, kind and caring of his sister's needs, yet wildly overprotective, and he was now showing that.

'So you should.' She rubbed her arms, trying to brush away his touch, the memory it evoked and the reality of the very reason she'd stood him up. If she told him right now what had happened, would he understand? He was the kind of man who wanted instant gratification. Although he'd shown kindness and patience with her, courting her in a way she was sure he'd not done in many years, he was the worst kind of man for her to be attracted to now that her confidence was so low.

'Perhaps we should go back to the villa and see if Xena is ready to visit your mother.'

He swore harshly in his native Greek and she had no idea why. Quite apart from that, it was hard to focus on the conversation when each deep breath he took made his muscled chest expand, snagging her attention in a way she didn't want, warning her he was at his limit as well as reminding her what could have been if only she'd been brave enough.

'I need your help, Rio. I can't stand by and do nothing while Xena becomes more and more frustrated at not remembering.'

The unexpected openness of his words touched her heart. He might be many things, but he *did* care about his sister.

'I will help, Lysandros. That's why I'm here now.' She could feel her resolve melting the highest peaks of her defences, making them begin to slide away.

He moved closer to her and she held her breath as he took her hand in his, fixing those intensely dark eyes on her face. 'Xena is right about one thing, is she not?'

Flustered by his touch, all she could do was look at him and whisper softly, 'What?'

'That we are attracted to one another.' The rush of the waves was drowned out by the thudding of her heart. He'd admitted he found her attractive. 'If we act on that attraction, we can convince Xena our romance is real.'

Rio knew it wouldn't be that simple. This wasn't just a case of Xena feeling low after an accident had left her arm in plaster, unable to play the violin. When Xena's memory did return, she would be heartbroken all over again. Not just about her own romance with Ricardo but about Rio and Lysandros's, and knowing why Rio had broken it off, she would be devastated to think the accident, her amnesia had pushed Rio into such an arrangement.

'I really don't think Xena would believe us.' The pads of his thumbs caressed her hands, making her voice a husky whisper. He was holding her captive with the gentlest of touches, and while it unnerved her, she wanted to remain there, wanted his touch.

'Xena has already gone to great lengths to bring us together.' Lysandros's accent had deepened. 'She will believe us. It's what she wants most of all for us.'

'But what happens when she remembers we split up?' He was beginning to convince her, making her feel it could really work and, above all, making her wish it was all for real.

He smiled, one that showed such self-assurance it made her fingers clench tightly into her palms, digging her nails into the soft skin. 'I hope that we can return to where we were the afternoon of the recital.'

'I don't know that we can go back to that,' she said, still unbearably distracted by the caressing of his thumbs on her hands.

'You said you would do anything to help Xena with her amnesia.' His voice had become a seductive purr and she was unable to form any kind of reply as she looked into his eyes, seeing the same desire in them she'd seen when he'd last held her close. 'All we need to do is set free the sizzling desire between us. The desire we were so close to discovering, Rio.'

'That's gone.' She tried to inject strength into her declaration, but knew she'd failed.

'I disagree.' He touched her face and her breath shuddered in as the spark of desire she was desperate to deny ignited inside her. 'There is desire, Rio, and you can't hide from it for ever.'

CHAPTER THREE

LYSANDROS WATCHED AS desire chased the panic from Rio's eyes, their velvet brown becoming darker as her gaze held his. Around him, the sounds of the waves quietened. It was just the two of them. Nothing and no one else existed, and the heady tension, which had always been beneath the surface, began to take over.

Rio's full lips parted, and all he wanted was to kiss her, to taste the sweetness of her lips and forget the madness of recent days. He didn't want to think about Xena's amnesia, to worry it could be more than temporary. He wanted to lose himself in the passion he knew lived inside Rio. He wanted to set it free, convince her what they had was far too powerful to ignore. Or walk away from.

'I can't hide from what I don't feel.' Rio's words were husky and very sexy. So she still didn't dare admit it. His instinct was to kiss her, to prove to her she did feel desire. But he held back. There was an air of fragility about Rio, weaving in with the innocence in her eyes. He remembered what Xena had advised him after Rio had ended things. The need to give her time and space.

The rush of a bigger wave drew him from the bubble of isolation his thoughts had taken him to. He took her hand as she stepped towards him, avoiding the wave, and eased her gently closer to him. 'I don't believe that, Rio.'

She sighed, her lips pressing together as if she knew how utterly kissable she looked and was doing everything possible to avoid that. 'But I do,' she said firmly.

He searched her face, looking into her eyes, convinced the attraction was there, if only she would allow it to shine through. 'Is that really the truth?' He kept his voice calm and gentle, sensing she was more like a nervous foal who could bolt at the slightest thing.

She pulled her hand from his, stepping back from him as the undertow of water dragged another wave back out to sea, seeming to take her too. She looked lost. More vulnerable than he'd ever seen her, and he wished now he hadn't adhered to Xena's advice. He should have demanded to know why Rio had abruptly ended things between them. Because he needed to know. If only he'd asked Xena to explain what had happened to make Rio change her mind so quickly, so unexpectedly, after the recital.

Rio made him feel unsure of himself. He hadn't felt like that since Kyra's betrayal ten years ago. The effect Rio had had on him had been different, right from the day Xena had introduced them. The attraction had been instant, but Rio's innocent fragility had made him want to take things slowly. For the first time in many years he had wanted to build a relationship based on more than just sex. A fact Xena had been quick to pick up on, goading him in the way only a sister could about one day making things with Rio more permanent.

Then something had changed. Rio had changed, and Xena knew why. If only he had asked Xena then, instead of allowing his pride to keep him wrapped up in work in Athens. Now he couldn't do anything to risk upsetting the fragile state of his sister's memory and confidence. And it was for that very reason he and Rio needed to act as if they were still a couple, around Xena at least.

'Yes, it's true.' She stood there, the wet sand gleaming in the sunlight around her, and she looked more beautiful than she'd ever looked. 'There is nothing between us, Lysandros. We should never have got together in the first place.'

He frowned at her, moving towards her as another wave rushed around his feet. 'Why is that, Rio?'

'We are too different.' Her explanation rushed at him faster than the waves were coming in, unbalancing him more than the undertow of water. The expression on her face left him in no doubt she believed that claim. He did not.

'If that is true, how did Xena manage to think we were so suited to one another?' As he spoke he realised the absurdity of the situation. His sister was the one person, apart from Rio herself, who could possibly tell him what had happened to make her change her mind. Yet Xena couldn't remember a thing about it. Not that he'd pressed her, not after the doctor's warning of not pushing her too hard too soon. But if Xena had blocked out all the bad events from her life in recent weeks and she still believed he and Rio were an item, there was only one conclusion he could draw. Whatever it was that had made Rio change her mind, it must have been bad. As upsetting for Xena as for Rio.

Rio smiled. A sad smile that held regret. 'Xena lives in a world of fantasy, where true love and happy-ever-afters exist. Surely you know that?'

He did. Only too well. His constant trips to London after he'd met Rio had certainly shown him that, as his sister had become convinced he and Rio had been on the path to one of those happy-ever-afters. He'd adopted the stance of ignoring her comments, hoping she'd find something new to focus on.

He nodded and smiled, wanting to lighten the mood, to put Rio at ease again. 'I do, yes. She has some very fixed ideas about us.'

'Except that she doesn't recall we are no longer dating,' Rio said, concern filling her voice. 'While I understand the doctors say she needs time to adjust to allow her memory to return and that it should be allowed to happen organically, I wish I could just tell her.'

'I don't think we should say anything yet.' Lysandros wasn't about to allow Rio to slip away from him so easily, not when he was finally beginning to break through her barriers. He looked at her, his gaze drawn to her lips, to the plump softness, and the urge to take her in his arms and kiss her rushed forward again. Maybe they should go back to the villa, back to Xena's company—before he lost the battle and kissed her.

'There you are.' Xena's voice cut through the tension in the warm air and Rio had never been so pleased to be interrupted. 'I should have known you two would be making the most of a bit of time alone.'

Rio smiled, but she was far from happy. Not only did Xena believe they were still dating, but Lysandros still wanted to know why she'd ended their relationship. She pushed her anxieties aside and walked towards Xena, relieved to move away from Lysandros. Away from the sensation that she was falling back under the intoxicating spell that was weaving around them again, just as it had the first day they'd met. She focused on Xena, trying to dismiss Lysandros from her thoughts. 'We thought we'd give you some peace to rest.'

'And we wanted a bit of time alone,' Lysandros said softly as he moved to her side, putting his arm around her, sending a rush of heat hurtling through her. His voice, filled with that lethal charm, always made her fall for him a little bit more. And now was no exception, but she couldn't afford to allow him to know that.

'What is it you shouldn't say to me?' Xena narrowed her eyes and pouted mischievously at Lysandros, and Rio held her breath. Would he tell Xena? Threaten the potential return of her memory by filling it with facts she needed to remember at her own pace?

'Did I say that?' Lysandros laughed and Rio felt the ice around her heart melt a little more as his genuine concern for Xena showed in his face. He might pretend to be the hard-edged businessman, but Xena could wrap him around her little finger in no time.

'Yes, Lysandros Drakakis. I distinctly heard you say, "I don't think we should say anything yet." What's it all about?'

'Isn't it time for us to be getting to your mother's?' Rio jumped into the conversation, trying to divert Xena's attention, but she just turned Xena's teasing suspicion on herself.

'You two are up to something.' Then her eyes widened and she looked at Lysandros, laughing. 'I wonder what it can be.'

'That's for me to know, little sister, not you,' Lysandros's voice teased as he turned Xena physically around, moving her back towards the villa. 'But right now it's time to go and see Mother.'

Rio began walking back to the villa as Xena continued to taunt Lysandros, but with that teasing now in Greek, Rio had little hope of understanding. Lysandros seemed to be denying whatever it was she was saying, but from the anxious look he cast at her as they entered the villa, Rio wondered just what had been said and what wild conclusions Xena had come to.

'Mother will be anxious to see you, Xena, and happy you are in such good spirits,' Lysandros said as he locked up the villa and they made their way to the jetty and his boat.

'She'll also be happy to see you two all loved up,' Xena taunted again, that look of mischief on her face getting ever stronger.

'We are not loved up,' Rio said quickly. Too quickly, if the warning look Lysandros shot her was anything to go by.

Xena laughed and teased Lysandros again in Greek. Whatever it was she was saying, it was making him distinctly uncomfortable. 'Stop fooling around,' he said lightly to Xena, and Rio was thankful he'd brought the conversation back to English. 'Mother will be waiting.'

After a short boat ride across the sea, they arrived at the villa, and their mother, who must have been watching for them, hurried from her villa and down to the jetty. Rio hung back, wanting to give Xena a few moments alone with her mother. After enthusiastic hugs, Xena and her mother went inside, leaving Rio once again alone with Lysandros.

'Xena really seems excited,' Rio said as Lysandros secured the final rope on the boat. He looked up at her, the wind tousling his dark hair, and she curled her fingers tightly into the palms of her hands, trying to halt the thought of running them through his hair, for fear of giving in to that temptation.

'A bit too much perhaps.' He stood up and suddenly he was too close again.

He looked down at her, his expression serious and intense, and Rio's heart skipped a beat. Why did she still react like this to him? How could he still have that effect on her? He was slowly dismantling every barrier she'd put in place around herself, along with the extra defences she'd built up after Hans had tried to claim something from her she hadn't wanted to give.

She couldn't take her eyes from Lysandros, couldn't break the eye contact. Her body began to sway towards him and she bit at her bottom lip. She wanted to kiss him, wanted to go back to that moment after the recital when she'd promised him so much with just one kiss. But she couldn't. She wasn't ready for that. Not now. Not yet.

'We should go,' Lysandros said, his voice deep and firm, dragging her mind back from the past, back from what could never be again. He was angry with her. She could sense it. See it in the firm set of his shoulders as he looked at her. Guilt raced through her. She'd been ready to take their relationship further, ready to give him her virginity, and then she'd stood him up. She really did owe him an explanation. But where did she start? And with everything else going on with Xena— how?

Memories of Hans as he'd spoilt everything she could have had with Lysandros rushed at her. Any hopes for a future with Lysandros were still spoilt, unless she could talk to Lysandros, tell him what had happened that afternoon. But she wasn't ready to do that yet and she couldn't go back to where she and Lysandros had been. She would be so far out of her depth with him, she might as well be plunging into the sea. 'Yes, let's,' she said quickly. At least with Xena and his mother around, she would be safe. Safe from Lysandros and herself.

When they entered his mother's villa, Lysandros watched as she enveloped Rio in a big hug, welcoming her in stilted English. Did Rio's presence also make his mother believe they were back together? Or, worse, did his mother share Xena's hopes? That Rio was the woman he would finally settle down with?

Xena's teasing, which mercifully had been in Greek, left him in no doubt how his sister saw the situation between him and Rio. It was more worrying than her lack of memory. To Xena, Rio's presence in Greece was not simply to keep her company while she recovered from the accident. It wasn't even about his need to find out why he and Rio had broken up, not when Xena didn't recall that event. It was about his and Rio's future—together.

Xena believed wholeheartedly he was about to propose to Rio. A thought that filled Xena with much happiness. That, in itself, was shocking, but so too was the realisation that if he did propose it could help Xena, could help her to feel safe and secure and allow her memory to return.

'She is very beautiful.' His mother spoke in Greek as she came to stand beside him. He dragged himself from his thoughts and back to the moment, refusing to acknowledge the idea that was solidifying inside his mind.

He looked at Xena and Rio as they laughed and chatted together, their friendship clear. Rio was beautiful. And he still wanted her. 'She is,' he said softly.

'Don't lose her, Lysandros.' His mother's words jarred his mind and he jerked his head to look at her. She was under the same misapprehension as Xena. He could see the hope in her eyes.

'Lose Rio?' he questioned in Greek, aware the use of her name had caught Rio's attention. Xena, understanding the discussion with his mother, came to the rescue as she took Rio's arm, wanting to show her around the villa.

'You are perfect together,' his mother said as Rio and Xena left the room. 'It's time to put aside the past and settle down. Both Xena and I agree. Rio is perfect for you.'

He should be angry they had been talking, but he couldn't get the thought of having Rio back in his life out of his mind. It would give him the chance to find out what had happened to make her stand him up and what he could do to get back to the moment she'd kissed him, telling him she wanted to be his.

'You and Xena have been discussing us?' he continued in Greek, aware that Rio and Xena could return at any moment.

'We have,' his mother said with a smile, along with a little embarrassment at being caught out. 'And if you and Rio are serious about one another, maybe now would be a good time to propose—for Xena's sake.'

He shook his head. Despite his earlier thoughts, he couldn't propose. Not when they weren't even dating. 'I don't have a ring.'

'There's Grandmother's.' Xena's voice startled him

and he looked around for Rio. 'She'll be back in a moment. Oh, I can't wait to see you ask her.'

How the hell was he going to get out of this? Lysandros couldn't miss the joy on Xena's face, the excitement in her voice. If he told her she was wrong, told her he had no intention of proposing—to anyone—it might unbalance her when she least needed upset. He could hear again the doctor's words.

'Your sister's memory will return if she is happy and relaxed, but she doesn't need any emotional upset.'

'I will fetch it now,' his mother said, and Lysandros wanted to shout, no, wanted to tell her to stop. He didn't want to propose. A proposal would mean marriage. He didn't want to get engaged again, much less married. His mind whirred. But a temporary proposal, one to help Xena's recovery, would not have to lead to marriage…

It would give Xena something positive to focus on and maybe he and Rio could finally find time to deal with whatever it was that had made her run out on him. Maybe they could then share the passion of a night together? The night her last kiss had promised him?

'I have kept it all these years, sure that after Kyra you wouldn't want to shower a woman in shiny new diamonds again.' She clasped her hands in front of her chest, her eyes now sparkling with tears and excitement. 'Rio is the perfect girl to give the ring to.'

As his mother went to get the ring he rejoined Xena and Rio, who were chatting happily as if nothing untoward had ever happened, their bond of friendship clear to see. He briefly considered if the idea of a fake romance would work without this added pretence, but one look at Xena as she gave him a conspiratorial glance told him it was absolutely necessary to achieve his objective. She believed he was about to propose and anything less would upset her.

But what about Rio? Would she play along? Would she do as she'd claimed and help Xena in any way she could?

Questions raced through his mind as his mother returned to the room, handing him a small box as she passed him, before she joined Rio and Xena. Rio looked apprehensive. She knew something was going on, but did she know he was about to up the stakes? Take everything to a level neither of them wanted?

He held the old and somewhat tatty box in his hand, knowing he was at a big turning point in his life. He was about to do the one thing he'd sworn he'd never do again. Ask a woman to marry him. He pushed the thought savagely aside, along with memories of the past. All he had to remember was that it wasn't real this time. It was easier to think of it as just an extra caveat in the deal between him and Rio to help his sister.

'I have something to ask, Rio,' he said, suddenly more anxious than he'd ever been in his life, not that he'd let anyone know. What the hell was wrong with him? He struck deals for shipping contracts and his new line of luxury yachts almost daily. Had faced all sorts of drama, yet he couldn't do this. Why?

Because you got it wrong once before.

Xena looked up at him, her expression anxious, making him wonder again what it was that was bothering her so much. 'Do it, Lysandros.'

He sensed Rio watching him as he held his sister's gaze. He could feel her scrutiny burning his skin, setting fire to the passion that had simmered dangerously close to the surface the last time he'd kissed her—just hours before she'd stood him up.

'Rio…' he began, turning to her, opening his hand to reveal the box his mother had just secretly given him. The squeal of delight Xena made as a hand flew to her lips fuelled his conviction that this was the right thing to do, and he moved closer to Rio, whose brows pulled together in confusion. 'Will you do me the honour of becoming my fiancée?'

The words came far more easily than he'd thought and he opened the box as Rio's eyes widened in shock. She looked down at the ring and then back at him, questions clearly running riot in her mind.

'But…' Her voice was barely a whisper and the whole room echoed with a heaviness of expectant silence.

Slowly he took her left hand, which shook, confirming she really was afraid of what he was doing. Carefully he slid the ring onto her finger. It was a perfect fit. She looked at him, the same shock he felt flooding her eyes. 'I want us to be engaged.'

CHAPTER FOUR

'I...' RIO BEGAN, stumbling over her words.

Lysandros's fingers tightened on hers, and the soft and caring expression in his eyes, which she wasn't going to allow herself to be fooled by, intensified. She forced out her words as her heart thumped and adrenaline raced through her. 'It's an engagement ring.'

'And I want you to wear it.' Lysandros's voice was deep, full of charm. If he was trying to win her round, he was almost succeeding. This was what she'd secretly wished for once, before...

Xena squealed again and Rio looked at her friend. She was ecstatic. 'This is perfect,' Xena said, clapping her hands together despite the cast on her wrist. 'It's exactly what I've always hoped for.'

Rio's heart sank. She was trapped. Not only by the expectant look on Lysandros's handsome face but by Xena's—and even their mother's—excitement. If she turned Lysandros down, said no, wouldn't it upset Xena? Stress her in a way the doctor had warned against doing?

But if she said yes? She would be engaged to Lysandros. It would be more than just acting as if they were still dating. Far more. Could she really do that? For

Xena? Could she become engaged to Lysandros, the man she'd once wanted—and still did, if she was truly honest with herself? Could she say yes? Just for now?

She looked at Lysandros. Did he really mean it or was he doing this for Xena? Had he also realised his sister had high hopes for them as a couple? Her throat felt tight, as if she couldn't speak, and she pressed her lips together, desperate to keep the answer she was considering—purely for Xena's benefit.

Rio was acutely aware of Xena's building excitement—of her happiness. Had Lysandros planned to do this all along? Even at the hospital? Was that why he'd been so insistent she go to Greece with Xena? He could have warned her. Could have discussed it with her. Anger simmered through her and she looked into his eyes, desperate to find some way out, a way to say no that wouldn't plunge Xena back into misery. But there wasn't one. Not now he'd done this.

'Rio?' Lysandros questioned softly. So softly it was as if he really did care. 'Say something.'

He drew her closer, still holding her hand, the heat of his touch scalding her. His increasing nearness made rational thought almost impossible as, despite everything, tingles of awareness sparked over her.

'I don't know what to say.'

'Yes, of course you know,' Xena burst out. 'You say yes.'

'That would be the preferred option.' Even though Lysandros was smiling and his touch on her fingers was light and gentle, there was a gleam of determination in his dark eyes and she knew there was only one answer he wanted her to give.

'I don't know.' Could she really do this? Become

engaged, even as part of a sudden plan to help Xena? Could she say yes to the man she'd never believed would become her fiancé? It was such a cruel twist of fate after all she'd been through.

'Rio, you have to say yes,' Xena said, her words finally breaking through Rio's thoughts. The roller coaster Rio was hurtling along on was getting faster and scarier with each passing second. She wanted it to stop. Wanted to get off. 'You and Lysandros are made for each other and planning an engagement party *and then* a wedding will be so much fun. Maybe it will even help me remember again.'

Rio looked back up at Lysandros, her heart pounding as nerves surged through her. Then he smiled. A smile that had self-satisfaction stamped all over it. Damn the man. He knew she wouldn't be able to refuse Xena. He knew he'd won. Got what he wanted.

'What do you think, Rio?' He brushed her hair from her face in a caring and loving gesture, forcing Rio to fight against the flurry of butterflies in her tummy. Xena cooed over the gesture. 'Shall we get engaged? Give Xena something that could help her remember?'

'How can I not say yes?' She forced a happy smile to her face as his gaze held hers, hoping he noticed the annoyance in her eyes. Behind her, she was aware of his mother and Xena talking rapidly in Greek. Probably already making plans, if she knew Xena.

'That is exactly what I'd hoped you would say.' Was that relief as his shoulders visibly relaxed? Had he thought she'd go back on the one thing she'd agreed to—anything to help his sister?

Rio dragged in a ragged deep breath. The look in his eyes, the intensity and desire, almost fooled her that this moment was real. That he loved her, wanted her in his life. Xena jumped for joy like a kitten after twine, hugging her mother, making her realise it *was* real. But not in the way it should be. She might have just agreed to an engagement with a man she had once loved, but she knew he didn't want commitment. That this wasn't in any way real for him. Now, more than ever, she had to guard her heart, protect herself and bury all she'd once felt for him.

'We need champagne,' Xena said as she came and hugged Rio before turning to her mother. 'Let's go and find some. Leave these two alone for a moment.'

'I can't believe you just did that.' Rio's shocked words were little more than a whisper as she watched his mother and Xena leaving, talking rapidly in Greek. What had just happened? The roller coaster she desperately wanted to get off looped violently. She touched the ring on her left hand. She was engaged. To Lysandros.

'You heard Xena. It will give her something to focus on, maybe even help her regain her memory.' Lysandros spoke softly and quietly, standing far too close. Her heart raced, and even though her head was warning caution, her body began responding to that nearness in a way that terrified and excited her. He'd decided how this fake engagement was going to play out and that was that. She had no choice but to go with it or risk Xena's chance of recovering her memory.

She looked into his eyes, the darkness full of warmth, and her stomach, along with her heart, flipped over. Was he doing this, making her feel like this, purposely? She refused to think about that, refused to be anything but detached from this whole situation. She couldn't let her heart get involved in his scheme. All she had to do was go along with it for now, string the engagement out for as long as possible and, above all, remember she was doing this for Xena.

'Champagne,' Xena called, as she returned carrying a bottle, her mother following with a tray of glasses.

'Perfect,' Rio said, trying to put some enthusiasm into her voice, trying to make this whole charade seem real. For her sake as much as Xena's.

'Now we really do have something to celebrate. I'm going to be busy planning an engagement party.' The pitch of Xena's voice rose to a crescendo in her excitement and for some bizarre reason Rio found this amusing and laughed. The whole situation was so far removed from reality it didn't seem possible.

Lysandros let go of her hand, putting his arm around her, drawing her even closer to him. The shock of his body against hers silenced the laughter, probably exactly the effect he'd wanted. 'There will be no need for fuss. Rio and I only want to celebrate our engagement with those closest to us.'

The reality of what she was doing finally filtered through like a mountain stream over the rocks. 'Nothing big.' Rio began to realise the implications of their engagement. It would be almost as binding as marriage.

'Only a small family gathering,' reassured his mother as she patted Rio's arm gently, a big smile on her face and happiness sparkling in her eyes. 'Here on the island.'

Rio's heart sank. Yet more guilt to carry. Had Lysandros even thought this through? The pretence of an engagement was a lie that had far-reaching effects. The happiness on his mother's face already chastised her, ratcheting up her guilt.

'My mother will ensure Xena doesn't get carried away while we are away.' Lysandros turned her to face him, lifting her chin upwards with his thumb and forefinger. A gesture that was so intimate all she could do was swallow down her nerves.

'Away?' Panic raced through her.

'Now I have officially proposed, we can spend some time together, making up for the weeks we have been apart.'

Rio's cheeks burned with embarrassment at what he was insinuating. Did he have no shame? To say such things in front of his mother and sister? She nodded, unable to break eye contact with him, becoming more unaware of what was going on around her with every passing second. As if they were already totally alone.

'That would be perfect,' she said softly, looking into his eyes, playing the role of adoring fiancée to the full. She might well be dragging them further into this charade, but she wanted him to feel the same way she had when he'd sprung his proposal on her.

'My yacht is ready to leave immediately. We will spend the weekend together.' He smiled at her, his thumb lightly brushing to and fro on her chin, causing sensations she had no right to be feeling.

'How romantic,' said Xena with a sigh, reminding them both they were certainly not alone right now. 'I *always* knew you two would be perfect for one another.'

Lysandros laughed. A deep sexy sound, adding to her current torture, and she was thankful for Xena's interruption, for the reminder they weren't alone, that this wasn't real. 'In that case, you would have no objection to me whisking my brand-new fiancée away right now.'

'Just go.' Xena laughed, the sound so light and carefree, so like the girl she'd been before the accident, it intensified Rio's guilt, adding weight to Lysandros's unspoken argument that getting engaged—temporarily—was the right thing to do. For Xena at least.

Lysandros took Rio's hand in his once more and led her away from the villa. Away from his mother and sister's scrutiny. He wrapped his hand tightly around hers, taking a deep breath as he felt the stone of the engagement ring pressing into his fingers. The shock at what he'd just done combined with a slowly intensifying desire for a woman who had turned him down, forming a heady cocktail.

'Xena looked pleased.' Rio's voice was hard and accusing, dousing the rising desire in him. He let her hand go, unable to bear the warmth of her skin on his, heightening his body's response to her.

'You told me you'd do anything to help Xena.' He couldn't keep the irritation from his voice, the growl reminiscent of one of the island's many wild cats when cornered. And right now that was exactly how he felt. Cornered by the hope in his mother's eyes. Cornered by Xena's excitement. But like any animal in that situation, he refused to show his weakness or his doubt. He had to remain strong and in control.

He could still see his sister, smiling. Could still see his mother, hope lighting her eyes, leaving him in no doubt she expected so much from him, from the marriage proposal. He saw again Rio looking up at him, the unspoken attraction between them clear in her eyes, felt the powerful passion she could so easily induce. He had to remember why they were really doing this, and that it was the right thing to do. Already there was a big difference in Xena.

'You took the idea of a fake relationship to a completely different level.' She hurled the words at him as they made their way to his speedboat, which would take them to his yacht anchored at sea. 'You're the one who suggested we stage a romance, and then, if that wasn't enough, you took the elaborate charade one step further by proposing.' She glared at him. 'What was that all about?'

Her voice had risen with each word, anger mixing with panic in her eyes as she turned to look at him. The sudden urge to pull her against him was too intense. He wanted to hold her tightly, kiss her until every drop of anger melted into the sort of passion he knew she would be capable of. Her outward appearance of innocence didn't fool him. Beneath that indifferent exterior was a passionate woman. He'd tasted it in her kiss after the recital.

'What was it all about?' He threw her question back at her, fighting hard to ignore his increasing need for her, drawing instead on exasperation that she was unaware of what he'd been doing. 'It was all about making our relationship convincing.'

'Convincing?' Anger slipped quickly from her voice, which had become a husky whisper of confusion.

She was giving in. He was going to get exactly what he wanted out of this arrangement. Their engagement had become far more than not stressing his sister. He now had Rio to himself and could finally get to the bottom of why she'd abruptly ended their relationship. A relationship that, despite not getting further than passionate kisses, had held the promise in each and every one of so much more, and not just physically. For the first time since Kyra, he'd wanted that.

'What happens when we split up? Because we can't remain engaged. What is Xena going to do then?' Rio's harsh words struck a chord. 'Or worse, what happens when she regains her memory?'

The image of his mother's face and the hope in her eyes flashed before him, reminding him of the one thing, as the only son, he had failed her in—settling down and having a family.

'I assume your reckless plan involves us splitting up as soon as that happens?'

'When the time is right, we will do exactly that.' That time would be once he'd found out everything he needed to know. In the meantime he'd enjoy being in Rio's company.

'I still can't believe you did that—and without a word of warning to me.'

'Engagement is the only way to convince Xena this is real.'

'But engagement?' she blurted out. 'That's so final. So permanent.'

'Not as permanent as marriage.' The truth of that hit him as he looked into Rio's eyes. 'Think of this engagement as a deal.'

'A deal?' Her eyes widened in shock. 'And what will this deal entail?'

'We will allow Xena to plan an engagement party, but once Xena's memory returns, we can call off the deal, end the engagement. Unless you can fill in the blanks for Xena—and me?'

She gasped and looked at him, her brows pulling together in an angry line. 'You are ruthless.'

She turned from him as if she was about to walk away. 'Yes, I am, Rio, and I always get what I want.' And right now he wanted her.

She swung back to face him. 'Is this really the way to help Xena?'

'It is the only way to help Xena. You and I will be engaged and we will remain so for as long as it takes for Xena to regain her health.'

'Then what?' she snapped at him.

'Then you can return to England.'

'You are quite something, Lysandros Drakakis.' The disbelief in her voice chipped at his conscience, dented his protective armour, rekindling the emotions she'd stirred in him before ending things between them.

'Your compliment is well received,' he taunted her, liking the flush of anger on her pale cheeks.

'What happens when Xena expects us to get married, when she—?' she began, but he cut across her before she had any notions of anything else.

'As I have just said, it's to help Xena. Once her memory has returned there will be no need for such a course of action. We can simply call off the engagement.'

She inhaled deeply as if trying to calm herself, and he smothered a smile of amusement. She certainly had hidden fire within her. 'And what will we do while we are engaged to make it convincing?'

'Give the outward appearance of a couple in love— madly and passionately in love.'

The sound of the clear waters of the sea against his boat as they stood on the jetty infiltrated his thoughts. He looked beyond Rio, to his mother's villa in the distance, and saw Xena and his mother standing on the terrace. He looked back at Rio.

'Xena and my mother are watching us right now, so if you meant what you said in the hospital, that you would do anything to help Xena, even make her believe our engagement is real, you will now put your arms around my neck and kiss me.'

'I will do no such thing.'

'Does that mean you lied to me, Rio?' He moved a little closer, so that Xena and his mother would think it an intimate gesture. Heated desire surged through him, catching him off guard. Just being that close to her was a temptation, making his voice fiercer than he intended. 'I don't like lies, Rio.'

If he wasn't mistaken, she actually gulped. Had she been lying? And if so, what else was she lying about?

'We don't need to go that far. We don't need to kiss.' Her voice wavered but his determination to do the right thing for his sister didn't.

'This is a deal, Rio, a deal between the two of us to help Xena overcome the effects of the accident. All you need to do is play out a romantic engagement, act the part of being in love and kiss me.'

She shook her head slowly, but her eyes still held his, her full lips parted slightly, igniting his desire once more. 'You really expect me to kiss you? Now? Here?'

'Neither Xena or my mother will be convinced by anything less than seeing us not only engaged but as lovers.'

Rio paled so rapidly he wondered if she was going to pass out. 'I can't believe I've agreed to this.'

'Think of it as sealing our contract.' He kept his voice low and gentle, her resistance beginning to dwindle. 'Remember how happy Xena was just now. All we need to do is provide the illusion of romance between us—for a couple of weeks at least.'

'I can't kiss you.' Her voice was a breathy whisper, sending shivers of passion all over him.

'You've kissed me before,' he said, watching the turmoil in her eyes. 'Do you really dislike me that much now?'

'Don't.' She looked down and he wanted to lift her chin, make her look at him, make her see the desire in his eyes.

'Kiss me, Rio.' His voice had become a hoarse whisper. 'The desire hasn't gone away, has it?'

'No, but things have changed.' She looked up at him, urgency in her gaze. 'I've changed.'

'Then perhaps you should tell me.' He brushed his fingers over her cheek, wanting to understand, wanting to know.

She shook her head rapidly. 'I can't—not yet.'

'But you will tell me? Soon?' he whispered, trying to keep the annoyance from his voice. Yet again she was backing out of giving him the answers he needed. Patience was what he needed—and charm. He'd seduce the answers from her, slowly and subtly.

She nodded and looked up at him. 'I will, Lysandros, I promise.'

'Then for now I will wait. Time alone will help. A long romantic weekend on my yacht to relax with one another will be just that. It's also the sort of thing Xena would expect me to do and will reinforce our engagement.'

'I'm not sure,' Rio said huskily, and he knew he was getting to her.

'I am.' He smiled down at her, saw her lips part, heard the ragged breath she drew in.

'What will happen afterwards? When we come back?'

'You want to spend more time with me, *agape mou*?' Her eyes widened in shock as she realised where she'd inadvertently led the conversation.

'That's not what I meant.' The defensiveness of her tone couldn't hide her confusion—or the attraction she was clearly fighting.

'I will spend most of my time working in Athens and you will be here with Xena.' He tried to put her mind at rest as well as tell himself what would happen. It was far more than having work to do; it was putting the temptation she aroused in him out of his reach. Give her the space Xena had told him she wanted, the distance he sensed she still needed.

'That's it? Nothing more?'

He smiled, using the charm he was renowned for. 'Xena and Mother are still there, still watching.' She frowned up at him, her lips pouting in an inviting way. 'Step into my embrace, Rio, and kiss me.'

Rio's eyes widened with shock and she stayed very still for a few seconds. She wasn't going to provide the evidence of being in love, the kiss that would seal their deal and convince his sister and mother.

'Kiss me, Rio.'

She hesitated then slowly moved towards him. He put his arms around her, holding her gently at her lower back as she put her arms up around the back of his neck, her sun hat dangling loosely from one hand on his back.

Lust leapt to life within him as he brought her body against his, the shock on her face leaving him in no doubt she'd felt it too. Her breathing was deep and slow as they moved closer, bodies pressing together, her eyes darkening and locking with his.

Seconds later he claimed her lips, the sweetness of them almost taking his breath away. He tightened his hold on her, pulling her closer, giving himself up to the intensity of the kiss. Rio murmured with pleasure and he kissed her harder, deeper, slipping his tongue into her mouth, demanding so much more from her. Passion exploded, and he forgot it was meant to be part of an act. Desire crashed over him, reminding him, if he'd needed it, how much he wanted Rio.

Without thought for anything else, his hands slid down her back to the curve of her bottom. Her arms tightened around his neck as he moulded her against the hardness of his erection. She groaned with pleasure, making him even harder as she moved against him, tormenting and exciting him.

Being temporarily engaged to this woman was not going to be a hardship at all.

Rio could hardly breathe and certainly couldn't think as hot pleasure rushed all around her, awakening the woman within her. The fear of being kissed by a man, of being held close against his body after Hans had tried to force himself on her, was swept aside by raw desire.

But wasn't that dangerous?

She shouldn't want to allow herself the pleasure of Lysandros's kiss, or the sensation of sparks of desire shooting around her as she felt the evidence of his need for her. She shouldn't want more than the kiss, but the desire was too powerful to resist. He was too powerful to resist.

He pulled back from her, whispering against her lips, intensifying the surge of pleasure pulsing through her so wildly. 'A kiss such as that would convince even me that you still desired me.'

'I was doing it for Xena.' She pushed herself away from the temptation of kissing him again, of giving in to the pleasure of his caresses, of needing to feel his body pressed erotically against her.

He laughed. A sound so sexy she shivered. 'Then I do after all believe you. You will do anything for Xena.'

'I meant it,' she said, stepping back from him, disengaging her heated body from his, acutely aware of the danger he presented to her uninitiated body. She needed to be far more careful. She *had* to resist his potent charms, his seductive caresses and his passionate kisses.

'In that case, we will return to Xena's villa so that you may pack for our *romantic* weekend aboard my yacht.'

'We are leaving straight away?' Did he really mean to whisk her off right now? How could she spend any more time in his company when she'd just reacted like that to his kiss?

'What about Xena?'

'She and my mother have much planning to do while we are away spending time alone—keeping up the pretence of being in love.'

That determined and powerful authority had returned to his voice. At least that was easier to deal with. It was far more preferable, leaving her with more control than the hard-to-resist seduction he'd just proved he was more than capable of—and which she'd proved she was far from able to resist.

CHAPTER FIVE

THE GENTLE ROCKING of the yacht had drawn Rio from her sleep. Sleep that had been hard to find the previous night with her body still humming with the need that kiss outside his mother's villa had evoked. A need that had only intensified during the evening as she and Lysandros had dined aboard his yacht. Every time his eyes had met hers, she'd seen the flames licking higher, making the air crackle with sexual tension, making her want to be kissed again.

The warm evening air had been heavy with desire and it had scared Rio. Scared her because she'd wanted to act on it, wanted to take herself back to the moment after the recital when she'd teasingly asked Lysandros to take her to dinner, to spend the entire night with her.

She'd wanted that same thing last night. Had wanted it so much but was thankful that, despite the desire in every look he'd given her, he hadn't acted on it. He hadn't tried to touch her in any way. When Lysandros had insisted she take the large and luxurious master cabin alone, she'd been grateful. He'd saved her from herself and as soon as she'd shut the door she'd locked it, not against Lysandros but against the urge to go back

to him and allow the passion between them to ignite—
fully and completely.

He was so powerful, so dominating. She wasn't ready
to let go of her fears and be intimate with him, despite
the burning need for him. The decision to spend a night
with him after the recital had taken weeks to come to
and Hans's attempt on her had taken her so far backwards she needed to start again. She couldn't allow
herself to be carried away by a heady kiss. She needed
to find again the woman who'd seductively kissed Lysandros that afternoon at the recital.

That would take time to rediscover and, no matter
how charming Lysandros was, she couldn't do anything
until she was completely ready.

'Rio?' As if conjured up by her imagination, Lysandros's voice sounded from the other side of the door,
making her heart pound erratically.

She opened the cabin door, looking into his handsome face. Her breath caught at the image he created
as he stood there dressed more casually than she'd ever
seen him but looking just as lethal as he did in his designer suit. The effect he had on her was so profound
she couldn't say anything.

'I have arranged a special breakfast for us as we are
supposed to be newly engaged lovers.' His dark eyes
held a hint of mischief, a smile playing around his lips.
Was that why he seemed more devastatingly handsome,
more charming than normal, because he was smiling
instead of betraying the hard-edged businessman she
knew he really was? Was the smile and charm part
of the act? Of course it was. She chastised herself for
thinking otherwise.

'Very thorough.' Rio finally found her voice and

joined in with the game he was playing, wondering what his crew thought about their separate sleeping arrangements. It certainly wouldn't look like they were lovers, and as he must have brought so many women to his yacht, she was sure they'd never occupied separate beds. 'But won't it have undermined your engagement plan as we spent the night apart?'

'Are you saying you would rather share my bed?' A wicked grin slipped over his face, sending her pulse rate soaring, setting her cheeks on fire.

'No,' she said quickly. Too quickly, if the look on his face was anything to go by. She blushed, remembering how he'd made her feel last night. How she'd wanted nothing more than to share his bed. 'But I'm sure it's not what you normally do when you have female guests aboard.'

'True.' He stepped closer, the spark in his eyes leaving her in no doubt the desire for her was still there and that he was enjoying her embarrassment. 'You are my fiancée and, as far as anyone else is concerned, we are waiting until we are married to share a bed, are we not?'

'N-no one will b-believe that.' She stammered over her response as an image of her sharing a bed with this handsome Greek filled her mind. She couldn't allow herself to imagine such things. 'Not when you are known for being such a...' She struggled for the right word.

'Playboy?' he offered, amusement mixing deliciously with his seductive voice. 'You, *agape mou*, have stolen my heart, made me turn my back on my bachelor playboy ways. What is so unbelievable about that?'

'I doubt many people will believe *I've* made you change.' She had to keep him at a distance, had to stop this light flirting. She wasn't the same woman who'd once been ready to give him her virginity, her love. 'What matters is that Xena believes it. I don't really care what anyone else thinks.'

He had the nerve to laugh at her and that sexy laughter almost unleashed the desire she was so determined to keep hidden. As if sensing her turmoil, he smiled at her, setting free his lethal charm. 'Breakfast, *agape mou*? A romantic breakfast for lovers?'

Could she do this? Act as if they were lovers? A newly engaged and happy couple? It had been everything she'd secretly wanted—once. She wasn't at all sure she could keep her heart from being broken, but she had to do this. For Xena. If it wasn't for the accident having wiped out Xena's memory, she wouldn't even be in Greece, let alone on this yacht with Lysandros. Whatever else she did, she had to remember that. 'Fine. I will be ready in five minutes.'

She used those five minutes to steady her heartbeat and compose herself. She needed to maintain a prickly hostility towards him, bury the attraction she was fighting. He had to believe there wasn't or couldn't be anything between them. It was the only way to keep her heart unscathed and play the role of temporary fiancée.

She picked up her sunglasses and sun hat and with renewed determination left the safety of the cabin. The sheer luxury of the yacht still amazed her as she walked up onto the deck. She recalled Xena's pride that he'd turned an ordinary shipping business into one that supplied the rich and famous all around the world with luxury yachts, and being here, in this almost fantasy setting, she could understand how it had become so successful.

'You look very beautiful.' The soft seductive purr of his voice as he took her hand, guiding her towards the stern of the yacht, sent a flurry of butterflies all through her. He was taking the role of a man in love with his fiancée very seriously, playing it out to perfection. How she longed for it to be real, to be able to go back to the recital and never leave to meet Hans, never go through that life-changing moment.

'You mentioned breakfast?' The teasing note in her voice was so unlike her that she couldn't help but blush. What was she doing, flirting with him? None of this was real. His proposal. Even the beautiful ring she wore. It was merely a temporary arrangement, one he'd already decided would end the moment Xena recovered her memory.

Yet despite knowing this, her attraction to him was getting stronger each day. She was in danger of losing herself, her heart to him. But she couldn't do that, not when she had no idea how he would react if he knew why she'd stood him up, why she'd ended their relationship so abruptly. He was a man who'd avoided all emotional involvement, so surely wouldn't want to deal with that kind of revelation, not when she'd need his support, his strength to make it.

She couldn't look at him, but the gentleness of his voice calmed her. 'I did. This way.'

He led her down the steps to the platform at the end of the yacht, climbing into the small boat and turning to look up at her. She hid her confusion over her emotions behind a question. 'Where are we going?'

He quirked a brow at her as she finally found the courage to look into his handsome face. That sexy devil-may-care smile tugged at the attraction she was desperately trying to ignore. 'Breakfast awaits.'

With his help, she stepped into the small boat, the motion of it unsteadying her, but not as much as Lysandros did as he held her arms, drawing her close to him. She looked up at him, that spark it was so crucial to ignore zapping between them, stronger than the sunshine sparkling on the sea around them.

'I wasn't expecting that,' she said, her voice far too husky for her liking. She couldn't do anything other than look into his eyes.

'Neither was I.' His eyes, dark and heavy with the same kind of desire she'd seen yesterday in the moments after they'd kissed, pierced into her soul. Her breath caught audibly and she bit her teeth into her bottom lip.

'I meant the wobble of the boat,' she quickly defended herself, but from his slow smile he was as aware of that desire as she was—and how it had made her feel.

The temptation to slide his fingers into Rio's hair, to brush them against the softness of her cheeks and taste the sweetness of her lips, as he had done yesterday, was almost impossible to resist. The memory of that kiss still burned on Lysandros's lips, and the heady desire, which had rampaged through him as he'd held her against him, surged forward again.

That kiss should prove to Rio they were good together. For him, it had rekindled all the desire for her he'd been keeping in check on each date they'd enjoyed. It had brought it all back. Stronger than ever—and harder to resist.

'Then we had better get to shore.' He focused his

mind on the task at hand instead of the memory of how she'd felt in his arms, against his body.

'Yes, I think that would be a good idea.' Her voice remained husky as she moved away from him, sitting down in the boat. He turned his attention to starting the motor and getting them to the beach. At least that was a normality that would take his mind off how she made him feel.

As the little boat moved quickly across the water Lysandros watched Rio, taking in her long, slender, tanned legs, still bemused by the fact that she'd chosen white shorts and a loose-fitting red-and-white-striped blouse. Any other woman he'd spent time on his yacht with would have emerged clad in the skimpiest of bikinis, even at the beginning of the day. It seemed that Rio wanted to conceal herself, but that didn't prevent him imagining her in a bikini.

'Here we are,' he said as the small boat pulled alongside the purpose-built jetty at the end of the beach, fighting the surge of heated lust as that image burned in his mind.

'This looks very secluded.' She stepped out onto the jetty, looking around the small sandy cove, appearing in awe of her surroundings. 'And very beautiful.'

'This is the perfect beach on which to have breakfast.' It was also a beach he'd never taken another woman to, and for reasons he couldn't yet fathom, that felt right. Everything about being with Rio was uncharted waters and he wanted this weekend to be the same.

For a moment she held his gaze, questions showing in her eyes, obliterating any of the desire he thought he'd seen earlier. Was she suddenly nervous of being here with him? Was the thought of being alone with him too much?

He sensed the need to tread carefully around her. If he was ever going to find out why Rio had abruptly changed her mind about dating him, he needed to be even more patient and gentle than before.

He still didn't understand it. One minute she'd been alive with joy at the recital, flirting playfully with him, letting him know she was ready to take their relationship further. Ready to be his—all night. Then it had all changed.

What had happened after she'd left him to meet the conductor? What had happened to make her stand him up? No message. Nothing. He'd never been stood up before and had tried to call Xena, not knowing how to deal with it. But Xena hadn't known—at least, not that night.

He needed to know why, what she felt for him, then and now. For some reason, one he wasn't yet ready to explore, it mattered to him what Rio thought. He wanted to reassure her that the undeniable attraction that hummed in the air around them whenever they were together was right on so many levels.

'My goodness,' she gasped in surprise as she saw the picnic laid out ready for them. 'When did you do all this?'

'A member of my crew set this up a short while ago.' That was the kind of reaction he'd hoped for when he'd planned this romantic picnic breakfast on a deserted beach.

She looked around the beach as if searching for that crew member. She was afraid to be alone with him. Was it because she didn't trust him or because she didn't trust herself? Was the attraction he was certain she felt for him the same attraction he felt for her, too strong to resist?

'And this is a private beach?' There was a definite tremor in her voice, a clear hint of anxiety.

'I had the distinct impression you would rather our romance and engagement were played out as little as possible in the public eye, so coming here like this seemed the perfect solution.' His motivation for this had been so far from that and guilt stabbed at him. All he'd wanted had been to resume where the kiss had ended yesterday. Take it to the passionate conclusion it had promised.

'Thank you.' Her voice was throaty and incredibly sexy.

He sat on the edge of the white blanket that had been spread out in readiness for them, opening the picnic basket, taking out waffles, fruit and the flowers he'd requested. Rio stood for a second, watching, before kneeling on the blanket. He could sense her suspicion, feel her wary gaze on him.

'We will, however, have to be seen out together at least once before our engagement party.'

'Seen out?' She looked at him sharply. The pleasure at the picnic he'd arranged had diminished the reality of their situation, but she must realise that while she played the role of his fiancée, she would be expected to be at his side when he attended important functions. Especially the charity ball in Athens. It was a charity he'd started and Xena would ask questions if Rio didn't go. He'd always had a beautiful woman on his arm at such events. This time it would be Rio. His temporary fiancée.

'It's an annual event I always attend. A charity close

to my heart. Xena and most definitely my mother would find it strange if you didn't accompany me.'

'Surely it would be better if I stayed with Xena? After all, that's why I came, to keep her company, help her recover.' There was an element of pleading in her voice, but he refused to be drawn by it.

He might have used Xena as the reason to bring Rio to Greece, but if he was completely honest, it had been for his own reasons. He'd always found it difficult to let anyone emotionally close and Kyra's deceit had only intensified that. From the moment he and Rio had met, she'd had a strange power over him. She'd begun to prise open the door to his emotions. A door he'd slammed shut after Kyra's rejection. But Rio was changing that, and he'd refused to accept they were over. Not when there had been so much desire simmering around them. She made him feel and he wanted that, wanted to open himself to her, to connect on a level he'd blocked out for so long.

He poured the coffee, allowing the strong aroma to sharpen his senses. 'You are a true friend to Xena, doing all you can to help her recover.' He didn't miss the slight lift of her delicate brows. He hadn't been referring to their engagement deal, but she'd taken it that way.

'You didn't leave me much choice, Lysandros,' she berated him, swiftly taking the opportunity he'd unwittingly created to let him know her true thoughts. 'Even in the hospital you made me feel I wasn't a good friend if I didn't agree to your suggestions.'

The annoyance in her face was clear and he tried to soothe her ruffled mood. 'Xena is happy, settled. Everything the doctor said she needed to be to get over her amnesia. I hope that happens soon. I don't like seeing her like this.'

Rio changed position, going from kneeling to curling her legs at one side, and she couldn't look him in the eyes. 'I hope so too.' She looked down, her attention intensely focused on the picnic before her, which they had both forgotten. He leant closer, needing to look into her face, to see the expression her beauty could so easily mask.

She still didn't look at him, still focusing all her attention on the picnic as if it were a lifeline.

'I want Xena to get better as much as you do. Why do you think we are doing this?' He paused, allowing the soft rush of the waves onto the beach to fill the silence.

'But now we are engaged.' She looked into his eyes, the passion of her words taking him aback.

'An engagement that will end as soon as Xena's memory returns.' He held her gaze, watched as her eyes darkened and, just as they had yesterday, her lips parted invitingly. 'Is being engaged to me really so bad?'

'No.' Her soft whisper spurred him on. 'There was a time when...'

Her words trailed off, taking him back to that afternoon in London. Back to the recital, the kiss that had left her glowing with desire. How could that have changed so swiftly?

'What happened, Rio? Why didn't you meet me that evening?'

Rio shook her head, refusing to say anything. He sensed he was closer to discovering why and he needed to know. This was more than just wounded male pride.

'Did you regret saying you wanted to spend the night with me? Did you change your mind?'

Rio looked at him as if she was considering her answer, as if she was trying to find a way to not admit what she really wanted to admit.

'It wouldn't have mattered if you had,' he continued when she didn't answer. 'I'm not in the habit of forcing myself on a woman.'

Her eyes widened, and she dragged in a long, deep breath. Did she really believe that he was like that? He touched her hand gently. 'Rio?'

'Yes. I changed my mind.' There was so much sadness, so much emotion in that answer that for a moment he couldn't say anything, the sound of the sea enveloping them.

'Why, Rio?' Eventually he found the words. 'Why, when you seemed so happy?'

He frowned. Why was she holding out on him? Suspicion and fury blended together. He looked at Rio as large tears sprang from her eyes and began to roll down her cheeks.

'Rio.' Shocked by the wave of protectiveness that had surged over him, he moved to take her in his arms and offer comfort.

She curled into him, her cheek pressing against his chest as he knelt next to her. She shuddered, fighting for control, and instinctively he pressed his lips against the top of her head. The fresh scent of her shampoo invaded his senses. Heated memories erupted, reminding him of the desire just kissing her could evoke. Even a compassionate kiss like that.

He looked up at the blue sky, the heat of the sun warming his face. As he looked back down, Rio pulled slightly away from him, looking up. Her eyes, still heavy with tears, searched his, and all he could think about was kissing her and making her sadness go away.

He lowered his head and moved closer, so close he was almost touching her face, almost kissing her. With a force that shocked him she pushed away from him.

'I can't do this.' She leapt to her feet, her breathing hard and fast. 'I can't kiss you again. I don't want to.'

She turned and walked away from him, stumbling as she hurried towards the jetty and the boat he'd tied up there not so very long ago.

'Rio. Wait.' He hurried after her, bemused by her sudden change of mood. She'd looked like she'd wanted to kiss him. Her lips had parted, waiting for his to claim them. Then her mood had changed, drastically and quickly, because he'd tried to kiss her. He'd done almost the exact thing he'd just claimed he wasn't in the habit of doing.

He caught up with her, grasping her hand, pulling her to a stop, needing her to look at him. When she did the wildness, the fear in her eyes shocked him.

'I should never have come to Greece. I should never have agreed to this, any of it. I can't do it, Lysandros. I just can't.'

He had to know what this was about. 'When you kissed me at the recital, it was a kiss of passion, full of meaning. It was there yesterday too, Rio. What exactly is it you're scared of? Me?'

She tried to pull her hand free of his, but he didn't want to let her go. He wanted to hold her closer still, keep her safe from whatever it was she feared.

'Yes.' She fired the word at him faster than a bullet from a gun. 'I'm scared of you, so just let me go.'

'Scared of me?' He couldn't help the incredulous

tone of his voice as anger and confusion mixed together, making a potent cocktail.

He saw the same fear in her eyes that he'd seen yesterday when he'd told her to kiss him. Then he'd thought it was just the fear of confronting the attraction between them. Now he wasn't so sure. This was not flirtatious and teasing. This was something more. Something that instinctively he knew would demand so much more from him than just proving he desired her.

Rio could hardly believe it had come to this. Lysandros had unwittingly unleashed that painful moment when Hans had taken advantage of her. Now Lysandros demanded to know exactly what it was that had made her end things between them. But she couldn't tell him. If their engagement were real, if he truly wanted more than just passion from her, she might be able to. She could tell him if he felt the same way about her as she did about him, although she was fighting it with every breath. But none of this was real. Not the romantic breakfast. Not the ring on her finger. Not even wanting her to kiss him. It was all an act. An elaborate charade from a man who didn't want a deeper or emotional relationship.

'It was more the situation than you.' Rio bluffed her way out of the corner she'd managed to back herself into. She couldn't tell him anything now.

Hans had most definitely taken advantage of all her barriers being lowered. He might no longer be a threat to her, or any other woman, but Lysandros was. For very different reasons he was a threat to her. She *did* want more. Wanted him.

She longed to be held by him. Kissed by him. Longed

for him to show her what passion and desire could truly be like. But she couldn't risk her heart. Not when she knew he'd already planned the end of their fake engagement.

'The situation?' His voice had deepened, impatience laced through it.

'I don't want to be engaged, Lysandros—to you or anyone else.'

'Neither do I.' The cold, hard truth rushed at her like an icy wave on the beach during an English winter. 'My ex-fiancée destroyed any ideals I had of marriage when she was unfaithful. Marriage is not for me.'

'But your mother is looking to you for grandchildren?' Curiosity forced the question out. Lysandros was finally allowing her to slip behind his defensive barrier.

'She is, but hopefully Xena will marry and one day have children—the next generation to inherit the family business.'

His emotionless words left her in no doubt how adamant he was about not being a father. It was another reason not to allow her emotions to become any more attached to him. She had begun to question her haste at ending their relationship, had started to see a different side to him. One that put her heart in danger, making her want a future with him, but now she knew it could never be.

'Lysandros…' she began cautiously, wishing she could tell him the truth, but the dark depths of his eyes, devoid of all emotion, snatched away her frail confidence, snuffed out the fleeting opportunity to say anything.

'I apologise for trying to kiss you just now.' The sincerity in his voice touched her heart, adding to her confusion of how she felt about him, what she really wanted. 'You have my word that I will not force you to do anything you do not want to do.'

He reached out and placed his hand over hers, sending a shock wave of pleasure rushing through her. It was a touch that told her he cared, told her he would be true to his word. 'If anything happens between us, it will be because *you* want it to.'

'What we had, before. It was good, but…' She paused as her heart and her head did battle. Her head won. The moment to tell him the truth had gone. 'I can never be what you need.'

'If that is what you believe then I must accept it.' The softness of his voice did untold things to her as her heart flipped over, disappointment filling her at what could have been, what could still be, if only she'd been brave enough. He made her feel unsure. She'd judged him harshly, believing his interest in her to be purely physical. Now she wasn't so convinced. Maybe beneath the hardened exterior he was far more tender and caring than he'd allowed her to think.

'And what about our so-called engagement? And the need to act out the romance?' She kept her voice brusque and businesslike, determined he wouldn't know just how much her heart was breaking right now.

'We need only return from this weekend as a happy couple. A bit of hand-holding and smiling should convince both Xena and my mother. I have business meetings all week, so you can have time alone with Xena on the island, but I would like you to attend the charity party in Athens next weekend.'

'Is that really necessary?' Her shoulders drooped

at the thought of being paraded around publicly as his fiancée.

'Just a few hours at the party by my side, but the weekend away in Athens will further convince Xena and my mother that after I vowed I would never marry, you and I are engaged.'

'Do you honestly think that is necessary?'

He nodded. 'I do, Rio.' He looked at her, his eyes searching hers. 'We are doing this for Xena, remember?'

The unspoken words hung in the air between them. He was wrapping it all up as something honourable he was doing for his sister. And if she too wanted to help Xena, she had little choice but to accept his terms.

CHAPTER SIX

SINCE THEIR CONVERSATION on the beach Rio had been on edge. Completely trapped by this charade of an engagement. Lysandros hadn't spoken of it again during lunch on the yacht and had disappeared below deck soon afterwards, leaving her to enjoy the warm sunshine. She tried to put everything—the kiss, the engagement and him—out of her mind and relax, but just knowing he was nearby, just remembering the way he'd held her so gently, as if he cared, made that impossible.

'Would you like to have a swim?' Rio looked at Lysandros and her pulse leapt. He was wearing only black trunks. She couldn't take her eyes off him, the afternoon sunshine showcasing his toned physique to perfection. His bronzed skin glistened.

She blinked rapidly, fighting for words—any words. 'A swim?'

His wickedly sexy smile left her in no doubt he'd noticed her reaction to him as she'd studied the muscled contours of his tanned body. His roguish tone made her heart flip and her stomach flutter as he stood there expectantly, waiting for her to join him. All she could do was look up at him. All that exposed flesh. That overpoweringly sexy masculinity. Damn him. Was he doing it on purpose? Pushing her to the edge? Proving a point? That their attraction was far from over?

'Yes, a swim.' He reached for her hand, his arms flexing as his muscles rippled beneath the sun's rays. 'It's very freeing, swimming in the sea. You should try it.'

She thought of the costume she'd packed, the daring one Xena had convinced her to buy last year and she hadn't yet had the courage or opportunity to wear. It was the only one she had with her but the thought of swimming in the cool, clear waters was very tempting.

'I will go and change.' She allowed him to help her up, allowed him to keep her hand in his, her eyes firmly fixed on his face as she came up close to his muscled chest. She inhaled deeply, taking in his scent, making herself dizzy with desire. She'd never seen a man naked, or even been this close to one who was all but naked. He was totally overpowering.

'Don't be too long or I'll have to come and find you.' The teasing note of his voice sent a shiver of pleasure down her spine and she smiled boldly at him, feeling the Rio Hans had almost obliterated pushing back to the fore. She could feel herself beginning to relent, beginning to want Lysandros all over again. Her body wanted him, longed for what could have been. As did her heart. But her head continued to reign supreme, keeping her safe.

She laughed lightly, desperate to find herself again, to once more be the woman who had told Lysandros she wanted to be with him all night. 'In that case, I will be back as soon as I can.'

He raised his brows, a smile on his lips, disarming that all-too-powerful control he usually radiated but in turn ramping up his sex appeal. 'Make sure you are.'

She changed so quickly she didn't give herself time to worry about how the black swimsuit looked on her, how the cut-away waist made it virtually a bikini. She was too flustered by the image of Lysandros, burned into her mind, all but naked.

As she reached the bathing platform at the end of the yacht she suddenly felt far too exposed. Lysandros was in the sea, his arms moving with ease as he trod water, his gaze all but devouring her. She could feel the heat of it from where she stood and the only way to avoid it was to either turn and run back to her cabin or jump into the water. His threat of coming to find her if she didn't join him filled her mind. It would be safer to be in the water than out of it.

Without any further hesitation she stepped off the bathing board and sank into the water. It was much cooler than she'd expected and she gasped with shock. She'd never swum in the sea before. At first there was a moment of panic as she sensed the depth below her, the vastness of the cool water around her. It reflected perfectly how she felt each time Lysandros looked at her, and those feelings were getting stronger. She panicked, unable to co-ordinate her arms and legs into anything that resembled swimming. The truth of her thoughts numbed her as rapidly as the cool water.

Just as she thought she was going under the surface of the water she felt Lysandros's arms around her, his body against hers as he pulled her close, powering them both the short distance back to the bathing board. Her breath was coming hard and fast as she looked up at him but it had nothing to do with the water. It had everything to do with the man who held her.

'Are you okay?' The same concern filled his voice

that he'd shown her at the hospital when he'd crouched before her. She could almost believe he cared for her.

She should look away from him, try to avoid all he was fooling her into. She should move her body away from his, but she couldn't. A spell had been woven around them, wrapping them together in the water. 'I haven't done this before.'

Her breathless declaration left her wondering what she was referring to. Swimming in the sea or being held by a man who was almost naked, a man whose muscled body was pressed against hers as he held her. The cool water accentuated every move he made as he kept them afloat.

It was wild. Erotic. After her experience with Hans, it should make her panic, but that was the last thing she felt. Right now, she wanted to stay in Lysandros's arms, to savour the protection and safety offered by them. She looked into his eyes and knew it was too late. She was falling for him all over again. She wanted him more than ever. If he tried to kiss her now she wouldn't ever want him to stop.

'I need a swim.' His voice was gruff as he let her go, leaving her clutching the bathing board rail. His eyes bored into hers and she couldn't find any words to hide how she felt right at this moment, to tell him she didn't want him to swim away from her.

With a rush of water, he pushed away from her, his strong arms taking him further away, further out of her reach. She should be glad because she'd been on the brink of kissing him, of allowing her body to beg for the kind of satisfaction she knew instinctively only he could give. But until she could tell him what had happened to her after the recital, there was too much between them still, even if the desire was burning higher than ever before.

She pulled herself out of the water, fighting the disappointment that he had kept his word. Annoyed with her warring emotions, she wrapped herself in a large towel, needing to calm the shivers that had more to do with Lysandros than the cool water. With a final glance back at his sexy body surging through the sea, she headed up onto the main deck. Even though she wanted to look back, to watch him, she couldn't. Not when she was losing her foolish and innocent heart to him all over again.

Lysandros had stayed in the sea long after Rio had gone back up on deck. He swam until nearly all his strength had gone, knowing he couldn't fight his desire for her much longer. Whatever it was between them, it was far more powerful than anything he'd ever known, and as she'd almost gone beneath the surface of the water, the overwhelming need to protect her, keep her safe from everyone and everything, had almost crushed him.

So much so that when he'd held that sexy body close to his all he'd wanted was to make her completely his, to show her that passion wasn't something to be afraid of, that desire—*their* desire—was something to be cherished.

But he'd let her go. He hadn't trusted himself. Not after the promise he'd made to her that nothing would happen she didn't want to happen. The only person who could set light to the passion that simmered between them was Rio. He'd given her his word and never went back on it.

When he joined Rio on deck he'd regained his control and that sexy black one-piece was thankfully well covered with a long black dress. Even so, the image of her as she'd stood at the stern of his yacht was there each time he blinked, as if he'd just looked into the brightest of lights.

Music, he decided, would take his mind off the erotic thoughts of Rio that crowded in on him, and he pressed the remote on the sound system. He stood with his back to Rio as the notes of the piano began to drift on the sea breeze. It would calm him and he fully expected it to please Rio as it was after all her instrument, but when he turned she looked more agitated than he'd ever seen her.

'This is one of Xena's favourites,' she said, her brow creased in worry, and all the desire he'd been fighting since he'd held her in the water threatened to take over. But he couldn't allow it, couldn't be the one to start things. It had to be Rio's choice, especially when the cloud of fear he'd seen on her face the day he'd arrived at the hospital still lingered around her.

'You should play for Xena when we return to the villa.' It was only now he realised he hadn't heard her play since she'd arrived.

'I'm not about to sit down and play for Xena when she has no hope of playing the violin for a long time.' The anger in her words raised his suspicion levels.

'Her wrist will heal, but it is more important to help her recover her memory. Listening to you play might do that.'

Rio paced away from him, the black dress moulding itself against her long limbs in the late afternoon wind, but their discussion meant he had to ignore that. She turned to look at him and he knew there was far more she was keeping from him.

'What is it, Rio? What are you worried about? Scared of even?' He watched her as she paced away from him, agitation in every step. Her whole body was tense and he knew for sure she was keeping something from him. Something big.

'You can tell me, Rio. Whatever it is.'

She turned to look at him, her face pale. 'That's just it. I can't.' Her voice had risen in exasperation and every nerve in his body was alert to the danger of being drawn into her emotions. But he'd been right. There *was* something she was keeping back.

Behind her the sun was sinking lower, creating a fusion of oranges across the sky, but all he could think about was his inability to deal with emotions. He didn't know what to do, what to say. Not when he'd spent his entire adult life hiding from all emotions but those that drove him in business, made him successful. Even as a child he'd remained behind a barrier so high that only the most determined family members had reached him.

His father had never been one of them. His father had been equally as unreachable.

As an adult Lysandros had decided his father must have been as emotionless as him, the pair of them so similar they'd retreated even further from one another. As a child, the only kind of sensible excuse for his father's aloofness he'd come up with had been that he'd never wanted to be a father.

That theory had been blown away after Xena had arrived. A baby his parents hadn't planned or expected, but one his father seemed able to shower with love and affection. The exact opposite of what he had received from his father.

Convinced he was somehow at fault, he'd buried his

emotions. Now Rio's obvious distress was slowly chipping away at his armour.

'Why can't you, Rio?' He wanted to go to her, take her hands in his and reassure her. He wanted to look into her eyes while stroking his thumb over the back of her hand, wanted to offer the kind of comfort she wouldn't be threatened by, but his long-held instinct to stand in the shadows of emotion prevented him from moving.

'I just can't.'

'Is it to do with Xena? The accident?'

She looked at him, wide-eyed with shock. She held his gaze as she hugged her arms around herself, giving herself the kind of reassurance, the comfort he should be giving her right now.

Again, there was that hesitation he was quickly realising Rio hid behind when forced to admit difficult things.

'As I told you, Xena and I had had a falling-out that night.' Her eyelashes covered her eyes, shielding her emotions from him as she looked down. He should be furious, should demand why, force her to tell the truth, but he couldn't summon any of those feelings. Strange new feelings were filling him and he crossed the deck and went to her.

Slowly he lifted her chin with his thumb and finger, wanting her to look into his eyes. When she did it was like being struck in the solar plexus. Never had he experienced such a strong urge to protect, to comfort.

'Why?' he asked gently, coaxing her, needing to know why she was so upset, so fearful.

'I should have supported her, but we'd been arguing and it seemed best to leave her to sleep. If only I'd known she would go out later, after I had gone to bed myself.' She tried to look down, but he kept her looking into his eyes.

'What were you arguing about?' Everything she was saying showed how jumbled her emotions were, and even though it would be pushing her when she was so very vulnerable, he needed to know this, sure it was crucial to Xena's memory loss.

'We'd fallen out over the man Xena was seeing.'

'Xena was in a relationship?' This was news to him.

'Yes, but it's over between them now,' Rio said almost in a whisper as she looked at him, panic in her eyes. 'Please don't let on to Xena that you know.'

A swift and uncomfortable knowledge that his own sister hadn't wanted him to know about her romance, that she hadn't felt able to confide in him, all but knocked the breath from his body.

'And has Xena remembered this man?'

Rio shook her head, the movement forcing him to let her go. 'He is just another of the bad events she seems to have blocked out.'

'Another bad event?' There were other things Xena couldn't remember besides the accident? Besides this man? Things that Rio clearly could.

Rio realised her mistake and moved away from him, away from his scrutiny. He needed to know what those bad things were but didn't know what to ask first. Should he demand to know the name of the man Xena was seeing? Or should he ask what other things his sister was blocking out?

The soft strains of the piano filled the warm evening air, the romantic notes in complete contrast to the wild emotions Rio had unleashed in him. The angry kind of emotions he was far more accustomed to dealing with.

'His name is Ricardo,' Rio began as she went and sat on the large luxury sofa, offering a view of the stunning sunset. 'He and Xena had been dating for several months.'

'Why didn't Xena want me to know?' He asked the question that had been racing round his mind. What had his sister been hiding?

Rio didn't know what to say. Tell him the truth and betray Xena's confidence or push Lysandros further away from her when she was finally beginning to rediscover the romance that had been between them before Hans had destroyed it?

Lysandros looked at her and for the first time she saw this powerful businessman, who was used to having everything exactly as he wanted, was struggling to understand what he'd learnt. He looked as vulnerable as she felt.

'Why, Rio?' His tone was soft but full of desperation. He really did love Xena. Even if he kept it well hidden from everyone—including himself. He loved his sister. Rio's heart wrenched and the need to go to him, to hold him, to let him know it was okay to be vulnerable, okay to feel love, rushed through her.

'You must never tell Xena I have told you,' she said with a firmness that surprised both her and him. 'I would never normally betray a friend's confidence like this, but Xena's amnesia isn't a normal circumstance.'

He frowned, his eyes full of questions. 'What is it, Rio?'

'Ricardo was married,' she said softly, allowing the implications to settle between them, to infiltrate the cracking barriers around him.

He turned from her and she dragged in a sharp breath. She hadn't expected that. Rage maybe, definitely anger, but not this. Xena had filled her in on his first engagement, on the fiancée who had had an affair and left him just days before the wedding ceremony. It was little wonder he was so against infidelity.

She crossed the distance to him, her attention fixed on his broad, tense shoulders. 'Xena told me why you would be angry she was seeing a married man. She said it was because of your father, the way he broke up the family when Xena was very young.'

He glanced down at her, the expression in his eyes unreadable. 'But she got involved with him? Continued the affair?'

Rio placed her hand on his arm, feeling the heat of his tanned skin beneath her fingers. 'She never wanted to hurt you. That's why she didn't tell you.'

For a moment his eyes searched hers, all barriers down, all the emotion he kept locked away showing in them.

'You must have loved your fiancée very much,' Rio said, hardly able to voice it. *She* was now his fiancée. His temporary fiancée. But he would never love her like that.

'My fiancée?' The barriers slammed back down. Firmness filled his voice.

'Yes. Xena said…' Rio stumbled over her words, caught off guard by the sudden change in him. 'She said you were engaged once.'

'I was, yes.' Now he sounded as if he was talking to a stranger. About a stranger. Every trace of gentleness had gone. 'She didn't want to get married—at least, not to me. Instead of being honest, telling me, she left with her new lover.'

'I'm sorry,' she whispered.

'It was one big web of deceit.' He looked at her, that dark coldness filling his eyes again.

'But we aren't being truthful to anyone now.' She grasped at her reasons for not wanting to accept his fake engagement deal—all the people who were going to be upset when he ended the engagement. Xena. His mother. Thank goodness she hadn't told her parents anything yet. They had always harboured hopes she'd meet the right man and would get married.

'Maybe we are,' he said softly as he turned to her, taking her hand from his arm, holding it in his. The expression in his eyes had changed. The coldness had gone, the building intensity of desire replacing it.

If only she could trust his desire, that softening of his demeanour. She blinked back the tears threatening to spill in the emotion of the moment, because when he looked at her like that she could forget everything.

'There is one truth, though, Rio.' His voice softened, the seductive sound making her heart flutter, raising her hopes, making her fall for him that little bit more.

'There is?' Was that husky whisper really hers?

His thumb caressed her hand, the sensation making her want so much more. She wanted him to hold all of her, not just her hand.

'I'm very attracted to you, Rio. That is very much true.'

She looked up at him, his declaration only confirming that for him what was between them was simply physical. She might have once started to hope it could be different, but those words warned that wasn't possible. And if it was, would he really want her after she'd given him such a clear message of wanting to sleep with him and then standing him up? He had no idea she was a virgin, no idea just how big a step that was for her. If they did continue their romance—for real, not because of a fake engagement—would he expect to go back to that moment? Expect her to sleep with him straight away?

She might be regaining the confidence to admit she was attracted to him, that she did want to have the night she'd almost had in his bed, but she wasn't ready to put her heart on the line yet. Before she could even think of being intimate with him, she had to tell him. Had to risk him turning his back on her for good.

'I know I said I wouldn't do anything you didn't want to do, but...' He paused, gently brushing her hair back from her face, and she couldn't take her eyes from him. 'I want to kiss you, Rio.'

Heaven help her, if she didn't move away, *she* would kiss *him*.

She could feel herself leaning towards him, feel the heat of need firing up within her. His gaze was fixed to hers, his eyes darkening rapidly, intensely. 'Lysandros...' she whispered huskily.

He took that as an invitation, brushing his lips teasingly and tantalisingly over hers. She closed her eyes as her need rose to new heights, and kissed him gently. He didn't reach for her, didn't take her in his arms, and for that she was thankful. Whether he intended it or not, he'd left her in complete control and she took it, opening her eyes and stepping back away from the temptation of all his kiss had offered—all she wanted.

CHAPTER SEVEN

THE IMAGE OF RIO, looking up at him as they'd stood so close together on his yacht, passion and doubt filling her eyes, had haunted Lysandros all week. The feel of her lips still burned on his as she'd lightly kissed him, almost relenting, almost giving in to desire. Then she'd stepped back from him, forcing him to honour the promise he'd given her. Her doubt, her pure vulnerability, had made him cut short their weekend and return her to the safety of Xena's company on the island late that evening.

He'd left for Athens immediately afterwards, needing to put as much distance as possible between him and the temptation she represented, hoping that a week of meetings and deals would smother the emotions, the need that just looking into her eyes created within him.

As soon as Rio had arrived at his penthouse apartment this morning, he'd known that hope had been futile. The desire between them now so high it was like tinder-dry grass being scorched in the summer sun. One tiny spark and it would ignite, but after his promise, the only one of them who could produce that spark was Rio.

He took a deep and steadying breath and waited for her to emerge from her room. Since she'd arrived, the apartment had become a flurry of activity as deliveries of everything from dresses to shoes and bags had arrived for her. She and Xena had obviously been busy after he'd left the island and, needing space and time to strengthen his resolve not to touch Rio, he'd left for the office. This evening, when she accompanied him to the charity ball, was going to test that resolve to the absolute maximum.

The door to her room clicked and opened and he turned to her as she emerged, but nothing could have prepared him for the elegant vision that stood on the threshold of her room, regarding him apprehensively—or the way his body reacted as lust throbbed urgently through him.

'You look stunning,' he said, walking towards her. The dark blue silk dress complemented her complexion perfectly and the plunging neckline did little to calm the desire he was already struggling to control for this woman. He wanted her with a passion he'd never known before. A passion that threatened to consume him totally.

All he could think of was how her body had moulded to his as he'd held her in the sea. The look on her face, her hair wet and slicked back, her eyelashes holding droplets of water, had created such a sexy image it would be branded for ever in his memory. Now this new sophisticated and daringly sexy version of Rio would join that memory.

'Xena assured me it was perfect for this evening's party.' She looked down at herself, picking up the soft silk of the skirt, pulling out the folds of the fabric, before dropping them and trying to adjust the daringly low neckline. So he was right about Xena's influence on all the purchases. She looked back at him nervously, the sexy and confident woman of moments ago slipping away. In her place was a woman very vulnerable, very innocent.

'Beautiful.' He wasn't referring to the dress but the woman wearing it.

'It is beautiful, but I haven't ever worn anything so daring. Xena is so much more adventurous than I am and you know how she is once she gets an idea into her head.'

He moved closer to Rio, unable to stop himself. He'd punished himself all week by throwing himself into his work and he hadn't realised how much he'd missed her company. 'You look amazing, Rio. Every man there tonight will be looking at you.'

'That's exactly what I don't want.' She almost gasped the words out. 'I don't want that kind of attention.'

He frowned, thinking of the gowns he'd seen her wearing before. Something wasn't making sense. 'The dress is beautiful, as are you.'

The level of protectiveness he felt for Rio was far beyond anything he'd known before. All he wanted was to look after her, care for her and keep her safe. It wasn't just because she was his sister's friend. It was deeper than that. It was also something he wasn't remotely ready to acknowledge, let alone explore.

'I just feel…' She searched for the right word. '… vulnerable.'

'Relax,' he said softly, and stepped close enough to inhale the light floral scent of her perfume. Instinctively he reached out and brushed back a stray strand of hair that had already broken free from her elaborately pinned-up hair. 'I will be at your side all night—if you want me to be.'

'I do,' she whispered, sending his pulse rate rocketing, and the heavy throb of desire struck up a constant drumming round his body. Were they finally getting back to that moment at the recital? The moment when she'd told him she wanted to be his all night?

'In that case, it will be an honour to have a beautiful woman on my arm.' He'd have to be blind not to have noticed the soft swell of her breasts, and he wondered if Xena was aware just how self-conscious Rio had become. He hadn't seen Rio like this before and Xena wouldn't be so insensitive as to insist such a dress be sent here for her if she was aware Rio felt like this. But then Xena still hadn't recovered her memory, and maybe, if things were normal, she would have known how uncomfortable Rio would be with a dress like that. 'All I can say is that Xena made the right choice.'

She blushed and looked down, but didn't step away. 'Thank you.' She paused and looked back up at him. 'For looking after me, for being patient.' She blinked as if considering whether to add something to that, finally succumbing to the temptation. 'And for not pushing me into anything, despite what I said at the recital.'

He took her hand in his and, looking into the depths of her eyes, he saw her pupils expand, saw the unveiled attraction shining in them. That pulse of desire leapt within him. She might be holding back on him, but she wanted him with the same kind of intensity with which he wanted her. Whatever her reason for calling things off, it couldn't be a lack of attraction or desire.

'We are in a strange situation,' he said softly as he stroked his thumb over her hand, the best way he could convey his respect for her. 'Our engagement is not real, and as you know all about my first encounter with engagement, I hope you can understand why it can't be.'

Lysandros imagined being engaged to Rio for real. Imagined planning to make her his wife, the woman he would spend the rest of his life with, and was shocked that the idea was far from unappealing.

'I do,' she said softly, so softly it sounded filled with regret.

'But there is one thing that is very real. The desire between us. I feel it every time I am near you. It tests my promise to you every time I look in your eyes and see desire in them.'

She took in a deep and ragged breath but didn't pull her hand back from his. 'It tests me too, Lysandros,' she said in a shaky whisper.

He lifted her hand to his lips, brushing a lingering kiss over her soft skin. That touch stirred all the longing he'd had for her since the first day Xena had introduced them. From their very first date he'd promised himself he would take things slowly, go at the pace Rio was comfortable with. He just hadn't expected her to shut him out of her life, not when they had been getting on so well and especially not when the sexual tension between them had increased with each date.

'There is something I should tell you, Lysandros.' Rio's voice wavered with emotion, or was it fear? 'Something that may douse that desire entirely.'

'Then tell me, Rio. Whatever it is, tell me. It's driving me mad.'

'I want to, but not now. There isn't time. We need to go to the charity ball.' Nerves hovered in those statements, showing him so much more than she knew, and he accepted that now was not the time to press her for more details.

'You can tell me, Rio,' he reassured her. 'Whenever you are ready, you can tell me.'

'Thank you.' She lowered her lashes, looking up at him shyly and smiling. 'I will. Soon. When I'm ready.'

He knew he'd have to accept that. Whatever it was between them, preventing the desire from flowing freely, would be removed, but not until she was ready.

'My car is waiting,' he said brusquely, pushing down his need for her. 'We should go now.'

Before I forget my patience and kiss you. Prove to you that nothing else matters.

Lysandros had been true to his word all evening and Rio had enjoyed the charity ball, where she was more than a little shocked to discover he was the patron for the charity. She stood now at the front of the gathered crowd, listening to the applause for the speech he'd just given. It might have been in Greek but she knew from the nodding heads of approval and the applause that he'd made an impact on those here tonight, that they respected him. It was clear that the charity to help families in crisis in Greece was one he was passionate about.

From the stage he looked down at her, smiling at her, before speaking again in Greek. As the applause slowed, her heart lurched, forcing her to suck in a deep breath. His tall, athletic physique, which she'd seen on the yacht and had tried desperately to ignore, couldn't be disguised completely by his black tuxedo.

He looked devastatingly handsome, the kind of man who would break a girl's heart, but he'd been so sweet, so gentle and patient since she'd arrived in Athens. It made her admit she'd missed him last week once he'd left the island. During the weekend on his yacht she'd almost forgotten her fears of being physical with him, almost forgotten why she'd ended things between them. Now, after his subtly seductive gestures, entwined with such caring patience, before they'd left the apartment, she couldn't help but want more. She wanted him to kiss her, to hold her and caress away that last lingering fear.

And she wanted that, wanted him—tonight. But first she had to tell him. Their engagement might not be real, but the raw sexual desire between them was. Despite always envisaging giving her virginity to the man she loved, the man she would one day marry, she couldn't walk away from Lysandros now and not know the joy of being completely his. Even if it was for one night only. Especially now she was sure it was what she needed to lock away the past for ever.

The lights dimmed, snagging her from her thoughts, and a round of applause broke out again, confusing Rio. Or was it the handsome Greek walking towards her, intent and purpose in his eyes as those around her moved back, allowing him through the crowd until he stood before her and took her hands in his?

'I ended my speech by saying I would open the dancing with my fiancée.' He smiled at her, mischief in his eyes, laughter in his voice, and her stomach somersaulted. 'Will you do me the honour? Or are you going to make me look a complete fool?'

She laughed at him, feeling more at ease in his company than she'd ever felt with any man. 'Just to save you from ridicule, I will dance with you.'

He took her hand and led her to the dance floor as the applause continued. When he took her in his arms she didn't feel awkward, as she'd expected to do. It felt so right to feel the heat of his body, his strength as he held her close. Right and exciting. It made that realisation of moments ago even stronger.

'I think I have shocked just about every person here.' He spoke softly as he lowered his head close to hers, so close that if she turned just a fraction she would be able to tilt her chin up and kiss him.

Heat coursed through her. Not because of her thoughts but because of how much she wanted it to happen. She wanted to feel his lips on hers once more. Really feel them. She wanted to taste the exquisite pleasure of being desired by Lysandros.

'Because you are dancing?' she teased with a coy smile, trying not to give in to the need surging through her so wildly.

'Maybe, but I think it has more to do with the fact that I am engaged to the most beautiful woman in the room.' His sexy, desire-laden voice sent a tremor of pure pleasure hurtling around her.

'Then maybe I should shock them too.' Her rediscovered desire for Lysandros gave her the kind of boldness she'd only just begun to explore the afternoon of the recital. That boldness now made her daring—flirty.

His brows rose suggestively as they moved slowly around the dance floor, other couples now joining them. 'And how would you do that?'

Rio lowered her lashes, suddenly shy, but when she raised them again and looked into the inky blackness of his eyes, swirling with desire, she knew fighting it was pointless. From the very first day they'd met something had sparked to life between them, something powerful and undeniable. She couldn't deny that she wanted this man to kiss her, to touch her and to love her.

Almost all the barriers she'd put up around herself, around her heart, long before Hans's attack, crashed down as she reached up to press her lips to his. The warmth of his lips melted to hers and she closed her eyes, savouring the heady sensation, wanting to lose herself in its pleasure for ever.

His hand brushed over her cheek, into her hair, pulling down some of the elaborate hairstyle she'd had painstakingly done only hours ago. It felt like they were swaying as the pleasure of his kiss took over. Why had she resisted him for so long? Why hadn't she been brave enough to admit she wanted him?

Because then you weren't ready.

Now she was.

The words swirled around in her mind as he slowly pulled away from her. 'That was magnificent acting,' he said in a hoarse whisper. 'Nobody will ever question our engagement now.'

'It wasn't acting.' She forced herself to continue looking at him, even though she wanted to look down, lessen the intensity of the emotions that shrouded them in a mist of desire.

His sexy, lingering smile made her surer than ever that she was finally ready to leave the past behind, finally ready to explore the joy of being loved by a man. She trusted Lysandros. He'd let his guard down, revealed the kind of man he truly was—a man burned by love, unable to trust the emotion again. That vulnerability helped her, as did his patience. Despite the tough devil-may-care attitude he showed to the world, the hard-edged businessman he portrayed himself as, he was a gentle, compassionate man. Hope began to grow within her. Hope that something more could come of their fake engagement, rekindling all she'd begun to feel about him when they'd been dating. Her emotions freed themselves from behind the defensive wall she'd retreated to after the attack.

'It's a good job we are surrounded by so many people at this moment.' His accent had deepened, his voice almost cracking with desire, heightening her need for him, her need to be kissed by him—and so much more.

'Why?' she teased, the power of being desired dizzying, as if she'd drunk far too much champagne.

'Why?' He tightened his hold on her, his hand at her back searing through the fabric of her gown. 'Because I would not be able to stop at kissing you.'

'I don't want you to.' She closed her eyes as a shudder of desire rushed through her. She swallowed, hardly able to believe what was happening, what she was about to admit, that she was finally ready to move on from that terrifying moment with Hans. 'I want you to kiss me.'

'Rio.' He whispered her name, the raw desire in his voice almost too much. 'Are you sure this is what you want?'

She could feel him breathing deeply against her, each breath pressing against her breasts, and she knew she would never be surer of anything in her life. She wanted Lysandros, wanted him to make love to her, but not until she'd walked out from beneath the shadow of what Hans had done. Not until Lysandros knew why she'd stood him up. 'It is, but…'

He brushed his lips over hers then spoke softly, his lips so close it was wildly erotic to feel his breath on her lips. 'I promised you nothing would happen until you want it to and I meant it.'

She looked into his eyes, saw the smouldering desire but knew he really did mean it. She was totally in control and that was exactly what she needed to know.

The hum of desire still ruled her body as Rio walked into Lysandros's apartment. The short time in the chauffeur-driven car hadn't lessened any of that sexual tension, hadn't made her change her mind, but nerves were beginning to rush over her. Before anything could happen, she had to tell him why she'd stood him up that night after the recital.

Nerves fluttered inside her. It was more than just what Hans had done. She was a virgin. She was choosing, this moment, to give him something very precious. Should she say something? Would he know if she didn't? Would he be able to tell that the emotions she was experiencing were so very new to her?

'Champagne?' His question arced through the air, pulsating through the heady desire that still had them in its grip. Nerves added to the powerful cocktail of feelings and made her skin tingle as if tiny flakes of snow were falling on her.

'Champagne sounds perfect,' she said, glad of the time to compose herself, to prepare to tell him what he deserved to know. Instinctively she walked over to the grand piano standing proudly by the windows that gave an unrivalled view of Athens. She wanted to reach out and touch it, to touch the keys, but not yet. 'There is something I need to tell you.'

She had his full attention now as he stood, the unopened bottle in his hand. 'What is it, Rio?' The gentleness of his voice gave her the strength she needed to finally tell him why she'd called off their blossoming romance.

'The reason I didn't meet you for dinner that night…' She paused, trying to gauge his reaction, but his eyes were full of concern and she knew she had to say it. 'It was because I was scared.'

'You were scared?' The incredulity in his voice was too much and she drew in a deep, ragged breath.

'Not of you, but of what I'd told you I wanted.'

'That you wanted to be with me all night?'

She nodded, her eyes locking with his across the apartment. He hadn't moved but the intensity in his eyes, the desire he couldn't hide, gave her the courage to continue. 'That was what I wanted that night—and it's what I want tonight.'

He put the bottle down and walked over to her, a frown on his face, his breathing fast and shallow. 'I want that, Rio, so much,' he said as he took her hands in his, and the sincerity in his voice almost broke her heart, it sounded so full of love. Or was that just her foolish heart believing what it really wanted to see, to hear, to feel? 'But I don't want you to be scared. I meant what I said about not doing anything you didn't want to do. You are in full control.'

'I'm grateful for that, thank you,' she whispered. 'But there is something else I need to tell you first.'

He brushed her hair back from her face so tenderly she almost closed her eyes, expecting him to kiss her. But he didn't. 'Tell me,' he whispered so softly it was almost impossible to hear him.

'After the recital I went to one of the practice rooms. Hans had arranged to meet me there, to go over some of my final pieces of the season. I was playing when he came in, so I didn't hear him. He'd been drinking and...' Her words stumbled to a halt and she swallowed hard as Lysandros appeared to hold his breath. She didn't know if she could finish, didn't know if she could admit it aloud. After she'd given her statement the only other person she'd told had been Xena. She'd understood why she couldn't see Lysandros any more, had supported her through it, but the accident had claimed those memories, along with the other bad events of recent weeks.

'What happened, Rio?' His voice was so gentle that it didn't fit with the hard lines of his jaw as he clenched it and looked down at her.

'He...he...' She looked up at him anxiously, not wanting to say it but knowing she had to, for herself as well as Lysandros. 'He thought I was interested in him, that I was playing just for him, and he tried to...'

Fury blazed in Lysandros's eyes, but he remained calm and still, giving her the strength to finish telling him. 'Only tried?'

'He took advantage of the fact that I was sitting at the piano and grabbed me. I managed to push him away and should have run, but I was too shocked. Then he tried to kiss me, tried to...' She shuddered at the memory of Hans pawing at her and the way her heart had raced as she'd lashed out at him, shocked by the intensity of it.

A harsh expletive tore from Lysandros and she blinked. 'Did he hurt you?' he growled.

She began to wonder if she'd done the right thing. Had she ruined the moment between them? 'No, thanks to Judith and two other men.' She closed her eyes against the memory, willing herself not to get upset all over again. Hans wasn't worth another tear. 'I went home with Judith after I'd given the police my statement. I just couldn't face you or Xena.'

'I understand, Rio.' He looked at her, full of compassion as he brushed his hand over her hair soothingly. 'Of course you didn't want to see me after that. Does Xena know?'

'Yes, but she seems to have blocked it out too,' she said, and finally looked down, away from his gaze. She'd just ruined the one chance she might have had at discovering intimacy with the man she loved.

'Can I hold you?' She looked up again. He still wanted her, but more than that, he was thinking of her just by asking.

'Yes,' she whispered, hope that he could one day love her blotting out the bitterness of all she'd just told him. 'Please, hold me.'

His arms wrapped around her, holding her to him. His gentleness was so unexpected after the firmness of his expression as she'd told him that her breath rushed from her in a gasp. She nestled herself against him, feeling safe and secure.

'Thank you for telling me,' he said as his lips pressed into her hair, but unlike the time on the beach she didn't pull away. It was a caring and loving gesture and exactly what she wanted.

'It scared me so much I just couldn't see you. I'm so sorry for standing you up.' Her voice was muffled by his tuxedo and she breathed in his scent, gathering strength from it.

'I understand, Rio, and it's okay. It wasn't your fault.' His voice was gentle as he lifted her chin with his thumb, and she looked up at him, seeing the sincerity in his eyes. 'We don't have to do anything you don't want to.'

'I know,' she whispered as desire began to sluice away the fear of a night that had almost lost her Lysandros. She wasn't going to allow Hans to dictate her future, her emotions any more. 'But I meant what I said. I want to be with you tonight.'

'Are you sure?' His eyes searched hers.

She smiled and stretched up to place her lips against his in a lingering and tender kiss. She didn't want to talk about the past any more, didn't want it to spoil things. She wanted to bring everything back to where they'd been as he'd been about to open the champagne, only now without that devastating secret between them.

'I am.' She smiled, pleased to see desire in his eyes once more. 'Did you say something about champagne?'

She watched intently as he popped the cork on the champagne, nerves and excitement whirling around inside her. She returned to the piano, reaching out her fingers, tracing them lightly over the keys, the past now banished by his understanding. She wanted him to make love to her, wanted him to be her first lover, and she would take this moment for what it was. Even though her heart was fast becoming his, she knew he was not the kind of man to give his. Not that it mattered now. She was beginning to fall in love with him and becoming truly his was all she wanted tonight.

Tomorrow didn't matter—just tonight.

Without thinking about what she was doing, she pulled out the piano stool and seated herself before the black and white keys that had tormented her for so many weeks since the attack. She could hear the fizz of the champagne as Lysandros poured two glasses and knew that placing her fingers on the keys and playing was as much a part of this healing process as giving herself willingly to the man who was, at least for now, her fiancé. She wanted to be loved by him, to experience a night of passion with him, but first she *had* to do this.

It was another way of putting aside that terrible afternoon.

He placed the glasses of champagne on the piano and stood at its side, questions in his eyes. She kept her focus on the piano keys in front of her, grateful he hadn't voiced those questions, hadn't broken the spell that was propelling her to do this—towards him.

She took a deep breath, lifted her hands onto the keys once more, poised and ready to play.

Lysandros remained silent but moved to stand behind her, out of her line of vision. After what Hans had done, it should have made her nervous, but she trusted Lysandros. Not seeing him but knowing he was there, that he was with her on this healing journey, enabled her to focus. She loved him even more for his patience, his understanding. As if he knew this was something she had to do before they could become lovers.

Her index finger pressed one note. She stopped. Was she ready for this? She didn't know, but whatever this was, it was far more than just playing the piano again. She sat, locked in her own world of turmoil.

Lysandros remained behind her. She was acutely aware of him standing there, of his presence, his patience, giving her strength. She took another breath, closed her eyes, slipping into that magical zone she always went to when she played. For the first time since the attempt by Hans to take from her what she hadn't wanted to give, she was ready to allow all her emotions to flow from her and onto the keys. She pulled back her hands.

She could do this. She could play the piano again *and* be with the man she loved.

CHAPTER EIGHT

LYSANDROS HELD HIS breath as he waited for Rio to play the first notes. The tension in the air was heavy. He'd seen her hesitation, knew it was because of all she'd told him and the worry of his reaction. He was as mad as hell, but he'd remained calm. For Rio's sake, he'd kept all his anger in, understanding now why she'd stood him up and then ended things.

If he was more able to connect emotionally with people, Rio may have confided in him, instead of ending things. But she hadn't because of his damned male pride, along with his inability to allow emotions in. But Rio was changing all that, smashing down barrier after barrier, allowing emotions to escape and be felt, not just him but her too.

He looked at Rio as she sat at the piano stool, his heart constricting so hard it hurt. He heard her draw in a deep breath and held his as she lifted her hands to the keys before pulling them back in hesitation. She needed to play right now, needed to let out everything she'd been holding back, everything about Hans, about him, about Xena's accident. He knew instinctively she needed that before anything could happen between them.

He also knew better than to break a musician's concentration and focus, yet he wanted her to know he understood. Not just that she needed to play now, but why. He moved back towards her, stood behind her, about to rest his hands on her shoulders when he remembered how she'd described Hans behind her. He moved away, relieved he hadn't destroyed the moment as she began to play.

The first notes were tentative, unsure. Then more notes followed until he recognised the first movement of Beethoven's *Moonlight Sonata*. The sound of the piano filled his apartment. The soft, slow notes, so full of emotion it was as if he was at his own private concert, as if she was playing just for him—for them.

He clenched his jaw, balling his hands into tight fists as need for Rio rocketed beyond anything he'd ever known. Each note smashed at the barriers around his emotions, the tension in the air increasing to almost suffocating levels. All he could think about was making love to her. He wanted Rio with a need reaching fever pitch, and as the notes were played with more conviction, he became convinced she was letting him know, through each seductive bar of music, that she wanted him too. That nothing else other than the two of them mattered. That tonight belonged to them alone.

He moved slowly away from the temptation Rio created, trying to focus on the lights of Athens, but it was too much. He had to see her, had to watch her, and turned his attention back to Rio at the piano. Her body swayed in gentle motion with the music, her fingers caressing and stroking the keys, making him wish it was his body she was touching so lovingly. The low-cut back of her dress was showing off her spine, each movement she made more erotic than the last. The ferocity with which he wanted her took his breath away, but he was careful not to scare her, not after what she'd just told him. He wanted this moment, tonight, to be special for her.

Several strands of her hair had fallen down and he longed to push them aside and kiss the pale skin of her neck. He wanted to inhale her scent, to taste her skin. How could a piece of music become so erotic?

Because the woman you want is playing it.

Rio stroked her long, slender fingers down the keys, her engagement ring catching the light and sparkling as she played the final notes of the first movement. Then, still locked in her emotional cocoon, she slowly laid her palms on her lap, her concert training still ruling despite the heightened sexual tension sparking around them.

The notes of the piano faded away and silence hung heavy as he stood, waiting for her to come back from whatever place it was musicians went to when they'd invested every ounce of emotion into their performance. His breathing deepened, became heavy, as if he had been kissing her for the last five minutes instead of listening to her play.

'There is only one thing more beautiful than hearing you play and that is watching you play.' His voice was husky with desire, and drinking the remainder of his champagne in one go, he tried to hold himself back, something he was not at all used to doing.

Rio turned to face him. 'I've never played to a man like that before.' She blushed and looked beyond him, out of the window, seemingly losing herself in the night view of the city he now called home.

'Then I am honoured.' He picked up her glass of champagne, not wanting her to think about the practice session she'd had with that vile man. He didn't want her to ever have to think about that again. With a smile he handed the glass to her, his fingers inadvertently brushing against hers. Had she crossed some sort of barrier by playing like that to him? 'Was that the first time you have played since…?' He didn't want to say the word 'attack'; he didn't want to bring it all back to her.

She looked up at him, searching his eyes, and he didn't miss the hesitation. 'Yes,' she whispered, so softly, so seductively he wanted to lean down and kiss her, but if he did, he wouldn't be able to stop. He'd want more, much more. 'I couldn't even sit at the piano. Then Xena had the accident.'

She stood up, bringing herself so close to him that he'd swear she knew exactly what she was doing, just how teasing it was to have her delicious body, only partially concealed by the dark blue silk of her gown, so very close to him.

'Xena will be okay,' he said softly as he reached out and stroked her cheek. 'I want you to be okay too.'

'Me?' Those long lashes fluttered down again, closing her off to him.

'Yes, Rio, you.' He lifted her chin with his finger until she looked up at him. 'I want you to be happy, I want to make things right for you, but I'm fighting really hard here because I want to kiss you so much.' All he wanted was to lose himself in the pleasure Rio's body promised and give her that same pleasure.

Rio didn't want to feel the pain crashing forward when he mentioned Xena. Neither did she want to remember the fear of the afternoon Hans had tried to kiss her, tried to touch her. She didn't want anything other than to abandon herself to the intensity of the desire that filled the air like the heat before a thunderstorm.

'I want you to kiss me,' she whispered. The sound was so tremulous she wondered if he'd heard her.

The fire of desire erupted in his eyes and doubts assailed her but she forced them back. She didn't want to hear them, didn't want to allow them to take away this moment. She wanted Lysandros, wanted him to kiss her and so much more.

His eyes grew darker than the night sky hanging above the ancient city beyond the windows. She couldn't look away, the fizz of desire arcing between them so powerfully. He didn't say anything, didn't acknowledge her words. Instead he moved closer, holding her face lightly in his hands as his lips gently met hers. A sigh of pleasure escaped from her and in her mind the happier notes of the *Moonlight Sonata*'s second movement played. This was right. So very right. She allowed the pleasure of his kiss to wrap around her.

She tasted champagne as his tongue slicked along her lips, then slid between them to entwine with hers. The stab of desire deep within her was so strong all she could do was answer his unspoken demands and deepen the kiss. The world swayed and she wanted to reach out to him, to put her arms around his neck and press herself against his body. It felt wanton and wild but so very right.

He let go of her abruptly, stepping back from her, the dim light of the apartment casting his face in shadow, making it impossible to read his emotions, his thoughts. All she could do was stand still, breathing deep and hard, her body pulsing with a hungry need that only he could satisfy.

'Don't stop, Lysandros.' The words were husky, sounding very unlike her.

'Rio.' He said her name hoarsely, moving out of the shadows slightly, his gaze intensely focusing on her. 'If I kiss you again I might not be able to stop. I will be in danger of breaking my promise that nothing will happen unless you want it to.'

Her heart thudded. He wanted her, truly wanted her. The man she was engaged to wanted her as much as she wanted him. 'You won't be breaking that promise, Lysandros.'

Rio could scarcely believe she was saying this. Lysandros was enabling her to be the woman she really wanted to be. She wanted Lysandros to be the man she gave her virginity to and she wanted it to happen now, here—tonight.

'I want to kiss you, Rio, and so much more, but only if you really want that.' His eyes were heavy with desire, his voice soft and seductive, melting her heart a bit more. He cared. Enough to consider what she'd told him, enough to recognise how big a moment this was for her. Enough to hold back, ask if it was what she really wanted.

'I want that, Lysandros.' Her whisper cracked with emotion, ratcheting up the tension surrounding them to unbearable levels. 'I want you to kiss me.' She faltered briefly, biting her lower lip, unused to admitting how she really felt. 'I want more too. I want you.'

'Are you sure?' The raw desire in his voice didn't quite conceal the doubt. 'After everything you told me...'

'I have never been more certain of anything.' She stepped towards him, wanting to show him how ready for this she was, wanting to hide her innocence behind the bravado of being an experienced seductress. His desire filled her with the kind of power she'd never known, emboldening her, unlocking the woman within her. She wasn't a nervous and inexperienced woman any longer. He'd changed that. He'd given her the confidence to free the woman within her.

He stroked the backs of his fingers down her cheek and she had to fight against the urge to close her eyes, to lean into his touch. She needed to see his face, read the emotions in his eyes. 'I promise you I will take it slowly.'

Was her inexperience that obvious? Had he guessed she was a virgin? 'Take me to your bed.' It was all she could do to whisper those words as he moved so close to her his chest brushed against her breasts, heightening her state of arousal.

'First another kiss.' Before she could say anything his lips covered hers once more. His hands held her face, tilting her chin up gently, enabling his tongue to explore her, to entwine with hers, sending so much pleasure rushing around her she wondered if she'd be able to remain standing.

Soft Greek words added to the tension around them as he pulled back from her, caressing her face again. She didn't want to know what they meant. She wanted to pretend they were words of love, pretend that whatever it was happening between them was real, that she'd found her dream of a happy-ever-after.

'I need more than a kiss,' she teased, emboldened by rising desire.

A slow, lazy and incredibly sexy smile spread across his lips, lighting the darkness of his eyes, allowing her to see the depths of passion within them. Her body trembled as his gaze slid down her, making her skin tingle as if he'd touched her.

He looked up into her eyes, pulling at his bow tie, letting it fall to hang down, giving him that roguish appeal she hadn't realised until now could be so erotic. Then he pulled off his jacket, dropping it behind him, still without breaking that powerful eye contact.

She had the urge to move closer, to reach up and spread her hands over his chest, to unbutton the white shirt and reveal his body to her. She knew how muscled it was from their time on the yacht, knew how it felt to press herself against it as the sea had formed the only barrier between them. Now she wanted to feel every contour, to explore him so that she could remember this moment for ever.

'If you want me to, I will do far more than kiss you,' he said as he moved towards her, passion making him suddenly more dominant. She backed away until she met the keyboard of the piano, the keys jangling in discord as her palms pressed them as if she'd never played a note before in her life. It made her conscious that her inexperienced body would be as much out of tune, that she was floundering in a sea of passion. Tasting the desire in the air, she bit her bottom lip, sure she was about to drown at any moment.

Lysandros moved a little closer, and embarrassed by her moment of hesitation, she moved to him, wrapping her arms around his neck, curling her fingers into his thick hair as she looked up at him. No words were needed as she looked into his eyes before kissing him, forgetting her innocence, her fears and demanding so much more from him than just a kiss.

He took her in his arms, a strange and wild tune playing as he moved her back against the keys, his kiss answering her demands instantly. In a flash of panic she remembered that Hans had done exactly this. It almost doused the passion. Almost. Until she reassured herself. *This is right, what I want and so perfect.* And it was right. It was perfect, and it was writing over that terrible moment, erasing it for ever.

Lysandros deepened this kiss, sliding one side of her dress down off her shoulder, the tape attached to prevent her exposing herself inadvertently now completely ineffective against his demands. Her nipple hardened, her breast bare as he kissed a trail slowly down her throat then torturously slowly down her breast. She let go of him, grabbing at the piano, arching herself towards him as he took her hardened nipple in his mouth. It was pure ecstasy, so intense she almost couldn't take it.

'Lysandros.' She gasped his name out, her breathing ragged with heady need.

He looked up at her with desire-hazed eyes. 'Do you want me to stop?'

She shook her head.

'Is it nice?'

'So nice.' She didn't even recognise her husky whisper. Her whole body was on fire, needing him, needing his kiss, his touch. She was losing control, losing the ability to think as her body demanded the satisfaction she knew instinctively only he could give her.

'If I go too fast, tell me.' His gaze held hers for a moment before his hand slid down her side, over her thigh, his lips returning to torment her nipple.

There was no way she wanted him to stop now. She drew in a breath of ecstasy as with alarming ease he gathered up the silk of the skirt, his hand spreading over her bare thigh. The touch was exquisite, but it wasn't enough. She wanted more. Much more. As he moved higher, finding the lace of her panties and sliding his fingers over the delicate fabric, she thought she might explode with pleasure. Now in her head the fast and wild notes of the third movement played, driving her to further heights of pleasure.

'Lysandros,' she gasped again, almost unable to speak, not wanting the moment to end. 'Don't stop.'

While his hand continued the tormenting exploration of lace, his lips moved away from her breast, the air cool on her skin, damp from his kiss. He looked at her with heavy eyes as she fought to keep hers open. His touch at the apex of her thighs was light and teasing, almost where she needed it but not quite.

'You are so beautiful,' he said softly, his accent deeper and more pronounced than ever.

She couldn't form any words, couldn't tell him that he made her feel beautiful as his fingers slid along the line of her panties, touching her where she craved it. She closed her eyes as he teased her, the only barrier to his touch the lace. Fire leapt within her and she moved against him instinctively, but still it wasn't enough.

Through a fog of need she looked at him, imploring him without words. She gasped in pleasure as his fingers pushed aside the material. The keys of the piano sounded again as she moved against his touch, opening her legs, feeling him going deeper as she looked into his eyes. She wanted to close her eyes, give herself up to the pleasure of what he was doing. At the same time she wanted to fight it so that it didn't have to end.

'Rio.' The gravelly whisper of her name was followed by words of Greek.

A wave of pleasure so powerful she had to close her eyes washed over her. She shuddered as he took her to the dizzying heights of orgasm, gasping his name and clutching at the piano. Slowly she became aware of his touch again, aware of her skirt dropping back down as he took her in his arms, holding her tightly against him. Kissing her hair.

He was thinking only of her pleasure, holding himself back, and her heart filled with love for him. She clung to him, savouring the moment, but her body still hummed with need, still rang with desire. She wanted him to feel the same pleasure. She wanted to touch every part of him, send him to the stars, just as he had done to her.

'Take me to your bed,' she whispered against his neck as she kissed him, the new growth of stubble prickling her lips.

As the pulse of desire thumped through him, Lysandros took Rio's hand, leading her away from the piano, across the wooden floors to his bedroom. Any misgivings about what they were doing, any doubts after her revelation, had vanished as she'd gasped out his name. There was now only one conclusion that could come of this evening. Rio would be his in every way possible.

Not just as a woman he'd made love to but as his fiancée. The thought filled him with a new emotion. He'd never felt this way before, never had that undeniable connection with any woman, as if his heart and soul were committed to hers for evermore. Unable to deal with that stark realisation with desire firing through him, he pushed it aside. Now was not the time for analysing.

His bedroom was bathed in soft light from the glow of the city and he wanted to see her naked on his bed as that light caressed her. He turned to face her as she stood by his bed, the innocence that always shone from her now muted by the desire still simmering beneath the surface, waiting for release.

He rested his hands on her hips, drawing her gently to him, smiling that she'd restored order to her dress, once again concealing the swell of her breasts from him—just.

'I want you to make love to me, Lysandros. I want to be yours.' She brushed her lips provocatively over his before looking up at him. Her beautiful eyes were so full of desire and emotion there was no longer any doubt in his mind of what she wanted.

'Rio, I want you so very much.' He kissed her, unable to restrain the passion and desire she roused in him any longer, but he remained gentle, wanting to keep the pace slow.

His fingers found the zip at her waist and slid it down as he indulged in the pleasure of her kiss. The fury of fiery passion consuming him once more, he pushed down each shoulder of the dress. He stood back, drinking her in as it slipped to the floor in a pool of indigo blue at her stiletto-clad feet.

He crouched before her, reaching up to pull the lace panties down her long legs. She clutched her fingers in his hair, stepping out of them as he kissed up her thigh, the tension in her fingers as she gripped tighter almost too much. He wanted to push her back onto the bed and plunge himself deep into her, but this was about her pleasure, not his.

Thankful he was still dressed, he continued to explore her thighs with kisses. He wanted to taste her and resumed where he'd left off at the piano. She gasped in pleasure, pulling at his hair as his tongue swirled against her, threatening to tip her over the edge once more. He took her almost to that edge again and then stood up in front of her, discarding his clothes, watching her breathe hard with passion, her desire-laden eyes locked with his.

Almost too late he remembered the necessary protection and opened a drawer behind him. He might be about to make their engagement far more of a reality than either of them had anticipated, but he had no intention of taking it further and creating a family.

Rio moved towards him, brushing her breasts against him as he tore open the foil packet. He rolled on the condom as he looked at her, then took her in his arms, kissing her as he moved her back towards the bed. Together they fell onto its softness, his body covering hers, her legs wrapping around him.

He'd wanted to take it slowly, to touch her, kiss her until neither of them could wait any longer, but as she lifted her hips, her legs pulling him to her, he lost all power of control, thrusting in deep and hard.

She cried out and stilled, her fingernails digging into his back. As questions raced for answers in his mind she moved, taking him deeper inside her, kissing his shoulders, and that final shred of control broke.

In a frenzied and wild dance that was anything but the gentle seduction he'd planned, his world splintered, her cries of ecstasy filling the room. She clung to him as her release claimed her, her legs wrapped tightly around him, keeping him deep inside her. It was so different from any other time, more intense, more powerful. Was that because he'd taken her virginity or because, despite everything, she was reaching a part of him long since closed off?

He didn't want to think of either of those scenarios right now. Instead he held her close and gave in to the need to close his eyes.

Rio lay in Lysandros's arms as darkness became day. She'd woken to feel the heavy weight of his relaxed body against hers. What had happened between them tonight had been totally magical. The pleasure of becoming his, of giving herself to him, had finally chased away those terrible nightmares, and she knew, without doubt, she was in love with Lysandros. She wasn't sure if he loved her, but did that really matter when they had a connection as powerful as this? Surely she had enough love for both of them?

He moved sleepily and she propped herself up on one elbow to look at him. The man she loved. Unable to resist the temptation, she kissed his lips, stirring him from his slumber, and with a suddenness that made her cry out he turned her onto her back and kissed her, his aroused body pressed against hers. Feeling wicked with the power she had over him, she ran her hands down his back and over his buttocks.

'Minx,' he said as he pulled himself away from her, throwing back the sheet. He went to the drawers and took out the packet of condoms, taking one and placing the box on the table next to the bed. Unable to take her eyes from him, she watched as he rolled the condom on.

Again he spoke in Greek as he crawled across the bed, kissing any part of her body he could as she laughed. Last night she'd done two things she'd thought would be impossible. Played the piano again and given herself to the man she loved. He'd been so gentle, so caring, thinking only of her. There was no way she could deny it any longer. She loved Lysandros.

Now she intended to enjoy being physically loved by him for as long as possible. Before reality crept back in.

CHAPTER NINE

AFTER AN EXQUISITE night of pleasure, making love with Lysandros, Rio had slept far later than normal. When she'd woken, she had expected Lysandros to be making excuses and stepping back from her, but the day had continued in the same passion-fuelled and romantic way of the previous night. Now, as the sun set over Athens, she sat on the roof terrace, a glass of wine in her hand and the man she knew for certain she was hopelessly in love with at her side.

'I'm sorry you weren't able to tell me about what had happened.' Lysandros's deep voice cut through her thoughts, his mind clearly on her revelation last night.

Last night, as she'd given herself to him, making her completely his, she'd known he'd guessed the truth, that it had been her first time. She hadn't told him the full details of what Hans had done to her, but at least now Lysandros knew he hadn't taken from her the one thing she'd been saving for the right man. The one thing she'd wanted to give Lysandros, leaving him in no doubt she'd been ready to be his all those weeks ago at the recital.

Was he angry she'd been unable to tell him she was a virgin? After telling him about Hans, it hadn't felt right to tell him that too.

He took her hand, leaning across from his chair. 'Why didn't you tell me?' he coaxed gently, that caring and protective touch still there. There was a new softness in his eyes and she hated herself for hoping there could be something good between them developing— something permanent.

'Admitting what Hans had done was hard.' She lowered her gaze briefly before looking back into his classically handsome features. She could so easily believe this was real, but she had to remember only the passion and desire were real. Their engagement wasn't real or intended to be long term. It was all about giving Xena the happiness and security she needed to recover her memory. And once she did, it would end.

'Not that, Rio. I can understand completely how hard that was, but why couldn't you tell me it was your first time?' She could see a hint of sadness in his gaze. Was it regret? Would he have slept with her if he'd known she was a virgin?

She sipped her wine, desperate to distract herself as his fingers caressed her hand so lovingly. If she thought her own emotional barriers were down then so were his. This was the real Lysandros, but could she keep him with her? Prevent him from retreating behind them once more?

'You normally date experienced women. I didn't think you'd want anything to do with a twenty-five-year-old virgin. I'd already made one big revelation.' She wanted to add how he'd made her feel, how she'd fallen in love with him, but held back. Such an admission would make her more vulnerable than ever.

'I wanted it to be special for you, after what you'd

told me, but if I had known you were a virgin, I would have been gentler, far more considerate.'

Rio closed her eyes, her heart flipping over. He was saying all the right things, looking at her in the right way, even caressing her hand gently as he spoke. He was doing and saying everything she would want from the man who loved her. But the sensible part of her knew there could never really be a future with him. He didn't want to settle down and certainly didn't want to fall in love. She was just part of the plan to help Xena. To him last night was another brief affair.

She opened her eyes and looked into his, her breath catching as desire swirled in his once more. 'It was special. And you were considerate,' she whispered.

'I am honoured that after all you've been through, it was me you chose to share in the moment you discovered the passionate woman within you.'

Lysandros took her glass of wine from her, placing it on the small table at his side, then gently pulled her to her feet as he too stood up. Her heart pounded so hard she could scarcely breathe, the intensity of the desire around them heavier than the humid night air.

She couldn't hold it in any longer and the truth broke free from her. 'You made me feel so special, so desired and loved. Last night made me forget.'

'I don't know how you can possibly forget the moment a man betrays your trust like that.' The anger in his voice only added to the tension in the air.

'It's hard to forget, but I don't want it in my thoughts. I will not allow that moment, that man, to define who I am, what I feel.' Her words sounded strong, her breathing rapid and shallow, but it was the expression on his face that obliterated that memory from the past, enabling her to finally move forward.

'Nothing bad will happen to you now. I will make sure of that.'

Rio searched his eyes as questions rang through her mind. Was he offering to look after her? Help her move forward and leave the past well behind and truly find the woman she'd been last night? Did that mean he wanted their engagement to be as real as everything they'd shared last night?

Hope flared to life within her. She was under no illusions that this man would ever love her, but as her own love for him was growing, she hoped he felt something, affection that would keep them together. If he could, then maybe there was a future for them.

She'd opened her soul to him, told him her dark secret. She didn't want any more untruths between them. Boldly she looked at him, determined to change the direction of the conversation, to find out more about the man who was now her fiancé—an arrangement she wished was entirely real.

'Last night, because of you, I got past the barriers that had prevented me from playing a single note on the piano since the night of the attack. I let go of a painful memory when I kissed you and asked you to take me to your bed.' Her voice wavered as the emotion of the moment he'd taken her by the hand and led her away from the piano rushed back. 'I wanted you to make love to me. I wanted you to be my first lover.' She looked at him cautiously. She needed to say something to make him see there could be something between them other than a temporary arrangement. 'It's liberating to come out from behind emotional barriers, Lysandros. Maybe you should try it.'

He brushed his fingers over her cheek just as he had done last night and the slow, steady thump of passion began to pump around her once more. 'And what barriers am I hiding behind?' Humour lingered sexily in his voice, a smile on his lips.

'You were nearly married. You must have really loved her to be so adamant you will not give any other woman your love again.'

His eyes hardened and the smile slipped away. Whether he admitted it or not, she had touched the demons of his past. 'Yes, Kyra and I nearly married.' Bitterness filled his voice. 'It is not something I ever think about and certainly doesn't have any lasting effects on me.'

'I'm not sure Xena shares that view.' Instantly she regretted her words. Xena believed he'd locked his heart away, shut himself out of reach of love, and hoped he and Rio would find love together. How could they? When their engagement was nothing more than a sham?

Lysandros looked at Rio's beautiful face, the setting sun casting a glow on her skin that was incredibly sexy. He stopped stroking the softness of her skin. Until she'd brought up his past he'd been hungry for her, wanting only to take her back to his bed. Now the ghosts of the past had emerged like shadows of the night, challenging him, despite what he'd just claimed. They challenged the way he felt about Rio, the way he wanted to protect and care for her. The shadows darkened. He was still the man Kyra's deception and rejection had made him. Still the man who couldn't open his heart, allowing in a woman's love, and he certainly wasn't ready to love her in return.

If only things had been different. If it had been Rio he'd fallen in love with and proposed to for real. Would he now have had the happy home life he had been desperate to avoid ever since the betrayal of his first love? Was it possible that he'd already have produced the grandchildren his mother still yearned for? Guilt stabbed at him. He was going to disappoint his mother all over again.

The gentleness of Rio's eyes coaxed the past even further from the darkness, and though their engagement would only last until Xena's memory returned, he *could* envisage more. Rio had opened up to him, told him all that had happened to her, so it was only fair that he bare his inner soul too.

'I was foolish enough to believe I had found love, to believe that Kyra and I would be together for ever.' His words were sharper than he'd intended, but the gentleness in Rio's eyes, waiting patiently for him to continue, eased the shame of admitting his male pride had got it wrong. The same pride Rio had attacked when she'd stood him up after the recital.

Rio dragged in a sharp breath, snagging his attention as she bit at her lower lip. 'That doesn't mean you can't fall in love again.'

He saw the hope in her eyes. Was she hoping to be the woman who changed that, changed him? It could never happen. He never wanted to be that vulnerable again. His childhood had made him cautious with his emotions and Kyra's betrayal had only confirmed his long-held belief it was easier, safer not to feel, not to get emotionally involved.

He must smother Rio's hopes. 'I can cope with the fact that maybe Kyra didn't want to marry me, that maybe she just got dragged along with things, but what I can't get past is the fact that she lied to me, that she was unfaithful.' He took a deep breath. Damn it. He *was* coming out from behind his barriers. 'My father was unfaithful to my mother. He destroyed their marriage. Our family. My faith in love.'

'I had no idea,' Rio whispered, her face paling with shock.

'That's why I don't want emotion. Why I don't want love in my life. Why I *can't* love anyone.'

And you almost changed that, but I can't let you.

Rio placed her hand on his arm, her head tilting to one side, her eyes looking beseechingly into his. She might have held back important facts, but he knew she could never lie, knew she was a woman he could trust, allow into his heart. He wanted to. What he felt for her was deeper than mere passion. Last night had been about more than just sex; that was why it had been so different for him. Yet the past clung, like a web spun in the moonlight, and only the brightest sunshine could free him.

'Kyra treated you terribly,' she whispered, making shame rush over him as he thought about all she'd been through. She'd survived the ordeal of being not only physically violated but emotionally too. 'And your father, I'm sorry.'

'I'm sure Xena has told you I haven't had a serious relationship in many years,' he said lightly, wanting to downplay the heaviness of the conversation, needing to extinguish that hope in Rio's eyes.

'She has, yes.' She smiled, her lips parting in that

inviting way, sending the hum of lust hurtling around him once more. 'She had hoped we would start a long-term romance.'

There was laughter in her voice, and despite himself, he couldn't help but smile. 'And that is why she believed our engagement.'

Sadness filled Rio's eyes. He'd achieved his aim. 'But she will remember soon.'

'She will, yes,' he said as he drew her closer to him. 'But for now let's enjoy tonight.'

He brushed his lips over hers, smothering the soft sigh of pleasure. Instantly the lust in his body increased and he wanted to sweep her into his arms, carry her from the roof terrace, back to bed.

'Our last night in Athens,' she whispered between kisses.

He'd never spoken his mind like that since the disaster of his first engagement, had never allowed a woman close enough to scale the defence he'd always had around him. His instinct was to deflect her from the truth of those words as well as prevent himself from analysing them. Instead he allowed desire to carry him out of the shadows of the past, making him realise he needed more nights with Rio, more passion, more desire. 'But not our last night ever.'

The hope that had started to grow within Rio burst open like a flower in the morning sunshine as the full impact of his words washed over her. He might not have said anything about loving her, but he still wanted her, wanted this moment. He believed whatever it was that had sparked to life between them was a good thing—for now at least.

'You want more nights like this?' she asked shyly, conscious of his body against hers, the way he caressed her face and the heavy look of desire in his eyes. There was no mistaking that there would be many amazing nights of passion ahead of them in this convenient engagement. Maybe it could one day lead somewhere else, perhaps be the beginning of much deeper and more meaningful things.

'We have something good, Rio. It proves that the misguided sentiment of love is not needed between us.'

'It's not?' She knew the smile had slipped from her face, even before she saw his frown.

'We are attracted to one another and the chemistry between us is nothing short of hot. Love would only complicate that.' That last sentence was said with conviction and the flame of hope within her heart spluttered slightly, as if a big gust of wind had raced across the roof terrace.

'Love always complicates things,' she said, quashing down any notion that one day he might love her as she now loved him. 'It will be different when we are back on the island with Xena.'

'In that case, we need to make the most of our last night here in Athens—alone.'

'Just what do you have in mind?' She was determined to do exactly that, to lose herself in the dream of love for one more night. Power raced through her as she teased him and, emboldened, she moved against him.

'Temptress,' he growled, his lips claiming hers in a kiss far more demanding and forceful than any of last night. She'd done this to him, pushed his legendary control to the limit, and that knowledge filled her with power, with excitement. 'What is it you want, Rio?'

Rio looked at him, her heart beating so loudly she was sure it echoed around them. His dark eyes watched her intently, waiting for her to say something.

'Another night with you,' she whispered huskily.

'Then you leave me no option,' he said, whisking her off her feet before striding across the roof terrace.

She feigned resistance, wriggling in his arms and laughing at the same time. She'd never been so happy, so carefree. She was going to make the most of this final night, allow herself to believe he loved her one final time.

As that thought lingered temptingly, she lay on the bed as his body covered hers, his kiss intoxicating and demanding. She met his passion head-on, losing herself in this bubble of happiness in which she now found herself. It didn't matter what happened tomorrow, next week or next year. All that mattered right now was that she was in the arms of the man she loved. She might not be able to tell him she loved him, but her body could— and tonight she intended to do exactly that.

CHAPTER TEN

ON THEIR RETURN to the island Rio had found it easier than before to create the illusion she and Lysandros were in love. Xena still hadn't recovered any memories but fully bought into the romance of their engagement. Once Lysandros had left for Athens Rio had faced a barrage of questions from Xena, but, not wanting to say exactly what had happened between them after the charity ball, she had been evasive in her details of the weekend away. Xena's satisfied expression proved she knew it had been a weekend for lovers. Were her deepening feelings of love for Lysandros that obvious?

In just two days Lysandros was due to return to his sister's villa for the family engagement party Xena had been planning. Rio was nervous. How should she act around him in front of his family? Would his desire for her have run its course or would he want more nights with her?

'You miss him, don't you?' Xena's voice interrupted her doubts and questions. She pushed them aside, focusing instead on Lysandros's impending return. Just knowing she would see him again very soon filled her tummy with butterflies, making her heart flutter.

'We have just got engaged.' Rio tried valiantly to answer Xena's question without admitting the truth. 'Of course I miss him.'

She missed what they'd shared for those couple of nights in Athens. Not just the intimacy and the passion of their lovemaking but the gentleness he'd shown her, the way he'd cared about her, his concern for her as they'd arrived at his apartment. That night, as she'd touched the piano and met his gaze, it had been as if he'd known, even before she'd told him the truth, exactly how hard it had been to do that, let alone play.

'You've fallen for him, haven't you? Really fallen for him.' Xena laughed, a sound so in contrast to her thoughts it made Rio feel even more anxious.

'Isn't that what people do when they get engaged?' Rio kept her voice light, determined not to show the depth of her feelings—her love.

'I knew all along you two were so right for each other.' Xena grinned, smug satisfaction on her face, her dark eyes sparkling, so like her brother's on the rare occasion he let his guard down. 'When did you make up, by the way?'

'Make up?' Rio feigned ignorance, despite the implications of that question.

'I can't recall why,' Xena began again. 'Not yet at least, but I do remember you had broken it off with him.'

'You remember something?' Rio was so pleased. Xena was recovering and her smile was full of excitement. 'Do you remember anything else?'

'I'm not sure,' Xena replied. 'But now it's started to come back, I'm sure I will begin to remember other things. That's not important now, Rio. You and Lysandros are. When did you get back together?'

'At the hospital. After your accident,' Rio said cautiously. 'It was the first time we had seen each other.' It was in part true. She and Lysandros had shared something special before Hans had spoilt it. Rio said nothing else, knowing it would be all too easy to give away the truth of their reconciliation, expose the fake engagement. If Xena's memory was slowly coming back, she didn't want to risk upsetting that, even though she would soon know the truth.

'There's something,' Xena said, a frown on her face. 'I can't quite recall it.'

'What is it about? The accident? Do you remember something new?'

As soon as she'd asked the questions, seen Xena's expression change, Rio worried she would remember everything. What Hans had done. The argument with Ricardo. The accident.

When she'd returned from Athens it had been to find Xena was much more the woman she'd been before she'd fallen for Ricardo. Before the time she'd admitted he was married. A time that had almost torn apart their friendship as Rio had tried to warn her friend that getting involved with a married man could only mean heartache and disaster. She'd never anticipated the scale of that heartache and had no idea why Lysandros shouldn't know anything about Ricardo.

Should she tell Xena he now knew? No. She wasn't even sure if Xena recalled her relationship with Ricardo.

Xena sighed wistfully. 'Everything that has happened, the accident, my loss of memory, will be worth it when you and Lysandros finally set the date. It's what I'd always hoped for.'

'Xena Drakakis, if I didn't know better, I'd say

that you had planned this.' Rio laughed at the mock wounded expression on her friend's face.

'Yes, I had always wanted you two together.' Her tone changed, and she looked down guiltily. 'But now I am starting to recall things.'

If Xena's memory returned fully, it would end the engagement. Lysandros had made that all too clear. She would lose the man she loved. Rio's heart was tearing apart—for herself and for Xena.

'Xena?' Rio questioned gently.

'I can remember other things, Rio. I can remember why you ended the relationship.'

'You can?' Rio tentatively asked.

'Yes, I can. It was what Hans did, wasn't it? The attack? That's why you ended things with Lysandros.'

Rio gulped, unable to say anything. It was all over now. Xena's memory was returning. The fog her friend had lived in since the accident was lifting.

'It was.' Rio finally spoke.

Xena shook her head, disappointment clear on her face. 'I didn't tell him why, but I do remember telling him to give you the space you needed. I warned him not to contact you. So, what happened? Are you really engaged to him? Did you two get back together, get engaged, purely to help me regain my memory?'

Rio was sure her mouth must be gaping open in shock. Xena had guessed their plan, had guessed she and her brother were acting out a fake engagement. What was she supposed to do now? Tell Xena the truth? How could she do that when all along her friend had wanted to see her brother happily married, and now that he'd told her about the marriage he'd almost made, she could understand where Xena's desire for that had come from. But did Xena realise he didn't want love in his life? That he couldn't love her, couldn't love anyone?

There was only one thing for it. Tell Xena the truth. 'I'm sorry, Xena; we thought if you were surrounded by happiness, it would help you recover—from the accident and the amnesia.'

'It did.' Xena looked so vulnerable Rio's heart went out to her. 'But you must feel something for him to get engaged?'

She owed Xena the truth. Owed herself the truth.

'I had been falling for Lysandros before I ended it. So much so that I couldn't face him after what had happened.'

'Hans?' Xena said sharply, making Rio look at her. She couldn't verbally acknowledge that so just nodded. 'And now? Do you love Lysandros now?'

'I do, yes.' She wouldn't tell Xena that Lysandros had said he could never love anyone again. That heart-breaking bit of information was something she didn't want Xena knowing.

'It's hard, isn't it?' Xena said softly, looking down at the floor, unable to meet Rio's gaze, but when she did, tears filled her eyes. 'I love Ricardo. I should never have run out on him like I did the night of the accident. He wanted time. He and his wife were separating; their marriage had fallen apart long before he first took me out. She even knows about me.'

Rio was stunned. Xena remembered everything.

'What do you want to do about Ricardo?' Rio asked gently, relieved the attention had slipped away from her and Lysandros. She sat next to Xena, who was making a brave attempt at holding back tears. Maybe she did need to cry. Maybe she did need to let out the pain of her broken heart.

Xena looked at her with big, wide, tearful eyes. 'I spoke to him yesterday.'

She'd contacted him? Yesterday? 'Did that help?'

'He and his wife have filed for divorce. He wants to see me, Rio.' The hope echoing in Xena's voice was the same hope Rio had clung to as she'd lain in Lysandros's arms after they'd made love the first time—and each time afterwards.

'If it's what you want, Xena, I will do whatever I can to make it happen for you.'

Rio knew the pain of loving someone so much it hurt. She recognised that pain in Xena's eyes.

'Thank you,' Xena whispered, sitting taller as if finding strength from somewhere. 'But first we have an engagement to celebrate.'

'You just told me you know none of it is real.' Rio's mind whirled. How could Xena possibly want her and Lysandros to continue with the engagement now?

'He is besotted with you, Rio. He watches every move you make. I've seen him doing it. There is no way I'm going to allow you two to go your separate ways again.' A new determination filled Xena's voice, but surely she realised there were some things even Xena couldn't make happen?

'We can't stay engaged, Xena. Not now.' The declaration was out before she could stop it.

'Of course you can. Everything is planned. Family invited. You are engaged, Rio. To be married—to my brother.' The enthusiasm in Xena's voice couldn't quell the anxiety bubbling inside her.

'It's not possible, Xena.' Desperation filled Rio's

voice and she wondered if she was trying to convince herself or Xena.

'You just told me you love him.' Xena spoke softly, her hand reaching out, touching Rio's arm in a reassuring gesture, her expression brighter now she was smiling once again. 'That's what you said, isn't it?'

'Yes, I did.' Rio couldn't keep it in. 'I love Lysandros.'

'Then there is nothing more to discuss. In two days' time we will officially celebrate your engagement and I'll be making sure he sets the date. Nothing would make me happier than for you to be my sister-in-law.'

Impatient to see Rio again, Lysandros had left the office at an unusually early hour, making his assistant smile as he'd claimed to be testing out another of his yachts. Were his feelings for Rio that transparent?

He'd arrived far earlier than planned after enjoying the freedom of the sea. As he'd neared the villa he'd heard, through the open doors onto the terrace, his sister and Rio talking, but he hadn't been able to make out exactly what they were saying. By the time he reached the terrace their words had become clearer.

'You just told me you love him.'

Rio loved him?

He stood on the terrace of the villa, trying to take in what he'd just heard Xena say, what he'd just heard Rio reply.

'Yes, I did. I love Lysandros.'

He'd thought himself hardened, immune to such emotions, but replayed again and again those words inside his head. Rio loved him? He had tried to convince Rio what he felt for her was just desire. Heated lust borne out of several nights of passion. Now he needed to convince himself. He didn't want it to be something stronger—something far more destructive.

He didn't want to fall in love with his convenient and temporary fiancée. The woman who was now playing out the role to perfection, claiming how much she loved him so that Xena wouldn't question their fake engagement.

Of course, that was it. She hadn't meant it at all. She didn't love him. It had been for Xena's benefit.

Relief surged through him. He could never be that vulnerable again. He didn't want to love anyone. He didn't want to lower the barriers he'd strategically built around himself, open himself to the kind of hurt and pain he'd known more than once in the past. He didn't want to risk that pain again, that rejection and devastation of trust.

Should he turn and go? The thought hung in the air as Xena laughed in delight and he could almost imagine her hugging Rio. 'You will be my sister.'

He didn't turn and go. Instead he walked into the villa, Rio and Xena springing apart, Rio's face ashen white.

'She would also be my wife,' he said as he moved into the room to stand by the large grand piano occupying the centre of the vast space. His voice was brusque, but Xena grinned up at him. She really was invested in their engagement. He'd have to make out he and Rio wanted a long engagement if Xena didn't start recovering her memory soon. The problem would then be that being around Rio for much longer would test him—test his vow never to become emotionally involved again. But he'd do it for Xena.

In a bid to release the tension suddenly in the air, he ruffled his sister's hair, knowing full well she hated it, and when she squealed in protest, he laughed. At that exact moment he made eye contact with Rio and it happened all over again. The spark ignited. The strong pull of attraction, so intense he had no option but to go to her. The sensation his heart was overflowing with the kind of emotion he'd never wanted tore through him again.

Oblivious to Xena's teasing words, he went to Rio. The woman who filled his dreams with heated memories, something no other woman had ever done.

'Lysandros?' There was a question in his name as she spoke softly. Was she trying to second-guess the next move they made or was she aware he'd just heard her declaration of love? A declaration he could believe or dismiss as part of the act.

'The Greek sunshine is enhancing your beauty. Giving you a healthy glow,' he said, taking her hand, raising her fingertips to his lips, pressing a kiss onto her slender fingers. It was all he could do to stop himself from remembering how they had caressed the keys of his piano when she'd finally played again. Then much later, as they'd lain in bed, how they had caressed his body. He could still feel her soft teasing touch on his chest, the slow lingering trail she'd made down over his stomach before touching him in a way that had driven him wild.

Enough. He pushed the memory aside, fighting with the words he'd just heard Rio say, aware his sister was watching every move he made.

Xena sighed as she sat back down. 'This is so perfect.'

Was it perfect? To be loved by a woman he didn't want to love, a woman he didn't want to occupy his heart? He needed to be alone with Rio, needed to know what her true reactions were, her true feelings. She must have been saying those words to Xena as part of the act, part of the deal he'd made with her. Exactly what he'd expect her to do, so why was that so unsettling?

Because you are falling in love with her. Despite everything you told her, you are falling in love with her.

He gritted his teeth against the knowledge he'd almost made a fool of himself. Almost believed the words he'd overheard Rio saying as part of her role play and exposed his growing vulnerability, his growing weakness.

'You two should spend some time alone. Take a romantic stroll on the beach.' There was mischief in Xena's voice, showing she was finally more her usual bubbly self. The Xena he knew so well was beginning to come back.

'Shall we take a walk?' He didn't miss the look of worry crossing Rio's face.

'I'd like that.' Her words were barely above a whisper, her face pale beneath the newly gained tan.

Together they walked along the sand until they were alone, and it was several minutes before she spoke hesitantly. 'Have you ever wondered if Xena might have guessed our engagement isn't real?'

'Our engagement is real. You are wearing my ring.' The words snapped from him and those beautiful eyes widened in surprise.

'But...' Rio began. Lysandros wasn't in the mood for discussion about anything other than what he'd just heard.

'The reason is different, that's all.' He cut across her words as emotions assailed him, bombarding him and pushing him out of his safety zone. 'I heard you and Xena talking just now.'

She didn't look at him, didn't even stop walking.

Damn her. Was she going to make him say it? 'You were telling her about us. You said you loved me. It was just part of the act, wasn't it? A way to convince her our engagement is real.'

She stopped, looking down at the sand, and he wished he hadn't been so harsh, but when she looked back up at him, her chin lifted in defiance. She'd become the same little spitfire he'd done battle with while Xena had lain in the hospital bed. The realisation crashed over him as if a storm had suddenly rushed in off the sea. He wanted her to love him. Hell, *he* wanted to love her.

'And does she still believe it is real?' He moved closer to her, wanting to prove how very real their engagement was beginning to be, wanting to remind her that last weekend she'd lost her virginity to him, giving him something special. If there was any chance those words he'd heard her say moments ago were real, then didn't he owe it to her to be honest? To tell her what he'd been denying since that night in Athens?

He wanted to love her, but he couldn't quite let go of the past. Just as she'd sat at the piano in his apartment, locked in her own world of regret, he too was there now.

'Yes,' Rio whispered, and he couldn't stop himself. 'She believes it's real, but it isn't. It can't ever be real— because you don't want that, you won't let me in.'

He took her in his arms, bringing her close against

him, feeling as if he'd been all at sea but had now found the port he'd never known existed. He'd found the woman who could make him forget the past.

'There is nothing fake about the way I feel when I hold you.' His voice became hoarse with emotion. Rio tried to look away, but gently he tilted her chin up, whispering against her lips, 'Neither is there anything false about this.'

The kiss was so powerful it totally consumed him. Her response was instant, her arms wrapping around his neck, her delicious body against his. It was paradise and as it ended he took her hand, beginning to walk slowly along the beach again.

She pulled away from him. 'It's real, yes, but it's just desire. Nothing more.' She hesitated. 'If… When Xena knows, we must end this. Stop this charade of being engaged—before it goes too far.'

'When she remembers, yes, we will.' He let her go, stepping away from her. Xena didn't remember yet, and until she remembered, he and Rio could continue to indulge in their desire. But what about that night in Athens? What about the heated passion that had filled that whole weekend? Was it really as she now claimed? Nothing more than desire? 'We need to talk to Xena.'

'And if she remembers?' Rio looked at him, worry startlingly clear in her eyes.

'Then we can end the engagement, but she has to tell us. We can't say anything, can't raise any questions over our relationship.' Lysandros found himself hoping Xena *hadn't* remembered anything, that he and Rio would be forced to remain engaged. 'I don't want to risk upsetting her.'

* * *

As she and Lysandros returned to the villa the hope there was a chance he could one day love her, as she loved him, was finally gone. Rio had felt desire in his kiss, had seen it in his eyes, but desire wasn't enough. She had to be strong. She didn't want to be part of a one-sided love affair. As soon as he found out Xena had regained her memory, she and Lysandros were over. And Xena had done just that. Time was ticking on their deal, on her illusion of love.

Voices sounded from inside the villa as they approached. Xena's voice and a man's. Ricardo's voice. Every nerve in Rio's body tensed. He was here? There was no escaping it now. This was the moment everything ended, the moment her heart broke.

'Xena has a visitor?' Lysandros asked, suspicion laced into every word.

Rio could feel the colour leaching from her face as she looked at Lysandros. Xena's memory was back; there was no point avoiding it. 'It's Ricardo.'

Before Rio could gather her scrambled thoughts, Lysandros marched into the villa and she rushed after him, remembering Xena's recent conversation about how she loved Ricardo. She recalled Xena saying they had spoken. Had she invited him, even knowing it would need massive explanations to her family? And worse, knowing how Lysandros would take it?

The air filled with furious Greek as he stormed into the room, Xena and Ricardo leaping apart like teenagers caught out. Rio had no idea what he was saying, what Xena was saying. It was more heated than she'd ever seen either Xena or Lysandros. This was brother and sister pitched against each other in a wild battle of words.

She couldn't let this happen. She had to stand up for Xena, even if it meant losing Lysandros—because she'd never really had him, his love. 'Stop.'

Her word rang round the room. Ricardo stepped into the spotlight, taking Xena in his arms, holding her as she tried to fight the tears.

Lysandros turned to her and Rio knew the moment of truth had come. 'What the hell is going on?'

Before she could say anything Xena had launched into the gap her silence had created. Rio stood numbly as Xena explained. How she'd remembered almost everything a few days ago and how she and Ricardo had made up, prompting him to come to the island. How she'd told Rio she knew they were pretending to be engaged, but how they *should* be.

Lysandros looked at her and Rio knew from the coldness of his eyes it was too late. She should have told him, but he'd completely shocked her by admitting he'd heard what she'd said to Xena, taking the urgency away from that as she'd tried to protect her heart. 'As you are already aware, we no longer need to keep up the pretence of being lovers—or being engaged.'

Lysandros turned to glare angrily at Ricardo, who stood his ground, looking back at him rebelliously. They remained like that for several minutes until at last Lysandros moved.

He went to his sister, taking her gently from Ricardo's arms, holding her tight, whispering in Greek, showing once again his compassion in the face of devastating news. She had no idea how long she watched the tender moment, but eventually Lysandros pulled away, returning Xena to Ricardo's embrace.

'Look after her,' he instructed Ricardo, then turned to go. 'I'm leaving.'

As he passed her he didn't even glance her way. Rio wanted to crumple to the cool marble floor, give in to the tears the whole encounter had evoked. She'd lost the man she loved.

CHAPTER ELEVEN

LYSANDROS COULDN'T BREATHE, couldn't think. Rio had known Xena's memory had returned. She'd blatantly asked him what would happen when it did, but hadn't told him. She'd kept something from him that changed everything between them. She'd deceived him.

He and Rio could really have had something special, but he'd fallen into the same trap all over again. Raw pain from the past opened up, snatching away all that he'd foolishly believed Rio was.

He couldn't stay. Couldn't look at Rio. Not when he'd finally taken down the last of his barriers. Dismantled them all—for Rio. Because he'd wanted her. Wanted to be with her. But now everything had changed.

He marched along the beach to where only a short time ago he'd kissed Rio. It was here he'd realised his heart had finally begun to open to love—her love. He wanted Rio's love, wanted to love her, wanted to share with her the emotion he'd locked out of his life for so long.

Raw and painful emotions had crashed over him as he'd heard Rio's conversation with Xena. To hear her say she loved him had confused him, shocked him. A whole range of emotions had assailed him. Finally, he'd acknowledged the truth he'd been desperately running from for the last few months.

Lysandros took in a deep breath, standing firm in the wet sand near the water's edge as the waves dragged it away from him, trying to unbalance him. It was as if the pull of the sea was forcing him to admit what he'd been avoiding all along. Right here, just a short while ago, he'd been on the brink of telling Rio how he felt, that he wanted their engagement to be real—because he was falling in love with her.

A larger wave rushed in, soaking him above his ankles, but still he didn't move. He'd already drowned, already slipped beneath the surface. It had happened the moment he'd first kissed Rio, but it had been in Athens that he'd lost the battle. That spark of attraction had fired into life, bringing love back to his heart. Only he'd been too damned arrogant to believe it.

Now the painful truth that he'd fallen in love with a woman who, despite what he'd overheard, had ripped his heart in two. He ran his hands through his hair in agitation. Her declaration of love for him to Xena hadn't been true. She wanted the engagement over. Before it went too far.

Should he go back into the villa? Tell Rio how he felt, or be there for Xena? Who should he put first? Xena, his beloved sister? Or Rio, the woman who had just told him that their engagement was over, rendering him as vulnerable as a newborn?

If he'd been a better man, a better brother, one able to connect emotionally, none of this would have happened. The solid wall of defence he'd built around him after Kyra's betrayal had shut out his sister—and pushed Rio away.

He walked further along the beach. He couldn't go back to the villa yet. Xena had Ricardo and it was all too obvious they loved one another. Whatever he thought about the man, Ricardo would look after her. But it was the image of Rio, standing there, that filled his mind. She hadn't even been able to look at him as the truth had unfolded, hadn't said anything, hadn't tried to stop him going.

He continued walking, brisk paces through the waves as they slid onto the beach. He couldn't face Rio yet. His emotions, his heart were all too vulnerable. He needed to lock them away, put them back behind the barriers. Only then could he talk to her, end their fake engagement—their deal.

Sensations of claustrophobia overwhelmed Rio. She needed air, needed to get out of the villa. Xena and Ricardo were deep in conversation, declaring love for each other and apologising. They didn't need her. Silently she slipped out onto the terrace.

From her vantage point she saw Lysandros on the beach, striding angrily along at the water's edge. The firm set of his shoulders showed his anger. He didn't want her. Didn't need her. Xena's memory had returned and their deal was over. Whatever she felt for him, she had to shut it down.

She couldn't stay on the island now. She had to leave. But how? She was marooned here, and the only boat belonged to the man who had just walked away from her, unable to even look at her.

There was only one thing for it. She returned to the villa, avoiding Xena and Ricardo and going to her room to pack. In the kind of haste she'd watched many times in the movies, she threw her belongings into her case. Then slipped the elegant ring off her finger. Placing it on the dressing table. Xena would find it.

Thankfully Xena and Ricardo had gone when she returned to the living area, and with her heart breaking, Rio left the villa. She glanced along the beach, seeing Lysandros had walked further away. She turned in the opposite direction, heading for the jetty where he'd moored his speedboat.

It bobbed ominously on the waves as she dragged her case down the wooden jetty. She looked down at the crystal waters, the sandy seabed clear to see, along with a starfish. How could she still see something so beautiful when her world was falling apart?

'You've blown it,' she told herself as she hefted her case up and over the side of the boat, careful not to scratch it, knowing the sleek craft was new. Lysandros had taken it out on its maiden voyage last weekend when he'd brought her back to the island after their time in Athens.

How had so much changed in one week?

In Athens they'd been lovers. She'd lost her virginity and her heart to him. Now a week later and with just two days until their engagement party, they were as far from lovers as a man and woman could be. Whatever they had discovered in Athens was over. She'd known it would never last but had foolishly hoped for love. Hoped that she would be the woman to mend his heart, enable him to love again, love her.

She closed her eyes against the threatening tears, placing her hands on her hips and tilting her face up to the sun, allowing the warmth to ease her pain, her despair. She'd hoped such an action would soothe her, calm the raging storm within her, but it didn't.

Deflated and humiliated, she knelt, trying to free one of the mooring ropes at the front of the long speedboat. She had absolutely no idea what she was doing or even what she'd do once the boat was free of the ropes. All she knew was that the gleaming white craft represented freedom and escape.

Despair filled her. She couldn't even free the rope. A strangled cry of frustration tore from her as she heard footsteps, turning to see the man who now possessed her heart striding down the jetty towards her.

'If you are that desperate to leave, all you had to do was ask.' Lysandros's icy and controlled voice cut through her panic.

Damn him. Why did he have to sound so sure of himself, so in control and, worse still, so sexy?

She leapt to her feet, boldly facing him, injecting haughtiness into her voice. 'Very well. I'm asking. Will you take me to Athens?'

'You seriously want to leave? After everything that has happened between us? Everything that has been said?'

For the briefest second, he looked out of control, vulnerable, but as he stepped closer she wondered if it had been a trick of the light. His eyes sparked with anger, strengthening her resolve to protect her breaking heart, to get away.

'Yes, and that's why I want to go. I want to return to the life I should never have left. Our deal is over, Lysandros. Just as you wanted,' she snapped as frustration surged through her. All he was doing now was proving he was the wrong man for her, the kind of man who demanded everything, the kind of man unable to be emotionally open and love her. How stupid was she that she'd hoped otherwise?

'At least allow me to help you. You'll be going nowhere until you release all the mooring ropes.' He was taunting her, but there was also firmness to his voice, anger lurking beneath the composed exterior.

Rio stared at him, completely taken aback. He obviously wanted her out of his life so much he would actually take her. Her heart broke into thousands of tiny pieces, like crystal shattering, splinters flying everywhere. There would be no hope of finding the pieces and putting them back together.

Within seconds he'd freed the sleek craft of its moorings and was aboard, starting the motor. Rio still stood on the jetty but finally roused herself into action, putting to one side the pain and hurt. She hastily jumped into the speedboat, as if her life depended on it, and sat at the very stern, as far away from Lysandros as she could get.

Seconds later the boat lurched into life and they began heading away from the island, the pace picking up over the clear waters, making them insignificant and small against the vastness of the sea.

The wind whipped at her hair, pulling the last part of her ponytail free, and Rio clutched it to the side of her neck, looking back at the island, now nothing more than a dark smudge on the horizon. Even though she felt sorry for herself, her thoughts turned to Xena. Would she be okay with Ricardo? What if he went back to his wife? The boat bounced over the water, taking her further away.

She swallowed hard against the tears threatening

once more. She didn't want to show weakness. The boat slowed and she opened her eyes, looking around her as the engine died. The boat began to drift to a stop on the blue waters that surrounded them.

'Why have we stopped?' She turned to look at Lysandros stepping down from the seat and away from the controls. What was he doing? Was this the moment he told her how much he despised her, how disappointed he was and, worst of all, that he never wanted to see her again? Well, she wouldn't give him the satisfaction.

'We need to talk,' Lysandros said, balancing with ease as the boat rocked and rolled on the swell of the sea. Rio, however, looked less comfortable with the sensation, but he pressed on with the plan he'd had to rapidly form as he'd found her trying to make her escape—in his boat.

He needed to talk to her alone. He had to know what had really happened. Right from the moment he'd kissed her in London at the recital to now. He couldn't let her go. Not like this. When he'd seen her heading to the jetty, her case rumbling behind her, he'd known that alone at sea would be the perfect place for such a discussion.

'There is nothing more to say,' she said, trying to stand but stumbling back a pace before sitting down, unused to being at sea in a smaller boat, obviously feeling every swell on the deep waters.

Her lovely hair was in disarray and her face very pale. She looked far more vulnerable and innocent than he'd ever seen her. Far more than she had appeared the night she'd played the piano in his apartment. The night he'd taken her virginity. A night that had changed everything. Changed him.

He crossed to the stern of the boat, sitting down next to her. Now was not the time to dominate. This was not a boardroom deal that required power and control of the situation. This was Rio, the woman who had penetrated his cold heart, brought love back into his life. This was also his last chance to convince her of that.

'You can't go like this. Not after everything that has happened between us.' He thought back to Athens, to the deepening desire that had claimed them both. He couldn't allow her to walk away yet. He needed to buy himself more time. He needed to come to terms with the revelations of this afternoon.

The fact Rio had kept Xena's returned memory from him and had manipulated the situation was at total odds with his own admission of how he felt about Rio.

'I have to go, Lysandros—*because* of what has happened between us.'

Rio looked at him, her eyes begging him, pleading him to understand.

'Doesn't that night in Athens mean anything?' He wasn't ready to allow Rio to walk out of his life—again.

'It does,' Rio said, pulling her hair from her face, holding it tight to prevent the wind snatching it back. 'It means too much and that is why I *have* to go.'

Lysandros's world rocked. His inability to acknowledge his emotions, to connect emotionally with anyone, was pushing away not just Xena but Rio—the most important woman in his life. That thought shocked him.

He'd failed the people he loved, the people who counted on him. It seemed to be what he did best.

Lysandros closed his eyes against the thought of the

two women he loved dealing with so much alone. Savagely he pushed the full implications of that acknowledgement aside.

'Why does it mean you have to go, Rio?' Even as he asked the question he doubted she would give him the answer. She had well and truly locked him out of her life, her thoughts, her emotions.

'We should never have got together, Lysandros, should never have got engaged.'

Even as he asked he knew why—knew it was because of him, because he was emotionally unobtainable. Anger and guilt fused inside him, thrashing around like a raging storm.

He swore savagely in Greek as the truth lashed at him. 'I should never have forced you to become engaged—not like that, not as part of a deal.'

'You did it for Xena,' she said with conviction, forcing him to look at her, to calm the furious bubbles of anger before they spilled over. 'Because you love her.' The warmth of her touch unleashed that spark of attraction, that fatal awareness of her he couldn't deny.

'And now she too will despise me for what I've done to you. If I had known about Hans, I would never have forced you into such a deal, Rio.'

Rio jumped up, the boat steadier now, and she stood over him. 'Xena could never despise you. She might be angry, but she will never despise you.' The passion, the truth of her words was as clear as the crystal waters beneath them.

Now he knew everything. Rio had wanted to protect Xena, proving her loyalty to her friend. She'd put Xena before everything, including her own happiness.

'What about you? Do you despise me, Rio?' He

stood, moving closer, his voice becoming a whisper as
he fought the overload of emotions he'd never wanted
to indulge in again, the kind he no longer wanted to
banish from his life—but was it too late?

CHAPTER TWELVE

'DESPISE YOU?' RIO'S heart thumped, hope flaring to life within her. She had to tell him. 'I meant what I said to Xena.' Lysandros watched her, saying nothing, making it even more difficult, his dark eyes searching hers. 'When I told her I loved you.'

'Was that true or was it merely part of the act of being engaged, something to make Xena believe it was real?' His voice deepened, becoming more demanding, and even though he sat next to her calmly, he still dominated the very air she breathed. His question went to the heart of the matter like an arrow to the bullseye.

Her nerves wavered in the face of his question. Had he understood what she'd said? She tried to find her courage after the admission he'd barely registered, too painfully true to make it again. 'I have told you a great many things as part of our deal, but I want you to ignore them all now. Xena has recovered her memory and I want to put this farce of an engagement behind me.'

He looked down at her hand, to the finger on which he'd placed the engagement ring such a short time ago. She remained firm, watching him, mimicking the same command he exuded so naturally, trying not to remember the heady sexual tension in the air as she'd played the piano at his apartment. She shut her mind against the pleasure of giving herself so completely to him that night. There was no alternative. She had to walk away from this—from him.

'You want what we have to end?' There was hurt and accusation laced into that question, neither of which she'd ever intended to inflict on him. 'You don't want to be engaged to me?'

'No, I don't. We can't truly be together, Lysandros. We want different things, need different things from a relationship. We are too different.' He sat back from her, from her passionate outburst, thankfully giving her space, room to think, to breathe, because she couldn't do either when he was so close to her.

'Different?' He touched her face, his fingers soft against her cheek, and she couldn't help but close her eyes to the sensation. She needed to get her emotions under control, needed to find some strength from somewhere. She'd just admitted she loved him, but he had casually sidetracked her words.

'From the very beginning I always thought that for you the attraction was purely physical. That once we'd spent a night together you would want to move on to the next woman.' Rio hung on to the strength she'd found, needing to tell him everything. After all, she had nothing to lose now. She'd already lost him, lost her hope of being loved by him. 'That was why I had to be sure.' She paused, looking at him. 'Before I spent the night with you. And then when Hans did what he did, I couldn't tell you. Not after I'd finally made the decision to make our relationship physical. I just didn't feel I could.'

'I never wanted you to feel that way, Rio,' Lysandros said, taking her hand in his. 'I was shut down emotionally against feeling anything romantic. I hadn't connected emotionally with a woman for many years. That was until you walked into my life. That's when I knew I wanted more. That I wanted you.'

She thought of the afternoon at the recital. He'd seemed different from his usual self that afternoon. More intense. But, then, she had been too. She'd been about to tell him she wanted to be with him all night.

'Me?' she asked, needing to know. Was Lysandros saying he'd envisaged more from their relationship than just a brief affair?

'Yes, you, Rio. At first it was only Xena who saw what we could be, that there was something special between us. I was still too locked up behind my protective wall, but that afternoon at the recital I realised she was right.'

'It would never have worked, though, Lysandros. I couldn't be the kind of woman you wanted, the kind you normally dated,' she whispered, her heart and soul being dragged out into the sunshine, laid bare before him.

'It's because you weren't the kind of woman I usually dated that I saw there was a future for us.' He smiled in that devastatingly sexy way she loved so much.

She had no idea what he was trying to tell her. No idea what the outcome of this conversation would be. All she knew was she had told him she loved him, and not once had he mentioned that word to her. He was doing all he could to avoid it.

She didn't say anything. She couldn't. Instead she allowed the motion of the boat to soothe her.

'In the hospital, you made it clear you only wanted me in Greece because I could help Xena recover,' she whispered, shocked to realise she'd spoken her thoughts aloud.

'I know.' He looked into her eyes, his own so dark she couldn't fathom out the emotion in them. He was the one hiding secrets now. 'I'm sorry.'

'What happens now?' She lifted her chin, looking directly at him, giving him the opportunity to be honest. To say they were over or to say he wanted her in his life—because he loved her. She didn't need an engagement or marriage. All she needed was him, his love.

'I want this engagement to end,' Lysandros said firmly, seeing raw emotions fill Rio's eyes. He should just say it, just tell her, but still he found it difficult. Letting go of years of caution wasn't easy.

'Then we both want the same thing.' Rio's voice faltered. 'To end the engagement.'

'I want you, Rio. You cannot deny you are as attracted to me as I am to you.' The air crackled as she looked up at him. His heart was pounding like a drum as he waited, cursing inwardly that he still couldn't tell her just how much he wanted her.

'It's true. I do want you,' she said in a resigned voice. 'But I want more than that, Lysandros. Much more. I don't want to pretend any more.'

'I'm not pretending, Rio. I want you. I want more too.'

She looked up at him and in the depths of her brown eyes he saw nothing but sadness. 'Want isn't enough.'

Was she going to force him to lay bare his heart? His emotions? Why couldn't he say it? What was holding him back? He cursed Kyra and her wicked lies, even cursed Rio's loyalty to his sister, which had played into all his doubts.

'Want is a good place to start.'

'No. Nothing is going to start. I need to go home. Now, please, Lysandros.' The firm determination in her voice was clearer than ever, but he wasn't going to give up. If he had to lay his heart on the line, he'd do it. He wanted Rio to stay, wanted what they'd had in Athens.

'I want you to stay.' Damn it. What was stopping him from telling her how he really felt?

'I can't,' she whispered, moving away from him. He could see tears threatening in her eyes and knew he had to prove to her how he felt or lose her for ever.

'Want isn't enough.' That was what she had said. Would his love be enough?

He took a deep breath, unlocking his heart, preparing to say the one thing he'd vowed never to say to a woman again. 'I love you, Rio.'

Rio looked at Lysandros. He just stood there, the only sound the waves against the side of the speedboat. She tried to process the words she'd so wanted to hear, tried to replay them because she couldn't bear it if they weren't real, if he hadn't meant them.

He moved towards her suddenly, taking her arms, urging her to her feet to look at him, into his eyes. 'Did you hear me? I love you, Rio.'

Her heart soared high into the blue sky. He had said it.

He spoke rapidly in Greek, shocking her from her stunned silence. 'But I thought…' She stumbled over her words, unable to voice her confusion, her shock, but more importantly her love.

'I know what I told you. That I never wanted love in my life again.' He looked into her eyes, and love, mixed with fear of her rejection, shone from his. 'But you changed that, Rio. You, and I want this fake engagement to end too, because I want you to be my wife.'

His wife? Her head spun as fast as her heart thumped. 'You want to marry me? For real?'

'Yes.' He laughed, holding her hands as if afraid she might disappear, but she had no intention of going anywhere. The man she loved had told her he loved her. He'd left his past behind just as she had. 'I want to marry you. I want the woman I love with all my heart to be my wife—as soon as possible.'

He began to say something else but she pressed her finger to his lips, silencing him. Desire flooded his eyes and she smiled at him. 'I love you, Lysandros, but should we rush into this?'

'I've never been surer of anything in my life.'

'You really want to get married?'

'I do, Rio. I do.' Those words flashed through her mind. The look in his eyes heated her body and the love she'd suppressed since she'd come to the island overflowed.

'In that case, you'd better take me back to the island,' she teased.

'Not yet,' he said, pulling her into his arms. 'I think we should kiss and make up first.'

She smiled up at him as he bent to kiss her, a kiss that showed her just how much he loved her. She could feel it, taste it. His love wrapped itself around her, caressing her entire body. The kiss deepened and her body trembled with shock at his revelation and the unfurling heat of passion inside her.

'I love you so much,' she whispered against his lips, unsure if the swaying was her or the boat.

'Then marry me, not just be my fiancée. Say you will be my wife.'

She smiled at him as she pulled back, held safely in his arms, looking into his handsome face. 'Nothing would make me happier.'

He answered by drawing her close against him, kissing her until she melted with pleasure. His hands caressed her and she wished she could show him right now just how much she wanted him, how much she loved him.

'Why the hell aren't we on my yacht?' The feral growl of mock irritation made her laugh and the urge to taunt him was too strong to resist.

'And why would that be?' She couldn't keep the coy smile from her face, revelling in the power of his love.

'Because I want to make love to you—right now. I want to prove to you how much I love you.'

'Then I will look forward to our wedding night.' Shyness made her blush and she looked down, away from the intensity in his eyes.

He lifted her chin back up gently, as he had done so many times. 'You are making me wait until we are married?'

'Yes,' she breathed in a husky whisper. 'And then I expect you to show me each and every night just how much you love me.'

His eyes darkened and the air became laden with desire. 'That will be my greatest pleasure.'

EPILOGUE

THE NEW SEASON for the orchestra was in full swing, and with Judith conducting, Rio had had no qualms about continuing her career. Xena too, fully recovered from the accident, was once more playing the violin.

Christmas was fast approaching and Rio had taken time off for a very important event. Xena and Ricardo were about to get married and Rome was filled with Christmas magic, the perfect setting for a wedding. It had also been the perfect setting in which to spend time with Lysandros.

As Xena and Ricardo had exchanged vows Rio had held Lysandros's hand. The small gathering of family members could be in no doubt that this couple belonged together as they were pronounced husband and wife. Rio looked up at Lysandros, standing beside her, remembering their intimate wedding day on the island at the end of the summer.

Only four months ago she had said the same words to him. It might not have been the big white church wedding she'd always dreamed of having, but the man she'd married far surpassed her dream. He was handsome and incredibly sexy, but far more than that, he cared for her and loved her.

Since that day on his speedboat when they had both put the past behind them, he had kept his promise, showing her just how much he loved her every day. Sometimes with passion that took her to another planet and sometimes with a gentle touch that held so much love.

He looked down at her as the happy couple turned to face their guests. 'Have I told you today just how beautiful you look?'

She smiled as he took her hand, pulling her against him, oblivious to those around him. 'Actually, you have,' she teased. 'At least a dozen times.'

'Come on, you two.' Xena's voice broke through the mist of desire that was building rapidly. 'We need you in the photographs.'

Lysandros smiled. 'I don't think we are going to be able to escape this. You know what Xena is like.'

'This is what she wanted all along,' said Rio as she reluctantly moved away from her husband. 'Two happy-ever-afters.'

'You girls are such romantics.' Lysandros's voice was full of mock irritation as they joined the bride and groom for photographs outside the town hall in the winter sunshine.

As Rio stood beside her husband, making the perfect photo for Xena's wedding album, of brother and sister both finally happily married to their partners, she wondered how Lysandros would receive the news that he was to be a father.

He'd reassured her often that the past was exactly that and he wanted children, but as she'd done the pregnancy test yesterday, she'd worried it might be too soon. Despite that, excitement had filled her. She would tell him once they were alone.

'We have good news,' Xena said as they stood in their family group on the steps, posing for the photographs. 'Ricardo and I are expecting a baby.'

'I'm so happy for you,' Rio said excitedly. She and her best friend would become mothers together. They were now like sisters, and after all that Xena had been through to find her true love, Rio knew how much that would mean for the couple. 'When?'

'It's early days yet, but I just had to share the news with you. Ricardo and I are expecting a summer baby.'

'There is only one thing that could please me more.' Lysandros added his congratulations as he shook Ricardo's hand, giving him a friendly slap on the back. 'And that would be to say the same thing to you.'

Rio took a deep breath before touching her husband's arm. When he looked down at her she nodded, the unspoken news bringing a smile to his face. She wanted to reassure him, to let him know the news they had both been tentatively hoping for was real. She didn't intend to take the spotlight from Xena's big day or announcement and hoped he would keep it quiet.

Lysandros, however, had other ideas. He picked her up, swinging her round, and when he set her back on her feet she looked at Xena, who wore that knowing smile. One so full of satisfaction and smugness that Rio couldn't help laughing.

'It appears that is exactly what I can say,' Lysandros said as Xena launched herself at him.

'I knew all along you two would make the perfect fairy tale,' Xena said, pulling away from Lysandros and taking Rio's hands.

The two of them looked at one another and Rio saw

her friend's eyes were as full of love and happiness as she knew hers were. 'We both have that,' Rio said softly.

Xena hugged her as the two men congratulated one another. Then Lysandros took her in his arms and kissed her, leaving her in no doubt how pleased he was about the baby.

As Xena tried to restore order to the unruly group photograph, Lysandros smiled at his wife, that desire-laden darkness in his eyes. 'I love you, Rio Drakakis, and I couldn't be happier. I'm going to be a father.'

Rio's heart soared. From a disastrous moment in London and a terrible accident had come total happiness for her and Xena. A perfect ending.

* * * * *